THE BOURNE ENIGMA

ROBERT LUDLUM was the author of twenty-seven novels, each one a *New York Times* bestseller. There are more than 225 million of his books in print, and they have been translated into thirty-two languages. He is the author of *The Scarlatti Inheritance*, *The Chancellor Manuscript*, and the Jason Bourne series – *The Bourne Identity*, *The Bourne Supremacy*, and *The Bourne Ultimatum* – among others. Mr Ludlum passed away in March 2001. To learn more, you can visit Robert-Ludlum.com.

ERIC VAN LUSTBADER is the author of numerous bestselling novels including *First Daughter*, *Beloved Enemy*, *The Ninja*, and the international bestsellers featuring Jason Bourne: *The Bourne Legacy*, *The Bourne Betrayal*, *The Bourne Sanction*, *The Bourne Deception*, *The Bourne Objective*, *The Bourne Dominion*, *The Bourne Imperative*, *The Bourne Retribution*, and *The Bourne Ascendancy*. For more information, you can visit EricVanLustbader.com. You can also follow him on Facebook and Twitter.

The Jason Bourne Novels

The Bourne Identity
The Bourne Supremacy
The Bourne Ultimatum
The Bourne Legacy (by Eric Van Lustbader)
The Bourne Betrayal (by Eric Van Lustbader)
The Bourne Sanction (by Eric Van Lustbader)
The Bourne Deception (by Eric Van Lustbader)
The Bourne Objective (by Eric Van Lustbader)
The Bourne Dominion (by Eric Van Lustbader)
The Bourne Imperative (by Eric Van Lustbader)
The Bourne Retribution (by Eric Van Lustbader)
The Bourne Ascendancy (by Eric Van Lustbader)

The Covert-One Novels

The Hades Factor (by Gayle Lynds)
The Cassandra Compact (by Philip Shelby)
The Paris Option (by Gayle Lynds)
The Altman Code (by Gayle Lynds)
The Lazarus Vendetta (by Patrick Larkin)
The Moscow Vector (by Patrick Larkin)
The Arctic Event (by James Cobb)
The Ares Decision (by Kyle Mills)
The Janus Reprisal (by Jamie Freveletti)
The Utopia Experiment (by Kyle Mills)
The Geneva Strategy (by Jamie Freveletti)
The Patriot Attack (by Kyle Mills)

The Paul Janson Novels

The Janson Directive
The Janson Command (by Paul Garrison)
The Janson Option (by Paul Garrison)
The Janson Equation (by Douglas Corleone)

Also by Robert Ludlum

The Scarlatti Inheritance
The Matlock Paper
Trevayne
The Cry of the Halidon
The Rhinemann Exchange
The Road to Gandolfo
The Gemini Contenders
The Chancellor Manuscript
The Holcroft Covenant
The Matarese Circle
The Parsifal Mosaic
The Aquitaine Progression
The Icarus Agenda
The Osterman Weekend
The Road to Omaha
The Scorpio Illusion
The Apocalypse Watch
The Matarese Countdown
The Prometheus Deception
The Sigma Protocol
The Tristan Betrayal
The Ambler Warning
The Bancroft Strategy

Also by Eric Van Lustbader

Nicholas Linnear Novels

Second Skin
Floating City
The Kaisho
White Ninja
The Miko
The Ninja

China Maroc Novels

Shan
Jian

Jack McClure / Alli Carson Novels

Beloved Enemy
Father Night
Blood Trust
Last Snow
First Daughter

Other Novels

The Testament
Art Kills
Pale Saint
Dark Homecoming
Black Blade
Angel Eyes
French Kiss
Zero
Black Heart
Sirens

ROBERT LUDLUM'S™

JASON BOURNE

RETURNS IN THE

BOURNE ENIGMA

A NEW BOURNE NOVEL
BY ERIC VAN LUSTBADER

First published in the USA in 2016 by Grand Central Publishing,
a division of Hachette Book Group, Inc

First published in the UK in 2016 by Head of Zeus Ltd

9 7 5 3 1 2 4 6 8

A catalogue record for this book is available from the British Library.

ISBN (HB) 9781784979478
ISBN (XTPB) 9781784979485
ISBN (E) 9781784979461

Printed and bound in Germany by GGP Media GmbH, Pössneck

Head of Zeus Ltd
Clerkenwell House
45–47 Clerkenwell Green
London EC1R 0HT
WWW.HEADOFZEUS.COM

Denial is the first impulse of a traitor.

—Josef Stalin

THE BOURNE ENIGMA

Prologue

Frankfurt, Germany

THE MOMENT JASON BOURNE stepped into the Royal Broweiser the hotel staff snapped to attention. Not that they had been standing idle. Herr Hummel, the executive director, would have had their jobs, and in any case they were too well trained. But Herr Bourne, well known to them, was a large tipper, and the staff scurried to take control of his three large, beautiful suitcases, each of which, they surmised, would have cost them six months' salary.

Bourne, a broad-shouldered, impeccably dressed gentleman of obvious means, had been staying at the Royal Broweiser over the past three or four months at irregular intervals. A businessman he might be, the staff speculated, but his physique marked him as a man who knew his way around a gym. He was always affable, loquacious, a font of slightly off-color jokes that never failed to delight the bellboys, who fell all over themselves to do his bidding. No request was too menial for them; they were happy to be put under his spell.

This morning, Bourne was shown up to his usual suite on the top floor, and, after a special delivery platter from Herr Hummel himself, was left to his own devices. The moment he was alone, he stepped to the window that overlooked Thurn-und-Taxis-Platz in the Old Town, took out his mobile, and pressed a speed-dial number. A moment later, the connection made, a female voice answered.

"I'm installed," he said. "How long do I have to wait?"

"A few days only." The voice in his ear warmed him. "We're tracking him; he'll soon be on his way."

"Days…"

"Don't be like that," she said. "Do you have any idea what it took to intercept an FSB confidential communique and substitute our own so Vanov was directed to you instead of to Bourne?"

"Who better than me, Irina?" The man posing as Bourne already felt a stirring in his groin. "Still. What am I to do here?"

"I know how deeply you despise Frankfurt, Jason."

"I love when you call me Jason."

"I'll bet you do." Irina chuckled. "You're too fucking tense. Find something to relax yourself."

"You," he said, almost wistfully. "Only you."

"Come, come, my animal," she whispered. "Surely you can—"

She must have heard his groan, though he thought it was barely audible.

"What are you doing, Jason?"

"You know what I'm doing." His zipper was open, his right hand rubbing his arousal. "Relaxing."

"Then, by all means," Irina cooed, "allow me to assist you."

Afterward, he wiped down the windowpane with a damp washcloth. Then, changing into the plush terry robe and slippers provided, he padded down the hallway, taking the elevator to the spa, where he stood under the rain forest shower for twenty minutes, cleansing both his body and his mind.

Upstairs in his room, he put on new clothes, went out and, under a sky burdened with gunmetal clouds, had a too-rich lunch at a café in Römerberg, then visited the Imperial Cathedral and St. Paul's Church. The following day he spent at the Zoological Garden, staring down a male lion who smelled like death. Bourne detested zoos even more than he hated Frankfurt and Germans in general. The thought of caging such magnificent creatures seemed to him a sin deserving of eternal damnation—if he had believed in such a thing, which, as a pragmatist and an atheist, he didn't.

Thank the gods and demons Irina called the next day.

"He just landed," she said. "He should be at the hotel in an hour."

The morning had dawned gray and ugly, just like the ones before it, except worse—it was raining. This city could drive me mad, he thought, as he broke the connection. But that was all done with now. At last excitement coursed through his veins.

It was showtime.

Captain Maksim Vanov, FSB, using the temporary title of cultural attaché, arrived at the hotel in a kind of controlled frenzy. It was his first time in Germany, Russia's longtime enemy. His grandfather had fought and died in the great patriotic siege of Stalingrad. He had been taught never to forget. As the bellman opened the door to his room at the Royal Broweiser, he shrugged the rain off his trench coat. The bellman hung it in the closet, explained the room's amenities, then loitered around until Vanov pressed a few euros into his damp palm.

Vanov took out the ancient bronze coin he had worn around his neck since General Karpov himself had given it to him, fingered it until it grew warm from his hand. Then, reluctantly, he let it go.

Unable to wait a moment more, he picked up the phone, asked for Jason Bourne.

"Is he in?" Vanov said in decent German.

"I believe Herr Bourne is taking breakfast in his room this morning. Who shall I say is inquiring?"

"Don't say a word," Vanov said. "I'm an old friend and I want to surprise him."

The eager tone in Vanov's voice must have persuaded the man at the front desk. He said, "As you wish, Herr Vanov. Good day."

"Good day to you," Vanov replied in the formal style so beloved of Germans.

Then he went out, riding the elevator up to the top floor. It was only when he stood before the door to Jason Bourne's suite that he hesitated, unaccountably gripped by an uncharacteristic bout of anxiety. General Karpov had handpicked him for this most secret and important mission. Having come under the great general's scrutiny, he did not want to fuck up. Everything must go precisely as the general had outlined it.

The door opened to his tentative knock and there he was: Jason Bourne in the flesh. He was dressed in a polo shirt, jeans, and loafers without socks. The physique, the face were more or less as they had been described to him.

"Jason," he said carefully. "I work with your old friend Boris." This is how the general had instructed him to begin.

Bourne frowned. "Boris?"

"Karpov," Vanov said. "Boris Karpov."

"Ah, well. Come in." Bourne gestured to a sideboard. "A drink?"

Vanov raised a hand, palm outward. "Not today."

"And you are?"

"Captain Vanov." Vanov glanced around the room, looking for signs of another inhabitant—a woman, perhaps—but didn't see any. "We have important matters to discuss."

"Indeed?" Bourne raised his eyebrows. "By all means." He moved toward the sofa in the suite's living area. "Shall we make ourselves comfortable?"

"I'd rather stand, if it's all the same to you."

Bourne threw him a curious look, but nodded. "Whatever you say, Captain." He returned to where Vanov stood. "Why didn't Boris come himself?"

Vanov laughed. "Surely you're joking. Preparations for his wedding."

Bourne silently cursed his lapse.

Vanov pulled out the bronze coin on its chain so Bourne could see it. "The general sent me to give you this." Reaching around behind his neck, he unlocked the chain, dropped it and the coin into Bourne's open hand. "He said you'd understand."

Bourne's expression was rueful. "I'm afraid I don't." He looked up at Vanov. "Why don't you explain it to me?"

Vanov opened his mouth to reply, but almost immediately shut it again. There was something wrong here, something he had felt almost from the moment Bourne had opened the door. What was it?

"Vanov?" Bourne was moving toward him. "Is something wrong? You look like someone just stepped on your grave."

"*Nichevo. Ya prosto chuvstvoval, kholod*," Vanov said. It's nothing. I just felt a chill.

"*Prostite menya za to chto y tak govoru*," Bourne replied without missing a beat, "*no eto ne meloche*." Pardon me for saying so, but that didn't seem like nothing.

Vanov stepped back abruptly, bumping into the end of the sofa. "You're not Jason Bourne," he said. "The general briefed me. Bourne's accent is pure Moscow. Yours is Chertanovo."

Bourne's smile widened. "I've spent more time in Moscow's slums, including Chertanovo, over the intervening years, Captain. Of course my accent has changed."

Vanov was shaking his head. "You cannot fool me—whoever you are."

He made to grab the coin out of Bourne's hand, but Bourne was ready. He slammed his knuckles into Vanov's throat. Choking, Vanov fell, his hands clutching at his throat. His eyes watered as he tried to gasp for air.

Bourne hunkered down in front of him. "I'm not going to waste time debating whether or not I'm the general's old friend Jason Bourne."

His fist unfurled to reveal the coin. Vanov kicked out, caught Bourne on the inside of his knee, bringing him down. Vanov managed to strike him three times with the edge of his hand, making Bourne's eyes water, before Bourne drew a steel baton out of a holster at his waist, snapped it against the back of Vanov's right hand, fracturing it. Then he struck Vanov a softer blow on the side of his head.

"Please," he said, "let's not make this more unpleasant than it already is." He touched the coin with the tips of his fingers. "Now tell me about this and the message you were told to give to Bourne."

Vanov spat a gob of blood onto Bourne's shirt. "I'm not telling you a thing."

Bourne sighed. "Sorry, Captain." His hand reached out in a blur, grabbed Vanov by his shirtfront, and hauled him to his feet as he himself stood. "I'm afraid we're going to have to do this the unpleasant way. Unpleasant for you, I mean." He grinned. "Fun for me."

He half-dragged a stumbling Vanov through the suite into the tiled bathroom. Without warning, he struck Vanov on the cheekbone, the baton opening a bloody line. Vanov staggered backward. Bourne caught him, stood him upright, and struck him again in precisely the same place. A bright red spray issued forth as the cut penetrated to the bone.

"You see how it is, Captain," Bourne said. "In here, with all this tile, it's so easy to clean off the blood." His smile turned sinister. "And, unless you answer my questions, there's so much more to come."

He struck Vanov again and again, and the tiles ran red.

Bourne sat on the edge of the bathtub, staring down at the thing that had been FSB Captain Vanov. He rose, crossed to the sink, washed his hands and dried them.

"How did it go?" Irina asked when he reached her on his mobile.

"Bad news," he answered. "There was no message per se."

"I don't understand." Irina's voice was no longer a purr.

"Instead, I have a coin."

"A coin?" Her tone had turned dark, ominous.

"That's it. The message was a coin. Old. Ancient, maybe."

"And what did he tell you the coin means?"

"He didn't. He wouldn't talk."

"Not a word?"

"He's a fucking FSB captain," Bourne said, "trained to withstand interrogation."

She sighed. "Plan B, then. You'll have to give the coin to Bourne and sell me to him."

"No problem."

"Don't get cocky," she warned.

"I'm only cocky with you."

"Listen to me, *moy golodnyy zver'*." My hungry animal. "If you underestimate Bourne even a little bit he'll tear you limb from limb, and that will make me very unhappy."

"We can't have that," he said. "I couldn't bear it."

Ringing off, he went to the doorsill of the bathroom, removed his blood-spattered loafers, and padded back through the suite to the bedroom. He snapped open one of the three large suitcases, removed an electric rotary saw with an extralong cord, rolls of thick plastic and duct tape, and a pair of shears. He returned with his haul to the bathroom. Stepping back into his loafers, he crossed to the bathtub and spread one of the rolls of plastic over the drain in the tub and the area of the floor closest to the tub. Navigating to a music app on his mobile, he activated the streaming service. Music flooded the bathroom; he turned up the volume. He plugged the saw into the wall outlet, set the shark-toothed blade against Vanov's right shoulder, and watched it cut a bloody path through skin, viscera, muscle, and bone.

Twenty minutes later, he had all the pieces of Vanov's corpse wrapped in sections of the plastic and sealed securely with the duct tape. He had saved the decapitated head for last, staring into the eyes, wondering what they had seen at the moment of death. He popped it into a smaller length of plastic, sealed it up. Then he spent another forty minutes sterilizing the bathroom of any trace of blood, bits of bone, and DNA, using chemicals he'd packed along with the saw, plastic, and tape. Humming to the music from his mobile, he filled the now-empty suitcase with as many pieces of the body as would fit. The overflow went into the second suitcase. Then he stripped naked, lay down on the bed, and took a nap.

Precisely an hour later, he woke, rose, crossed to the dresser, and ate every single item on the platter of food Herr Hummel had sent up. Fastidiously wiping his fingertips and his glistening lips, he opened the third suitcase, which was filled with what seemed to be an entire wardrobe of clothes. He needed to pick out an outfit that most resembled the one Vanov had worn.

Ninety minutes after that, he called for the porter, accompanied him down in the elevator with the three shining suitcases. He was checked out by Herr Hummel himself. The man who had been Jason Bourne and was now Maksim Vanov, unbeknownst to the hotel's executive director, made sure he thanked Herr Hummel for his generous welcoming gift.

"*Fantastisch*! Much appreciated, *mein Herr*," he said as he took back the credit card in the name of Jason Bourne.

Herr Hummel, beaming, all but clicked his heels in delight. "I and all the staff are already looking forward to your next visit, Herr Bourne."

He exited the Royal Broweiser, his three bags wheeled behind him like ducklings all in a row. With the suitcases neatly stowed in the boot of his rental car, he handed the porter and the valet each generous tips, slid behind the wheel, and drove off.

On the outskirts of the city, he stopped at the edge of a deserted lake Irina had previously scoped out, into which he rolled the two suitcases containing the remains of the real Captain Vanov. They disappeared in tiny bursts of bubbles, like a child playing underwater. Then he dried off his feet and shins, pulled on his socks, rolled down his trousers, and laced up his shoes. He drove back into the city, arriving just after seven p.m. at the Meisterstuck Hotel in Stresemannallee. He entered as Maksim Vanov, cultural attaché.

It was not yet dinnertime in Frankfurt, and when he knocked on the door to the room at the end of the third floor, Jason Bourne was still there, packing for his flight to Moscow.

"Jason," he said, when the door swung open, "I've been sent by Boris."

Bourne frowned. "Boris?"

"Karpov. Boris Karpov. Your old friend."

"I don't know who you are." Bourne stood in the doorway, blocking Vanov's way.

"Maksim Vanov, Captain, FSB, at your service."

Still Bourne hesitated.

"I've been sent by a friend. May I come in?" Vanov's murderer said in Russian. "The matter is urgent and talking like this in the hallway isn't—"

"*Derzhite vashi ruki, gde ya mogu videty ih.*" Keep your hands where I can see them. Vanov lifted his hands, palms outward, Bourne stepped aside and allowed him in.

"*I vash russkiy yazayk prevoshoden, mne govorili.*" Your Russian is excellent, as I was told.

"*Ya imel prevoshodnayh prepodavateley,*" Bourne replied. I had excellent teachers.

Bourne stood silent, observing Vanov in such a studied, intense fashion that the person beneath the Vanov identity actually felt slightly unnerved. If he were to be honest with himself, he hadn't felt that watery sensation in the pit of his stomach since the time he had been jumped in a back alley of Chertanovo. He'd just celebrated his thirteenth birthday by drinking himself half-blind on 180-proof slivovitz. Five punks had surrounded him, deriding him in Fenya, the language of Russian prisons. They used the slurs like weapons as they herded him into a cul-de-sac and their leader began the beatdown. He was carrying little money and no items of value, such as a watch or a ring. Infuriated, they surely would have killed him, if Irina hadn't interceded. She shot the leader dead with an old Makarov she had somehow managed to purchase on the black market, despite her tender age. How she had managed this he could not imagine. In any event, the dead punk's compatriots vanished like yesterday's newspapers. That was the precise moment—when he had seen her applying her trade for real—that he knew he loved her more than he would love anyone else during his lifetime.

Bourne, glancing at his wristwatch, said, "Time, Captain. I leave for the airport in less than an hour."

"Then my timing couldn't be more perfect," Vanov said, brushing aside his brief upsurge of memory. Irina could do that to him, often at the most inopportune moments. He couldn't stop it; he was helpless to control anything about her, even his own memories—as if part of her had lodged itself inside him just before the moment of their separation in their mother's womb.

Vanov produced the bronze coin, holding it out in the palm of his hand. "Does this knock out any cobwebs?"

Bourne stared at the coin for a moment before looking up to study Captain Vanov's face with every ounce of his experience and skills. Boris had told him Vanov would be coming to see him when he had called to invite Bourne to his wedding.

"You don't seem happy for me, my friend," he'd said.

"Happy enough," Bourne replied. *"I'm just wondering about the rush. I've never heard you mention Svetlana before."*

"Love comes to all of us, my friend, if we're lucky. Even you, Jason. Even you."

Bourne had momentarily stiffened, wondering if Boris, with all his tentacled sources, knew about Sara. But how could he? He'd met her, of course, but that was before there had been anything between her and

Bourne. Still, when it came to love Bourne found it imperative to be paranoid. He had vowed never to put Sara in more danger than she was used to, even if that meant walking away from her and his feelings for her. He'd done it before; he'd do it again. On the other hand, he was becoming aware of the increasing difficulty in cutting off his feelings at the knees, and this, a weakness for someone in his line of work, was cause for concern.

"Don't worry," Boris had continued, *"I know you were on your way to Moscow anyway. Are you any closer to finding Ivan Borz?"*

"When it comes to Borz, 'closer' is a relative term."

"But you will *find him."* It hadn't been a question. Boris never questioned Bourne's abilities.

"Yes."

"Just make sure you kill him this time. The sonuvabitch has a knack of cheating death almost as often as you do. He's so slippery, so full of changes in identity if I didn't know better I'd think you'd tutored him."

"Now that would *present a problem."*

"I'm sending Vanov with something for you." The darkening of Boris's voice had alerted Bourne that they had entered the real reason for the call. *"Keep it safe, at all costs."*

"What is it?"

"A lifeline."

"What?"

"A lifeline for the end of the world."

And with that cryptic comment Boris had rung off.

Now, in the hotel room in Frankfurt, Bourne took the coin at last—Boris's lifeline. He turned it, looking at it from all angles. "Clearly, it's ancient, from the Roman Empire. Other than that…" He glanced up at Vanov, shook his head.

Vanov looked crestfallen, an emotion that was genuine. "Ah, pity. The general instructed me to bring it to you. He said you would know what it means."

Bourne nodded noncommittally.

"There was no verbal or written message with it?" Bourne asked.

"There will be many people you don't know at the wedding. Some may know you and not be pleased to see you. I'm to set you up with someone who will be of use to you in this and other matters. She will help in whatever you may require." Captain Vanov handed Bourne a slip of paper. "Here is her mobile number. When you land at Sheremetyevo, call her."

Bourne frowned "Who is this wonder woman?"

"Her name is Irina. Irina Vasilýevna. She is very well connected in many of Moscow's influential *siloviki* and oligarch circles. She's also conversant with other—or, how shall I better put it—unofficial personnel."

"She's into Moscow's black market?"

"Her father and brother were."

"They're dead?"

Vanov nodded. "Three years now." Strange, he thought, how speaking of his own father's and brother's deaths meant nothing to him. It was as if he were speaking of fictional characters—or ones who had never existed. Of course, it was different for Irina. She and their father had been very close. Their father had confided everything in her, and for this he had been supremely grateful.

"I won't need her," Bourne said.

"The general insists his wedding run perfectly smoothly. These are his explicit orders." With an obsequious smile, Vanov moved toward the door. With his hand on the doorknob, he turned, "Good luck, Mr. Bourne. I trust you've brought a heavy overcoat. In Moscow you will hear winter's footsteps hard on your heels."

Part One

Of all the aphrodisiacs in the world,
the most powerful is being a twin.

—Irina Vasilýevna

1

"MY BEAR, WHERE have you been?" Svetlana asked.

"Working, my pet," General Boris Karpov said as he came out of the enormous bathroom of their palatial Moscow hotel suite.

"Working?" Svetlana evinced an exaggerated pout. "On this day of all days?"

Karpov sighed as he plucked his freshly pressed dress uniform jacket off the wooden caddy. "Unfortunately, the world doesn't stop to celebrate our wedding."

Svetlana Novachenko had a face like a porcelain doll—a porcelain doll with killer cheekbones, emerald eyes, and hair the color of champagne. That she was half Ukrainian, rather than full Russian, was no impediment to Boris Karpov marrying her. He was the head of the combined FSB and FSB-2, the inheritors of the KGB, the president's infamous alma mater. As such, he was in a highly privileged position in the Russian Federation, medaled, feted at the Kremlin, invited to every glittering political affair, surrounded by the czars' jewel box interiors. He'd even had dinner once or twice with the president himself. All this was to say that Boris Karpov could marry whomever he wanted, so long as she wasn't a Jew.

Svetlana Novachenko wasn't a Jew. She was a member of a wealthy and powerful mixed Russian and Ukrainian industrial family that traced its lineage back to Czar Nicholas I.

"What were you really doing, Boris?"

She was stretched out now on a velvet chaise longue, her slim, magnificent body naked and glistening. Her arms were raised over her head in a provocative pose deliberately mimicking Francisco Goya's *La Maja Desnuda*.

"If you must know," Boris said, fastening the brass buttons of his jacket with its six rows of medals emblazoned across its left breast, "Cairo Station was in a bit of a muddle, having discovered the Israelis had been spying on them electronically."

"Cairo, is it? So far from where we are here in the bosom of Mother Russia."

He gave her a sideways glance. "I rarely know when you're being facetious."

"Oh, yes you do, darling." Svetlana smiled with her small white teeth. "You simply won't admit it." She extended her arms over her head even farther, throwing her breasts into high relief. "You're sure you're not carrying out yet another stage in the Sovereign's pernicious campaign against Ukraine?"

Boris frowned, trying his best to ignore her attempt at seduction. "You don't believe me?"

"The Sovereign seems to have bent all his energies on reclaiming what Russia has lost over the years. Aren't you part of that?"

"Don't be absurd."

"Do you not credit what he just stated publicly?"

"He makes many statements, Lana."

"This one is more despicable than the others. Last night he defended the treaty the Soviet Union signed with Nazi Germany on the eve of the World War Two, under which they secretly carved up Poland and other countries like the butchers they were. The Sovereign is no better than Molotov and Ribbentrop, proof positive he's a madman."

Boris said nothing. He was irrationally resentful that she had exponentially expanded the knot of anxiety in his stomach that for weeks he had been trying to control. And on their wedding night!

"And what has this war stance gotten him? Privation here at home for the populace as Western embargos cut deep, the ruble is at an all-time low, and the stock market is in free fall. Even the billionaires' concerns grow daily as they see their money hordes receding like the tide. Face it, the Sovereign is in trouble. He's shoved the entire Federation onto a slippery slope."

"What slippery slope are you referring to?" Though Boris knew all too well to what she was referring.

Svetlana sighed, which only served to thrust her breasts out even more. "Vankor," she said with that canny look in her eye that had made Boris fall in love with her.

"What about it?" He felt a stab of fear rush through him. Her combination of intelligence and uncanny intuition was bringing her far too close to the nub of the matter.

"My bear, do you think I don't know how the Sovereign has severely altered the Federation energy strategy? Russia owns the oil-rich Vankor fields free and clear; through Vankorneft it has the expertise and the infrastructure to run it, and yet the Sovereign has just struck a secret deal with the Chinese, allowing them to buy ten percent of Vankorneft." She eyed Boris. "Why on earth would the Sovereign chip off a piece of one of the Federation's crown jewels?"

Boris said nothing, knowing she liked to answer her own questions.

"Because, my bear, the Sovereign is frantic for money. The economy is deteriorating at an alarming rate. It takes billions to keep an army on the ground away from home. Mother Russia has to feed all those breakaway rebels in Eastern Ukraine, not to mention subsidize all of Crimea now. And with the ruble in free fall, the stock market so depressed that yesterday Apple's net worth exceeded that of our entire market, where is the money coming from? Desperate times call for desperate measures—and you caught in the middle. This is what worries me the most."

Svetlana misinterpreted his pained expression. "My bear, you are programmed to lie—even to me. I might say, *especially* to me."

He turned to face her. "And why would that be?"

"Your 'important business' on your wedding day wouldn't happen to be *maskirovka*?"

Karpov laughed. There were times, like now, when her intelligence and intuition truly frightened him. "My entire adult life I've been spinning webs of concealment, plausible deniability, and carefully leaked *dezinformatsiya* designed to confuse, befuddle, and lead astray our enemies so that they cannot predict what we will do next, let alone be able to respond to it."

Svetlana's arms came down as she sat up straighter. "You know, there are some who claim your wanting to marry me is nothing more than *maskirovka*."

"What?"

"Because of my family."

He stared at her as if he'd suddenly found a viper in his room.

"That you don't really love me. That you have agreed to enter into a marriage of convenience."

"Hey." Boris laughed again, but it was all sharp edges, nothing amused about it. "I have the ear of the president. I don't need your family." But seeing the serious look on her face, he sobered quickly. His face clouded over. "Who?" he said. "Who would be passing such disgusting *dezinformatsiya*?"

"If you knew would you cut out his tongue?"

Boris grunted. "I'm not medieval; I'm not Ivan the Terrible."

"Also up for debate."

Boris's heavy eyebrows lifted. "Who is feeding you such nonsense?"

"You know perfectly well who: First Minister Timur Savasin. But don't worry, my love. If I believed a word of it do you think I'd be marrying you?"

But now Boris looked truly unhappy.

"It's true you have the ear of the Sovereign. But if his right-hand man is passing lies, I can't believe the Sovereign isn't aware of it. You have to admit the Sovereign is a piece of work, adoring his Hemingway, going hunting, riding around half-naked on a horse."

"He longs only to repair what was sundered decades ago. He wants the repatriation of the countries that were part of the Soviet Union."

"Countries whose faltering economies put such a strain on Moscow it was forced to let them go. Good riddance, I say!"

"The Russian Federation is too small for this new world order, Svetlana. We need to spread our wings once more."

"Now you sound like Hitler."

"Bite your tongue! The president wants only what was once his. And so do all Russians. His popularity is soaring."

"'What was once his.' Do you even hear yourself? Ukraine, Lithuania, Poland, Latvia, Estonia, and all the rest were occupied by Russian troops at the end of World War Two. They never belonged to Moscow, and they sure as hell don't belong to the Sovereign, the Czar-Batyushka."

"I wish you wouldn't call him that."

"Why not? I'm not the one who traffics in lies and deceit."

"If I thought you had a Ukrainian heart..."

Svetlana's flush had crept from her cheeks to her throat and the tops of her shoulders. "You'd do what? Dispatch one of your hooded terrorists to kill me? Order one of your tanks idling at the border to run me over? Or arrange this very marriage? After all, takeover by proxy is the Sovereign's latest methodology for waging war."

He rolled his eyes. "There's no use talking to you when—"

"I hate it when you treat me like a child, Boris Illyich."

He knew she was really angry. She almost never called him by his patronymic. Nevertheless, he couldn't help himself: "If you act like a child you'll be treated as such. You're jumping at phantoms, letting your imagination run away with you. That's the Russian definition of *paranoia*, you know." His voice turned abruptly conciliatory, all self-defensive barbs retracted. "My field of expertise is the Middle East, as you very well know. As for Ukraine and the other countries of the former Soviet Bloc—"

"And yet you question my loyalty."

"I did no such thing. Our discussion—"

"Is that what this is?"

Once again, he stood watching her. "Our discussion was purely hypothetical."

"This is all about economics, isn't it?" she continued, off on another tack now that she had made her point. "The economics of greed. The Sovereign and his *siloviki* made billions of dollars on Russia's oil. But now that's all coming to an end. From where will the money come to keep the Federation going? That uncertainty—that fear—has given birth to all this talk of *repatriation*. Russia now needs the former Soviet countries in order to remain—?"

"Strong."

"But in the past they brought Mother Russia to the brink of insolvency."

Boris once again marveled at this woman's grasp of the tangled threads of economics and geopolitics. It was one of the reasons he fell in love with her, though her prowess in bed was indescribable. She was right, all the way down the line. Privately, he thought the president's goal was one that would certainly bankrupt Russia. The satellites had to be let go; they had been dragging Moscow into insolvency. The USSR had been too vast, too unwieldy, and now with Chechen and other Muslim ethnics feeling they were owed the world, this was not the time to try to corral them back into the pen. Those horses had left forever.

"But you see how wrong you are, Lana. The president has already announced a pact with Ukraine to keep the natural gas spigot open through the long, cold winter that will be upon us in months."

She shook her head. "You think I don't know what the sovereign is planning, Boris, but I do. Russians don't want war; they don't want him. Already the Western sanctions are strangling us—and it's the men and women in the streets who are suffering.

"That so-called pact with Ukraine will fall apart before it is even signed. The Sovereign will blame NATO for tampering with Ukraine. The temperature has already plummeted. As the winter arrives, he will turn off the natural gas spigot, not only to Ukraine but to all of Western Europe, triggering a recession that will race around the world."

Boris barked a mirthless laugh, his expression darkening. "What an imagination you have, my pet. The president won't risk starting World War Three. He may be crazy, but he's not insane."

She laughed. "Of course you're right. I got carried away. Oh, come on, darling, don't pout. It makes you look like a willful child." Even at low wattage her smile was irresistible. "Besides, you'd never have fallen for someone who wasn't this spirited." Her smile widened as she beckoned him with her crooked forefinger, its tip lacquered bloodred. "Come here, my bear. You look so handsome in your dress grays."

Boris shook his head. He still appeared put out by their friendly argument, even though verbal sparring was a staple of their relationship. "No fucking until after the ceremony."

"Who said anything about fucking?" Svetlana said with a seductive smirk.

"Later." Staring into her eyes, he straightened his jacket by pulling down on the hem with both hands. "As much as we both want, but later."

"Boris, you're so bourgeois."

"No, my love, merely practical." He came and bent over, kissed her lightly on the lips. "Now it's time for you to bathe or apply makeup or do whatever it is you females do to get ready."

"Idiot!" But her smile was warm as she kissed him back, more passionately, her soft lips opening as her hand went behind his head. "Now go," she said, releasing him, in her mock-command voice. "Mingle with our guests." And as he crossed the room, "And be nice!"

"I'm always nice," Boris said.

Her throaty laughter followed him out the door.

The moment the door closed, Svetlana wrapped herself in a royal-looking floor-length silk robe. Veniamin Belov entered from a narrow door that connected to the next room. He was a small man with pale skin, thick black hair, and round-lensed glasses behind which were dark, restless eyes that seemed to constantly be looking for a safe exit. He held a small device in front of him, waving it back and forth, searching for electronic bugs.

When he was satisfied there were none, he came toward Svetlana. "So," he said, "has he declared himself one way or another?"

Svetlana's mouth twitched. "Veniamin Nazarovich, you mean you didn't have a stethoscope pressed to the door?"

Belov's tense lips twitched in reply. "This isn't a game, Lana. How many times must I tell you?"

"Come here, love," she said, her arms reaching out. "Your tie is too tight."

He shook his head. "Don't make me regret—"

"What?" Her eyes flashed a warning. "This plan would be a non-starter if it weren't for me."

He remained silent for a time, as if trying to reset the temperature in the room, which had turned decidedly frosty. At length he sighed. "All apologies, Lana. Perhaps my impatience—"

"—is showing like a slip beneath a skirt," she cut in curtly. "And is just as careless."

"*Mea culpa.*" He laced his fingers. "*Mea maxima culpa.*"

This produced a smile from her and, though small, managed to raise the temperature of the room. "With such fluency you could infiltrate the Vatican hierarchy with ease."

Belov relaxed visibly. "Your assessment of the general's state of mind, then."

Svetlana frowned. "Frankly, I don't know. With Boris facts are in short supply. Always." She wet her lips. "He evinces the Sovereign's line, even here with me in private."

"Disappointing. He has a reputation for being his own man."

"However"—Svetlana raised a forefinger—"were I to hazard a guess, I would be willing to bet that his personal opinions are the polar opposite."

"Aligned with ours, in other words." Belov tapped a long, narrow finger against his lower lip. "How much would you be willing to bet on the general?"

"What do you imagine?" She shrugged her shapely shoulders. "I'm all in."

Something in her tone must have struck a chord inside him. "Lana, please don't tell me you've fallen in love with him."

"That's none of your business," she said a shade too quickly.

"Oh, but it is." He perched on the edge of the sofa cushion nearest her. "Love has a way of distorting reality. I know you understand this. We've been through it with other people. You've seen the failures caused by the distortions. We are all counting on you; you're the straw that stirs the drink. In the eleventh hour where we find ourselves, you cannot afford to make a mistake."

Svetlana drew herself up. "And now in the eleventh hour have you lost faith in me, Veniamin Nazarovich?"

"That was a gut check."

"Nothing wrong with my guts."

"Good." Belov rose. "Because without the general—"

"Don't say it," she admonished, unfurling off the sofa at last. "Don't you dare even think it."

2

BORIS STRODE ALONG the tapestried hallway through thrown open double doors, Army and FSB guards on either side, into the glittering ballroom mobbed with people in fancy dress. He felt a wild surge of pride. They were all here: the president, the first minister, the prime minister, the head of the presidential administration, the first chief of staff, the foreign secretary, and so many others—they were all here to honor him on his day of marriage. Champagne and caviar were flowing, along with copious shots of the finest triple-filtered vodka, passed around on silver trays by uniformed waiters. In one corner a string quartet was playing a transliteration of a Tchaikovsky symphony that, to his ears, sounded strained and ridiculous.

But in all the seething ocean of Kremlin hierarchy and elite members of the oligarchic *nomenklatura*, the men who feasted off the Federation's economy, the one person he searched for and found was his old friend and comrade in arms Jason Bourne.

As he waded through the hand clasps, the shoulder grips, the murmured words of congratulations, the barely hidden looks of jealousy and, yes, fear—for he was a feared man within the Federation as well as in far-flung climes—he was surprised to see that Bourne wasn't alone. By his side was a small, slender, catlike woman in a deep-purple dress whose bodice was slit so far down that the inner halves of her heavy, globular breasts were visible in a most inflammatory manner.

Boris flattered himself that he knew Bourne as well as anyone on the planet, which was not to say in any way completely. No one did, not even Bourne himself, Boris surmised—not since his memory loss. But one thing he was sure of was that Bourne was the quintessential loner. He never had a woman on his arm, yet the way this handsome woman had wrapped her arm possessively around his it didn't look as if she was about to let him go anytime soon. Even more oddly, Bourne didn't seem to notice. He moved as if she were not there at all. An enigma, to be sure, Boris thought pensively, that he must ask Bourne about after the ceremony when they could slip out for a quiet, unsurveilled talk. He felt a measure of shame that he had had an ulterior motive when he had extended the wedding invitation to Bourne. Wouldn't life be nice, he thought, if the only reason he wanted Bourne here was to celebrate the marriage. Nice, perhaps, he reflected, but that was someone else's life, not his.

Then, as he moved closer, his heart skipped a beat. Was that...? Could it be...? And then the thought exploded behind his eyes: What the hell was Jason Bourne doing with Irina Vasilýevna? It didn't seem possible that the two of them could know each other. And if they did, why hadn't Jason mentioned it? Surely he knew... Boris's eyes became slits. But the way he was acting, Boris was almost certain he didn't know.

Irina's father, Vasily, had been a wealthy and powerful oligarch, but even the wealthy and powerful could run into serious trouble if they were in business with the wrong people. This was what had happened to Vasily and his older son, his firstborn. Boris had not ordered the dual termination; he'd been in Damascus with Jason, as their interests had intersected. The order, so he had been told subsequently, had come from the president himself. He returned in time to save the twins from the same fate, arguing truthfully that, unlike the firstborn, they could not be blamed for Vasily's crimes. Of course, the twins never knew how close they had come to death, or who had saved them. But their grandfather did, and he had been grateful.

Now, with a titanic effort of will, Boris broke out in a broad smile as the two men embraced one another, not only as old friends but also as brothers who had shared peril after peril, who had saved each other's life not once but numerous times. This was the world in which they both lived, and the embrace was to acknowledge their mutual survival to see this momentous day dawn. *At least this much is genuine*, Boris thought.

He kissed Bourne on each cheek, and when he did so on the cheek away from the woman at his side, he whispered in his ear: "You received the coin in good order?"

Bourne gave a slight nod.

"Good. We have urgent matters to discuss. Meet me at the far end of the hotel loggia directly after the appetizer is served." As an added measure of security, he had spoken in Arabic, a tongue they both knew well.

The moment of intimacy over, he pulled back, and with an official smile now plastered on his face, moved off to a flurry of handshakes and well wishes from knots of guests clamoring to congratulate him.

Though Bourne was acutely uncomfortable with Irina clinging to him, no one—not even his friend Boris Karpov, and certainly not Irina herself—was aware of his inner turmoil. She exuded sex the way other people gave off body odor. She smelled as if she had just had sex or was enflamed by it. It was a constant strain to keep his mind clear.

He had called her after he had cleared customs and immigration at Sheremetyevo. She had offered to send a car for him, but Bourne was not in the habit of climbing into cars sent for him. He gave her an address where he'd meet her in the city center, and took a taxi in past the Garden Ring Road.

She had smiled when she saw him—a megaton smile as heavy as it was wide. "Good evening," she'd said in Moscow-accented Russian, and kissed him on both cheeks, just as if they were old friends. "Your flight was acceptable, I trust?"

"It was fine," Bourne had said, getting his first exposure to her heady musk.

She saw his nostrils flare, and the answering curl of her lips told him all he needed to know about her self-awareness.

"Captain Vanov described you perfectly," she had said, taking his arm in the possessive way she had.

Bourne did not trust her, much as he hadn't fully trusted Vanov. For one thing, Boris had never mentioned this woman, would not have had someone waiting for him. Knowing Bourne's preference for being alone, it was out of character. On the other hand, Vanov had given him Boris's coin. So right away he was confronted by an anomaly that only Boris could clear up. In the meantime, it seemed best to allow the string to play out with Irina, to see what she really wanted from him. There were so many cross-currents—political as well as business—in Moscow, more treacherous than anything in Washington, it was easy to lose your way and find yourself entangled in a web of someone else's making. This possibility seemed magnified to him as Boris had chosen this moment of his marriage to send Bourne a mysterious coin and refer to it as his lifeline.

Bourne drank in the sight of Irina. She wore a flared coat in deep red, high black boots, spit-shined, high-heeled. Her hair, loose and dark, framed a face that seemed made to kiss. He felt the press of her breast as she walked with him through the reddish-green Moscow night, filled with flashing lights and the roving eyes of members of every state agency imaginable.

A black Land Rover 5.0L SUV was waiting for them two blocks away, idling at the curb, its enormous 510 hp V-8 engine panting like a lion after a kill. A uniformed chauffeur opened the rear door as they approached. The uniform was unfamiliar to Bourne; it was certainly not from any official government agency. He must be employed by a private company, then, or an extremely wealthy oligarch.

The SUV cut its way through the heavy traffic, heading out of the heart of the city. The driver took an exit on the north side, onto an impeccably maintained road, something of a novelty in Moscow, lined with flowering cherry trees. Up ahead was a dense pine forest into which the road plunged, as if into a mountain tunnel. The SUV's headlights split the otherwise impenetrable darkness, picking out a blur of needles and upthrust branches. Not even the star-strewn sky was visible.

Just as abruptly they emerged from the forest. The headlights picked out a glossy green wall at least twenty feet high. As the vehicle slowed electronic gates opened, then closed behind it. Before them was another world, entirely separate from the rest of Russia, in which enormous gilded mansions sprawled over gracious estate grounds. Some looked Victorian, others Georgian, Japanese, Art Deco. There was even a mansion built like a Bavarian castle.

They passed all these over-the-top residences, turned into a long driveway composed of white marble chips that glittered like stars in the headlights. On the way, they passed a pair of great stone sphinxes amid the exquisitely manicured gardens, their enigmatic smiles exactly duplicating the Egyptian originals.

The mansion, lit up as if for a holiday, was in the Art Nouveau style: ornate stone facade, sculpted female faces crowning windows that looked like eyes, hemispheric balconies iced with swirling verdigris copper railings that seemed to be melting, like something out of a Dali painting—or a drug-fueled fever dream.

"Thirty-two thousand square feet, indoor pool and ice skating rink, two movie theaters, a ballroom," Irina had said as if reciting a multiplication table. "What else? At the moment, I can't remember." The SUV rolled to a stop opposite the front door. She had turned to him, smiling. "Home."

Now, as the crowd made its slow march into the ballroom where the marriage ceremony would take place, Bourne was put in mind of a *Financial Times* article he had read on the flight over: not only were there more billionaires living in Moscow than in any other city on earth, but fully one-third of the Federation's economy was owned and controlled by just thirty-six men, all of whom stood in the shadow of one man: the president. The concentration of wealth was one of the main reasons dealing with anyone with power in Moscow was so treacherous: their enemies instantly became your enemies.

They paraded between two lines of guards, grim-faced and certainly armed despite the festive occasion. They scrutinized every face that passed them by, save for those who could have their heads with one spoken word.

The ballroom was huge; nevertheless, it was filled to capacity. Pinpoints of light from the ornate chandeliers caused disco fireworks to spark off the luxe jewelry hanging from the women's necks, ears, and wrists, and from the brillantined hair of their husbands, lovers, and escorts.

As the last to enter took their seats, ten guards moved into the ballroom, ringing the walls while the remaining six kept their stations in the wide, wood-paneled hallway. Bourne had not had to count; his eyes, surveying the immediate environment, had communicated the information, along with a boatload of other trivia to his brain, to be sorted at lightning speed, filed away should it be needed.

He had done the same with the interior of Irina's mansion, from the marble statue of Michelangelo's *David*, spewing recycled water from the tip of his penis into a carved alabaster shell three feet across, to the antique Isfahan carpet in the study, to the titles of the books on the oiled teak shelves.

She had ushered him to a seat on one of twin hand-stitched Italian leather sofas. A servant entered with a silver serving tray stocked with small plates of caviar and a variety of drinks—from tea to vodka. Everything screamed money—vaults of it. Bourne had a brief but amusing vision of Scrooge McDuck diving into his swimming pool of silver dollars.

When they were alone, Bourne said, “Do you live in this place all by yourself?”

Irina’s smile was both cunning and prurient. “So Captain Vanov tells me you don’t know why the coin was sent to you,” she said, ignoring his question.

“That’s right.” Bourne noted her reluctance to talk about herself, filed it away for further reflection.

“May I see it?” She held out a perfectly manicured hand. She was studying him with the almost obsessive intensity of a lepidopterist.

“I don’t think that’s a good idea.”

Instantly, she pouted, using coyness to try and mask her interest. “I simply want to look at it. What harm could that do?”

“Tell me about this house,” Bourne said, a half smile fixed to his face.

She regarded him for a moment from beneath half-closed lids, then shrugged. “As you wish. I respect your need for privacy.” She offered him a small pile of Beluga on a tiny blini, balancing it on her fingertip. “I’ll talk while we eat.” Her smile turned prurient again. “I don’t want to be accused of letting you go to bed hungry.”

3

SUCH A HORROR to be good friends with the head of the FSB," Irina said.

"What?"

"I said it's an honor to be good friends with General Karpov."

"What you said was 'Such a *horror* to be good friends' with him."

Irina laughed. "I can't imagine I would say such a thing. In any event, it's not at all what I meant."

"We've known each other a long time," Bourne replied, "so he tells me."

"And you believe him."

"I do."

"Why would you? Government men are trained to lie."

"I live in that world," Bourne said. "I know it from the inside out."

She shook her head. "I simply find it odd that the general would be so close with an American."

"I suppose we've found our own private détente. It's been beneficial for both of us."

"You didn't ask him about the coin."

Bourne found her intense interest in the coin curious. "There'll be time after the ceremony."

The invitees had settled. The string quartet had been replaced by musicians who played a song that seemed vaguely martial. An odd choice for a wedding—though in Moscow, maybe not.

"And yet this man, General Karpov," Irina said under her breath, "he is frightening, yes? He and many others like him."

"There is no one like him," Bourne said.

"You are not Russian. You wouldn't understand."

"There you're wrong."

Her gaze was cautious and reappraising. "It seems improbable, but . . . you two are aligned in your politics?"

"We talk ethics, not politics."

"I'm relieved to hear it." But her eyes still radiated caution.

"Just think," Bourne said, "if Boris and I weren't good friends you wouldn't be here now, rubbing shoulders with the Moscow elite."

"Now you're cross."

"I'm never cross," Bourne said shortly.

Irina took a breath. "I suppose I'm having trouble seeing you as a friend of that man—of anyone in the FSB, for that matter."

Bourne turned to her briefly. "In my line of work you tend to meet the strangest people. Often it's the ones you least expect that wind up helping you."

She hesitated a moment. "That's what happened with you and the general?"

Bourne nodded. "Many times."

Her eyes were still clouded over. "Well, that's something to think about."

"Here's another," he said. "Boris assigned you to me, but you seem to hold a dim view of him."

She laughed. "He's FSB. I hold a dim view of them all. Doesn't mean I haven't learned to work with them. I mean, is there an alternative that doesn't get me killed?"

Before Bourne could ponder her reply in earnest, a pair of French horns heralded the beginning of the ceremony.

As Bourne held Irina in his arms he was wondering what the Kremlin *siloviki* had thought of the Russian Orthodox ceremony. For that matter, he wondered what Boris had made of it. So far as Bourne knew, his friend had never shown the slightest interest in any organized religion. The idea must have come from his new bride, whom Bourne had yet to meet.

The chamber orchestra was playing a waltz, and Bourne and Irina were dancing along with scores of other couples across the vast ballroom floor, beneath glittering chandeliers as big as meteors. The ceremony was over, and the newly married couple had yet to make an appearance. In another part of the grand hotel photos were no doubt being taken of the wedding party.

"I was here once with Boris," Bourne said. He whirled her away from an FSB colonel and his mistress, but not before he saw the man shoot Irina a filthy look. He was handsome in a saturnine way, with the heavily mannered bearing of an aristocrat, odd enough in a Wild West city full of clattering, snorting beasts, but particularly in the buttoned-down FSB. "We were hunting an arms dealer."

"Did you catch him?"

"When it happened it wasn't pretty. It took the staff days to clean up."

"You bad boys."

Bourne didn't yet know how she meant that comment. He glanced around the ballroom. "This hotel used to be one of the czar's many palaces," he said. "I wonder what that was like, rattling around in these huge rooms. No matter how many servants and lackeys you had, I imagine it was an incredibly lonely life."

A flicker of a shadow passed across Irina's face. Tiny as it was, a crack seemed to have formed in her facade. "I've had enough dancing. Do you mind?"

They picked their way through the jostling throng, toward the French doors that led to the tiled terrace. Bourne grabbed a couple of flutes of champagne from a passing waiter's tray. Irina had already downed four glasses, and it wouldn't hurt to keep them coming. Alcohol had the almost magical effect of loosening people's tongues.

The scents of night-blooming jasmine and orange came to them. They passed a pair of guards, who gave them a cursory look before returning to their scans of the overlighted hotel grounds. Somewhere, not far off, a dog barked, then returned to its snuffling.

"Nothing to complain about as far as security is concerned," she said so softly that once again Bourne had the impression she was talking to herself.

He looked out over the grounds, but all his other senses were attuned to her, trying to work out the true nature of the woman beneath the dazzling, erotic surface.

"I live with loneliness all the time," he said. "It's my world—but I don't know whether I've chosen it or it's chosen me. Normally, I don't think about it much, but there are times"—he gave her the briefest glance—"when I do."

Irina sipped her champagne thoughtfully. "Is that a compliment or . . . ?" She shrugged her beautiful, square shoulders. "Doesn't matter."

The sounds of the dog came again, closer this time. They saw its shadow first, huge and distorted. When it came into view it was at the end of a thick chain leash held by a guard: almost as big as its shadow, its coat bristling, nosing around the bushes for the scent of an intruder. It was wholly intent on scent, until it paused, lifted its leg, and almost disdainfully peed on the bush.

Irina laughed softly. "I feel sorry for the animal, chained and bound."

Bourne said nothing, waiting. And then his patience was rewarded, but not in the way he had anticipated.

"Tell me," she said, "have you ever been in love?"

He kept surprise out of his voice. "Why do you ask?"

"Last night. You spoke her name."

"I don't believe I spoke anyone's name."

"But you did. While you were asleep. You were restless, dreaming. Perhaps it was a nightmare."

"I don't have nightmares."

She smiled at him. "I have nightmares. Everyone does."

"Nevertheless, I never spoke a name."

"But you did. I heard it."

"I don't believe you."

"Sara. You called 'Sara.'"

Bourne did not care for the turn the conversation had taken. Had he spoken Sara's name in his sleep? "I don't know any Sara."

"You love her."

Something hardened inside him. "Irina, what is this about?" and then she surprised him again.

"I was in your bedroom last night. I heard you call out her name. 'Sara,' you said in the tenderest voice I have ever heard. I was jealous, I admit it. I've always wanted a man to speak my name so tenderly."

What to make of this woman? It was as if she were many people. "It's you who were dreaming."

She ignored this. "I sat for hours watching you sleep."

"I would have known."

She took the slightest sip of her champagne. "I was engaged once. I was young enough to have fallen deeply in love. He was just like you, that's how stupid I was. He worked in your world, on the margins, in the shadows. He was very good—very good, indeed. Many people were terrified of him. But he inhabited this world fully and completely. He stepped out of the shadows only briefly. I soon discovered there was no room for me. Well, you must know all about that." She wet her lips. "As I say I was young and stupid. I was too besotted to break it off. One day he left for god alone knows where. He never came back. He never left a trace. He vanished off the face of the earth. Poof! Up in smoke, like a magician."

"There are no magicians," Bourne said. "Only illusionists."

Her smile was ironic just before she turned away. She took a deep breath, let it out slowly. "So many things can kill you, so many ways to die."

Once more he didn't know whether she was talking to him or to herself.

"Have you ever thought about dying, Bourne?"

"Every day," he said. "But I've already died once. I'm on my second life."

"What's that song? 'You Only Live Twice'?"

"Nancy Sinatra." Bourne laughed. "That's part of a life long ago and far away."

Irina finished off her champagne, reached for his untouched flute. "I want to live twice," she said.

A dark note in her voice put him on alert. "Has there been a threat to your life?"

"This is Russia, Bourne." She downed his champagne in one long swallow, set the empty flute on top of the balustrade next to hers, peered at them as if they were a psychic's crystal ball.

"This estate," she said, after what seemed a long time. "This palace, so huge and forbidding. Like a knight's castle, it might as well have a moat around it." She moved the flutes together until their lips touched. "I know what that kind of loneliness feels like." Her eyes caught Bourne's, then slowly drifted away. "I live alone in my house," she went on. "Three years ago it was different, of course. I had Father and my brother."

"Where are they now?" Bourne asked.

"Dead." Irina's eyes searched his for a reaction. "They were murdered."

"By whom?"

She shrugged. "Many guesses, a show investigation by the police, no arrests." She shrugged again. "I expected nothing more. It's Russia, after all."

"But your family is wealthy."

"That was the problem, wasn't it? It's the *siloviki*—the security wonks—who have the political clout. All the oligarchs have is money, and in the dawning of this new era of conservatism and isolationism, money isn't nearly enough." She gripped the balustrade, as if for security. "Still, in my father's case, there was another issue: All oligarchs cast shadows. Some shadows—very, very few, to be sure—are almost as long as the Sovereign's." She pursed her lips. "Mikhail Khodorkovsky was lucky. He only got ten years in prison for defying the Sovereign."

"So your father was a dissident like Khodorkovsky." When she nodded, Bourne said, "How were he and your brother killed?"

"The estate was infiltrated. At night. Alarms were deactivated."

"Professionals."

She nodded again. "They slaughtered my father and brother in their beds."

"I imagine nothing was taken."

"That's right."

In America, the place would have been ransacked to make it look like a robbery. Here, there was no need for such a ruse. "And you?"

"Mercifully, I was away on business." Her eyes had darkened as her vision turned inward. "This was three years ago. I returned four days after the home invasion. My family was at the mortuary, awaiting my identification." She wet her lips. "I buried them, alone."

"Your mother?"

"Ah, my mother." Irina produced a wan smile. "I visit her once a week, twice whenever I can. The sanitarium is in a beautiful location, but it's difficult to get to."

"Your mother," he said at length. "She was hurt in the home invasion."

"Oh, no." Irina swung around toward him. "She's been locked away ever since we . . . I . . . was born. She's been diagnosed with paranoid schizophrenia."

"These days there are a number of drugs—"

"She's tried them all." Irina's fingers wrapped around the wrought-iron balustrade as if they were bars on a cell. "Nothing's changed for her.

It's been years now. Years and years. The same for her, but increasingly difficult for me. Sometimes she seems fine, other times she doesn't know me or mistakes me for the devil."

"The devil? Really?"

Irina nodded. "She hallucinates; it's all quite real for her, I assure you." She gave a little laugh that turned into a half sob. "When she mistakes me . . . I've taken to speaking like the person or . . . entity she thinks I am. The doctors caution me not to do this, but I don't listen. At least then I can converse with her. Isn't that better than watching her talk to an invisible demon for an hour?"

Whether she was seeking a form of validation or simply asking a rhetorical question was unclear. Either way, Bourne said nothing, wanting to give her more space. The trick was simple but effective. The more she talked the better sense he had of her. But as the silence grew longer, it was clear she was in need of prompting.

"Why the devil, do you think?"

"Oh, that's clear enough," Irina said. "My mother is convinced her disease is actually a demonic possession. She feels she's doing penance for her sins."

"What sins?"

"No idea, but, well, you know they could just as well be imagined as real." When Irina unwound her fingers from the balustrade they left damp marks.

Bourne did not need that telltale clue to know she was lying, just as she had been lying when she had confirmed Bourne's statement that her father was a dissident. He could see the truth hiding behind her eyes. She knew perfectly well what her mother's sins were. He was beginning to wonder whether they were knowing what her husband and son were really into.

4

FOR VENIAMIN BELOV, the hotel—the former palace—was nothing less than a prison. It was only when he was quits with it, having driven his car outside the grounds, that his breathing returned to normal. Not that Belov breathed easy anywhere in Moscow these days. He would have liked nothing more than to flee the country entirely, make himself a new home somewhere where Jews weren't hated and persecuted. Where might that be? he often found himself wondering. These days, the dangers in Jerusalem and Tel Aviv were ever more serious. Hamas, Hezbollah, ISIS, these were all implacable enemies bent on Israel's destruction. And with the way the Israeli right wing was acting—pushing Israel's borders further and further into the Gaza Strip—was it any wonder? He felt a terrible sadness at the political direction Israel had chosen. He had no love for the Palestinians per se, but didn't they deserve their own land as Israelis did? The exigencies of the implications had made him realize that all the paths laid out before him would put him in harm's way. After much fretful consideration, he had chosen. But was it the right one? He had yet to find out.

Several miles from the hotel, Belov consulted an app on his mobile that showed the location of every traffic surveillance camera in Moscow in real time, since the police and FSB were continually adding more. Satisfied, he turned off, went down a side street, and pulled to the curb. There he switched license plates, using one—one of many—stowed in a secret compartment in the trunk he had built himself.

In a burned-out lot in Chelobityevo, a Muslim slum of unrelieved squalor not far from the Garden Ring Road, Belov disposed of the identity that allowed him access to the hotel. The lot was a pit that stank of unwashed flesh, human excrement, and despair. Ignoring the furtive life all around him—old men sleeping while young boys copulated—he made a pile of his passport, driver's license, and *siloviki* identity card. From the inside pocket of his jacket he retrieved a small box made of thin sheets of granite. It was cool, despite having been near his body. From within, he extracted a disc not larger than a throat lozenge. This he placed atop the pile, then he lit a match and dropped it. The result was a sudden flare of green-white as the phosphorus compound ignited.

Forty minutes later, a new identity intact, he was down on the right bank of the Moskva River, beneath the shadowed bulk of the Bolshoy Kamenny Bridge, a surveillance-free zone, at least at the moment. At the western edge of the Kremlin, it was the first span across the river, its earliest fifteenth-century incarnation being a live bridge of boats, linking the Kremlin with Zamoskvorechye, on the southern bank. The more modern stone bridge had given way to the present-day span made of steel.

In deepest shadow, Belov saw the tiny red glow of a cigarette end, and he slipped down the bank toward it. The moon was full and riding high in a sky largely devoid of clouds. He felt its cold, silver light on his shoulders like a mantle. He did not believe in werewolves or elves. He did not even believe in the Golem forged in the ghetto of the Polish Jews. But he did believe that demons stalked the earth. The horror that was being visited on Ukraine by Russia on his own doorstep was proof enough.

The question of how well Svetlana knew General Karpov, whether he would willingly or unwillingly follow her direction in undermining the

Sovereign's planned full-scale invasion of Ukraine, was to be the subject of tonight's rendezvous. His contact claimed to possess intel Svetlana needed to help keep their beloved Ukraine free of the Sovereign's pernicious influence. It was too sensitive to be transmitted. Any electronic transmission, no matter how secure, was a potentially lethal liability to people like Belov. In these days of complete network surveillance the old-school methodology had returned as the most secure way of transferring information from one agent to another.

The contact threw down the butt of his cigarette, mashed it underfoot as Belov came up.

"Yasha," he said, "what have I always told you? Leave no sign."

"It's one of those terrible cheap Russian brands. The kind found around here all the time." With an almost theatrical sigh, Yasha bent down, snatched up the flattened butt, put it in his pocket. He was a small man, pale, his eyes big in his skull-like head. With his undershot jaw, he looked harmless as a mouse, which was the point. "We have only six days," he said.

Belov sucked in his breath. "So short a time. I was sure we had more."

"Well, we don't. The economic sanctions imposed by the West have put enormous pressure on the Sovereign. The ruble is plunging, along with the stock market. Food, already scarce, is getting scarcer. There are daily demonstrations in the Moscow streets. Far worse, the oligarchs are getting restless; their holdings are shrinking daily. He has to act before his coalition of *siloviki* and oligarchs fractures." Yasha's voice, which should have been triumphant, was instead sulky. He was a bit of a drama queen, but he was a fine agent for all that—slippery as an eel. "Our plan now seems untenable at best—at worst, impossible."

"That's why we have someone on the inside working for us."

Yasha made a disgusted sound in the back of his throat. "How can you trust her? I mean, she's Russian."

"She's half Ukrainian, which makes all the difference. Besides, I'm Russian, Yasha."

"Sadly, that's true," Yasha said with a crooked smile.

Belov opened his mouth in time to eat the bullet fired from the Makarov that had appeared in Yasha's hand. As he staggered back, blood spurting, clawing at his mouth, Yasha whirled, reacting to a movement in the periphery of his vision.

He blinked as he saw an unexpected figure in the wavering light of a passing ship.

"Rebeka!" he said. "Why are you here?"

She landed a vicious kick, sending his Makarov spinning out into the river.

"Rebeka, please! I was taking care of the leak!"

"You're not the solution, Yasha," she said. "You're the problem. Belov wasn't the leak; it was you. You sold him—and the people like us—out to the FSB. We stood ready to help the Ukrainians' pivot to the West succeed. But now..."

The ship's horn sounded mournfully, ushering Yasha into oblivion as a bullet fired from a Glock fitted with a noise suppressor entered his forehead and penetrated his brain.

5

AT ROUGHLY THE same time Belov was gasping his last breath, the final table of wedding guests was served their appetizers. Boris Karpov excused himself from the crowd of well-wishers surrounding him and Svetlana at their table in the hotel's ballroom and rose to slip away. With a hand on his forearm, Svetlana held him up.

"Where are you going?"

"What? Now I'm married I can't even take a piss without explaining myself?" he said only half jovially.

Svetlana stared hard into his eyes. "I don't believe you."

Boris's expression hardened. "Shall we proceed directly to the divorce without even the bliss of our wedding night?"

She laughed suddenly, her face brightening like the moon in the sun's reflected light. "There will be many things for us both to get used to, my love, not the least of which is sharing the same space. I know you were a confirmed bachelor."

Boris laid a hand on her cheek. "Until I met you."

"With many, many female conquests."

"Every man is required to sow his wild oats."

"As long as they're not too wild." She leaned in and kissed him hard on the mouth. "Don't be long, my love. We've more dancing and toasting to do."

In truth, Boris's bladder was not the pressing issue of the moment; it was his preplanned meeting with Jason Bourne. He knew why Bourne had come to Moscow, and it wasn't primarily to attend the wedding. He was on the trail of Ivan Borz, the master terrorist-arms dealer, who might be Chechen or might very well not be. Even the FSB wasn't sure, just as they had in their possession over a dozen surveillance photos claiming to be of Ivan Borz, all of them of different men. Bourne had thought he'd killed Borz twice last year, only to discover that both men were not Borz at all, but stalking horses. Borz had been running El Ghadan, the terrorist who had attempted to force Bourne to kill the American president. How Bourne had managed to wriggle out of that spider's web was still a mystery to Boris, one he meant to have his friend answer tonight. But before they got to reminiscing there was vital intel Boris needed to impart to Bourne—intel that concerned Ivan Borz.

In fact, Borz had been the reason Boris had been in cipher communication with his team in Cairo earlier in the evening. Goga, his lead man there, claimed he had found traces of Borz—the real Borz this time, so his contacts swore—in the Egyptian capital. It turned out that Borz had peculiar sexual proclivities, a bit of information Boris had shared with Bourne during their last phone call several days ago. If true, it was a decided weakness, one Boris was only happy to exploit. His honeymoon would have to wait until he returned from Cairo, possibly with Borz's head. He would ask Jason to accompany him. The arrangements had already been made; it would be like old times. Boris suddenly felt in need of old times.

Being the director of the newly merged FSB and FSB-2 was draining—overseeing the daily intel, devising infiltration plans, as well as dealing with the Kremlin hierarchy in which a terrible schism had appeared, dividing the conservative and the liberal members in constant feuds, backstabbing, and ideologically motivated purges. Picking his way through that land-mined territory was like dancing on the head of a pin, but Boris hardly thought of himself as an angel. Too much blood had run under the bridge for that fantasy. It was a good thing he had his second-in-command, Colonel Vladimir Korsolov, to count on. Korsolov came from a family of high-ranking *siloviki*, mother and father both. He knew all the trapdoors and a good number of the skeletons, hiding out deep in the Kremlin closets. He made Boris's job a good deal easier.

He thought of all this as he hurried down the wide corridor. He was picked up by a pair of bodyguards, who flanked him as he headed toward the bathroom. He waved them off as he went inside, stayed there for three minutes, then returned to the corridor, heading toward the loggia where he had asked Jason to meet him. He wanted no FSB personnel around when he met with his American friend, no CCTV, either, which was why he had hit upon the loggia.

Pushing through a swinging door, he found himself beneath the east side of the loggia, whose tiled roof was held up by twelve pillars in the shape of caryatids. The women in their Grecian robes regarded him with solemn grace. In the courtyard itself, cherry trees rose up from the four corners. Then it was roses and zinnia all the way to the center, where a marble fountain with water overflowing an urn carried by a female water bearer filled the night air with the sounds of what seemed to him children playing. It recalled to him scenes from his youth, before his life in the service of the *siloviki* was even a gleam in his eye. How simple everything was then. His parents had a country house, with a cherry orchard ragged from inattention. One morning in early summer when he was ten, his father roused him from sleep. He did so with his great walrus moustache, the feel of which always made Boris giggle.

"You and I," his father said, as Boris dressed, "are going to have an adventure!"

That entire summer, father and son labored in the cherry orchard, raking, watering, feeding, pruning, and later, spreading nets over the budding fruit to keep the birds from stealing it. All of June, July, and August, when they came out to the house, Boris worked from morning till dusk. He and his father scarcely said a word to each other, but his father's proud smile, and a kiss on the top of his head each night, meant everything to him. It was the happiest summer of his life. Looking back on it, it was perhaps his only happy summer, for his father keeled over and died on the coldest day of the following winter—the ides of February—when snow covered the ground from horizon to horizon. Boris, ever the stoic, watched his father lowered into his grave with dry eyes and nary a sound escaping his lips. But days later, out at the house, he awoke to an icy dawn, drew on his clothes, and padded out to the cherry orchard.

The trees were bare, pale as bone stripped of flesh and sinew, dead looking. Behind him were the dark imprints of his snow boots. In the center of the orchard, he removed his boots and thick wool socks. He stood in his bare feet, sunken into the snow until they reached the frozen, black earth, and there he sobbed without respite, until he was as dry and empty as the husk of an old and forgotten tree.

He stepped out into the garden, the light of a full moon falling on him like the memories of his childhood. The memories of a father he rarely thought of now and had all but forgotten. How could he have pushed such a powerful figure into the obscurity of time, cobwebbed and dim, he berated himself, when all that he had accomplished, all that he was, was due to his father's strict but fair teaching?

It was a question he was destined never to find the answer to. At that moment a length of shining piano wire, thin as a nerve, was whipped around his neck, pulled so quickly across his throat he didn't have time to get his fingers up to protect the vulnerable spot, so tight he could not draw another breath.

Boris struggled. He was not a young man, but he was as fit as any soldier, and a good deal more canny. He had been in numerous lethal situations in his time and had survived them all. At what point he became aware that this time was different he'd never be able to say. But when that moment did come, when he knew that his unknown and unseen assailant was implacable, unstoppable, and would within moments succeed in killing him, he was prepared. In a sense, he had always been prepared. From the moment his father died he had taken a path through life that would familiarize him with death. And now, at the end, he knew why.

He'd known this moment would come, sooner rather than later. There was no surprise, no sorrow, not even a sense of loss. But then into his mind came all the people he had killed and had ordered murdered, and he grew afraid that their souls were waiting for him, to judge him, and to cast him down. That instant passed as in the misty distance the cherry orchard of his childhood appeared. He made out his father standing in the center of it, looking at him, waiting. As if in a dream, he moved closer to his father. He was in the mist now. It should have felt cold, but instead it was warm and welcoming. Closer and closer he came to his father, until they were one.

6

COLONEL VLADIMIR KORSOLOV had the indifferent gaze of a doctor or a gravedigger. He held the appearance of a man who knew he was different and didn't much care for it. Perhaps as a child he had been beaten up for it. In any event, he seemed to regard everyone else with a disdain he could not afford to turn inward.

This assessment ran through Bourne's mind when Korsolov and three of his FSB minions intercepted him as he hurried toward the loggia. He was late. It had been easy enough to break away from Irina, but then, on his way out of the ballroom, he had been detained by Svetlana, and it had been difficult to cut short his conversation with the bride. To his surprise, two of the agents held Irina between them as if she were a prisoner.

"Halt," Korsolov ordered. "Stay where you are, Bourne. Do not move."

The third agent positioned himself directly behind Bourne, so close Bourne could hear his stentorian breathing, like a farm animal.

Korsolov, having introduced himself, now stood in front of Bourne, his eyes steady, his countenance perfectly blank. "Why are you near the loggia?"

With events clearly overrunning Boris's timeline, Bourne felt the truth was the best course. "I was on my way to meet Boris."

"General Karpov, you mean. Is this correct?"

"It is." Bourne craned his neck. "Why is Irina Vasilýevna being held?"

"I'll ask the questions, Bourne." Korsolov took a step closer. He was the FSB colonel who had eyed Bourne and Irina while they were dancing. "Why were you meeting with General Karpov?"

"I've no idea," Bourne said evenly. He was getting a very bad feeling in the pit of his stomach that he couldn't shake no matter how hard he tried. "Boris told me he wanted to talk. He suggested we meet in the loggia after the first course was served."

Korsolov waited a beat before he said, "And?"

"And nothing. I'm on my way to meet him, and instead here I am talking to you and your goons."

Korsolov frowned. "'Goons'? I don't know this word."

"It's American slang for 'FSB agents.'"

Korsolov's frown deepened, but behind his back Bourne saw Irina's brief ironic smile. The colonel took another step closer to Bourne. He lowered his voice. "Listen, Bourne, I don't like Americans—especially Americans who think they have special privileges in Moscow. Going forward don't for a minute think you'll get the kind of lax treatment General Karpov afforded you."

Bourne reacted to Korsolov's use of the past tense. "What do you mean?" The falling sensation in the pit of his stomach accelerated. "Has something happened to Boris?"

Without a word, Korsolov turned on his heel, led the way down the remaining length of the corridor. Bourne was keenly aware of the goon at his back. He saw Irina shake her head before she, too, was marched down the corridor. The unmistakable sound of a generator threw harsh decibels at them, and Bourne's heart sank. In this context a generator could only mean one thing: a crime scene.

Double doors opened onto the loggia. Floodlights used to illuminate the hotel entrance for the wedding were being relocated, their electrical cords snaking away behind them, all connected to a large, ungainly-looking generator, coughing like a dragon with emphysema.

The moment Bourne caught a glimpse of the body, he broke away from the close-knit group. In the periphery of his vision he was aware of the goon who had been behind him start to sprint after him, but be arrested by a hand signal from Korsolov, who, smartly, was more interested in Bourne's reaction than in keeping him on a close tether.

Bourne had seen plenty of corpses in his day, some at his own hand, but the sight of the too-wide red smile that ran across Boris's throat brought him to his knees.

"Jesus, Boris," he whispered, "how could you have let this happen?"

Boris lay on his back, his arms splayed to either side, palms up as if in supplication. Bourne noted the fresh dirt on the knees of his friend's trousers. What were his last thoughts as the life pumped out of him? Bourne could not guess, but his own thoughts turned to the many times he and Boris had shared both danger and laughs, had gotten drunk on good vodka and bad, had hidden each other, lied to each other when they needed to, but mostly told each other the truth, backed each other up, saved each other. A deep sadness welled up in Bourne where moments before agitation and dread had uncomfortably mixed. Friends of Boris's nature came only rarely into people's lives, and in their profession possibly not at all. Boris was a rare bird, and this was no way for him to die.

He resisted the urge to get up, smash the generator, plunge the loggia into shadows and moonlight, the better to hide the atrocity. Murder was bad enough, but the harsh light stripped Boris's corpse of all dignity and sense of, if not peace, which was never a word in Boris's vocabulary, then proper rest.

With these thoughts threatening to overwhelm his uncanny powers of observation, Bourne brought himself from the brink of despair back to the moment at hand. Tough though it might be, he knew the only way to honor Boris's memory was to solve the enigma of his murder. He had little doubt that his friend's sudden demise had something to do with whatever it was Boris had wanted to talk to him about. Even on the evening of his wedding Boris felt it couldn't wait. The urgency of whatever situation Boris had found himself in was as clear and hot as the spotlights illuminating him.

The piano wire that had killed him was still embedded in his throat, the center having sawed through the cricoid cartilage. The entire front of Boris's suit, shirt, and bow tie was black and glistening with the blood that had gushed out of him as he was dying. On either end of the piano wire were wooden handles. They looked like they had already been dusted for fingerprints. Bourne could see none; unsurprisingly, the killer had worn gloves.

"What do you see, Bourne?"

With a start, Bourne realized that Korsolov was standing over his shoulder. He realized he'd better get his mind fully in gear. He could mourn for his friend later.

"There are defensive abrasions on his hands and fingertips."

"He tried to fight back. So what?"

"So there's material under his fingernails. Maybe it's shreds of the gloves the killer was wearing, maybe an analysis will lead us somewhere. Or we could get really lucky and a bit of the killer's skin might be lodged under there."

Korsolov seemed unmoved. "What else?"

"This wasn't just a murder by a professional, it was a ritualistic killing."

"What makes you say that?"

Bourne pointed. "The dirt on his trousers indicates he was on his knees when he died. From that position it's impossible for him to have then fallen onto his back without having his legs doubled beneath him. And look at how the body is laid out—with precision, with clear religious implications."

Korsolov leaned forward. "What d'you mean?"

"It's obvious," Bourne said. "The Christ image."

At once, Korsolov hauled Bourne to his feet. "Are you fucking kidding me? I told you . . ." With a seemingly great effort he caught hold of himself, and in a lower tone of voice, said, "Maybe you could get away with being a wise guy with General Karpov—"

"I wouldn't have had to explain the implications to Boris," Bourne said. "He would've seen it himself."

As the colonel made a gesture to one of his goons, Bourne added, "If you take me into custody I won't be able to help you solve Boris's murder."

"Who the fuck needs you? My men are quite capable—"

"No," Bourne said, "they're not." He looked Korsolov in the eye. It was the only way to stand up to a bully. "No one knew Boris the way I did—not you, not anyone inside the FSB."

"If I thought for a minute that you had killed the general—"

"But you don't. I was on my way to see him when you waylaid me."

"The only reason I don't—"

"He was my friend."

"You're an American. That's three strikes against you in my book." Sensing he had gained the upper hand at last, Korsolov's lips twitched in a bitter smile. But he was wrong.

"As his second in command you had more of a motive than I did," Bourne observed.

"What?"

"That's right. You're an ambitious man—what deputy director of FSB wouldn't be? But as long as Boris was alive you'd gone as far as you could." Bourne sensed the stirring in the rank of goons, and he forged on. "Boris told me about you." That was a lie, but no one had to know. "He told me you'd become restless as his number two."

"That's a lie!" Korsolov snarled.

"So restless that he was contemplating assigning you to a post overseas."

"That's preposterous."

Bourne shook his head. "But the truth will never come out, now that Boris is dead."

"You are fabricating a monstrous lie."

"You'll never know." There was satisfaction in hammering nails into the supercilious ass's coffin. "Not that it matters. As a Russian you know firsthand if you repeat a lie often enough it becomes the truth."

Now Korsolov's grin widened. "You've overplayed your hand, Bourne, because where you're going no one will hear you, let alone begin to wonder about me." He nodded to one of his goons, who shook out a pair of manacles, preparing to cuff Bourne's wrists behind his back.

"You have forgotten many things tonight, Colonel," Bourne said, "but the most important is the hit Boris's murder will exact on your reputation. Do you think the president is going to promote the man who allowed his boss to be murdered under his own nose?"

The goon snapped the manacle around Bourne's right wrist.

"The man whose security failed to spot the assassin, the worst kind of criminal who infiltrated the venue where the president himself was vulnerable, gorging himself on caviar, champagne, and vodka."

The goon had grabbed Bourne's left wrist when Korsolov raised a hand to halt him.

His eyes narrowed. "Sooner or later, Bourne, I will bury you."

"You aren't going to pound a tabletop with your shoe?" Bourne shook his head. "You need me, Colonel, if you're going to survive this disaster."

"No, Bourne. All I need is a perp. And I have a ready-made one in this woman." He pointed to Irina. "Her father and brother were known criminals. She despised the FSB doing its job and flushing them down the drain. The general was its head. You see where this is going? Who better to kill than him? And what better suspect could I have?"

"The one who actually murdered Boris."

"And if she's guilty?"

"First, garroting is more a matter of leverage than strength, and she lacks the height. Boris was like a bull—even you know that, Colonel. Second, this is a fetish killing, which means whoever did it isn't going to stop with Boris. If you charge Irina with this crime you'll find another FSB officer dead in a week, maybe only a couple of days. There's something to look forward to while you contemplate the end of your career."

Korsolov gave a snort of derision, but at the same time he signed to his minion who freed Bourne's right wrist and stepped back.

"Okay, smart guy, it seems I'm stuck with you, at least for the moment. But I need an insurance policy to keep you on the straight and narrow, because I know the straight and narrow isn't your long suit, to say the least." He made another hand sign, and the goon who had been behind Bourne stepped behind Irina and snapped the manacles on her. "The woman is going into the Lubyanka, Bourne. Nothing you can say will change that; it's set in stone." He glanced at his watch. "You have precisely forty-eight hours from now to identify the murderer and bring him to me. Otherwise, Irina Vasilýevna will be bound over for a show trial for the murder of General Karpov. And what a show it will be, believe me. Then she'll die."

"You mean in true Russian fashion the outcome has already been decided."

Colonel Korsolov's lips twitched again, giving him the aspect of a particularly evil marionette. "Her fate is in your hands, Bourne. And when she dies, I personally guarantee you'll be watching front row, center."

7

I WILL NOT sit here another minute," Svetlana Karpova said. "I want to see my husband now."

"Please, madam, I urge you to calm yourself." Lieutenant Andrei Avilov was doing his best to soothe Karpov's newly minted widow. Married and widowed on the same evening, he thought. If his wife had been killed on the day of their marriage no one would be able to calm him down. "I promise you will see the general in good time."

Avilov was a thick-bodied man with the typical Russian trait of occasional melancholia. However, between those troughs he was a tough-minded, canny, politically savvy *siloviki* who was absolutely loyal to the deputy prime minister, also called the first minister. To the Kremlin inner circle Timur Savasin, first minister, was known as the first among equals, ironically just like the director of the Israeli Mossad. Timur Savasin was the Sovereign's number two, in charge of all security matters, as well as much of the Federation's economy. He wielded more power than the Federation's actual prime minister. He was also Boris's boss, but he was as unlike Boris as the moon was to the sun: Where Boris was a prototypical Russian bear—wide of beam and brawny—Savasin was tall, slim, an athlete of some repute in martial arts circles, and a charismatic. He was also a traditionalist, a conservative who longed for the good old Soviet days of the KGB's iron-heeled boot. He hated Americans almost as much as he hated Ukrainians. He had only contempt for the Europeans; he loved squeezing them on the issue of natural gas. He also smoked like a chimney, a habit he claimed calmed him and cleared his head of the idle chatter of *siloviki* and oligarchs alike.

Avilov had made himself his boss's shadow, and thus had ingratiated himself with the first minister. Even better, he had managed to make himself indispensable to Timur Savasin. As a corollary, he was now bent on destroying Colonel Korsolov's career so that he could step into the vacuum created by General Karpov's sudden demise that had so shocked the president and Timur Savasin. This, he knew, would be no easy matter, considering the muscle behind Korsolov and his family. Korsolov knew things about so many people that Avilov had plotted his best course to keep away from the FSB colonel. He had to be eliminated, just as his boss had been. How Avilov was to accomplish this exceedingly difficult goal was, at this very early stage, unknown to him. But he had faith that within the labyrinthine corridors in which he lived lay the answer. He just had to recognize it and use it.

But back to General Karpov: As far as the other guests were concerned, a story had been circulated that a minor security breach necessitated the premature end to the wedding reception in order to protect everyone's safety. Following Timur Savasin's express orders, Avilov had spirited Svetlana back to the suite she and Karpov had shared, where they would have spent their first night as a married couple. Now there would be nothing for her but grief and agony.

Still, Avilov observed Svetlana as through a bureaucrat's cloudy lens, unmoved by her earthly emotions. She was half Ukrainian, after all; half a Western-loving traitor to the ideals of the Federation. Why should he have sympathy for her? She had lost her husband, true enough, but he had lost his sister to an ice fall, when they were teenagers. Nina hadn't wanted to go climbing with him, but he had bullied her into joining him. He had been thinking about his lording it over her, grinning to himself, seeing the tears freezing on her eyelashes and cheeks, reveling in the physical torture he must be putting her through. With an ear-shattering crack, the ice fall came out of nowhere, a rush of blue-white, the mass sweeping her away. He'd almost been pulled off the mountain, too, would certainly have died with her if he hadn't cut the line between them. He hadn't even seen Nina fall, so swiftly and completely had she been swept under. Climbing back down the mountain on trembling legs, the frozen tracks on her face were all he could remember. Two teams of mountain rangers had spent the better part of a week trying to find her, but she was buried too deep, or had been pitched into a crevasse. Dead, with no body to mourn, his father had descended into depression, his mother almost lost her mind. The family was done. Finished. But for Avilov, freed, it was the beginning of his new life.

Now as he stared implacably at Svetlana's tear-streaked face, he tried to recall those last moments with Nina, but could not. Even her face seemed clouded over, as if he were peering at her as the ice fall took her from him.

"My husband!" Svetlana screamed now. "Where is he? Why am I cooped up here like a prisoner? You must tell me!"

"Madam, please. Calm yourself. The general is in protective custody. He is safe and sound, I assure you." Why Savasin had ordered him to take this line with the widow was unknown, but he trusted his boss and so did not ask questions or overthink the matter. "*Overthinking*," Savasin was fond of saying, "*can only end in tears*."

On the other hand, the cruelty of the order was not lost on Avilov. But again he viewed it through his highly evolved lens, not allowing it to affect him in the least. He was watching a specimen react, and whether it was in a vented cage or a kill jar was yet to be determined, and not by him. He was merely following the orders of a man he loved and revered, a master chess player from whom he would continue learning the nastiest tricks of the trade as he climbed to the loftiest reaches of the *siloviki* ladder on his mentor's coattails.

"But why isn't he *here*?" Svetlana insisted. "If you're protecting me, surely you can protect him."

"That's not how the system works."

Svetlana's eyes flashed. "The system, the system, it's always the system with you *siloviki*. You are slaves to it."

"The system is what makes the Federation work, madam."

Svetlana's laugh was harsh, almost, Avilov would say, cruel. "Idiot! The Federation isn't working. That's why we're at war with Ukraine, why there are terrorist bombings in the south, why the Chechens have sworn vengeance, why we are at odds with the West."

"We've always been at odds with the West."

"Glasnost—"

"—was a failed experiment by a deluded bureaucrat."

She came toward him, with a kind of determination he wasn't fully prepared for. "You're all deluded, Avilov—*siloviki* and oligarch alike. It's every man for himself and damn the public." She was so worked up spittle flew from her lips to the lapel of his uniform. "All you old-line reactionary Soviets are so proud of your Revolution. What Revolution? You're no different than the czars. In fact, you're worse—greedier, more arrogant, and so very bloodthirsty." She was closer still, backing Avilov toward the door to the hallway. "You suckle at the teat of disinformation. Lies are all you know—and that makes you, what? You're not human, Avilov. You're not even alive. You're an automaton of the Federation, a toy soldier with a gun too big for you to handle."

Avilov hit her. He had meant it only as a slap, but somehow, some way, her words had slid between the plates of his armadillo armor, and it was his balled fist that slammed into her cheek. He saw the blood fly, heard the crack of bone fracturing as she fell—almost flew—sideways beneath the force of the blow.

The next second she was on the carpet, bleeding, her hand tenderly cupping her cheek as he stood over her, splay-legged and panting like a cheetah at the end of its food run. If he had indeed been everything she said he was, he would have knelt beside her, sunk his teeth into her flesh, and ripped out her throat. Wouldn't he?

But the fact was, deep down, where he feared to look, Avilov recognized himself in the dark mirror she had held up to him. He saw it in the moment he had cut himself free of his sister, he saw it as he had climbed down the mountain, avoiding the ice fall. And he saw it in his elation at severing himself from his family. Timur Savasin was his father now; the Federation was his family. Without both, he was nothing, lost on a sea without sight of land or even a horizon to guide his direction.

Hearing Svetlana's whimpers, Avilov came back to himself, squatted down, intending to investigate the severity of the damage he had inflicted on her. Instead, her long nails rushed at his face, digging in, flaying skin and flesh from just under his left eye socket to the corner of his mouth.

He was so shocked he punched her again, connecting with her jaw this time, so hard her head spun from side to side. A cut beneath her left eye leaked blood. She winced as she smiled up at him.

"Go ahead, Avilov, kill me. See what happens to you then."

Avilov felt himself losing control. "I'm not afraid of you." He didn't care. "I'm not afraid of your husband." Fuck her. Fuck Boris Karpov and his damned FSB minions. "You know why? Because your husband is dead."

"What?" Svetlana's bloodshot eyes opened wide. "What are you saying?"

"General Karpov was garroted." His voice was a cruel drawl, as cruel as her laugh had been. "That's what this emergency is all about, not the crap we handed out to you and your guests."

"I don't believe you. You're lying." Svetlana's voice was a deep gurgle as she worked her words around the shards of pain in her jaw.

"Why do you think he isn't here with you? Because he's lying in the loggia, in a pool of his own blood."

"Fucker! I'll see you fry in hell for this."

And then, all control lost, his body did what his brain bade it to do. Jamming a knee between her legs he pried her thighs open, pushed up the layers of her wedding dress, the shiny white satin and lace splattered with their mingled blood. If he expected Svetlana to put up a fight he was disappointed. She now lay quiescent, her limbs pliable as rubber, staring up at him with tears streaming down the sides of her face, while he reared up over her, unbuckled his belt, unbuttoned his trousers, and shoved them down to his knees. His erection made a tent of his undershorts. He grabbed them by the elastic, fumbled them off. He was in a frenzy of lust that went far beyond the physical. He was not only possessing her, he was taking something precious from Boris Karpov, never mind that the General was dead.

He thrust into her with such swift rage he didn't care that she was dry and unwelcoming, that the back-and-forth friction was painful. If it was painful for him, it was painful for her. But she was no longer staring up at him. She had turned her head to one side, her eyes lost within themselves, looking at nothing in her surroundings. She might have been a million miles away, and this disassociation angered him all the more. He slammed into her over and over until he felt the warm gush of her blood, and this proof of his mastery over her sent him over the edge. His eyes squeezed shut as he shivered, the muscles of his buttocks and thighs clenching over and over.

He stayed in place even after he felt himself deflating. He wanted to keep the feeling of pressing her down into the carpet, of knowing he was where Boris Karpov had wanted to be, but would never be again. He had taken his pound of flesh, but, Avilov being Avilov, he needed more.

"Now my blood's on you," he whispered into her ear, "you'll never be able to wash it off."

As he lay atop her, as she lay weeping uncontrollably, he began to figure out how to turn that need into reality.

8

NO FINGERPRINTS, NO footprints, but the murder weapon had been left behind. Deliberately. Why? Bourne pondered this question as he studied the forensic photos of Boris's corpse. He had spent an hour inspecting the entire loggia with Korsolov as his uncomfortably close shadow. He had found nothing. And why, he thought now as he sat in a salon of the hotel hastily converted to an FSB processing post, had his friend been arranged in a Christ-like pose postmortem? There were professional killers and then there were psychopaths, some of whom were obsessed with rituals. But inevitably psychopaths made mistakes—sometimes glaring ones—simply because of their pathology and their unshakable confidence that they were smarter than everyone else. In this, as in so many things, they were mistaken, but self-delusion was also part of their pathology.

The conundrum was this: On first blush, Boris's killer seemed to be both a careful professional and a psychopath fixated on ritual. Bourne knew better than to assume the two were mutually exclusive, but he had never run across a single person who might fit the bill, had never read or heard about one, either.

"Bourne, what are your thoughts?" Korsolov said as he stood beside him. He grinned like a bear with a fresh-caught fish in its paw. "Found the murderer yet?"

Bourne stared down at a photo of the gaping wound across Boris's throat. "You'll be the first to know, believe me."

"Oh, I believe you. I just don't believe you'll find the killer."

"Opinions are like assholes, Colonel," Bourne said. "Everyone has one."

Korsolov bent down, almost breathing down Bourne's neck. "You think this is a joke, American?"

"You must if you're going to show-trial Irina for Boris's murder."

Korsolov's smile broke open his face again; it wasn't a pretty sight. "You love her, that's it, isn't it?"

"I just met her yesterday. You really are an idiot." Bourne looked up at him as he said this, noting with a flicker of pleasure the scowl that replaced the colonel's grin. It was a petty victory, he knew, just as he knew that he could only push Korsolov so far. And yet during the course of the next forty-seven hours he intended to find out just how far this imperious *siloviki* could be pushed. For Boris he would do this, and much more. But for now it was back to the nuts and bolts of the grisly business at hand.

"What have your forensic experts found under Boris's nails?"

"No fibers," Korsolov said, clearly pleased to have intel Bourne didn't. "The killer wore latex gloves, we know that much."

"So. A professional," Bourne said flatly. He was studying a pair of close-ups of Boris's palms. "DNA?"

"Not a trace. The general's nails weren't able to dig in that deep."

There was something on one of them. Looking closer without Korsolov asking what he'd seen wasn't easy. "Two pairs."

Korsolov bent down far enough for Bourne to smell the shreds of rotting meat between his teeth. "What?"

"The killer must have worn multiple layers of gloves, which meant he anticipated Boris's strength and determination." Bourne thought he recognized what was on Boris's right palm, but a crease—his heart line—was partially obscuring it. "This killer was a professional. He was meticulous in his planning."

"Which also tells us nothing." Korsolov's tone was as sour as his breath.

"On the contrary, it tells us a great deal. There are very few people capable of this obsessive level of planning."

Korsolov's eyebrows lifted. "You know their names?"

"I need to see Boris's body," Bourne said, rising so abruptly that Korsolov almost lost his balance. "Now."

They had temporarily stored Boris's body in the kitchen's walk-in freezer. It wasn't the morgue, but it was the best they could do until everyone in the hotel had been completely cleared and they could safely transport the body to the morgue without attracting any attention. The space was huge, filled with sides of beef, racks of chops, and armies of aging steaks. To one side were shelves housing bins of ice cubes and sealed plastic bags filled with chopped liver, ground sausage meat, and pirogi filling.

Boris was laid out in the center, his thick brows rimed with frost. His lips were purple-blue, as if he had stayed in the Black Sea for too long. His eyes were staring up at the ceiling. The congealed blood, oil-black in the freezer's harsh fluorescent light, was like dried paint on an unfinished canvas. But there was no transmuting the dreadful blood-grin across the width of his throat, an appalling reminder of his violent death.

As Bourne stared into his friend's face he recalled their time in Reykjavík, the grave danger they had faced, and their private celebration afterward. Boris had poured them glasses of chilled vodka, but before Bourne could take his up Boris had shaken pepper into both glasses.

"*In the old days*," Boris had said in all seriousness, "*you had to be careful with your vodka. Some of it was made with fusel oil, which is poisonous. The pepper, you see, drew the fusel oil out of the vodka, making it safe to drink.*" Boris was always full of useful warnings concerning life's little dangers.

Bourne missed him already. Boris had always been more than a vital resource; he'd been a true friend, despite being Russian down to the marrow of his bones. Like all the best people working in espionage, he was a master at compartmentalizing the different areas of his life. Without that ability you'd go mad, which was why often enough spies put their own guns into their mouths and pulled the trigger.

Bourne had fully expected his shadow to be right over his shoulder, but at the last moment Korsolov had received a mobile phone call and had stepped back out of the freezer, walking far enough away so that Bourne couldn't hear his end of the conversation.

Silently thanking his good fortune, Bourne took Boris's right hand in his, brought it up for closer inspection. Rigor mortis had not yet begun to set in so he was able to bend the wrist to bring the palm into the best light. He stretched the skin on either side of the heart line, did the same for the left hand, but found nothing.

It seemed barbaric to have his friend staring sightlessly, so he bent over to close his eyes for the final time. But as he did so, he noticed something shining deep in the slash across Boris's throat, a tiny golden bit, twinkling like a far-off star. Using a thin-bladed boning knife he found in a wooden rack of butcher's tools, he quickly dug out the star—for star it was: a Star of David. And not just any Star of David, he saw, as he wiped off the blood and gore clinging gooily to it. Sara's star, the one that was usually around her neck, the one she was, in any case, never without. He knew it was hers, because one of the six points was damaged, where it had scraped the orbital bone of the man trying to kill her in Doha last year, before she jammed the star through his eye, pushing it with her fingertip into his brain.

Korsolov's voice rose. He was ending his conversation, coming back toward the meat locker. Bourne's time had almost run out. Quickly and expertly, he pocketed the star, washed the blade in the slop sink, dried it, and returned it to its rack.

Korsolov stepped into the freezer, and from his now familiar too-close perch said, "Well?"

Bourne stepped away from Boris's corpse. He was rattled—shaken to the core, more accurately. The thought that Sara had murdered Boris was unthinkable, unendurable. But the more he thought about it, the more likely it became. The FSB was one of Mossad's main antagonists. The two organizations had been at each other's throats for decades over the treatment of Russian Jews. Sara, a trained Kidon assassin, would have been able to handle Boris without difficulty. And it would be just like her to use the trappings of a psychopath and religious fanatic to deflect suspicion away from Kidon.

"I need a car," he said, masking his feelings entirely. His heartbeat drummed maddeningly in his ears. "An official car. I don't want to be hassled by the police."

"Of course." Korsolov grinned. "An official car you shall have."

Bourne drove the FSB vehicle out of the hotel parking lot, along the Ring Road, and into the heart of Moscow. Night was in full flower; the moon seemed to follow Bourne as he drove very fast and very accurately through the maze of the city. He was looking for something specific, and when he found it he pulled into the curb and parked a block ahead. Walking back, he thought of why Korsolov had been only too happy to lend him an official car—all FSB vehicles had a powerful tracking device hidden in their undercarriage. Korsolov had no need to suggest a driver for Bourne; he'd know where he was at every moment.

Until now.

Bourne mounted the motorcycle, hot-wired the ignition, and took off, leaving the FSB car and its tracker behind.

It took him twenty-three minutes to find the correct apartment building, but repeated rings on the buzzer went unanswered. He checked the time, then returned to the motorcycle, and drove it a half mile southeast to Kutuzovskiy Street. He parked down the block from where Eyrie's uniformed valets were taking charge of behemoth SUVs and limousines disgorging a mix of sleek *dyevushkas* in short skirts, plunging tops, and five-inch heels and the sons of overstuffed oligarchs, whose night was just starting. Expensive cars cruised by at five miles an hour. Young men whistled at the dyevushkas, most of whom had the decency to give the guys the finger before turning away, laughing into their palms. The atmosphere was sweaty, grimy with menace. Which appeared to be just how the denizens of the Eyrie liked it.

Bourne was stopped at the door by a bald-headed bouncer with more muscles than Arnold Schwarzenegger. He put a mitt on Bourne's chest, said with a sneer, "American, English, Dutch?"

"I'm here to see Ivan Volkin," Bourne said in perfect Moscow Russian.

A blank face. "Who?"

Bourne repeated the name.

"Never heard of him."

"Then you should be fired. Ivan owns this club."

Bourne's reply brought the glimmer of expression to Muscles's craggy face.

"Tell Ivan that Fyodor wants to see him. Fyodor Ilianovich Popov."

Muscles squinted at him. The line behind Bourne, lengthening every second, was growing restless. "And if I don't?"

Bourne shrugged. "It's your funeral." He began to turn away when Muscles said, "Hold on."

He tapped his wireless earpiece, then spoke several words Bourne couldn't make out over the rising noise of the crowd clamoring to get in. He tapped his earpiece again, finished. His eyes snagged Bourne's for an instant, a sign that he might be human after all. "Upstairs," he said laconically. "All the way."

The best action—and, paradoxically, the quietest space—was a roped-off section of Eyrie's rooftop, which had earned it its name. Two permanent tents took up the bulk of the space. Inside there was music, dancing, and who knew what else. The views from the open section of the roof were unmatched: the wide moonlit Moscow River, the massive tiered juggernaut of the Stalin-era Ukraina Hotel at the bend in the river, and the White House, from where the prime minister and his deputy steered the Federation.

It wasn't long before Bourne spotted Ivan. He wasn't hard to pick out, a furry bear of a man, salt-and-pepper hair standing straight up like a madman's, a full beard white as snow, small but cheerful eyes the color of a rainstorm. Even sitting, it was clear that he was slightly bandy-legged, as if he'd been riding a horse all his life. His lined and leathery face lent him a certain dignified aspect, as if in his life he'd earned the respect of many, which he had, being the eminence gris of the most powerful Moscow families in the *grupperovka*, the Russian mob.

Bourne had met Ivan some years ago through a mutual friend, and though he hadn't seen him in years, the old man looked as if he hadn't aged a single day. As was his wont, he was sitting in a remote corner, away from the two permanent tents, amid the shadows of potted palm trees, surely dragged out of hothouses only when the beastly Moscow weather permitted. With him were a pair of dyevushkas—twins: svelte, blonde, and looking very young—who rose and, on hypnotically swaying hips, vanished the moment Bourne was let through by a porcine bouncer. Not so the man sitting with Volkin. He looked like a younger version of the late, unlamented Dimitri Maslov, and for good reason. After rising and enveloping Bourne in his bearlike hug, Volkin introduced his companion as Yegor Maslov, Dimitri's son, though Volkin called him by the familiar diminutive, Gora, a sign of how close the two were.

"Gora, I'd like you to meet an old friend, Fyodor Ilianovich Popov,"

Volkin said with a mischievous twinkle in his eye only Bourne noticed. “He works for Gazprom. Upper management now, isn’t it, Fyodor Ilianovich?”

Bourne presented his card. “Second vice president,” he said, playing along with the legend’s profession as he had described it to Volkin. Shaking Gora’s hand was like trying to crush a lobster claw.

The last time Bourne had spent time in Moscow Dimitri had been head of the Kazanskaya *grupperovka*. Now, clearly, his son, Gora, had taken over. In those days, the Kazanskaya had majored in drug-running and black market cars. These days, who knew what they were into? One thing was for certain: with the greeting Gora gave him, he had no idea that Bourne had been responsible for his father’s death.

Volkin waved a hand to an empty seat, “Please, Fyodor, join us.”

When Gora smiled he looked like a little boy, so different than his father. “I’m afraid it will be just you, Uncle Ivan. I have a pressing engagement.”

Volkin raised an ironic eyebrow. “At this hour? You should be in bed, Gora.”

“That’s just where I plan to be,” Gora said with a laugh. And then he was off, crossing into one of the tents presumably to take the elevator down to the ground floor.

Bourne sat in the seat Gora had vacated. Ivan didn’t even need to lift a hand. A waiter appeared, took their drink orders, and vanished into the tent where techno music pulsed and young men and women danced, drank, and got high.

“So. It’s been some time.” Volkin rubbed his hands together with a kind of grim anticipation. “What do you have for me this time?”

9

"KAKÓGO CHËRTA!" Colonel Korsolov said. What the hell!

Captain Pankin handed Korsolov two passports.

The FSB officers were standing under the Bolshoy Kamenny Bridge, where Belov and Yasha had had their clandestine meeting and had met their abrupt end. Now, however, it was a brightly lit crime scene.

Korsolov paged through the documents disinterestedly. His nose wrinkled. "Two men meeting under the bridge. Homosexuals. A perfect end to this shitstick night. Frankly, I applaud whoever shot these degenerates." He tossed his head in the direction of the three uniforms standing at the edge of the cordoned-off area awaiting orders. "Let those fucking *govnjuki* at the MVD handle this mess." He meant the bastards at the Ministry of Internal Affairs. "Why the hell did you call me out here? Two less pussies in Russia is a cause for celebration, not an investigation."

"Homosexuals, possibly," Captain Pankin said.

Korsolov screwed up his face. "What are you getting at?"

"Take a look around," Pankin said. "See any closed-circuit TV cameras?"

"Perfect for their degenerate trysts. Yes, so?"

"Knowing your directive regarding homosexuals I thought it prudent to call you in."

"You did the right thing, Captain, but as of this moment, as I said, my plate is full." Korsolov considered. "Well, as long as we're here we might as well do some good. Get a CCTV camera for this dead spot." He chuckled at his double entrendre.

Pankin got on his mobile immediately, barking orders in double-quick time, which pleased Korsolov. It was about the only thing that had pleased him tonight. Nevertheless, he made a mental note of the captain's name. These days, smart young men who took the initiative when they saw an opportunity were increasingly hard to find.

While Pankin had been on his call, Korsolov took another look at the victims' documents. One of them, Veniamin Nazarovich Belov, was a Russian citizen. He went closer to the two bodies, took a good look at the two faces. He frowned. Neither of them rang a bell, but of course there was blood and dirt all over them. Still. He looked back at Belov's passport photo, stared at it.

Pankin looked at him quizzically. "Is there something wrong, Colonel?"

"There is," Korsolov said, "but I'm damned if I know what it is."

"I was very sorry to hear about Boris Illyich." Ivan sipped his heavily sugared tea. "He was a constant pain in my ass, for certain, but he was a good man."

"I wasn't aware you knew the general that well."

Ivan grunted. "The sentiment is mutual." He eyed Bourne with that amused twinkle in his eyes. "I highly doubt a Gazprom bureaucrat such as Fyodor Popov would have known the general, either."

Ivan watched Bourne sipping his tea, possibly waiting for a response. When none was forthcoming, he shrugged, and said, "You know, it was impossible not to like Boris. When he was just a lieutenant, I recognized a man on the way up. He was smart and ambitious. I wanted him, so one night I took him to dinner and then to a brothel I own. Do you know he was offended? Can you picture it?"

"Knowing him as I did, I certainly can."

Ivan shook his head. "I don't think you can. Do you know he hit me? Even in those days he was canny enough to wait until I had taken him into a private room of the brothel. We were alone, waiting for the girls I had picked out. And he sucker-punched me." He chuckled. "It was a smart move, because if he hit me in public, so to speak, in front of my men I would have had no choice but to have them hold him while I beat him senseless."

Ivan swallowed some tea, stared down into the glass as if he could see the past reflected in it. When he looked up, his eyes seemed brighter, more alive. "Even as a young lieutenant he understood the nature of power, the consequences of losing face. That was our Boris." He shook his head ruefully. "I tell you this. He will be missed."

Ivan shook his shaggy head. "If we're being melancholy we need vodka." He lifted a hand, and at once a waiter was by his side. Ivan ordered. By unspoken mutual consent and a deep sense of respect the two men remained silent until the bottle of vodka arrived in a container of ice. Ivan waved the waiter away, filled two shot glasses with the icy liquor.

The two men lifted their glasses, clinked the rims together in a silent toast. The full moon hung low in the sky, paled out, as was the rest of the night, by the glittering lights of the leviathan Ukraina Hotel.

Ivan sighed. "Up until then I had never met a man who couldn't be bribed. Everyone covets *something*. But for Boris there was only Mother Russia in all her resplendent heritage and mysteries." Ivan swirled the dregs of vodka, coating the bottom of his glass. "That night at the brothel, well for him. He had principles; it was easy to admire such a man. That was the beginning of an on-and-off friendship that lasted—well, until tonight. Poor bastard. No one should die in that fashion." He cocked his head. "Is that why you've come to see me? Are you a detective now instead of a bureaucrat?"

"Partly," Bourne acknowledged.

Ivan leaned forward, refilled their glasses, lifted his. "Let us now toast Fyodor Ilianovich Popov. He had a short and happily uneventful life."

The two men drank.

Ivan smacked his lips. "You know, I didn't believe your legend when you first came to me, and that was before I discovered who you really are, Jason." He smiled at Bourne's stony expression. "Oh, come on, it wasn't so difficult—not for a man like me."

Bourne put down his empty glass. "Does it matter who I am?"

"Not to me. You were Boris's friend." Ivan shrugged. "What else do I need to know?"

"I killed Dimitri Maslov."

"Yes, well, he was a shit, wasn't he?" Ivan refilled their glasses again. "The son's another matter altogether."

"Meaning you can control him."

Ivan smiled, shaking a forefinger at Bourne. "I genuinely like him. He's got excellent instincts." He tipped his head. "Like you."

He sat back and sighed deeply. "Do you know who garroted Boris?"

"I think I'm headed in the right direction." A direction that would lead everyone away from Sara.

"Difficult to believe he could be taken by surprise like that."

"Which makes me think he knew his assailant."

"Ah." Ivan tipped his glass, drank, swallowed. "Enlighten me, please."

"Here's a riddle for you. What do you get when you combine a meticulous homicidal mind with one psychopathically obsessed with ritual?"

"Obviously you have the answer," Ivan said.

Bourne smiled grimly. "A Russian politician."

Ivan's echoing laughter stopped everyone in their tracks, even those who were too stoned or too ignorant to know who he was.

10

I'M AFRAID I'M not following you." Colonel Korsolov massaged his forehead with the tips of his fingers. The assassination of the head of the FSB, now a double murder. This night was one for the homicide books.

"It may be nothing," Pankin said. "But there are other reasons two men would meet at night under a Moscow bridge where no security camera would record the meeting."

"Such as?"

"Sir, these men weren't simply murdered. One shot each to the head. They were executed."

Korsolov peered darkly at his captain. "If you have a point, make it."

"Homosexuals would meet out of sight under this bridge at night, true," Pankin said. "But so would spies."

Korsolov looked from the two victims back to Pankin, then he snorted. "Captain, you've been reading too many American thrillers. You have no proof—not even a clue, is that correct?"

"Except for the manner of their murders."

Korsolov waved away his words. His mind was wholly occupied with

General Karpov's garroting, which had not yet been made public even among the FSB rank-and-file, as well as with the wild card he had been dealt. He wouldn't wish Bourne on his worst enemy, but there he was, in Korsolov's face, like a hyperactive kid too damn smart for his own good.

"That isn't a clue," Korsolov said sourly, "that's extrapolation, Captain." He handed back the passports. "I urge you to reign in your flights of fancy."

"Yes, sir," Pankin said. "But here's the thing. We found no murder weapon. Further, we found no shell casings."

Korsolov shrugged. "So our murderer was careful. The American military call it 'policing your brass.' Have your people dredge the river here. Maybe our killer threw the pistol away." He looked out at the scimitars of moonlight on the Moskva. "That's what I would do."

Pankin gave the order, which sent his men scurrying to comply, then turned back to his boss. "Sir, I don't think this was a homosexual killing. As long as I'm here I'd like your permission to nose around a bit more."

"Jesus, Captain, you are one stubborn sonuvabitch," Korsolov said as he stalked away.

"That's what makes me a good detective."

Korsolov snorted again, but lifted a hand as if in salute. "As long as you're at your desk at nine this morning, knock yourself out."

Three FSB agents were in the official Skoda SUV, two on either side of Irina in the backseat and the driver up front. As the vehicle lumbered through the Moscow night, Irina closed her eyes and took ten Zen breaths—sucking air deep into the bottom of her lungs through her nose, out again through her partly open mouth, completely deflating her lungs. When she opened her eyes she saw the FSB agent on her left staring down her cleavage. She arched her back slowly as if stretching, and his eyes almost popped out of his head. If there was one thing she had learned as a child it was how perfectly mesmerized men became with her female form, no matter how young. She could have been victimized—in fact, she had been victimized, multiple times—but eventually she had learned to put her degrading lessons to good use. She became stronger, smarter, more wily than any man she had ever had dealings with as an adult. Once she engaged a man's primitive lizard brain the rest just flowed toward her like liquid gold. She got what she wanted, and often more. That was her life—perhaps every beautiful woman's life—if they had the presence of mind, the will, the inner strength, the courage to reach out and grasp it.

She slammed her elbow into the left-hand agent's nose, at the vulnerable place where it met the upper lip, so rich with nerve endings. Blood spurted, the agent grabbed his nose, his eyes watering in pain, but Irina was too busy to notice. As she had been taught in martial arts classes, she had pinched the aortic carotid of the agent on her right, stopping the blood flow from his heart to his brain. The agent tried to swipe at her, but there was waning strength in his left arm, and she batted it away without trouble. He was reaching for his handgun when his eyes rolled up in his head and he pitched forward, slamming his forehead against the back of the front seat.

By this time, the driver, with one hand on the wheel, had his own pistol out, but Irina, leaning forward, slapped both palms against his ears with such force he almost blacked out. Taking his pistol from him was a snap. Now she held it against his temple, giving him instructions on where she wanted him to take her and by what route.

Fifteen minutes later, she told him to pull into the curb adjacent to a burned-out building. The street was deserted; the streetlights were blown out. A shadowed night had fallen over the block and its surroundings. Dogs barked, a gun was fired, followed by raucous laughter. High-decibel music shot out of an open window like water from a fire hose.

The driver licked his lips. "You sure you want to get out here?"

Irina clubbed him behind the ear with the butt of the handgun, and he fell sideways, insensate. She leaned across one of the unconscious agents, opened the door, then kicked him into the curb.

Stepping out onto the agent's broad back, she looked around, breathing in the soot and ashes that identified the block. Glass shards littered the sidewalk, garbage skittered everywhere, fetching against piles of dog shit. She had been here before many times, years ago. She had been taken into this building, now a rancid shell of its former self, just like the block. Her nostrils flared. Funny how strong some memories were. She could still smell the sweat, tobacco, liquor, and fine Italian leather that in her mind were associated with her uncle. At once overcome, she turned, gagging, and vomited onto the FSB agent sprawled in the gutter. Damn her uncle to hell, she thought as she wiped her lips with the back of her hand. The acrid taste of bile was in her mouth, along with the memory-taste of what her uncle spewed down her throat. His big hand pressing like a vise on the top of her head, so powerful, but for an instant trembling as he cried out. And then the hand pushing her roughly away into a shadowed corner of the empty apartment in the building he owned. Then him near her again, his rasping voice in her ear: "*This is your fault, understand? If you weren't so damned pretty . . .*" Breathing heavily, like an overheated engine. "*If you tell anyone, your shame will be the death of you.*"

Irina looked into the interior of the Skoda. She knew she should kill these men; they were like the green-headed flies of high summer that would not give up trying to bite you until you brought the hammer down, flattening them. But there was another way, a better way.

She could feel them all around: the eyes watching her. Petty thieves, local drug dealers, the indigent, the long-suffering, all holding a grudge against the system that reveled in grinding down the have-nots to little nubs, shadows on a graffitied wall. She wondered what they made of her in her fabulous low-cut dress and satin fuck-me heels. Holding a handgun at her side. It didn't matter. She wasn't afraid. Why should she be? Like all predators they could smell what she really was, the wildness inside her. Despite her moneyed background she had more in common with them than she had with Colonel Korsolov's federal minions.

"*Vsë puchkóm*!" she yelled. It's all good. "They're FSB motherfuckers, boys!" Her voice echoed hollowly. But she knew they heard her, were listening with every fiber of their being, as she would have done had she been in their place. "There's a treasure trove inside this Skoda and no one to stop you." And then to herself, "Happy May Day, you poor shits."

As Irina strode swiftly down the block, she heard their furtive scurrying, like hungry rats awakening from a troubled slumber. Before she had reached the cross street, they had surrounded the Skoda, were picking clean the three unconscious agents, tearing and rending, stomping and kicking as they cursed through gritted teeth. At last, the sweet revenge of the underclass!

Irina continued on her way, leaving her memories behind with the new wave of violence. She felt free, redeemed, defiant. And why not? She knew precisely where she was going.

11

SVETLANA AWOKE TO see Misha's pale, handsome face looming anxiously above her.

"Where—?" She winced at the pain in her jaw. Her head throbbed. It felt like it was three times its normal size.

"You're in the hospital," her brother said. "You were drunk, you stumbled and fell in the hotel room. Luckily, one of Colonel Korsolov's men found you."

"Yes. Lucky," she managed to get out, not without considerable pain. Then full consciousness overwhelmed her. She stared up at Misha with bloodshot eyes. "Boris," she whispered, her voice tremulous and reedy. "He's dead, isn't he?"

"Oh, Lana, I'm so sorry."

She squeezed her eyes closed. Even that caused her pain, or maybe it was the blood pulsing in her temples. Good God, she thought, how could so much go so wrong so quickly?

"Lana—"

"Don't," she said sharply. "Don't even."

Silence. Just the inhuman breathing that filled all hospital rooms, along with the sickly sweet smell of sickness, old age, and the aftermath of operations.

She opened her eyes. They were enlarged, filled with tears that welled up and cascaded down the sides of her face. Misha popped a tissue out of a box and wiped her eyes. She wanted to tell him to stop, but she lacked the strength. Or perhaps it was real desire. She loved Misha—despite everything.

"I shouldn't have snapped at you."

"You had cause." Misha balled up the damp tissue and threw it into a plastic can. Everything in the room seemed to be made of plastic. He cleared his throat. "Nevertheless, Lana, I am genuinely sorry. I know you loved him."

The ghost of a half smile lifted one side of her mouth, all she was capable of at the moment. "You never understood that, did you?"

"Considering who he was—"

"He was Boris Illyich Karpov, Misha. You mean *what* he was."

Misha nodded. "All right."

"You never knew him so you don't get to judge him, especially now."

"I'm sorry."

"Stop saying that. For God's sake."

"What do you want me to say, then?"

"Where's Mama and Papa?"

"Downstairs. Mama's in tears, of course. And Papa's pacing a hole in the linoleum. Still, I thought it better I came up to see you first, in case…" His voice drifted off into a kind of darkness Svetlana recognized.

"In case I was unfit to be seen, yes?"

He hesitated, but her eyes bored into his and, as usual, he acquiesced to his sister in warrior mode. He nodded. "I didn't know how badly you were hurt in the fall."

"I didn't fall, Misha."

"What? But we were told—"

"Since when do you believe what you're told by government goons?"

"But at your wedding…I mean, there was no reason to lie. Was there?"

"Don't be a fool. From their perspective, there's always a reason to lie."

He perched on the edge of her bed so he could be closer to her. "Tell me, then."

She licked her lips. "Water, please."

He filled a plastic cup from the plastic pitcher, pressed a button for the top half of the bed to lift her up. When she'd drained the cup, he said, "More?" She shook her head, winced again, and he took the cup from her, put it aside. "Now."

She closed her eyes again for a moment. She felt dizzy, the room was spinning, and she was falling, her stomach seeming to rise up into her throat so that she was certain she was going to vomit. She popped open her eyes, Misha saw her distress at once.

"Lana." His hand on her forehead, smoothing back tendrils of hair, soothing her, cooling her as it had when, as a little girl, she'd come down with a fever. Then he'd stay with her, tell her stories so goofy they'd make her laugh, no matter how ill she was. Now, looking at him, she wondered if he would have rather been out playing ball or running with his pals during her confinements, and a wave of tenderness she hadn't felt for him in many years overcame her.

"Misha." She took his free hand in hers. "I love you."

And there was that smile she had come to rely on all through her girlhood, radiating out, encompassing her, making her feel everything would be all right. But it wasn't all right—not now, maybe never. With Boris gone, everything changed. Everything had turned to ash. Boris had been their last, best hope, and now he was gone. Still, she wasn't powerless; she had made sure of that.

Misha leaned over, kissed her carefully on both cheeks. When he drew back, he said, "Lana, what happened to you? Please tell me."

She shook her head, though pain shot down her neck. "Absolutely not. Misha, you're the golden boy, the chosen one of the family. Papa counts on you as heir to the business. You must remain innocent—beyond reproach."

He shook his head. "I don't understand. What has that to do with—"

"I'm the black sheep of the family, Misha. The less you know about my life the better."

"Lana." He took her hand in both of his. "Don't do this to me. Don't shut me out."

"I'm protecting you, Misha."

"You've always protected me," he said with the kind of gratitude tinged with regret. "But this . . . I mean if it's true it wasn't an accident, I absolutely have to know. I'm your brother. You must tell me what happened. I know you won't tell Mama and Papa."

"Misha . . ."

"Please."

So she did. She told him how Lieutenant Avilov had held her captive, provoked her, at last told her what had happened to Boris. "Then he took me by force," she said.

"He . . . Lana, he *raped* you?"

"You should see what I did to his face," she said grimly. "No, I take that back. I don't want you anywhere near that pig. He's far too dangerous—for you, toxic."

"*Bljákha-múkha!*"

Svetlana tried to smile. Even his curses were G-rated. "My face will heal. I'll be fine," she said. "He's going to need plastic surgery to be able to look at himself in the mirror."

"Good for you." A wan smile flickered across Misha's face, was quickly replaced by his look of concern. "But, Lana, he raped you. Say the word and Papa will press charges."

"I'm not going to press charges, Misha."

He reared back. "What?"

Svetlana gingerly touched her wounded jaw and cheek with the tips of her fingers. "Avilov works for Timur Savasin."

"The first minister." Misha's face had drained of blood.

Svetlana nodded. "The first minister."

"It doesn't matter." Misha seemed to have recovered his equilibrium. "It doesn't matter who he works for, he can't—"

"You see, Misha, this is why I didn't want to tell you. You know nothing of this kind of business."

"I'll explain the situation to Papa. I—"

"No!" She gripped his hand, her nails making white crescents in his palm. "I forbid it. Misha, do you hear me? You'll tell Papa nothing of this. You'll go back to work and do nothing." Her eyes searched his. "Promise me."

Misha hesitated, then nodded. "All right."

"Say it, Misha." Her voice had become anxious and urgent. "You must say the words."

"Okay, Lana. I promise."

She relaxed then, leaned back into the pillows, her eyes falling closed once more. "Good. No one can touch Avilov, not even Papa."

12

IVAN VOLKIN HAD a smile like a fox. He might have cultivated it, but Bourne was of the opinion he'd been born with it.

"You know, we're lucky, you and I," Ivan said.

The bottle of vodka was half empty. An hour or more had passed in talk of Boris, Maslov *pére*, the *grupperovka* clans—in other words, the old days. Boris's death had turned Ivan nostalgic and a touch melancholy. There was no use fighting it; Bourne went with the flow, in the process gleaning nuggets of information that one day might serve him well. Now, at last, Ivan was emerging from that faraway world.

"We love what we do," he said, "which is more than you can say for ninety-nine percent of the world."

"How do you know I love what I do?" Bourne said.

"Why, it's clear as a virgin's conscience," Ivan said, his crafty smile spreading to his cheeks and eyes. "Otherwise, you'd be dead by now." Then he laughed. "You know, you drink like a fucking Russian."

And once again Bourne thought of Reykjavík. "One of the things Boris taught me."

"Of course." Ivan nodded. "He would have."

Bourne put the dregs of the vodka aside. He'd had more than enough for one night.

"*Alë, garázh!*" said a familiar voice just over his shoulder. "You have strange friends."

Ivan laughed at her ironic address.

Bourne turned. "Irina."

Ivan, still laughing in delight, lifted a hand in an almost Roman hail, "Ah, Jason, I see you have met my granddaughter, Irina Vasilýevna Volkin." He shook his head. "Now why am I not surprised?"

"What are you doing here?" Bourne said with a frown.

Ivan waved her to a seat. "Irochka, come, sit between us."

Bourne turned to her as she sat, poured the last of the vodka into Bourne's glass, and swigged it down. "You're supposed to be in custody."

"Custody?" Ivan's great whiskery brows knit together. "Irochka, what does this mean? Why should you be in custody?"

"I'm afraid it's because of me," Bourne said. "I made a deal with an FSB colonel. He's allowed me forty-eight hours to find Boris's murderer or he's going to charge Irina with the crime. She was supposed to be in custody to keep me honest, he said."

With each word Ivan's countenance darkened like a rainstorm blowing in over mountain peaks. "Colonel? What colonel?"

"His name is Korsolov," Bourne said.

"*Chërt voz'mí!*" Ivan cried. Goddammit.

"You know him, I take it."

"I knew that goat fucker when he was just a snot-nosed kid." Ivan grunted. "Used to wet the bed, he did. Had dreams of falling and dying, his father told me once. He'd wake up in a puddle of pee." He grunted. "Probably still does." He looked out onto the river, at the moonlight reflecting off its surface. "He thinks he's a man now, but I know the truth. He's still that little boy. No time has passed. Boris did not understand this. Or perhaps he understood it too well. Korsolov was someone he could control. Life is like that sometimes. In his line of work, you choose not by competence but by who you can be sure of."

His eyes cut to Bourne. "He's not going to touch a hair on my granddaughter's head, you have my word on that. Is he making your life miserable, too?"

"Peering over my shoulder every chance he gets," Bourne said. "He's a real *ljubopýtnaya Varvára.*" A Curious George.

"Now?"

"I ditched the company car with its tracking device, stole a motorcycle, and came here. I'm clean."

"So am I. The three goons who tried to take me in are no longer among the living." Irina said this as if she were making small talk at a social tea.

"Did you take care of them yourself?" Ivan shook his head. "No, *króshka*, you're too smart for that."

"Now you tell me what's really going on," Bourne said.

Irina sighed. "I need more vodka."

No sooner had Ivan raised a hand than another bottle in its iced container and another shot glass appeared tableside. Ivan made no move, watched as Irina hefted the bottle, unscrewed the top. Filled the shot glass. Then she tilted the bottle to her lips. The contents gurgled down her throat. Ivan appeared unperturbed. She slid the bottle back into its bed of ice, licked her lips, then addressed Bourne.

"My father and older brother worked for Ivan—beneath the table, you understand. Somehow, the FSB found out."

"Boris didn't order the raid," Ivan added. "He was out of the country."

"He was with me in Damascus, as it happens," Bourne said.

Ivan nodded, and Irina continued. "In his absence, the raid was authorized by Korsolov."

"If Boris had been in Moscow," Ivan said, "the raid never would have taken place." There seemed no rancor against Boris; he was, it appeared to Bourne, stating a fact as much to reassure his granddaughter as to inform Bourne.

Irina only shrugged. Whether or not she believed Ivan was unclear.

This told Bourne something crucial about her personality. She trusted no one—not even blood. Rare for a Russian.

"Why did you lie to me?" Bourne said, already knowing the answer.

She shrugged again. "What did I know about you?" Then a tiny smile crept across her face like a water spider skimming the surface of a pond. "Now I find you with Krýsha."

Krýsha literally meant "roof," but it was street slang for the head of the *grupperovka*. Also the protection money for a business demanded by the mob. Bourne wondered how many of those definitions applied to Irina's use of the word.

"How did you two meet?" she asked now.

"Years ago," Ivan said. He appeared to check his fingernails. "Jason killed Dimitri, you know."

Something came over Irina's face, but it was so enigmatic Bourne couldn't tell precisely what it was.

"Really?" she said. The word was a placeholder, used when an idea or emotion wasn't allowed free rein.

"Scout's honor." Ivan turned to Bourne. "Isn't that what you Americans say?"

"Some of us," Bourne allowed.

"Not you, I would think."

Irina seemed to be mocking him, but as gently as a mother rocks a baby. Her face was devoid of cruelty or scorn. Could she be flirting? Bourne wondered. What could Dimitri Maslov's death mean to her? Obviously, they had had some kind of relationship, since Ivan referred to him only by his given name. In any event, she did not appear to have been broken up by his sudden, violent demise. She must have hated him, Bourne thought. Was that enmity merely an echo of her *krýsha*'s feelings, or was it caused by her own encounter with Maslov? Another mystery that required solving.

However, with Irina here it was time to get to the heart of his business with Volkin. "I need a list of names, Ivan—politicians who had a reason, the will, and the wherewithal to plan Boris's assassination." *But it wasn't any of them*, an insistent voice inside him whispered. *It was Sara.*

Ivan grunted. "Boris had a long, productive life, which, in Russia, means he had many enemies. Most of them, however, were so afraid of him they would never make a move against him."

"This person," Bourne said, "is a homicidal psychotic as well as a religious fanatic."

This produced a deep laugh. "A religious fanatic? In Russia? You must be joking, Jason."

"I am perfectly serious, Ivan. And, in this instance, our working definition of religious fanatic is a broad one. Our man might just as well be someone who harbors a deep grudge against organized religion as a closet Christian."

"Psychotics are a dime a dozen in politics, never more so in Russia." Ivan tapped a forefinger against his lower lip. "Give me a couple of hours to consider and draw up a list, for all the good it will do you."

"What do you mean?"

"You're looking in the wrong direction. I have it on good authority that Boris wasn't killed by a Russian—politician or otherwise."

There was no denying Ivan Volkin's authority, Bourne knew.

"It seems likely that Boris was murdered by Ivan Borz."

"Borz?"

"You know him?"

"I've tracked Ivan Borz from West Pak to Singapore. I've killed two men claiming to be him; neither of them were."

"This is unsurprising." Ivan crossed one leg over the other. "Let me explain. Boris was most recently in Cairo. He was running a top secret op—secret even, I think, from the Sovereign or the first minister."

"Borz?"

Ivan nodded. "Boris had sworn to get the sonuvabitch. No one else has been able to get close to him, let alone know what he actually looks like. He's got false Borzes all over, as you yourself discovered. But Boris got a lead he was certain was legitimate. That Borz is a Chechen and has set up an HQ in Cairo."

"A Chechen?" Bourne said. "That sounds unlikely."

"Precisely why Boris thought the lead was genuine." He spread his hands. "And I mean, really, who would look for him in Cairo? The place is a stinking zoo, not to mention hot as Hades."

"Do you have any evidence that Borz himself was in Moscow tonight?"

"Well, if he was, he's gone now, that's almost a certainty." Ivan grunted. "In any event, I've got my antennae up, but I have to tell you that a *svóloch* like him is not on my compatriots' radar screen. They don't deal with Chechens, they don't hire Chechens. They shoot Chechens on sight."

13

IN THE DEAD of night Andrei Avilov awoke in an oversize, luxe room decorated with a definite feminine eye. Outside the curtained window, spotlights lit a thick forest of conical fir trees. It took him a moment to realize he was in the private clinic funded by the Sovereign, overseen by Timur Savasin himself. It was no wonder the décor was frilly enough to give Avilov the willies: the clinic usually housed the discarded mistresses of both the Sovereign and Savasin, the first-class plastic surgery a parting gift, supposed to lessen the blow of rejection for a young woman. The turnover, Avilov thought idly, must be remarkable, to keep three full-time surgeons on staff.

Which reminded him that the left side of his face felt like weasels had ripped his flesh.Not so far off the mark, he thought wryly. Dimly, he recalled his hurried consult with the plastic surgeon. At first, he had balked because she was a woman, even when he saw himself reflected in her canny eyes. He was in no mood for another female, but he'd had no choice. Orders from Timur Savasin himself. Now, hours later, he wished he had a mirror.

"Not to worry," Dr. Nova had said, *"I can save the original look of your*

left eye. If you had been taken to any hospital inside the Ring Road you'd have a permanent droop in that eye and it would water continually. You'd have to keep blotting it, especially outside in the wind."

If she expected him to be grateful she was sorely mistaken. He'd been as sour as an unripe cherry.

"*Cheer up, Andrei,*" she'd said with what seemed to him a metallic smile, "*you'll come through this encounter relatively unscathed.*"

He resented her calling him by his name instead of formally by his rank. "*I'll be scarred?*"

"*In the beginning.*" She shrugged. "*Then, who knows? It will depend on how elastic your skin and muscles are.*" That sharp-edged smile again. "*You can always tell the women you meet it's a dueling scar. That should get them tumbling into bed.*"

Quits with lying down and feeling woozy in the anesthetic's aftermath, he levered himself up, froze as he felt an immediate throbbing, as if a fistful of pinballs was ricocheting around the inside of his skull. Black spots appeared in his vision, and he blinked them away with grim determination. He drank some water, held ice chips in his mouth, letting the frost soothe away the pain.

"I imagine you're wanting a mirror." He turned at the sound of her voice. Dr. Nova. She had entered the room without him being aware of it—another symptom.

"Didn't I tell you I only wanted a local?"

"I didn't hear that," she said drily. She came and stood by the side of the bed. She seemed entirely unafraid of him. He didn't like that at all.

"Now I need to flush whatever you gave me out of my system."

She was dark-haired, raven-eyed, with an aggressive nose and jaw that helped form the illusion of her being taller than she actually was. "What are you going to do, Andrei? Report me to Daddy?"

Her laughter made him grind his teeth, which, considering his condition, was a mistake. He tried not to wince, missed by a mile.

Her mouth was wide, her lips like ripe fruit. "Face it, Andrei. You're human, after all."

That's not what that bitch Svetlana Novachenko said, he thought darkly.

"You don't think much of women, do you, Andrei." That laugh again, so mocking, so knowing—almost like a man's. "That's all right. I'm used to men like you."

Now she sounded downright contemptuous, and he felt a kind of panic to be trapped under her thumb.

"I'm getting out of here," he said, swinging his legs over the side of the bed.

"You'll do nothing of the kind." Her hand on his shoulder was firm, strong, incontestable. "You're under my care now, Andrei. Orders from on high."

He knew what that meant. Savasin must have received a report about the incident in the hotel room, no doubt drawn up with all requisite venom by Colonel Korsolov or one of his damned minions. Avilov cursed the day he had ever been in the same room with Svetlana Novachenko. Was this Boris Karpov reaching out from the grave? He dismissed the thought almost as soon as it bubbled up, was furious with himself that it had ever occurred to him.

"Time to change your bandage," Dr. Nova said. "I'll just be a moment."

She crossed to the bathroom, closed the door behind her. The room was like a ticking clock or a body laid out on an operating table, turned inside out, its beating heart exposed. He looked over to the door, which, he saw, she had not fully closed. He moved from the position into which she had pushed him, edging down the bed. A gap between the edge of the door and its jamb revealed her to him, as if he were watching an X-rated movie. She had her skirt rucked up around her hips. One gleaming leg was exposed. Her thigh gleamed, substantial, hard-muscled, ending in the deep-shadowed dell of unfulfilled promise.

As he watched, she rose slightly, wiping herself, and his eyes were transfixed by the erotic boundary of curling hair, black as a moonless night. Her legs were spread as she hunched down, her pelvis canted slightly forward. Had she been aware he was watching he would have sworn she was offering herself to him. But that invitation was merely a product of his fevered thoughts.

Then she was finished, the toilet flushed, the water ran. When she emerged he was precisely where he had been when she had left.

She came over to the bed. "Ready?"

Her hands rose, pink and fresh from her thorough scrubbing.

"This might hurt, but only a little."

He felt a tremor begin along the insides of his thighs, traveling inward and outward at the same time.

She bent over him. Involuntarily, his nostrils flared: she smelled of gardenias and musk. "Is that perfume you're wearing?" Hyperaware of his lengthening penis, he was having trouble breathing normally.

"I don't wear perfume."

He closed his eyes, his senses swirling with the scent of her. He drew his knees up.

"Stay still, please."

He was as hard as a rock. "Couldn't a nurse do this?" he asked as he felt her cool fingers, and then the surgical scissors on his skin.

"I like to admire my own work," she said, her mocking laugh reduced to an impertinent smile. "An impulse you can surely understand, Andrei."

Stung, his eyes flew open. "I'd prefer you call me by my rank."

"I'd have preferred not to work on you, Andrei, but we all have our crosses to bear." Having peeled the last layer off, she stood back. "There."

"How does it look?"

Only afterward, when he was alone again, did it occur to him how much like a child he had sounded. And then he couldn't get Dr. Nova out of his mind. Or any part of his body.

14

NO," IRINA SAID when they returned to her mansion, "don't turn on the lights."

"Are you worried that the FSB has staked out the property?" Bourne asked.

She shook her head. "You took care of that. It's just . . ."

He stood close to her, felt rather than saw her shrug.

"Sometimes I prefer being in the dark."

Perfect, Bourne thought. My normal state of being.

She moved, and he saw the glitter in her eyes. The illumination from the security lights, striped through the curtains, limned her in profile like an old-fashioned cameo. He thought she might take his arm then, but she didn't. Instead, she headed for the marble-and-gilt staircase.

"Time for sleep," she said, and he didn't contradict her.

But an hour or so later, when she was safely tucked in bed, Bourne crept out of his room barefoot, down the curved, baronial stairs, along the hallways until he reached the room that had been her father's study. It smelled of old cigar smoke, leather book bindings, and carpet fibers.

On the floor above him, Irina was on the phone with Aleksandr.

"He's here with me now," she said softly into her mobile.

"What about the coin?"

"Patience, my love."

"Patience is not my strong suit."

She gave a low, seductive chuckle. "Except in the most important area." She lay back against the pillows, one hand behind her head. "Not to worry. This is a man who cannot be hurried. He is suspicious of everything. I need to move slowly and with exceptional caution. As we have discussed, gaining his trust won't be a simple thing."

"If you move too slowly," her brother said, "we'll never find out the secret of that coin."

"Without Bourne we would never find out. And I have a couple of tricks up my sleeve for when the time is right. He'll come around, you'll see."

"And when will I see you? I'm dying for—"

"Not now, my love." She rose off the bed. She had not changed out of her clothes. "It's time for me to see what there is to see."

"Keep me apprised."

"Always."

"Wherever you go," Aleksandr said, "my love is with you."

Closing the heavy wooden door behind him, Bourne crossed the Isfahan carpet to the oversize burlwood desk, where with a small squeak he sat in the old-fashioned swivel chair and switched on the task light. Rummaging through the drawers he found a magnifying glass, set it on the leather-framed baize blotter, drew out from his pocket the Star of David. Perhaps he was mistaken. Perhaps the point wasn't damaged. Perhaps this wasn't Sara's star. Setting it on a clean sheet of notepaper, he held it under the light, peering at it in its small puddle through the magnifying glass.

At once, his heart sank. There was the damage—the same damage he'd seen on the star the last time he and Sara were in Jerusalem. Quickly tucking the star away, he drew out the Roman coin.

"*We have urgent matters to discuss*," Boris had whispered in his ear when they had met in the ballroom. Had he already had intimations of his death? Was that why he'd had the coin prepared, just in case he couldn't tell Bourne in person what was so urgent?

Bourne peered at it through the lens, turning it this way and that. It took him some moments but at length he saw it, and moved the coin on end, closer to the lens. There it was: a hairline juncture running all the way around the coin's edge. It was a fake, then, but a damn fine one. And what had Boris secreted inside it?

He was just thinking of trying to open the coin when the door swung open and Irina floated through.

"I couldn't sleep, either."

The task lamp lit the lower half of her, leaving her in shadow from the waist up. She had not turned on any of the lights on her way downstairs to find him. Not that it mattered. Sometime previous a troubled dawn had stumbled past the heavy drapes, and now spilled across the floor like mercury.

"May I ask what you're doing?" she said, as she rounded the desk and came to stand over his left arm.

He lifted the coin. "It's genuine. A Dupondius—that's a measure of its worth—from sometime after twenty-five BCE."

"Very old, then."

"Yes."

"As you said."

He watched her as she plucked the coin from his fingers, rolled it around. "Again, why did the general send it to you?"

"I still have no clue."

She threw him a hard look. "How is that possible?"

Bourne sighed. “I told you that I had to take Boris’s word that we were old friends. Remember?”

She nodded. “I do.”

“Years ago, I was shot in Marseilles. I was pitched into the Med, lost consciousness. I would have died if fishermen hadn’t pulled me out, if their doctor hadn’t nursed me back to life. One thing he couldn’t do was give me back my memory. Everything from before I was shot is lost to me, including, I’m thinking, what this means.”

He took the coin back from her. It was too precious for her to keep long, especially with the magnifier around. He put both the coin and the magnifier away, switched off the task lamp.

Sunlight shimmered through the gap in the drapes. A new day, a new mystery.

15

WHY DIDN'T YOU ask Ivan about the coin?" Irina asked now in the ghostly, dawn-lit study.

"How do you know I didn't?" When she didn't reply, Bourne said, "I was waiting to see if you would ask him. Why didn't you?"

"I think you can work that out for yourself."

"Why didn't you want him to know about its existence?"

She sighed. "Because then he'd take it away from me, just like he's taken everything away from me." She looked hard at Bourne. "He thinks he's doing me a favor, making things easier." The tip of her forefinger made tight circles on the desktop. "I don't want that kind of help—from him or from anyone."

"Meaning me," Bourne said, rising.

Her eyes held steady on him. "When I *ask* for help that's another matter entirely."

He nodded. "Fair enough."

She made a disdainful face. "Whoever said 'All's fair in love and war' never read Tolstoy."

"Or any other Russian novelist, for that matter."

She gave him a wry smile. "True. We Russians aren't ones for happy endings. So few of us ever had one. You can't fill your belly on hope."

It was odd, Bourne thought, hearing these proletariat sentiments from a scion of a wealthy father. But he'd already figured out that Irina wasn't like any other member of her family. Defiantly so, if he was any judge of character. What had happened to her along the way to make her so filled with rage, so fiercely independent?

Irina watched him with a curious expression. "What are you thinking?"

"I'm interested in Ivan's theory of who killed Karpov."

"Ivan's evidence is circumstantial. Until we determine that Borz is in Moscow—or was up until last night—we can't be sure of anything."

"But it's a theory that makes perfect sense," Bourne said. "General Karpov had made Borz a target. If he discovered something vital about him, it figures Borz would want him dead."

"Now that the general has been murdered you should be more interested in the mystery of the coin, but you're not. Why?"

"I already told you."

"Meaning?"

"Borz," Bourne said. "He's the real reason I came to Moscow. To find him."

"To kill him."

"Yes."

"Why?"

"A terrorist perpetually in the shadows, who pays men to impersonate him. Do I need another reason?"

Irina gave him a hard look. "A man like you? Yes."

Bourne hesitated. The worst thing he could do was to underestimate this woman. He didn't trust her, but he had to respect both her intellect and her cunning. "Borz was behind a plot to force me to kill the president of the United States. He had a friend of mine and her two-year-old daughter abducted to make sure I did."

"And yet the American president is alive and well."

Bourne smiled. "Two Borzes down, one to go."

"Otherwise it falls apart, the center doesn't hold."

"And what rough beast slouches toward Bethlehem."

"That would be Ivan Borz, a devil, it's safe to say, that William Butler Yeats never met."

"Though it seems he anticipated him." In the intervening months since he had been in Singapore, the last stop in his hunt for Ivan Borz, Bourne had heard incessant chatter from many different sources all concerning the rapid rise of Ivan Borz, who had, it seemed, overnight, expanded from arms dealer to recruiting specifically for ISIS, which, to Bourne, made no sense. Why would a stone-cold businessman like Borz turn to recruiting terrorists, a time- and resource-consuming endeavor without rich remuneration? He knew he was missing a connection somewhere.

At the same time, he was continuing to work out who Irina really was, though it seemed increasingly clear that what she wanted from him was Boris's coin. Why? What did it signify? And why did he harbor the growing suspicion that Borz and Irina were somehow tied together in a Gordian knot?

A peculiar silence grew up between them, like a stand of high grasses, through which they began to see flashes of each another from a different angle. There was something about her that reminded him of Sara—though her Kidon code name was Rebeka, which was how she had first introduced herself to him on the flight that had taken him to Damascus. Since then, he had seen her dying once and dead another time, in the back of a taxi in Mexico City. She had survived both times, and though they hadn't spoken in a long while, there was a sense that their shadows intertwined. A powerful magnetism drew them together, a shared sorrow that dissolved only when they were together. With her, he felt a peacefulness that was so foreign, so complete, it seemed in some way forbidden, as if he was undeserving. And, strange to say, it seemed as fragile, as easily lost, as a whisper in a crowded stadium. Maybe it was that she and Irina were both constructed of secrets, both enigmas that defied solving. It was this tide of unknowing in Irina that reminded him so strongly of Sara.

In Irina's case, however, there was the distinct sour tang of danger. Bourne saw in her a doorway into something dark and tragic, something as yet beyond his understanding. And even though he knew she was trying to play him—possibly even because of it—he continued to reel her in closer and closer, not only to find out the nature of her game, but to see beyond to the person who had instructed her.

"Well," Irina said, breaking his train of thought, "the least I can do is help you."

Again there was that sense of unknowing, of secrets within secrets. "You have an idea?"

Irina nodded. "I do. One Ivan doesn't know about."

Just past dawn Captain Pankin took a break and plodded the three flights down to the FSB commissary. Even by former Soviet standards the commissary was bleak and flyblown. Gray, gray, and more gray wherever you looked. Even the melamine tables and molded plastic chairs looked exhausted. In fact, only the lower-echelon FSB officers—the proles—inhabited it. Officers of Pankin's rank and higher invariably went out of the building for their meals. FSB was nothing if not fiercely hierarchical.

Pankin was bleary-eyed from staring at a computer screen for hours, trying to glean information on the two men found murdered under the Bolshoy Kamenny Bridge. He had come up empty, and was now in desperate need of fuel, though he was beginning to think that his search was going to remain fruitless. It was times like these, he reflected, as he took a tray that looked like it hadn't been adequately washed in several months, when he hated being in the FSB, hated being a Russian, come to that. The levels of bureaucracy he had to deal with were soul crushing. But, on the other hand, one of the things you were taught in the FSB was to exile your soul to Siberia, never to be heard from again. Gulaged, Pankin thought now, as he halfheartedly placed plates of gray food on his gray tray, that's what I am. He looked around the cavernous room at the smattering of young men hunched over their food. That's what we all are. Workers of the Federation unite! he thought sardonically, knowing there was no desire for revolution left in the Russian people. They'd been bled white.

Bars of pale sunlight slanted through the windows high up in the east-facing wall, adding to the impression of a prison. Pankin poured himself a cup of coffee, added creamer and more sugar than was good for him, then chose a table, and sat down. He stared at his food unhappily. Took a swig of coffee instead, which was just this side of ripping a hole in the lining of his stomach.

I should have left the building, he thought, to get food fit for humans, not dogs. He was just about to do that when he noticed Piotr at the next table. Piotr, one of the young-gun IT techs, a recent hire through General Karpov's initiative to bring a cutting-edge sensibility to FSB hardware. Even Karpov had run into resistance from hidebound conservatives who loathed any innovation that reeked of American know-how. Piotr had widely abandoned his wedge of very bad pie. His pimply face was lit up by his laptop. The screen flickered with a face whose features kept changing, morphing it from Piotr's to increasingly bizarre hybrids.

"Piotr," Pankin said, "what the hell are you doing?"

The tech started as if given a galvanic shock, turned his head in Pankin's direction as he slammed down the lid of his laptop. "Nothing, Captain," he said breathlessly.

"That's *Herr* Captain to you, sonny." Pankin laughed, for the moment his frustration forgotten. Then, seeing the stricken expression on the young man's face, he added, "At ease, Piotr. That was a joke."

"Oh. Of course." But the poor kid couldn't even meet his superior's gaze.

Pankin leaned over, intrigued. "No, let me see what you were doing." He waved a hand. "This is all off the record."

Piotr took a deep breath, reopened his laptop. The hybrid face popped back up onto the screen. "Me and a bunch of pals have this game we play. We each upload a selfie, pair up, and then keep changing one aspect of our partner's face. When we're finished, the other guys have to guess the identity of the original face." He shrugged. "I suppose it sounds stupid."

"To an old man like me," Pankin said glumly.

"No, hardly." Piotr's throat and cheeks shone red. "I only meant..."

"Forget what you meant." Pankin stood up, moved his chair closer, then sat next to Piotr, which seemed to alarm the boy. "How does it work?"

Piotr expelled a barely audible sigh of relief. "It's simple, really." His fingers flew over the keyboard, altering features of the image faster than Pankin's eyes could follow. "It's based on our facial recognition software."

Facial recognition software. A light went on in Pankin's head. "Is it any good?"

"The program? It sucks, light-years behind the times," Piotr said. "Compared to the American or Interpol database, ours is pathetic. You couldn't ID the Sovereign's niece."

Pankin felt a spark of excitement in his chest. What if he could find his two victims in the American or Interpol databases? "How could we expand it?"

"We can't," Piotr said flatly.

"There's got to be a way."

Piotr shrugged.

"Oh, come on, man."

Piotr, finally picking up on Pankin's urgency, turned shrewd. "Like I said, you'd need the American and Interpol software, and we don't have access to it."

"But there *is* a way."

"Not officially. And for me the danger would be extreme," Piotr said steadfastly.

Pankin closed his eyes for a moment. "What?"

"I want to run the new IT department and I want the budget to run it correctly."

"How about I throw in a night with Emma Stone and the Moon, as well?"

Piotr snickered. "Hey, Captain, wouldn't it be nice if I didn't have to hack into another country's servers to get your job done?"

Pankin knew it would, but there was a lesson for Piotr to learn first. "Or I could cite you for improper use of FSB software," he said.

Piotr looked stricken. "I thought you said this conversation was off the record."

"Sonny, one thing you'd better learn is that when it comes to the FSB nothing is ever off the record." He grunted. "But okay, you have a point, especially if the program finds that, as I suspect, my two murder victims aren't who their papers say they are." He sighed, thinking of how he was going to convince Korsolov. "Whose servers are you going to hack into?"

"I'm going to need, um, unofficial help on this."

"Money is no problem," Pankin said, knowing it would be, but he'd deal with that some other time. "Again. The American federal government's or Interpol's?"

"Neither," Piotr said, regaining his equilibrium. "You'll like this." His head bobbed up and down, a sign of his building excitement. "We'll be drilling into China's servers. Those People's Liberation Army pricks have hacked into practically every important database on the planet. They're aces at it, but my friend claims that for him their own firewalls are porous as shit."

"And you believe him?"

"Captain, this guy is my mentor. Computer-wise, he can run rings around everyone I know."

"My age, more or less?"

Piotr burst out laughing. "He's fifteen years old."

16

COLONEL KORSOLOV WAS in the process of chewing his lower lip into hamburger meat when the FSB courier rode up on his motorcycle. Pale lemon sunlight shouldered its way through the morning's low-hanging cloud cover. Korsolov was standing on the sidewalk in front of the burned-out building that, so far as it was able, anchored the crippled block in a neighborhood so foul he could imagine only Chechens living in such abject squalor. Before him were the three savaged bodies of the guards he had sent to take Irina Vasilýevna to detention. They were sprawled in the filthy gutter by the side of the blackened skeleton of the Skoda SUV.

"Look at this. Have you ever witnessed such desecration?" He gestured as the courier dismounted and stepped to his side. "A fresh turd on the floorboards, a sign of their utter contempt for law and order."

The courier stared wide-eyed at the massacre. "Sir, what happened to our men?"

"What happened to them?" Korsolov rounded on him, his face inflated with rage. "They were stupid, that's what happened to them." He lifted a hand, let it fall to his side. "In our business, stupidity deserves its fate."

"But, I mean, look at them."

"Rent by wolves." Korsolov was still staring into the bare, blackened interior of what had once been the Skoda. "So what the fuck are you doing here in this shithole? I have to be here, at least temporarily, but you . . . ?"

The courier handed over a manila envelope. "Ballistics report on the weapon used in the Kamenny Carnage."

"Is that what we're calling the murders now? It's been given a headline?"

The courier was justifiably rattled. "Just internally, sir."

"Where are we? America?" Korsolov ripped open the envelope. "I'll soon put a stop to that."

The courier, eager to atone for his transgressions, though he hardly knew what they were, said, "One of the murder weapons was found in the river, not a hundred yards from the bridge. A Makarov. The groove markings indicate that it's an old weapon, well used. The bullet that killed victim number one came from that pistol, sir."

"But not the other one?"

"No, sir. The bullet that killed victim number two was from a Glock."

"And?"

"We've combed the area, dredged the river. No sign of that weapon."

Korsolov nodded dolefully; half a glass was better than an empty one. "The Makarov was probably bought locally on the black market." He ran his forefinger down the pages as if he were scanning them. But at the moment he had no patience for words, so he was grateful for the verbal summary. Not that he would tell the courier that. He was rageful at every member of his department, even the ones scrubbing out the toilets at three in the morning. Briefly, he was annoyed that these three were dead; he would have felt a modicum of pleasure assigning them to latrine duty.

Korsolov came to the end of the report, which was brief and concise. "Why are you still standing here with your mouth half open?"

"A message from Captain Pankin."

"Well?" Korsolov snapped his fingers. "Cough it up."

"It's verbal, sir."

This caught Korsolov's attention, which it was supposed to do. He looked around at his men in riot gear returning from scouting the nearby buildings. They were carrying nothing; they had found no one. What a surprise.

"Tell me."

"Captain Pankin has possession of the Makarov. He wishes you to meet him at this address at your earliest convenience." The courier dutifully recited the address the captain had made him memorize.

"Though I welcome any excuse to bid adieu to this sewer, why the fuck should I? Did he elucidate on his request?"

"Yessir. He said he'd tracked down the man who sold the gun to the Kamenny—" The courier swallowed hard. "To the murderer."

"You mean one of the murderers. Two guns, two shooters." On the other hand, good news does come once in a while, he thought. Even here, waist deep in excrement. He dismissed the courier with a curt "That will be all."

Then he beckoned to the leader of his team. As the man was about to report, he said, "Don't bother." He held up three fingers. "Three dead comrades. Three blocks. You are to raze them entirely, starting with this one. Use grenades and flamethrowers and whatever other ordinance you deem necessary. Not a brick, not a building stone left standing. When the fuckers who did this return home, they'll find whatever shit they own or have stolen as useless as this Skoda."

Mik was not a man you would care to meet in a dark alley. In fact, he was not a man you would choose to meet anywhere, any time. But this wasn't any time, this was, so far as Bourne was concerned, the end-time for Ivan Borz.

He and Irina confronted the large man with the sloped shoulders, overlong arms, and low brow of a simian. He was hairy as hell—black fur sprouting everywhere, including from small ears high up on the sides of his egg-shaped head. His shaved skull made him look older, no doubt the idea, since Bourne judged him to be no more than twenty-one or twenty-two years old.

They were in a warehouse owned by this *vosdushnik*—an airman, so called because he made dollars appear out of thin air through false bank accounts running across the globe, transferring money electronically stolen from legitimate accounts so fast the authorities couldn't catch up to it or to him.

"Watcha bring me, Irochka?" he said to Irina, in the harsh accent of the city's slums.

Two muscle-bound ex-cons with oiled biceps, tats up and down their arms and necks, and submachine guns at the ready stood off to their right and left. Another appeared behind them, blocking the exit.

"It's your turn, Mik," she said, clearly unintimidated. "I brought the goods last time."

He laughed, showing yellow teeth better suited to a horse. "Right, right, right. I forgot."

"As if you forget anything, Mik. Your memory is your business."

"So true, Irochka." He shifted from one huge foot to the other. "If I ever get Alzheimer's they'll have to take me out to a meadow and blow my faltering brains out."

He didn't ask for Bourne's name and Irina didn't offer it. In fact, he scarcely looked at Bourne, not even giving him the once-over. This spoke to the intimacy and trust he had with Irina. Bourne wondered whether Ivan knew anything of his granddaughter's wild-child life in Moscow's new wave underbelly.

It was at this moment Bourne felt the presence of one of Mik's guards behind him. A moment later he felt the muzzle of the submachine gun in the small of his back.

At the same time, Mik said, "Irochka, you know better than to bring a stranger here."

"He's a friend, Mik."

The *vosdushnik* shook his head. "Strangers are a security risk. You never know what they're gonna—"

He got no further in his thought. Bourne had taken a step backward. With the heel of his shoe he stamped hard on the guard's instep. At the same time, he twisted his torso. One forearm shoved the submachine gun to the side and, as he spun, he drove his fist into the guard's side with such force the blow cracked two lower ribs. The guard buckled, and Bourne grabbed his weapon.

The two side guards brought their Kalashnikovs to bear, but Bourne's was aimed directly at Mik's chest. "Which one of you wants to be responsible for your leader's death?" he said to them in idiomatic Russian. No one moved; no one said a word.

Mik lifted a hand slowly and carefully. "You bring this *psikh* into my midst?"

Irina shrugged. "What can I say, Mik? He's a scorpion. You know what they're like when provoked." Her gaze dropped to the man writhing on the concrete floor, holding his side. "Your man made a mistake."

"I suppose he was lucky it wasn't a fatal mistake, eh?" Mik was now staring openly at Bourne. "Why are you here, Irochka?"

"I'm looking for Ivan Borz," Bourne said.

Mik laughed. "You and three hundred thousand people." He shook his head. "Sorry, you came to the wrong roost."

"You move money for him, Mik." Bourne did not know this for certain, but sometimes with these people a shot in the dark was better than keeping your ammunition dry.

Mik pursed his lips, as if tasting a lemon. "I won't even dignify that with a response."

"None is needed," Bourne said as he approached the *vosdushnik*; the two guards moved away from the walls, closing in. "It's the truth."

Mik, seeming truly annoyed now, angrily waved his guards to stand down. "If Ivan Borz is a client of mine, that's no business of yours."

"It's very much my business."

"*Yob tvoyú mat'!*" Go fuck your mother! "*Ty menjá dostál!*" I'm sick and tired of you!

Bourne held out the Kalashnikov he had been pointing at Mik.

"What is this?" Mik said warily. "Some kind of fucked-up peace offering?"

"In your business," Bourne said, "you need this more than I do."

A deathly silence pervaded the interior of the warehouse, after which Mik's boisterous explosion of laughter sounded like a volley of rifle shots. As he took possession of the Kalashnikov, he said, "Jesus wept, I can see why you're fucking this *stvol*, Irochka." Referring to Bourne as a weapon was about as big a compliment as he was likely to pay anyone.

He turned, motioned to his guards to deal with their fallen comrade, then bade Bourne and Irina to follow him across the empty floor of the warehouse, through a door he unlocked with a key around his neck. The door, Bourne observed, was as thick as that of a bank vault. Doorways on either side of a hallway revealed phalanxes of teenagers hunched over laptops, earbuds stuck in their ears. They were as oblivious of the outside world as Chinese factory workers. At the far end was an archway inscribed with snippets of Arabic from the Qur'an. The small room beyond was lined with prayer rugs aligned with Mecca.

They stopped in front of a locked door on their left, which Mik opened with a second key. Inside was what appeared to be a room in a pasha's seraglio. Large jewel-tone cushions were scattered about, an incised hookah sat on a low table, and the cloyingly sweet scent of pot hung in the close air, thick enough to get a small dog high.

"Sit," Mik said, gesturing. He picked up a pair of women's panties and moved them so he could recline on his favorite pillows. "All right," he continued when they were all seated. "Why do you want to find Ivan Borz?"

Bourne told him.

"Your friend and her daughter—they're okay?"

"They're mourning their husband and father, who was shot to death in front of them."

Mik waved a hand. "The two-year-old will forget, but her mother . . ." He shook his head. "That's another story. She will mourn a long time."

"Where is he?" Bourne said.

"Listen, my friend, Ivan Borz is one of my best clients—I move millions of dollars around the world for him." He spread his hands. "Where's my incentive?"

"Billions," Irina said.

"What?" Mik came out of his slough as fast as a missile out of a launcher.

"Give us Ivan Borz's location," she said, "and I'll deliver a client worth billions."

Mik laughed. "And who would that be, Irochka?"

"The Sovereign's inner circle, the Kremlin's elite guard."

This set Mik off as if he had been watching a posse of clowns pour out of a VW Beetle and repeatedly strike each other with mallets. Russians loved clowns, the more idiotic their behavior the better. Otherwise, belly laughs were few and far between.

"Please, Irochka." He wiped tears from his eyes. "You're killing me."

Bourne turned to Irina. "You mean he doesn't know?"

She gave him a lopsided smile. "Why give away for free what will one day demand a price?" She leaned forward, tapped Mik on a knee. "Finished with your fun?"

"Unless you have another joke to tell me."

"Ivan Volkin is my grandfather. He knows everyone in the Kremlin personally. In fact, over the years he's had dealings with most of them. He knows where all the skeletons are buried. He also knows that in the current climate anyone with hot money is desperate to stash it outside Russia." Her smile was slow and enticing. "A few choice words from me . . ." She allowed the rest of the sentence to hang in the air, unspoken, and all the more powerful for that.

Bourne watched the change come over the *vosdushnik*'s face in precisely the same way Irina did.

"Is this the truth, *stvol*?"

Irina took out her mobile phone, showed him the selfie she had taken of Ivan and herself just before they left Eyrie. Ivan's eyes were gleaming as he kissed his granddaughter on the cheek.

"And your grandfather can deliver these apparatchiks?" Mik was practically licking his chops. "If you can do that, then I'll give you whatever you want."

17

YOU CALLED ME over here to listen to this pathetic shitbird?"

Colonel Korsolov was still fulminating over the humiliation his men had heaped on him by their carelessness and stupidity. He glared at Captain Pankin. If he was to disappoint him as well, there would surely be hell to pay.

"And by the way," he said, peering more closely at Pankin's face in the pallid light at the rear of the store, "are you on amphetamines?"

"No sir," Pankin said. "What you're seeing is lack of sleep."

"Because if your judgment is in any way impaired—"

"No worries there, sir."

Korsolov sniffed, disdainful as the fucker who had defecated in his Skoda. "The next few minutes will tell the tale, Captain. Proceed."

Pankin pointed to the man behind the filthy counter. He was small and emaciated. His hair seemed to be falling out. Behind them, the shop sold plumbing supplies, but back here in the fetid dimness of what stunk like a sewer, Anatoly Levkin sold black-market pistols and ammunition.

"This is the man who sold this Makarov." Pankin meant the murder weapon, which he had placed like an unwanted guest on the counter's glass top, scored as an old man's face.

Korsolov squinted at Levkin. "You're sure about this? There are a million old Makarovs hiding in plain sight in Moscow."

"No doubt." Levkin bobbed his head like any servant worth his salt when confronting his master. "But this one I sold two days ago." A forefinger curved as a talon reached out, showed them the tiny letter-number combination stamped on the underside of the trigger guard. "There is no doubt."

"And who, pray tell, did you sell it to, comrade?"

"Well, here's where it gets interesting," Pankin broke in. He withdrew a photo of the two victims found under the bridge. His finger tapped a spot on the photo. "He identified one of the victims."

Korsolov's face screwed up. "That makes no sense. Captain, I am not in the mood for another enigma, piled on top of the ones I'm already dealing with."

The wisp of a smile passed across Pankin's lips. "You're right, sir. It wouldn't make sense if this man who bought the Makarov was who his ID papers claimed he was."

"But he's not."

"No, sir."

Suddenly, Colonel Korsolov's morning turned significantly brighter. "Have you identified him?"

"I have, sir. With the help of the Chinese."

Korsolov looked alarmed. "The Chinese?"

"It's a long story." Pankin drew out of his breast pocket a sheet of paper. "The man who bought the Makarov, the man who is now dead, is named Lev Isaacs."

"A Jew."

"Better."

"An Israeli."

Pankin's eyes glittered in the low light. "Better still." He was clearly enjoying himself. "Lev Isaacs was a Mossad agent."

Andrei Avilov, having checked himself out of the *siloviki* clinic in the densely forested countryside, sat in his car, waiting. Checking his watch, he knew the night shift was over. He had already seen one of the surgeons on call drive away from the clinic. Where was Dr. Nova, the surgeon who had worked on him?

He lit a cigarette, drew smoke deep into his lungs. He was not normally a smoker, but when he was anxious or nervous it became a compulsion. His eyes went from the front door of the clinic to his hand holding the cigarette. It was trembling—not much, but enough to alarm him. What had gotten into him? But he knew. Dr. Nova had gotten into him just as if she had stitched a part of herself to him while sewing him up. The entire left side of his face was a mask of pain, stiff as if it had been dipped in plaster. His left eye throbbed, seemed to be about three times its normal size even though the upper lid remained at half-mast. He clutched the wheel and the tremor ceased.

Movement at the door, and his gaze sprang toward it. His heart labored like a trip-hammer when he saw her coming down the stairs. She crossed to her car, wrapped in a coat of maroon cloth in which she appeared lost, like a little girl wearing her mother's clothes.

He waited while she started the car, backed out, and drove away. Then he fired the ignition and left the clinic behind, intent on following her. They drove in a kind of tandem, with him matching her speed as if their two vehicles were connected by a stout line. He kept three or four cars between them. He was very good. There was no way she knew she was being followed.

When she pulled into the Gorki-Intern Medical Clinic on Soloslovo in the Odintsovsky district, he was unsurprised. She was a surgeon, after all. It was not uncommon for the medical personnel at the *siloviki* clinic to have second jobs at the hospitals and clinics inside the Garden Ring Road.

He watched, smoking his third cigarette in a row, as she parked her car. He got out, took a last, deep drag, then dropped the butt onto the tarmac, went after her as she trotted through the automatic sliding glass doors.

Inside, he might have been in an aquarium: blue walls, green chairs, a fish stenciled onto the information booth dribbling bubbles up toward the stern-looking woman on duty. She was as wide as a weight lifter and twice as ugly. She stopped him with a scowl as he tried to pass. Scanning his official ID did nothing to improve her mood, but she wasn't his concern—Dr. Nova was.

He saw her step into an elevator alone. It rose to the sixth floor and stopped. He took the next elevator in the bank up to the same floor, and stepped out onto the gleaming linoleum floor. He looked one way, then the other, and was just in time to see her turn a corner to the left.

Striding down the hall, past the sick rooms, he wondered what he was doing. He hadn't run after a girl since he was a teenager. He'd been a pole vaulter and a sprinter. Boys like him were the apple of the girls' eyes. Girls came to him like bees to flowers. All except the one he wanted. Tanya. It was Tanya he ran after, and it was Tanya he finally got. Now he wanted Dr. Nova in the same highly charged hormonal way, and he was certain he would get her as he had Tanya.

He turned left at the corner, went slowly down the new corridor, checking the open doors to the rooms as he passed. A bit more than halfway down he saw a flash of maroon—her coat. He remembered with vivid clarity how he had followed Tanya into the section of the gymnasium used by the ballerinas. She was at the barre, one leg up, the underside of her ankle resting on it. She was engaged in herself or in her stretches. He was able to take advantage of a vulnerable moment to ask her out. She said yes, mouthing her answer to him in the mirrored wall.

As he hurried along the hospital corridor, he imagined himself catching Dr. Nova at such a vulnerable moment, her turning and saying yes to him. He entered the room she was in.

The moment he did so, the door closed behind him, and he looked from Dr. Nova to the figure sitting up in bed. It was Svetlana Novachenko.

18

TIME FOR YOU to be judged," Svetlana said.

"Who by?" Avilov grinned. "You?" His eyes shifted. "Dr. Nova?"

"Neither of us." Svetlana swung her legs over the side of the bed. "You will be judged by God."

Avilov laughed. "I don't believe in God."

A curious Mona Lisa–like smile played at the corners of Svetlana's mouth, despite the pain movement caused her. "Then you will be left with nothing when you die."

"What are you saying?" Avilov shook his head. "I'm not dying."

Svetlana cocked her head. "By the look of you, you got the worst of our . . . encounter."

"Huh! I doubt it. Dr. Nova here said when I heal fully even I will hardly be able to tell anything happened."

"You're never going to heal fully." Grabbing the sheets with both fists Svetlana let herself down onto the cool floor. "In fact, you're never going to heal, period."

Avilov's brows knit together. "Your foolish attempts at frightening me are useless."

Svetlana's gaze moved to Dr. Nova, who had remained silent all through the dialogue, and Avilov turned toward her now with a smug expression on his face. "Yes, Dr. Nova, please tell this poor deluded woman the truth."

"The truth, Andrei." Her eyes were never larger or darker than they were at this moment. "The truth is that you will, in fact, die ten minutes from now."

"What? I don't believe you." And yet he looked stricken. And then, as if a switch had been thrown, anger replaced consternation. "The federation takes a very dim view of lying to its personnel." Contempt added itself to his anger. "Punishment will be exacted and, trust me, it won't be pretty."

"Neither will you be, Andrei," Dr. Nova said without inflection.

"What?" His anger was undercut by a terrible vertiginous sense of betrayal. "I... What have you done to me? When—"

"Before I so carefully and, I must say, beautifully stitched you up I inserted venom from a Komodo dragon into your wound."

Involuntarily, Avilov clapped a palm to his cheek, unmindful of the pain. And then, abruptly, his eyes cleared. "You're lying. This is just something cooked up between you two—"

"Cousins," Svetlana said. "Rada and I are cousins."

"I rushed from the wedding to be at the clinic to treat you."

Avilov smirked. "And you just happened to have a drop of—what was it?—Komodo dragon venom on hand? I never even heard of a Komodo dragon."

"They are the largest living lizards," Dr. Nova said, as if speaking to an ignorant student. "They live on an island—Komodo—in the Indonesia archipelago. Their venom contains several poisonous proteins which cause shock, severely lowered blood pressure, swift blood loss, muscle paralysis that will affect your ability to breathe. When one bites you it's a toss-up as to whether your lungs will be paralyzed or you'll go into shock first."

Avilov snorted. "Women! You make me laugh, the two of you."

"Actually," Dr. Nova said, "we have a number of rare and exotic poisons in an iso chamber. If you were FSB you would know that the clinic isn't just for Kremlin *siloviki* and discarded women. It's also for field agents sent overseas on termination contracts. The poisons are useful when neither a pistol nor a rifle is practical."

Avilov's face grew ashen. Dr. Nova kicked a chair over, and he slithered into it.

"Did you think I didn't see you outside the clinic, smoking your cigarettes, waiting for me? I could feel your lust even from that distance. When I was standing next to you it was all I could do not to be sick." She sighed. "But I think a man like you, a pragmatist so far from the benevolence of a god in whatever form he or she might take, requires a practical demonstration." She gestured. "Take a deep breath. Please."

"Why?" he asked dully.

"See for yourself." Svetlana had taken two small, careful steps away from the bed, and now she swayed a little as she watched, as up close and personal as he had been with her during the assault. "Let's see how you're doing."

Avilov tried to suck in air. This effort produced a fit of coughing so racking it brought up blood.

"Andrei," Dr. Nova said, backing away, "you are going to die. Very, very soon."

"Christ," Avilov said, head in hands. "Jesus Christ."

"You don't believe in God," Svetlana said, and turned away.

Three of Mik's men lounged around Irina's Range Rover, admiring it as if it were a hip-sprung dyevushka. As Bourne and Irina approached, she began to shoo them away. Wrapping his fingers lightly around her wrist, he said softly, "This isn't going to end well."

"For us or for them?" she asked. At that moment, her mobile vibrated. A text from Aleksandr. Not now, she hastily texted him back.

Bourne let go of her wrist, moved in front of her. He could see the tats writhing on the backs of the men's hands as if they were parts of a serpent. These were gimlet-eyed, battle-hardened men, once the property of the brutal Russian prison system, and very likely experts at bare-knuckle fighting.

"What is going on here, Irina?"

"You know—"

"All I know is that you've been lying to me from the moment we met. Boris didn't send you. I saw his expression at the wedding. He was stunned to see you. All you're interested in is the coin."

Irina's eyes flicked over his shoulder to where Mik's men stood. "This isn't the time or the place."

"It's now or never, Irina. Otherwise, I walk away and you'll never see me again."

"No! I . . . There are records in there you need to see. Something terrible has been going on. What I'll make Mik show you will explain everything."

The level of alertness in Mik's men ratcheted up, their eyes watchful, their muscles taut, as they approached.

Bourne turned to them. "Keep your distance," he warned.

"I don't think so," the one in the middle responded. He was the tallest. A livid scar ran down the side of his face, tugging the outer corner of his eye down. "Not until you've paid for what you did to Foka."

"Maybe," the one with the torn earlobe said with a grin, "you won't leave here at all."

The third one, with a forest of facial hair down to his chest, drew his Makarov. "Let's just give him a third eye."

"Nah," said Scarface. "We need to do to him what he did to Foka."

"Worse," said Lobeless. "Pain, pain, and more pain."

He came at Bourne, swinging his Kalashnikov butt first. The edge seemed to catch Bourne on the chin, because he went down to one knee, Lobeless grinning over him. Bourne's fist drove into Lobeless's crotch, then his fingers opened, grabbed, and pulled hard.

Lobeless's scream startled the birds out of the trees, their cries melding with his. Bourne wrenched the Kalashnikov out of his hand, swung the barrel hard into the midsection of the Beard, whose lips drew back from teeth sharpened to points. They snapped at Bourne's cheek as he doubled over. He grabbed Bourne behind the neck, bringing Bourne's face closer to the snapping jaws.

Dropping the Kalashnikov, Bourne slammed his forehead against the Beard's, heard his teeth clack together, then thrust the ends of his fingers up into the soft triangle beneath his jaw. The Beard's eyes rolled up in his head as blood gushed out of him.

Scarface, his disfigurement livid against his engorged face, shouted in rage as he squeezed off three rounds from his handgun. They struck the Beard's torso, shaking it like a high wind will a tree. Bourne shoved the Beard into Scarface, disarmed him while Scarface was wrestling with the dead weight of his compatriot's body.

Scarface freed himself and lunged for Bourne, expecting him to resist. Instead, Bourne waited, patient as the sea, until Scarface was inside his defense. Scarface delivered the first blow—a rock-solid punch to Bourne's ribs. Bourne immediately locked his extended wrist and pulled while swiveling his own torso to the left. Using Scarface's momentum as a fulcrum, he dragged his assailant off balance. As Scarface stumbled forward, Bourne drove an elbow into his eye socket. Scarface went down, his face in the dust, and Bourne landed on his neck, knee first, cracking three cervical vertebrae, depriving Scarface's brain of blood and oxygen.

As he rose, he saw Irina running back toward the entrance of the warehouse where Mik was standing, watching the carnage unfold. He had a peculiar expression on his face—one Bourne had seen too often. It was the beatific serenity of the Muslim extremist martyr. Into his mind came the glimpse he'd seen of the Arabic arch, the prayer rugs aligned toward Mecca.

"Irina!" he shouted as he ran toward her.

But it was too late. Mik had his thumb to the keypad of his mobile phone, and even as the first bullets flew from the Makarov Irina had picked up when Lobeless went down, his thumb depressed the key.

Bourne, too far away from Irina to rescue her, dove behind her Range Rover. An instant later, the explosion took out the warehouse and everyone in it, along with Mik and Irina.

19

LIEUTENANT AVILOV LIFTED his head out of the protective bowl of his hands. The darkness was the only way to keep reality from frying his brain. "You deliberately kept the door ajar."

His beloved, lusted-after Dr. Nova cocked her head. "What did you say?"

"In my hospital room. The bathroom door," he said miserably. "You wanted me to watch you."

Svetlana stirred, moving from one leg to the other. "What a filthy pervert you are."

"You did, didn't you?" He kept his eyes on Dr. Nova's, though it cost him in both pain and anguish. "You knew I would take the chance. What do you want from me?"

"You're bleeding, Andrei," the blindingly beautiful Dr. Nova observed.

He put a hand up to his cheek. It came away bloody. "Something is wrong with your stitches."

"My stitches are impeccable," Dr. Nova said icily. "As always."

"Then why am I bleeding?" He felt slow, stupid, his thoughts muddling along like icebergs.

"You know why, Andrei."

And he did know why. The dragon venom had performed a miracle. It had transformed his blood into water, was casting it out of his body through the weakest link of his defense. He held his hand tight against his cheek, but the blood kept coming, seeping through the gaps between his fingers.

Svetlana held up her right hand. To him it was beautiful because it was bloodless.

"Do you see what I've done?" she cried. "I've bitten my nails down to the quick. Made them ugly as sin. Why? Because I had scraps of your skin embedded so deeply under them I had no choice."

Avilov stared at her dully. He was damned if he was going to apologize to this bitch. He was damned if he was going to give her the satisfaction—any satisfaction. "What's to stop me from heading to the nearest hospital once I leave here, get an antivenom injection?"

"Go on," Svetlana said. "We won't stop you."

Avilov made to stand up. His knees and calves shook so badly he was obliged to grab on to the back of the chair as if for dear life. When the trembling reached his thighs, he collapsed back into the chair.

"So you see," Dr. Nova said, "it's too late. As you've already demonstrated yourself. You'll die here in this room while Svetlana stares into your eyes." She smiled wolfishly. "We're clever things, us Russian women, despite what you think. When we target someone, we want to be assured our mission is accomplished."

"But surely you have the antivenom," he said in a voice so shaky it appalled him. "What do you want? Name it."

"For many years, no one believed a Komodo dragon's bite was venomous, even though they routinely took down and killed cape buffaloes," Dr. Nova said with a pitiless voice. "There is no antivenom for a Komodo dragon bite."

He had no response to that—the last possible avenue closed. It was only then the ironic absurdity of his situation washed over Avilov like a tsunami. These two crypto-Muslims had trapped and infected him all because of what, a quick diddle and poke? If he had ever been inclined to believe in a supreme deity, this made it clear to him what a fantasy that was. And to top it off, the one woman who had made him feel anything turned out to be a traitor to him and to the Federation. What kind of god would fuck him up so utterly? But he could see now that the Soviets had it right: All was chaos. Best to grab whatever you could from the maelstrom before your time in this veil of tears was over.

Now he knew what it must be like to be incarcerated in the bowels of the Lubyanka. Worse, to be straitjacketed in the prison's depth. He'd seen men like that—confined like Russian *matryoshka* dolls within the Lubyanka's terrifying walls, a ghastly hall of mirrors with no exit save one. In time, they'd all gone mad. He had no time.

Dr. Nova leaned over, took his chin in her hand, jerked his head so that he was forced to look her in the eyes. Little did she know how much pleasure and anguish that caused him.

"How do you feel, Andrei?"

"If you kiss me," he whispered, "all will be well."

She laughed, and he drew in the scent of her.

He accepted his fate, just as he had accepted the possibility of early death when he had entered the Kremlin. It was a Russian thing, something these Muslim fanatics would never understand. He held one consolation close to him, like a flame in winter. As Dr. Nova had deceived him, so had Svetlana deceived General Karpov. *Honey traps* was the old-school term for how field agents trapped their enemies with tainted women, liaisons they could use to turn their enemies, manipulate them to doing their will. He never thought it would happen to him, but it had. Fucking women, he thought, darkness descending over him like a shroud, like an endless night. You love them only to find they're nothing but trouble.

"I feel," he said, the words squeezed out of him, "distinctly unwell."

Then his eyes rolled up in his head and he keeled over.

Wind in the willows on the left bank of the Moskva caused a rustling, as of a swarm of insects. The sun, pale and haggard, struggled to provide heat, any heat at all. A boat horn hooted, as mournful as the cry of a little lost boy. This sound and the reverberations it set off was not uncommon in Moscow.

"Mossad," Colonel Korsolov said. "A Mossad field agent infiltrated into Moscow executed with a single bullet. Why?"

"I have a theory," Captain Pankin said.

"Let's hear it."

The two men walked along the bank, heading toward the Bolshoy Kamenny Bridge, where it had all begun.

"I think the double execution is related to General Karpov's assassination."

"You think Lev Isaacs murdered Karpov and then was himself killed to erase any trace."

Pankin nodded. "That could be. Or whoever killed the general also killed these two men."

Korsolov stopped, hands dug deep in his pockets. "Explain."

Pankin bit his lower lip as he sought to order his thoughts into a theory. "It's like this: Isaacs being in Moscow the same night the general was murdered cannot be a coincidence. Therefore, we have to surmise that the Mossad killed him. The murder was meticulously planned. Moreover, the killer knew not only that the general would be at the hotel last night, but where he would be within the hotel and at what time."

"Which argues for an accomplice inside."

"Precisely."

It was at that moment that Korsolov remembered where he had seen the man who had been murdered with Isaacs—the hotel! The papers on his body identified him as Belov, Veniamin Nazarovich Belov, a Jew. But that certainly wasn't the name the man had used at the hotel. "Good Lord, Pankin, I think they were both Mossad agents." And he told Pankin what he had just remembered.

"Do we have any proof?"

Korsolov snorted. "With Mossad there's never any proof. One need only go on instinct." He touched the side of his nose. "And I can smell them like a ratter."

"Two Mossad agents, one an inside man, and then shortly after the general is killed, they're both executed. You said Belov was in the hotel. He could have murdered Karpov."

"Perhaps," Korsolov said. "Or there's a third Mossad agent we don't yet know about. An assassin who killed all three."

The two men looked at one another, and said at the same time, "Ki-don."

20

YOU DID YOUR best, Jason." The old man shook his head. "It's not your fault."

Bourne sat on the old, blowsy sofa in Ivan Volkin's homey apartment. Sun streamed in through the windows, setting up diagonal columns in which dust motes rose and fell, as if the sunlight was breathing. He was surrounded by souvenirs from all over the world, old photographs of family and friends, Volkin with a dizzying number of world figures. And then the photo of Irina as a child.

"Even then she wasn't with her parents," Ivan said as he served them tea, "but sat alone, by herself, off to one side." He lowered himself into an overstuffed chair, sighed. "I'm afraid she was born a wild child." He plopped six sugar cubes into his glass but forgot to stir them in, perhaps the only outward sign of his distress. "She had secrets, Jason. The life she chose for herself was built on them. I understand that." He sipped his tea, made a face, set the glass down in the center of its saucer. "But I never understood her. She was a complete enigma to me." He shook his head again, possibly for the first time in his life bewildered. "Why she would get involved with a *vosdushnik*—well, that's just beyond my comprehension." He looked up at Bourne, his eyes beseeching. "What did she want, Jason? What was she seeking?"

Bourne wrapped his hands around his glass, felt the heat from the tea stealing into his palms, and from there up his arms. The heat felt good. He'd been cold as ice on the drive away from the ruined warehouse to Ivan's unprepossessing neighborhood.

"I didn't know her that long, Ivan, but if I had to guess I'd say that she was searching for a place for herself in the world."

"Why? She had everything she could possibly—"

Bourne's expression stopped him dead. "Imagine, Ivan, having you as a grandfather. Imagine feeling stifled by your power, all the things you did for her."

"Isn't that what a grandfather does with his grandchild?"

"Maybe all she wanted, Ivan, was to do those things for herself."

"But she didn't have the wherewithal. She was young. Worse, she was female. In this world—"

"Stop," Bourne said. "Listen to yourself." He leaned forward. "Ivan, Irina was obviously a woman who knew her own mind, who flouted convention. She must have worked hard to devise her own ways of getting what she wanted. And I can imagine she felt the need to be secretive about them to keep you at arm's length, to keep you from continually stepping in, intervening in every decision she made."

Ivan sat back, seemed somehow shrunken by the chair or perhaps by his realization of what Irina had been and of what he had missed at every turn.

He put a hand to his temple. "I failed her. Her death is my fault. She never would have gone near that *vosdushnik*."

"She would have found Mik no matter what you did or didn't do, Ivan. Your exalted position has affected the way you see the world. You can't manipulate everyone. You're not God."

Ivan glared at Bourne for a moment, his fingers at his temple trembled. "No. No, you're right, Jason." He sighed. "The truth is power disconnects you from the real world. Great power even more so. I've had it for so long that I often forget what life must be like for the little people scurrying around their little lives."

Bourne could have made a comment here but he chose to keep his own counsel.

"So." Ivan picked up his glass, stared into the depths made murky by the semidissolved sugar cubes. "What *was* she doing with the *vosdushnik*?"

"I couldn't hazard a guess," Bourne said. "They seemed on intimate terms, but then he tried to kill us both, so who knows?" He paused for a moment. "Unless it had something to do with what her father and brother were into."

Ivan was still staring into his tea, as if he wanted nothing more than to be a million miles away from his granddaughter's death.

"Ivan?"

Volkin finally stirred. When he looked up his eyes were for a moment vacant, dead. "I've lost a son, a grandson, and now Irina. Where does it end?" Then his eyes snapped into focus. "No death happens in a vacuum, Jason. At least not in our world, eh? Like ripples spiraling out from a stone thrown into a lake I think now there are implications to Irina's death." He lapsed back into silence, his concentration as wavering as the dust motes trapped inside their shafts of sunlight.

Bourne sensed this was a crucial moment, felt that if he pushed Ivan now the old man would only push back, and Bourne would get nothing more out of him. He finished his tea and rose.

"I need to get back to Irina's, clean up, change my clothes."

Ivan possibly didn't hear his words but he registered that Bourne was about to leave. He raised a hand. "Hold on." His finger pointed. "Sit back down a moment."

Bourne complied. He'd taken the right course.

Ivan scrubbed his wrinkled forehead with the tips of his fingers. "Forgive me, Jason, I misspoke before. I know exactly why Irina went to Mik."

He placed his hands in his lap, stared at their veiny backs as if they were road maps that could get him to a different destination. “My son and grandson were up to their armpits in shit. Their under-the-table dealings were draining their legitimate business. They were becoming more and more desperate. When I tried to help them, when I discovered what they had gotten themselves into, I backed away. They were in so deep even my associates wouldn’t help them.”

He looked up suddenly, his eyes enlarged, rheumy. Every year of his life seemed etched on his face. “You already know my position on the Muslims of the Federation. I despise all Chechens. You say some are good, hardworking men and woman. I say they’re all a scourge. They won’t be content until they have exacted the full measure of revenge for the two wars we waged on them.” He raised a hand. “Don’t try to dissuade me. I know I’m right.”

“Mik and his associates were of interest to me only while they were alive,” Bourne said. “I’m interested in only one Chechen: Ivan Borz. He’s assumed to be Chechen, but frankly I have my doubts. In any event, Mik moved Borz’s money around, but now that lead is in ashes.”

“Perhaps not.” Ivan laced his fingers over his thin belly. He seemed to have come back from the misty graveyard he had retreated into when Bourne had given him the news of Irina’s death. “One thing I did find out—because my grandson told me before the FSB raid—is that the money Mik appropriated out of thin air for Borz was all headed to Cairo.”

Where Boris had set up his operation on Borz, Bourne thought.

“I need to get to Cairo yesterday,” Bourne said. “Can you get me there?”

Kidon. A Hebrew word for “bayonet.” Used to describe Mossad’s elite corps of infiltrators, wet work specialists, the best of the best when it came to combat and silent killing.

Korsolov and Pankin were looking for a Kidon assassin—an exterminating angel. Their best bet was to study the CCTV tapes from Moscow airports and train stations, searching for a face that found a match in the FSB's admittedly incomplete and slightly out-of-date database.

Not that they were alone in the endeavor. The colonel had dragooned upward of a hundred people into the search, and their computer screens were all running hot as they sifted through the constant flow of people coming into the Federation through Moscow, two to a screen to ensure nothing was missed. He had considered sending a contingent to the nearest seaport but, as Pankin was quick to remind him, the Kidon relied on speed—in and out before anyone knew one of theirs had ever been there. That argued against transport by sea. Pankin would have liked to go back to Piotr and his mysterious contact to harness the facial recognition system the Chinese had hijacked from Interpol and the U.S. Feds, but he knew FSB's Kidon database, incomplete though it was, was far better than that of either of the foreign agencies. Mossad was, after all, the Federation's enemy. The FSB's threat assessment directorate had cause to keep track of its agents as best it could.

They had been at it for over four hours when Korsolov pulled Pankin away. They went down the hallway eerily lit by overhead fluorescents, buzzing like angry flies. Korsolov bought them coffee out of one of the vending machines and they drank, leaning against a wall on which was a poster exhorting those within range to take their next vacation in the paradise of Crimea. A bright yellow sun shone down on azure water and a buff-colored beach. A gaily striped umbrella completed the fantasy.

"Captain," Korsolov said, "do you know what a field promotion is?"

"Of course, Colonel."

Korsolov smirked, dug in his pocket, extracting a pair of shiny objects which he pinned on the epaulets of Pankin's tunic, after first removing his captain's insignia. He dropped them into Pankin's cupped palm. "Keep these as a souvenir. Give 'em to your firstborn son, so he'll join the FSB like his father."

"Sir?"

"In recognition of your help in the matter of identifying the perpetrator of General Boris Illyich Karpov's heinous murder, and to celebrate my imminent promotion to general, you have been promoted to colonel. In addition, you are now my adjutant. You'll report to me and to no one else."

"Sir, I don't know what to say."

Before Korsolov could respond, one of his men hurried up. "Sir, I think we have something. Only..."

"Only what?"

"Well..." His man pulled out a digital copy of a photo taken off one of the CCTV cameras in Sheremetyevo. The time stamp was two days ago at 20:08 hours. A female face, half hidden by the head of a passing man, was circled in red grease pencil.

"Who am I looking at?" Korsolov said.

"Maybe no one," his man said. "Maybe a ghost."

Korsolov handed the photo to Pankin. "This face mean anything to you, Colonel?"

Pankin, who during the long night had made it his business to refamiliarize himself with all Mossad personnel in the FSB records directorate, said, "It does. But like this man, I'm a bit puzzled."

Korsolov was rapidly losing patience. "And why is that?"

"Well, hard as it may be to believe, this member of Kidon was knifed to death some three years ago in Mexico City."

"Do we have proof of that, Colonel? I mean incontrovertible proof."

"When it comes to Mossad we are rarely able to dig up incontrovertible proof."

Korsolov's forefinger stabbed out, tapping the red bull's-eye drawn on the surveillance photo. "And yet here is incontrovertible proof that she is still alive." He eyed Pankin, the messenger all but forgotten. "General Karpov's exterminator. What's her name?"

"She's had many over the years, legend on top of legend. By all accounts, she was—excuse me, *is*—Kidon's best agent." Pankin cleared his throat. "We know her only by her code name: Rebeka."

Part Two

Life? It's simple: manipulation through ideological doctrine.

—Ivan Borz

21

SARA YADIN, KNOWN by her code name Rebeka, returned to Israel as Jenny Parker, an Australian national, a historical researcher at the University at Perth, the legend impeccably fabricated by Mossad's Scrivener Directorate.

Jerusalem was under war skies, a seemingly endless occurrence these days. The bleak grayness of Moscow was replaced by a riot of deep, life-affirming earth tones, the spikes and thorns of Russian were replaced by a molten torrent of Hebrew and Arabic, warming her from the inside out. She walked out into the heat, colliding with the scalding sunlight on her face and bare arms, which she nevertheless welcomed as an old and trusted friend.

She took a taxi from the airport, had it drop her off in front of an anonymous, blank-faced office building that housed law firms, import-exporters, and the like. She took an elevator up to the third floor, where a discreet sign announced GOLD JEWELRY. Pushing through the door, she went straight to the glass-topped counter, bought a Star of David identical to the one she had lost and a thin gold chain that was close enough. She paid in cash, fixed the clasp at the nape of her neck, and walked out, feeling the familiar weight of the star against her chest, but plagued by a vague unease nevertheless.

She walked a mile in a circuitous route to make certain she wasn't being followed, then entered the executive offices of Mossad and surrendered herself to the usual scrutiny by the security team whose members she knew by their given names.

Above her head was the motto, "*Where there is no guidance, a nation falls, but in an abundance of counselors there is safety*," Proverbs 11:14, inscribed in Hebrew into the midnight-blue marble.

The Caesarea division was on the eighth floor of the nine-story building. Another security search was mandatory before she was allowed entry. The Kidon offices were in the rear, a series of windowless rooms, protected from electronic surveillance, monitored around the clock in three shifts of two men and two women each.

She was met by Mossad's director, who welcomed her back with a brief nod and a curt "Well done." He led her along the corridor and through a door that could be opened only by highly restricted iris ID. Beyond was a narrow spiral of steel treads, which they ascended. It gave out onto a tiny landing that was between floors eight and nine. Through another locked door was a suite of rooms the polar opposite of the Kidon offices. In fact, the space, with its modern leather furniture, plush beige carpet, and tasteful but innocuous prints on the walls, looked more like an expensive suite in a five-star hotel.

The Director turned and, as soon as the door to the suite closed behind Sara, grabbed her in a bear hug and kissed her on both cheeks.

"Well done." His voice was warm and affectionate. "Well done, Sara!"

"Thank you, Father."

Eli Yadin released her, and he and his daughter took a step back to assess one another. "Your mission went well," he said.

"It was flawless," she replied.

A shadow crossed his face. "Not entirely."

"What do you mean? My target is dead."

"Of course he is. There's no doubt of that. None whatsoever. Had you not terminated Yasha he would have given Belov—and, eventually, Svetlana Novachenko—"

"Svetlana Karpova."

Eli Yadin regarded his daughter for a moment. "The late General Karpov was not a friend of Israel's. Sara."

"He helped Bourne—and, indirectly, me—in Damascus. Have you forgotten?"

"I forget nothing, daughter. But our mission had been, through Belov, to secretly help Ukraine break away from Russian influence. Now, because of Yasha's treachery, that plan is as dead as he is."

"I will not debate Boris with you," she said tightly. "You implied a problem."

Nodding his shaggy head, he guided her to one of the sofas, poured coffee from a pot on a nearby sideboard, brought the cups over and sat down beside her. "You were made at Sheremetyevo airport." He handed her the coffee, which she accepted but did not drink.

Unconsciously, she fingered the gold star, as if to make sure it was still there. "Who?"

There was a discreet knock on the door, the Director, frowning, said, "Come," and Dov Liron, head of the Caesarea unit, Sara's boss, came in. She rose, shook his hand, then kissed him on both cheeks.

He hoisted a manila folder. "You asked for this as soon as—"

Eli lifted a hand to still him. "Just leave it on the desk, Dov. Thank you."

Liron complied and left without a backward glance. The Director discouraged curiosity inside Mossad headquarters.

"Well, that's the odd part," Eli said, returning to her question. "At first, it seemed as if the interest came from our Chinese enemies. They like to keep tabs on us as best they can." He shrugged. "Though we always manage to be at least one step ahead of them."

He sipped his coffee. "Drink, drink, darling. The breach isn't anything we can't deal with."

Sara eyed him, took a sip, but didn't taste it.

"No, it wasn't the Chinese who spotted you; it was an old enemy of ours that has tapped the Chinese faucet. They must have found some piece of evidence of our presence."

He leaned over, took up three cubes of sugar. "Here. I forgot." He dropped them in her coffee, watched her sip again with no little pleasure. "No, it was the Russians who made you." He sat forward, elbows on knees. "Bottom line, I want you away from here. We have to assume the FSB has traced your flight back here."

"Away from Jerusalem? Where?"

Her father shrugged. "I don't know. The Maldives, maybe. You could use some rest and relaxation. The scuba diving is fantastic, and I know you've been dying to see the reefs. Now's your time."

Before she could reply, his mobile buzzed and he lifted a finger as he answered it, listening for some minutes, then saying, "All right." He disconnected, and rose. "Excuse me a moment, darling. I have a small fire to put out. I won't be a moment."

When she was alone, Sara stared into her coffee. She didn't want to go to the Maldives, even if it was to scuba dive. She did not want to go on vacation; she did not need rest and relaxation. After what happened, the suggestion of a vacation smacked of failure. Her mission in Moscow had been difficult—not technically, though it had involved more than one target, which was unusual enough without the other circumstances involved. It had somehow taken a toll on her emotionally. This was so odd it caused her no small degree of concern. One of the basic elements of Kidon training was to kill quickly, silently, efficiently, and dispassionately. Otherwise, your survival—your basic humanity—was at risk. Involuntarily she shivered, as if the ice that had crept into her bones in Moscow had not yet left her. It was like waking from a dream that, unaccountably, seemed just as real with your eyes open.

Unsettled, she rose, wandered around the suite, until she found herself at her father's desk. There, as if spotlighted, was the manila folder Dov had left, so urgent he had instructions to come at once to the Director's inner sanctum.

Sara reached out, touched it with the tip of her forefinger. Then she turned it around to face her, flipped it open. She had just enough time to see the words: "Mission Mounted," "Ivan Borz," and "Cairo" before she heard the scrape of the door. Hastily, she flipped the file shut, moved away from the desk. When her father entered, she was watching the city through one of the castle-like slits between the vertical blinds hanging in front of the layers of bulletproof glass.

"So," Eli said, "I've made arrangements for your flight to the Maldives."

"That's what was so important?" Sara did not turn around.

"Of course not. But while I was—"

"I'm not going to the Maldives," Sara said.

"Oh? All right. Where do you want to go?"

She turned around to look him in the eye when she said, "Cairo."

"Cairo? You're joking, yes?"

"No, Abba." She folded her arms across her breasts. "I'm not."

Eli took a step toward her. "But, Sara, you can't be serious." He stopped abruptly, turned toward his desk, where the folder lay slightly askew. He turned back to her. "Sara, no. The operation has already begun."

"Without me."

The Director snorted. "Of course without you." He spread his hands. "You were on assignment."

"And now that assignment is over."

"And you need rest."

"What I need, Abba, is to leave Jerusalem. You said it yourself."

"Don't use my words against me, daughter!"

Sara's heart beat faster. Her father only called her "daughter" when he was very angry with her. Still, it was not in her nature to back down. "Just the facts, Abba. Just the facts."

The edge of his hand cut through the air like a knife. "You're not going anywhere near Cairo, and that's final."

Her eyes flared. "You know you can't stop me."

"Sara, Sara, Sara." Eli shook his head. "I only have your best interests in mind. Your body may be healed from your near-death experience in Mexico City, but your mind—"

"My mind is as clear as a bell. I can see for miles."

He put a hand on her shoulder. "Where is this defiance coming from?"

"You know very well," she said.

Eli closed his eyes for a moment. "Ivan Borz."

"You cannot deny me this, Abba." She placed a hand atop his on her shoulder. It was a very Roman gesture, one legionnaire to another. "This of all things on earth and in hell."

Enrobed in silence, father and daughter bowed their heads and prayed together.

A pack of wolves, that's what I've raised, Ivan Borz thought. With the grace and all-knowing guidance of Allah. The Wahhabis are the perfect foils. They were born to be raised as wolves, all they needed was a voice coming to them from out of the wilderness. And this they found. Allah brought them to me, first in ones and twos and then, as word spread, in handfuls, in entire villages, in an ever-widening gyre.

Borz sat cross-legged, as was his wont, on an ancient Egyptian rug, faded and frayed, of oxblood camelhair and Chinese silk, which was set, per his instructions, in the precise center of the mosque's central prayer room. Around him were arrayed his acolytes, his fearless warriors, his cannon fodder, male and female alike, some as young as seven or eight, in concentric circles. Like the planets of the solar system, he thought, around the sun whose heat will warm them forever, even when they are among the angels. Which, for some of them, would be very soon.

"*Al-ʔamdu lillāh*," Ivan Borz said. All Praise and Thanks to God. "Terrorism is victory. They are one and the same. Terrorism is what unites us under the banner of Allah. Terrorism is what makes us strong." His black eyes picked out acolytes here and there, poured his intensity, his fervor, into them as one pours boiling water from a pot. "The infidel has money, comfort, indolence, perversions beyond measure. The infidel wishes to impose his countless perversions on us. He has come to our shores, like tar washing up on the margins of our land, befouling us and our sacred way of life, our path to Allah, to Ar-Rahman the Beneficent, to Al-Quddūs the Purifier. He has come armed with weapons and lies.

"And that, my family, is why we are gathered here today, at this time, in Cairo, the beating heart of Islam. To be purified in Allah's grace and holy spirit." Islam has many hearts, he thought. Cairo is but one of them. These people need to believe in their relevance, they need to know that their lives matter, that they can, in death, make a difference, because their lives are a misery of poverty and hopelessness. They need to believe in victory. In that belief lies strength—and power. Their belief is a vital part of my victory.

"We have been marginalized by the infidel, pushed into the shadows, run up into the mountains that so terrify and confound our enemies. The infidel needs us to feel helpless. The infidel feeds on our hopelessness. Our poverty strengthens him, our bitterness emboldens him as he seeks to grind us under his decadent Gucci shoe.

"Nevertheless, we are not helpless. Allah, the All-Seeing, the All-Knowing, Ar-ḥīm the Exceedingly Merciful, has provided for us. He has armed us with a weapon so powerful that we will find victory, my family. Terrorism is what Allah has given us. Terrorism is all we have to fight the infidel, to fight him as he seeks to destroy us. But terrorism is all we need. Terrorism does what no other weapon on earth can do. Terrorism plunges a dagger into the minds of the infidel. Terrorism strikes fear in the rich, the indolent, the perverted. He cannot sleep for fear of us. He cannot feel happiness because of us. He drugs himself up because of us. He does not know when or where we will strike next. He fears for the future."

Ivan Borz moved a five-sided box to a place between his knees. The box was made of a dark metal with a rime of frost at its angles. It was icy to the touch, kept cold by the packs of blue gel lining the inside. Ivan Borz lifted the box's heavy lid, and every pair of eyes was riveted to the movement of his hands. Setting the lid down, he reached into the box and lifted high the severed head, holding it by a fistful of dark greasy hair. The hair hadn't been washed in months. Neither had the body to which it belonged.

"An American journalist, captured, interrogated, turned to Islam, martyred in the name of Allah the merciful. His sacrifice is your rallying cry." His legs unfolded like that of a praying mantis as he rose to his full height. He lifted the head higher so even those in the back rows could see clearly.

"Witness now how the infidel will be defeated. Terrorism will defeat the infidel. This I promise you."

22

NIGHT HAD OVERTAKEN the cauldron of the day when Bourne arrived in Cairo. The heat was like an oven with the door open instead of closed: stifling yet tolerable. He was almost killed twice in the maelstrom of the city traffic, once when the taxi he was in was nearly broadsided by a truck, another when it overtook and cut off a bus with barely an inch between the vehicles. The taxi left a tail of diesel particulates behind it. It belched more noises than a dyspeptic stomach. The interior stank of falafel grease and stale sweat.

Ah, Cairo! Bourne thought as he vigorously cranked down the window. How do you miss a city and at the same time wish you had never been here?

But then that was Cairo, a seething chaos of contradictions, where ten million vehicles and one stoplight made for a dark and exhilarating passage.

He checked into the nearly deserted El Gezirah Hotel, washed up, changed, then called for a taxi. It took him crosstown in a dizzying, zigzag pattern in order to beat the insane traffic, letting him off at Midan Kit Kat. From there, he walked down to the Nile, through the charcoaled meat and stew scents of the evening. An uneasiness compressed the reddish atmosphere of the city, like a bow drawn too tight from which a launched bolt would at any moment cause devastation.

On the near bank wooden gangplanks led individually to a line of one- and two-story houseboats, some painted, others simply of beaten boards, all weather furrowed and weary. Many of them had once been gaily painted, serving as nightclubs and casinos, but that time was long past. Though remnants of their former glory were everywhere to be seen, in bits of signage, boards of painted gilt and silver, they were dulled now as if viewed in sepia photos.

Bourne found the houseboat painted a Nile blue. As he crossed its wooden gangplank, the muezzin started his call to prayer. The rising and falling voice from the filigreed wrought-iron balcony high up on the soaring minaret several blocks north floated over the wide river, as if it were a bird diving for its supper.

Bourne stood absolutely still before the wooden door. The sounds of the thick water lapping, the soft, fitful breeze on which was carried the supple voice of the muezzin—all these together brought Cairo rushing back to him as if he had never left.

This was Feyd's home. Bourne had met him before he broke away from Treadstone. Feyd was a Treadstone stringer, one of many the organization had maintained in its worldwide network. For as many years as Bourne could remember he had used Feyd, and Treadstone had, in turn, paid him well. His information was always impeccable and so accurate it inevitably breached the heart of the matter.

Bourne remembered Feyd as a sturdy man, short of leg and arm, with a wrestler's deep chest and shoulders. His face, quick to smile, seemed to have won a hard-fought victory over time, each line and crease a misfortune overcome, a face that was at once crumpled and triumphant.

Bourne raised his hand and knocked on the door.

It wasn't long before he heard soft footfalls approaching, then an instant's silence before the door was wrenched open, and the muzzle of a pistol was aimed at his chest.

A girl with huge coffee-colored eyes, black hair, and an oval face dark as stained teak peered out at him from the dim interior of Feyd's houseboat. The handgun she held was steady as a rock. Her forefinger lay alongside the trigger guard but the safety was off. She knew what she was doing.

"Did Feyd teach you how to use that?" Bourne asked.

As she looked at him, her initial alarm faded. She cocked her head, her brows drew together, as did her lips into what might have been misinterpreted as a pout. Bourne, however, knew it was not.

Recognition illuminated her face as from a lightning flash at night. "Uncle Samson!" She lowered the gun and flew into his arms, her body pressed against his. Samson had been his operational name when he had been in Cairo.

"Amira." He inhaled the scents of cinnamon and incense wreathing her like a halo. Then he held her at arm's length. "You were a tiny thing the last time I saw you."

Her heavy eyelids fluttered. "Not *so* tiny, Uncle Samson." She twitched her narrow shoulders. "But, yes, I suppose I've grown taller."

"Grown in every way."

"I was eleven the last time you saw me. I'm sixteen now—seventeen in five months."

"Don't push it. Time goes too fast." He smiled. "May I come in?"

"Of course." She stepped aside, pulled him over the threshold. "What an idiot I am!"

"I've come to see your father. Where is Feyd? Is he home?"

Her expression seemed uncertain, then darkened as she turned from leading him into the living room. "My father was killed two weeks ago."

"Amira, I'm so sorry." He stepped toward her, embraced her for a moment before stepping back. "And you've been alone since then?"

She nodded, for the moment mute.

"Amira I need to ask. Was it an accident or—?"

"Murdered," Amira said.

"Will you tell me about it?"

She nodded, ringlets bouncing shadows across her cheeks. "But first we must drink and eat, or what a poor host am I?" She made a sound deep in her throat, which could be interpreted either as joy or sorrow, or both. "What, then, would my mother have thought of me, had she been here?"

She slipped silently into the open kitchen, began preparing food. Behind him, Bourne heard the fairy tinkling of myriad wind chimes made of seashells, an ethereal accompaniment to the muezzin's controlled wail.

All around Bourne were photos of Amira's mother and father, haphazardly placed on shelves, bookcases, side tables, as if often moved according to Amira's mood or where she was in the room so that some were always in her view. The photos were of the parents alone; there were none of them together.

The photos, the cheap mementos crowded in around them, spoke of a life well lived, of marriage, of family, of time passing and remembered in all its marvelous complexity.

Bourne had none of this. Try as he might, he could not remember his parents, where he had been born and raised, whether or not he had siblings. All of this reminded him that he had no idea who he was or where he had come from. It brought home to him again that he had nothing of his own. He was an unmoored creature on a sea without any sight of land, drifting with the current or fighting against it, in the end it didn't matter. And yet in his dreams he kept being drawn back to the moment off the coast of Marseilles. He could hear the shot, a crack of thunder splitting the low sky open, but he couldn't feel the bullet strike his body. Then the freezing water of the Mediterranean, inky-black, oily. Blackness, blankness. Pulled from the sea by fishermen, part of the early morning's catch. Their doctor had saved his life, but his memory had died, leaving a great void yearning to be filled.

This great void inside him was why Sara had become so important to him. Her life, her father, she herself loomed large in his present as well as in his recent past, which meant his entire life. It was why the death of Boris had hit him so hard. When you take a penny from a pauper, what has he left?

"A penny for your thoughts," Amira said as she carried two plates of stew to the table on the balcony. "Let's eat outside where we'll catch a river breeze." She inclined her head toward a shallow bowl. "Would you bring the pita?"

She lit a string of fairy lights. The wind chimes turned and sang in counterpoint to the muezzin's voice.

When they were seated, she said, "You taught me that: 'A penny for your thoughts.'" She laughed. "At the time, I didn't even know what a penny was." Her expression grew solemn. "But, Uncle Samson, you looked so lost in thought."

Bourne began to eat, breaking off a section of pita, shoveling up some stew onto it using only his right hand. "I lost a good friend yesterday," he said, once again pushing down his anguish. "And now I find that Feyd is dead."

Amira rose, went back inside, crossed to the refrigerator, and returned with two frosty bottles of beer. For a time, they drank and ate in companionable silence broken only by the soft lap of the water, the cry of a bird. Some raucous music played, then abruptly stopped. The muezzin's call to prayer had ended.

"But it seemed to me more, as if you were lost in the past," Amira said, engaging him with her coffee-colored eyes.

"I have no past," Bourne said, "to speak of."

"That can't be true. I know you for—"

"I mean before that. I have no memory of where I was born, who my parents were, if I have sisters or brothers. But you have a brother, I recall."

She nodded. "El-Amir, yes. He is in the West. You never met him. He's so smart, so clever. He finished his A-levels, then went on to the London School of Visual Arts, where he met and married an heiress, and was installed at a high-level position at CloudNet satellite TV, one of his father-in-law's media companies."

"So you must have seen him recently."

With a sad smile Amira shook her head. "My father used to say that we Egyptians must look to the future, always. 'The future is our salvation, my children,' he would say, always with a kindly smile. 'Honor the past, yes. But for us to dwell on the past brings only sadness and more loss than we can bear.'"

"So he left you here on your own."

"El-Amir is a big shot now." Tears sparkled at the corners of her eyes, but did not spill over. "Apart from the occasional postcard and the money he sends us I don't hear from my brother."

"Amira—"

"It's no big deal. I still love him. El-Amir is all that's left of my family. And he looks after me in his own way. He's very generous." She continued to look at him, studying his face as if she were an artist about to sketch out an idea on a fresh canvas. "I don't begrudge him leaving." Her mouth half open, she seemed on the verge of continuing, then apparently thought better of it.

He pushed his plate aside. "Tell me what happened to your father."

Amira sighed, looked out over the Nile, where the moon's reflection rippled and coalesced in an age-old rhythm. "After Treadstone was shut down he fell on hard times. Everyone associated with the organization was discredited. He tried to talk to representatives of the U.S. government, but got nowhere. He was, as he said, radioactive.

"For a while, he did odd jobs, whatever he could get, nothing much really, but enough for us to make ends meet. Then about a year ago he began to work as a guide for one of the big tourist hotels. He expected great things, but, you know, after the Arab Spring almost no tourists come to Egypt anymore. He was left with boring businessmen, always with one foot out the door, waiting to be contacted." She shrugged. "One day his past caught up with him. I suppose he knew it would happen sooner rather than later." Her expression grew pensive. "I think now he was marking time, waiting for it to happen. Maybe that's why he took the job—so he would be more visible, easier to contact."

"Who contacted him? CIA? Typhon?"

"Neither."

A boat drifted into view, lying low in the water. The sound of its diesel engine came to them like the sputter of an old man clearing his throat.

She turned to look at him. "It was the Russians."

A tiny chill slithered down Bourne's spine. The boat, clearer now across the water, looked like a tourist barge. Dual sphinxes rose from the curving prow. It was almost empty.

"Who?" he said. "Who was it who contacted him?"

"He said he was a general in the FSB." Amira had been fiddling with the last piece of pita. Now she set it down on her plate. "His name was Karpov. Boris Karpov."

23

THE MOON SILVERED the edges of the Pyramids of Giza, which otherwise glowed a pale melon in the powerful uplights buried in the sand. Ivan Borz, sitting with his legs up, ankles crossed on the top of the wrought-iron balcony railing of his residence in Giza, peered across the desert at the immense Pharaonic necropolis that had cost so many their lives. "And for what?" he wondered aloud. "The ancient Egyptians had it all wrong."

He looked from the Pyramids to the five-sided box sitting on the chair next to him. The top was off, the face of the head turned toward him. The American head. So beautifully preserved.

He drew his computer onto his lap, opened it, and displayed one TV show after another to the head. "You see this shit?" He pointed to the screen on which grotesquely built men and women were vying for control of something—different things on the different shows that flickered across the screen—but always control. "These must be familiar to you, yes? European and American reality shows. This is the soul-rotting drivel we must protect our people from. There are no Muslim values here—no values whatsoever, except greed, avarice, and betrayal."

With an angry gesture, he closed the laptop, put it away. He stared down at the head for a moment. Then he smiled. "You know," he said, "you are my only friend in this godforsaken wilderness, the only one I can talk to. The only one I trust." He sighed deeply. "Being Muslim, being a student of history, I know how to talk to the downtrodden, the disenfranchised, the poor shits who have nothing, no prospects ever to be anything. But you already know this, don't you? You know everything that's in my head, every thought, every memory. No crevice too deep." He laughed. "But I digress. Where was I? Ah, yes! I give them martyrdom. After I'm through with them, that's all they long for." His smile, though widening, had turned rueful. "But, let's face it, who wants to be stuck here in Cairo or in Syria or Iraq recruiting? Not you. Not I. But for the amount of money I'm being paid, for the assurance of being left alone by the FSB to do whatever the fuck I want, it's worth it." He tousled the black hair. "Don't you think?" He laughed. "Of course you do."

He pulled out a Cuban cigar from a secret inner pocket, bit off the end, lit it slowly with a solid silver lighter, took his first few puffs. "Have patience, my friend. The one who murdered you will pay, this I have sworn. You will be revenged."

Footfalls came to him, soft and delicate as a woman leaving her bath. "Keep your own counsel now," Borz whispered to the head. "We do not want this one to know our business. I recruited him in a dazzling display of Muslim activism, the twisting of the Qur'an that suits our aims. He is a believer, my friend. I am not. But soft now. He comes."

But it was no woman who came up behind him now, breathing softly as a lover.

"El-Amir," he said without turning around. "Punctual as usual."

"I smelled the smoke from a distance," the young man said, stepping around to face his boss.

"In this godforsaken shithole one must take one's pleasures, tiny though they may be."

El-Amir was clothed in an outfit straight from the best tailors in London. He had the dirty-blond hair and light eyes that set the British upper classes and the polo masters off from everyone else. On close inspection, however, it was possible to discern that his hair was dyed, that he wore blue contact lenses. His upper-class British accent might have been fake, as well, but none save a linguist could tell. He carried a slim, crocodile-skin laptop case that, like the powerful computer inside, had been handmade expressly for him.

Ivan Borz produced another cigar, held it up. "Here." He flicked open the lighter as El-Amir took the cigar from him, rolled it between his fingers, inhaled its rich aroma. "I'll light it for you with the present you gave me."

When the second Cuban was lit, El-Amir took a seat on the other side of the boxed head. He was tall and lanky. His face seemed to belong to a long-dead age. Three hundred years ago, he might have been mistaken for a crafty Jesuit, save for his lens-clad eyes, which were like stones weirdly glimmering underwater.

"How long are you going to keep that thing?"

"For as long as I can converse with it."

El-Amir shook his head. "You're bonkers."

Borz leapt up, was at El Amir's throat all within the space of a single heartbeat. "Shut your fucking mouth." Eye to eye, breath mingled, the two men stared at each other, each thinking their own thoughts. All at once, Borz stood back, stared down at El-Amir. "Speak not about things of which you are ignorant."

El-Amir swallowed hard, held his hands up, palms outward in a gesture of calm and peace. "Apologies. I didn't—"

"I saw the video, by the way." Borz retook his seat. His demeanor serene, as if nothing untoward had happened. "Magnificent production values."

El-Amir nodded, not knowing whether or not to smile. "That's what you get when you hire professionals." Leaning over, he slipped the laptop out of its case, fired it up. He inserted a flash drive into one of the USB slots, navigated to the files therein.

Up popped one video after another—beautifully lit, exquisitely framed, even though they were obviously shot with a handheld camera. The camera's movement added to the urgency of the images of black-clad Islamics taking over one Syrian town after another. Jump-cut to a map of the area, showing how far the movement had spread, how close they now were to the Turkish border.

"Here's our latest, and it's killer." He laughed. "Literally." He focused the screen on a video of terror chieftains sitting around a campfire in what might have been a desert, except for the fact that bombed-out buildings like the cracked, rotten teeth of a wino formed the dramatic backdrop.

There was no talk, no subtitles. Instead, the men passed around a series of weapons: submachine guns, mortars, bazookas, flamethrowers, antitank missiles. The metallic sounds of the war matériel seemed somehow heightened, to come at the viewer like shots. They were passed from left to right as one reads the Qur'an. As each weapon was handed to the last man on the left, he gave it to a female, fully clothed in black from head to foot. Only her eyes were visible, gleaming, lambent from the firelight. The camera zoomed in slowly, lovingly on her eyes.

El-Amir hit the Pause button. "Look at those eyes," he said admiringly. "I spent five days finding this young woman. Those eyes are huge, dark, exotic, and, most of all, expressive. These are eyes the viewer falls in love with. The way this section is framed you can't help it. Now the viewer, in thinking 'How beautiful!' has become complicit in the video. He's drawn in despite himself. In such beauty the camera finds power."

El-Amir hit the Play button and the image unfroze. The camera moved back to show the upper half of the young woman. She brought each weapon toward the camera like a religious relic, offering it up to the viewer. In extreme close-up one could see that the weapons were American made. The camera raked over their serial numbers in pitiless slow motion, so there could be no doubt that the Islamic terrorists were using American weapons that had been "liberated" from the Syrian military.

Now the fire-lit group broke up, the camera followed them closely as they approached a towering cache of weapons and ammunition, still in their original shipping crates. Jump-cut to the terrorists using the weapons to kill everyone who stood in their way as they moved through the last Syrian town before the border to Turkey.

The screen went black, but the sounds of weapons fire, the shouts and screams of the dead and dying, persisted, heightened not by increased volume but by the lack of visual. At last, one line in Arabic appeared, and, below it, the English translation: *THANK YOU, AMERICA! WE WILL NOT FORGET YOU!*

"Beautiful, El-Amir." Borz stomped his booted feet as if he were at a sporting event. "I commend you, my friend!"

"It's as I told you," El-Amir said as he removed the thumb drive and packed away his laptop. "The production, framing, and editing of violence into a memorable entertainment package takes old-school Hollywood theory and modern electronic know-how."

Borz nodded. "This will go out?"

"It's already up on YouTube and our own six channels with links on Twitter, Facebook, pins on Pinterest, and Tumblr. I got it out as soon as I finished the editing." He sat back, puffed on his cigar. "And how was Moscow?"

"Shitty," Borz said. "Why anyone would choose to live there is beyond me."

"Most of them don't."

"Killing Karpov," Borz said, hopscotching topics to see how well El-Amir would keep pace. He was well aware of how he had terrified the man. All well and good. Periodically, everyone needed to be reminded of their place in the scheme of things.

"Killing General Karpov was a positive pleasure," Borz said with admirable alacrity. "Plus, I got to spike an old friend of mine—a Kidon assassin named Rebeka."

"I'm happy for you."

"What are friends for?" Borz's lips formed a curdled smile. "Even the ones who can no longer talk. *Especially* those."

El-Amir tilted his head back, blew smoke into the sere wind off the desert. "Where does the bad blood between you and Rebeka come from?"

"A poisoned well." Hell would freeze over before he told anyone, let alone El-Amir, the origin of his animus toward Rebeka. Mossad had been trying to shadow him for some time, with only limited success. Frustrated, they had gotten Kidon involved. They had given Rebeka the scent and set her loose in Cairo, where they suspected he was hiding out. They were only half right. He was in Cairo, all right, but he was there to broker the biggest arms deal of his career. Unusually, the deal was complicated. Borz had had to handle two separate clients, two murderous personalities, two outsize egos, two hateful human beings—which for Borz was saying a lot—in order to close the deal. For all these reasons and one other—he alone was the arms dealer with a large and diverse enough inventory to satisfy these people—they had come to him. As such, he had tripled his usual fees. Neither of the clients seemed to mind. For Borz himself it was the payday of a lifetime and, as an added incentive, a good portion of the war matériel he would be supplying was going to be used against Israel.

How it happened to this day Borz was unclear, but somehow Rebeka had discovered the site for the meet, where the deal would be consummated. A crack sniper, among her other infernal talents, she had shot dead both of his clients and just missed killing him by a hairsbreadth. Since then, he had been trying to run her down to exact the revenge she so richly deserved. She had not only cost him his enormous payday but had also humiliated him in a manner he could not abide.

El-Amir, unaware of the inner workings of his master's mind, took the cigar out of his mouth, studied the tip. "You know what I love most about a good cigar?"

Ivan Borz watched a thin streamer of cloud occlude the moon for a moment. Then the silvery light returned to the Pyramids. "I can't imagine."

"The ash," El-Amir said. "It never crumbles. It stays together no matter how extended it gets."

Ivan Borz wanted nothing more than to strangle the life out of this ego-inflated balloon, but for the moment El-Amir was crucial to his current work. Borz laughed silently. Pity, really. "Is that part of Existentialism One at Cambridge?" He blew out a stream of smoke, watched it hide the moon as the cloud had moments before. Then it was gone.

El-Amir laughed. "Don't tell me you're jealous of my education?"

"Hardly," Ivan Borz said. "Do the professors at Cambridge teach you how to kill? Or how to die?"

24

THE MOMENT BOURNE left Amira's houseboat he put in a call to Eli Yadin. Ever since he had worked with the director of Mossad he had Yadin's private mobile number. He heard the electronic ring, then a click, the sudden hollowness on the line that indicated the switch to a secure line, then more buzzing as the various security sweeps processed the origin of the call. Only then did Yadin answer.

"Where are you?" The Director was never one for small talk.

"Cairo, looking for Ivan Borz."

Yadin grunted. "Good luck finding that fucking chameleon."

"Eli, was Sara in Moscow two nights ago?"

"Why don't you ask her yourself?"

"Because I'm asking you."

Yadin's voice grew grave and dark. "What's happened?"

"I was hoping you could tell me."

"Unfortunately, I have nothing to tell you."

"Eli, listen to me. I'm standing here on a bank overlooking the Nile and I have in my hand Sara's Star of David."

Silence.

"I know what you're thinking, Eli. I know it's hers."

"It can't be. She was here this morning and she was wearing it."

He told Yadin about the dented point. "She must have bought a replacement."

"She hardly had time; she came here directly from the airport."

"Where did she fly in from, Eli? Where was Sara?"

Silence.

"I wouldn't ask if—"

"I know."

Another silence.

"Sara had a target in Moscow," Yadin said.

"Did her assignment include killing Boris Karpov?"

"It was not."

"The truth, Eli."

"I'm pleased Karpov is dead. He was no friend of Israel's."

"He was a friend of mine."

"So Sara tells me. Curious friends you have, Jason."

"That would include you, Director."

Again, silence. And all the while Bourne was watching every movement, every shadow, the passing of every vehicle and boat, scrutinizing them for a hostile motion, or surveillance. He was in the enemy's camp; from now on there would be no rest, no letting down his guard.

"How does your friend's death involve Sara?" the Director said at length.

"His throat was slashed by a garrote. I found Sara's star embedded in the wound."

"That's not possible—"

"Deep inside the wound, Eli." Bourne took a breath. He hated the drift of this conversation, but he had to go there. "We both know Sara has used her star as a weapon."

"On more than one occasion," Eli said with some deliberation, "it has saved her life."

Time to get it over with. "Did she have orders to terminate Boris Karpov?"

"She did not."

"Eli—"

"This I swear to you, Jason. But your information explains why the FSB is after her. They were checking all exits from Moscow. They pulled her face off a CCTV at Sheremetyevo, and now the entire organization's out for her blood."

"Imagine what Mossad's response would be if you were terminated, Eli."

"I can't say I'm sorry he's dead, but she didn't come anywhere near your friend."

Now came the question Bourne did not want to ask. "Eli, do you think she might have deviated from her assignment? Boris was a whale of a target."

"We don't work that way. Sara doesn't work that way. End of story."

Bourne felt relief spread through him. "Okay. Then I think I know who did kill Boris."

"Someone known to me?"

"Ivan Borz."

"Your own private ghost. It happens we have a line on him in Cairo. I assume you know that."

"Lines intersect, Eli. Let's make sure they don't cross."

"Lev Bin." Yadin recited a mobile number.

"I'll contact him," Bourne said. "Now tell me why the FSB thinks Sara killed Boris. I'm the one who found her star. No one saw me, no one knows."

"Perhaps it was simply her presence, along with the discovery of the man she did terminate. Consider: the head of FSB is murdered and that same day a Kidon agent is spotted leaving the country."

"How did they make her? I thought Kidon personnel were—"

"A story for another time, Jason. Right now my concern is for Sara."

"Where is she, Eli? Jerusalem?"

"She was. I wanted to hustle her off to the Maldives for a vacation and for her own protection. Only—"

"Only what, Eli?"

"She took a different flight."

A clutch in the pit of Bourne's stomach. "Where did she go, Eli?"

"When you see her, Jason, and you *will* see her, sooner rather than later, tell her she's in a shitload of trouble from me." A heavy intake of breath, audible even over the secure line. "And, Jason, don't let anything happen to her."

A young woman brought the tea on a tray she held aloft with one hand. A rolled prayer rug was beneath her free arm. Her black robes covered her from head to toe so only her eyes could be seen, which was the way women were obliged to present themselves in public. Anything less modest was wicked, wanton, an affront to the strict teachings of Allah.

"Time," she said. The two men had long since finished their cigars, the smoke dissipating on the late-night wind that scoured the desert, created tiny sand devils, whirling dervishes that turned the uplights brown.

As the woman set the tray down on a side table, El-Amir said, "Borz, look into her eyes."

Borz did so, saw those magnificent eyes from the new video El-Amir had shot, edited, and uploaded to the Net.

"Congratulations," Borz said. "You're a star."

El-Amir smiled. "No doubt," he added. "No doubt at all."

Ivan Borz reached beneath his chair, unfurled his own silk prayer rug. The woman handed the rug she carried to El-Amir. She looked askance at the severed head in its box.

"Remind you of your homeland?" Borz said, because he couldn't help himself.

Her eyes lifted to his. There was no hint of amusement in them. He had learned rapidly that she had no sense of humor whatsoever.

"I am reminded of the oppressor every time I see drones in the sky, see missiles pulverize a home where someone I knew lived."

Borz grunted. "How well you express yourself in Arabic."

"My parents speak Arabic," she said. "They wonder where I've gone."

"To a better place," Borz said.

She lifted a bowl of water from the tray, handed it around so that the men could wash their bare feet and hands. In this sere wind a towel was superfluous; their extremities dried almost immediately. Then, without another word, she turned and left them.

The men knelt on their rugs, and the sacred ritual began. Their voices were joined in prayer, as synchronous as the movements of their torsos.

Prayers finished, they rolled their rugs, sat back in their chairs, sipped tea in companionable silence.

At length, El-Amir said, "We have almost more recruits than we can handle. Social media has not only raised our profile a thousandfold, it has given us direct access to those who are weak-willed, easily radicalized, immanently susceptible to our cause."

"You have put us in an enviable position," Borz said as he and El-Amir sipped tea beneath the gaze of the Pyramids, of the ghostly moon. "We are actually ahead of schedule."

"I aim to please," El-Amir said. "We both have great ambitions that supersede religion or ideology."

"Tell me," Borz said, because he had no interest in talking ambition with anyone but the boxed head, "do you ever miss your sister? She's just across town, still living on your father's houseboat."

"I always miss Amira, or at least the part of me that died back in London does." El-Amir's voice was low, level, seemingly without emotion. "The person that is here, that films, cuts, and edits your videos doesn't remember who she is."

It was perfect—the best answer he could give, and Borz was pleased.

"And you," El-Amir said. "Are you still seeing this woman, this tour—?"

"What of it?" Borz snapped. He disliked probes into his personal life.

El-Amir shrugged. "I wondered whether you'd see her one more time before we left."

Borz kept silent. All around them dawn crept across the desert, and with it began the parade of tour buses, bringing tourists who braved the international news reports to visit the glories of Egypt's past. These days the buses were two-thirds empty, sometimes never ran at all for lack of customers. Borz felt some pride in that.

The dawn. They had acknowledged it with prayer; now it was time, once again, to work. Four days, he thought as he rose. Four days until the end of the world.

25

SVETLANA KARPOVA SAT on her hospital bed, dressed, overheated, and impatient. She was ready to leave; her doctor had given his consent, had signed all the paperwork. She should have been gone hours ago. Instead, here she sat with a pair of military officers standing guard outside her door. She had tried to step outside her room but they had stopped her, gently but firmly. These were not FSB men; who had given them the command to keep her here she could not say.

She had been moved, of course. The room where Andrei Avilov had died had been cordoned off as a crime scene. Through the open door of her new room, she had caught glimpses of forensic experts coming and going, lugging their mysterious equipment. But for all their vaunted expertise they had found nothing, for the simple reason there was nothing to find. Andrei Avilov had died in that room, but he'd been murdered elsewhere. They, of course, did not know that. They would never know it. And soon enough the case—if you wanted to call it that—would be closed.

These were the facts, as Svetlana knew them. Then why was she being kept here, clearly against her will? She had no idea, but she'd had just about enough. She needed to grieve for her dead husband in solitude and quiet. And a hospital was about the least quiet building in the city.

She stood up, determined to confront the two officers once and for all, bully her way past them if need be, when a striking man walked into her room. He was accompanied by an even more striking young woman, never introduced, who said not a word through the entire interview.

"Mrs. Karpova, I am so very sorry for your loss," the striking man said. His voice was a purr, almost like velvet, a difficult thing to accomplish using the Russian language. He had piercing eyes, a mustache and goatee combination that had gone out of style with Trotsky, and pitch-black hair, slicked back from his window's peak with some kind of pomade she could smell from across the room. He appeared fit and strong. Nevertheless, he was smoking a cigarette, the stench of which made her want to vomit. Smoke curled lazily, lending him a penumbra, like some minor deity, which, in a very real way, he was.

Boris had introduced them at the reception. But even had he not she would have recognized him from the many news photos she had seen of him. His presence answered a number of questions, including the nature of her guards. He advanced across the room to stand between her and the door. She found herself face-to-face with Timur Savasin, the first minister, the most powerful man in the Russian Federation, bar only the Sovereign himself.

"The general was a great man. Great. He will be missed most acutely." Smoke emanated from his nostrils, as if he were a drowsing dragon.

She noted that Savasin said "the general," not "Boris Illyich." So Boris hadn't been kidding about this guy, she thought. Dangerous as an electric eel, and just as slippery. He was no friend of Boris's, he's no friend of mine.

She briefly put on a thousand-watt smile before she allowed her features to return to those of a grieving widow, who had been manhandled. "Thank you, First Minister. Your kindness is greatly appreciated. Now. Can you tell me who killed my husband?"

He waved a hand in dismissal. "Now, now, that's nothing for you to concern yourself with. The matter is being dealt with, trust me."

Trust you? she thought. Not for a second. "I'm afraid I must insist, First Minister. The government owes me that much, at least."

Timur Savasin appeared to consider her request. At length, he stubbed out his cigarette, nodded. "All right, Mrs. Karpova, as a special favor I will tell you what we know. The general was killed by a Mossad agent—a member of their Kidon branch—the assassins. How she gained access to the hotel we'll never know. But rest assured, we know where she's fled to, and agents have been dispatched to ensure her termination."

"A name," Svetlana said. "I want a name, First Minister."

"We don't divulge names," he said flatly.

Men had been saying no to Svetlana all her life. She knew how to deal with them, even the powerful ones. "My husband was the head of FSB. You owe me this, First Minister."

Timur Savasin sighed, apparently decided that telling her could do no conceivable harm. "The only name we have is the one Kidon has assigned her. Rebeka."

"Her operational name is as far as you've gotten."

"That's all we need, Mrs. Karpova," he said darkly, slamming the door on the subject.

He rubbed his hands together. The unpleasant necessities dealt with, he was at once all business. "And now, if you would, please tell me in your own words what transpired between you and Andrei in your hotel suite the night of your wedding."

"I was attacked," Svetlana said. "Assaulted."

"Sexually?"

"Surely you've read the medical report."

"I'd like to hear it from you."

"Of course." She nodded, careful for the moment to be obedient. "I was physically and sexually assaulted."

"My apologies for being so blunt, Mrs. Karpova. It cannot be helped."

"I understand." You shit, she thought.

"Who assaulted you, Mrs. Karpova?"

This was the tricky part. She must not show that she had the slightest motive to kill Avilov. If she told the truth, if she implicated Avilov in the assault, there would be her motive, laid out for Savasin on a silver salver. There was also her cousin Rada to protect. She recalled with vivid clarity the deep and abiding enmity between FSB and Savasin's military cadre, and particularly Andrei Avilov's hatred of Colonel Korsolov burning bright. She needed to gamble that Avilov's prejudice was a reflection of his boss's.

"I was with Andrei when the door burst open and one of the FSB guards advanced toward me. Andrei stepped between us, they grappled. My view was partially obscured, but I saw blood on Andrei's face. Then Andrei crumpled to the floor and the guard…" Here she caused her voice to falter. She forced a tear or two from her eyes, kept her head held high, the better for Savasin to observe the tears rolling down her cheeks. Boris always said she should have been an actor. She cleared her throat, said in a clogged voice, "Well, you know the rest."

"And the FSB guard—how did he die?"

"I think you can guess, First Minister. Andrei came to, pulled the man off me, and knifed him."

"I see." Timur Savasin moved so that he was no longer between her and the door. "Do you know why FSB guards were posted at your suite?"

"I assume to protect me." It was crucial, she knew, to sound rational. No mention must be made of her hysterics, or her trying to get out of the suite to see Boris. "At that point, I knew something must be wrong."

"Your guards were under the direct command of FSB Colonel Korsolov. Have you any idea why one of them would want to assault you?"

Sell it, Svetlana told herself sternly. *Sell it by telling him what he wants to hear.* "It was all so confusing."

"I understand. Still if you could—"

"He was enraged. Well, his boss had just been murdered. He called me a Ukrainian whore, a filthy traitor, a fucking bitch, more." She wanted him to see that she wanted to turn away, couldn't, was trapped in the memory of the violence and humiliation of the assault. "Much more."

Timur Savasin appeared unmoved, but perhaps that was only her take.

"And Andrei?" he asked. "Why was he with you?"

"He came to tell me what had happened to my husband."

"Yes, Korsolov was otherwise engaged at the, ah, crime scene." Savasin sighed. Of course, he knew why Avilov was there, but there was always the hope that the widow would say something to incriminate herself, to tell him that she was lying, that she was hiding something. Because he knew she must be hiding something. Ukrainians always did. "What an ordeal you've been put through. Again, I am most terribly sorry. Words cannot express . . ." His train of thought seemed to change midsentence. "Retribution for Andrei knifing one of his men . . ." His fist clenched. "Colonel Korsolov—though he has just been promoted by the Sovereign to general—must bear responsibility for the wickedness of retribution."

"I don't see how that's possible, since you yourself have said that the Sovereign has promoted him. Is he also the new head of FSB?"

"He was the great General's choice." Savasin's tone made clear his distaste. "I can't fathom why he chose to personally oversee Korsolov's rise through the ranks to become his adjutant. The man's a dangerous psychopath."

No wonder the Sovereign promoted him to fill the void, Svetlana thought. But on one subject she agreed with the first minister. "On that we agree," she said. Now to hammer the last nail home, she thought. "First Minister, those FSB guards—General Korsolov's people—are you aware that they were keeping me prisoner?"

"What do you mean?"

Of course it had been Andrei Avilov who had kept her prisoner while he had abused and assaulted her, but she knew revealing the truth would do her no damn good. "As I told you, I knew something was wrong. After Andrei told me what had happened . . . I told them I wanted to see my husband—they refused. They pulled weapons to make their intent clear. I was imprisoned on my own wedding night."

"That is unacceptable behavior. It cannot—it will not—be tolerated." Savasin popped another cigarette from a pack at his hip, held out a hand. "You have my word, Mrs. Karpova, that these incidents will not go uninvestigated. The culpable people will not go unindicted. Andrei's death will not go unavenged."

His smile was quite frightening, as if she were confronting a hungry wolf. "Now here is what I have set up for you. A nice long cruise. We'll fly you to Amsterdam, where you will board the liner. A top suite has been reserved for you using your maiden name."

"My maiden name? But why?"

"So you can get on with your life. Leave all this unpleasantness behind." That smile again, sickening her. "It's for your own good, trust me." Timur Savasin lit his cigarette, spread his hands. "I mean, let's face it, as Mrs. Karpova you're damaged goods. Here at home, what man will look at you twice?"

She felt the heat sweep up her neck into her cheeks. Her heartbeat felt like a sledgehammer, and there was a red rage behind her eyes. It was all she could do not to leap at him, scratch his eyes out.

Already, she thought, her answering smile a rictus of pain and humiliation, the outrages perpetrated against me are multiplying exponentially. Is there in truth no justice?

Early morning and it was already broiling. Sara, in the midst of Cairo's traffic chaos, realized she hadn't been back in more than five years. Back then, she had arrived uninvited and unsanctioned, to take care of a bit of business that would otherwise have gone unattended because it was a minor matter to everyone at Mossad save her.

As she made her way through the exhaustingly clogged city she kept reminding herself of what would be awaiting her when she returned to Jerusalem. By now her father must know she was in Cairo, and why. Ivan Borz. She had history with him. In fact, Ivan Borz was the reason she had come to Cairo five years ago.

As the world's largest arms dealer, he was well known to Mossad, deemed a major threat, and therefore targeted. After three frustrating years trying to find and terminate him, her father had had enough. He sent her to find Ivan Borz and eradicate him. She had been warned that, unlike the majority of Kidon missions, this one was likely to be long-term. She didn't mind; she had nothing going in either Jerusalem or Tel Aviv. She was, in fact, bored—the first and most definitely the last time she'd feel any form of tedium.

In the pursuit of her objective she had met an Egyptian money broker. Over the course of a month and a half she gained his trust. He wasn't a bad man, per se, but he was up to his neck in them. Sara should not have had a moment's compunction in using him, nevertheless in one of those moments in time that change everything, a moment you wish you could take back, she had. By one of those astonishing strokes of luck that sometimes happen in the ever-fluid field, he was lending money to one of Borz's two current clients. Which was how she gained knowledge of the site of the gathering between Borz and his clients to consummate an enormous arms deal. Shortly thereafter, the moneylender was found beheaded in his office. Whether it had been Borz or one of the men working for his now-deceased client, Sara never found out. Not that it mattered to the moneylender. Dead is dead. Her larger regret was that she had failed to kill Ivan Borz.

If Eli was disappointed in the outcome of her mission he never mentioned it. Instead, his sole message to her was that Cairo—anywhere in Egypt, for that matter—was off-limits to her until further notice.

Further notice had come to her in the form of the dossier Dov had left on her father's desk. Five years on. And now here she was, back in Cairo. She exited her taxi, walked a mile and a half, turned into a shop selling hijabs. She bought one, wrapped her head, then went into the rear of the shop. An old man with a face the color of a betel nut and as creased as tree bark looked up from his work, smiled as she said, "How is your daughter, Uncle?" in perfect Arabic.

"You mean Sidra?"

"No. Ermina."

His smile widened. "She is well and thriving."

Finished with their recognition parole, the old man rose, beckoned her to follow him down a dimly lit corridor. He opened a locked door, led her into a tiny storeroom lined with shelves on which were piled fabrics he would fashion into stylish hijabs, along with ready-made ones.

Stronger than he appeared, he pulled on one set of shelves, which swung out on massive hinges, and they stepped into a deep alcove. This space, too, contained shelves, but they were piled with weaponry of all kinds.

He stepped back, gestured for her to make her choices.

As always, Sara chose wisely.

26

AS THE SUN rose Bourne slept in a lumpy bed in a groaning hotel in a seedy neighborhood, while the ancient air-conditioning unit gasped and struggled to mitigate the heat that was only just beginning.

He awoke, showered, and dressed, and was out the door, enduring the blinding glare of sunlight that accompanied the inchoate roar of the city. He had made three calls to the best jeweler shops in the city, hitting pay dirt on the last one.

Across town, he purchased a loupe and a beautiful set of jeweler's tools in a soft velvet-lined case. He paid cash and walked out of the shop. He needed a quiet place—certainly not his hotel room—where he would be undisturbed.

Designed in the neoclassical style by Marcel Dourgnon, the dusky-rose-colored Egyptian Museum of Antiquities, at Tahrir Square, was the first purpose-built museum edifice in the world. In 1902, the thousands of artifact treasures, spanning five thousand years of Egyptian dynastic history, were transferred there from the palace of Ismail Pasha in Giza, where they had been displayed for more than a decade.

Bourne found his way to the museum's library, an oasis of calm and virtually silent. The room was subtly perfumed by the scent of paper and bindings from the eighteenth and nineteenth centuries, and possessed an atmosphere he found appropriate for the work at hand. He settled himself at the far end of one of the long refectory tables, near one of the small, green-shaded lamps, and unwrapped his new jeweler's case, then took out the fake Roman coin Boris had sent him. He peered at it through the jeweler's loupe. In the pool of aqueous light cast upon the table, he examined the coin on end. There was the hairline join that circumnavigated the edge.

Choosing a .8 precision screwdriver, the smallest available, he placed the tip against the join, began to carefully apply pressure. At first nothing happened. He applied more pressure, this time from a slight angle. Still nothing. He was just wondering whether the hairline was a join at all, when he felt the tip of the implement sink inward. It was a tiny bit, but it might be enough. He twisted the screwdriver, the tip applied torque to the two sides of the join, and the coin opened like a clam.

Inside he found a piece of onionskin, tightly folded and refolded in upon itself. Taking up a tweezers from his kit, he slowly and carefully opened the bit of onionskin. Little by little, the text Boris had laboriously written revealed itself. Morning mists lifting off a graveyard.

"This town is just fucking weird," Boris had said, as he and Bourne sat at an outdoor café in Jerusalem, drinking strong coffee and eating couscous.

A square of undyed muslin flapped overhead, keeping the scorching sunlight off them. The voices of hawkers were everywhere, and the passing parade of people moved with aggressive, purposeful strides or with the delicacy of deer. It was a clear day four years ago.

"I mean who's going to tell you the truth—Mossad? An Arab? From which sect, from which faction within that sect? The trouble with Israel is that it's controlled by the religious right. Those fanatics have the prime minister and Mossad in their pocket. Everybody falls in line; everybody does what they're told." He shrugged his big, meaty shoulders. "So what are you going to do? Everyone has an axe to grind, and believe me it's an ancient one, buried so deep in their bones even Hercules couldn't wrench it out."

He dug into his couscous with an uncharacteristic fury. "Fuck all organized religion, that's what I say. Think of what the world would be like without any religion."

"We'd all be Communists," Bourne said with a small laugh.

Boris saw no humor in that. "Communism is a dead end, my friend. Does it exist in Russia today? We learned our lesson. In China? They know better. Even Cuba is beginning to see what they've done to themselves. Okay, maybe North Korea, but a sadder, more deluded, more threadbare country never existed in the history of the world."

Boris sat, hunched over, brooding for some minutes. Bourne had seen this mood before, and he was loathe to interrupt it.

"Speaking of the history of the world, I've been working on a private side project. Ever since cyber-spying hacks have become so sophisticated and supercomputers are being used to decode even the most sophisticated ciphers, I've been on a hunt for new ways to communicate securely. The FSB now uses typewriters for all internal memos and project reports. Nothing concerning ongoing projects is on our servers, otherwise GhostNet would be all over us." He meant PLA Unit 61398, the Chinese Army's hacking unit. "But how to communicate to agents in the field? That was the more vexing problem."

He grunted as he called for more coffee. "I thought about this long and hard, then did some research on my own. What I came up with was this: Sumerian."

He sat back as the coffee was set down in front of them. When they were alone again, he segued smoothly from his preface to his thesis. "Sumerian has many unique qualities, not the least of which is that it's riddled with homophones. That, and the fact that there are two branches—the so-called male and female—makes it, in my opinion, a perfect cipher language. You can bunch the glyphs into groups, like looking at Morse code. And, of course there's always the false group hidden somewhere in the message in the event a hostile figures out the cipher key."

He lifted a forefinger as if testing the air for a change in the weather. "So now I will show you the glyphs while I pronounce them in Russian, and, naturally, you will memorize them as I draw them. Finally, we will each write a cipher for the other to decode. A game, if you will. *Our* kind of game. And like all our games, one with the possibility of deadly consequences. If you're ready, we'll begin." And dipping the tip of a finger into his coffee, he started to draw cuneiform glyphs on the tabletop.

Twenty-four glyphs, each one representing not a letter, not a word, but a concept, arranged into four groups, written in Boris's own hand, an artifact that seemed to have resurrected him from the dead. It was as if he were sitting across from Bourne now, in the dim antiquity of the museum library.

This was what Bourne was staring at now, written on the unfolded bit of onionskin. Boris had drawn the mixed male and female Sumerian symbols, just as he had four years ago on the café's tabletop in Jerusalem. This time, however, they were in a different progression. Boris had left him a cipher.

Now Bourne had hard evidence that his friend had had an intimation of his death. Why else send a courier on an urgent mission to Frankfurt to find Bourne and deliver the coin? Boris could have waited until he saw Bourne at the wedding, but obviously he felt there was no time or he didn't want to chance a direct handoff. He had diligently followed decades of security protocol.

Momentarily overcome with emotion, Bourne looked up at the dusty windows, where light filtered in, so weakly he could have been underwater. The shadows of palm fronds fluttered like sea anemones. Being aboard ship with Boris had always been difficult; the man was continually green about the gills. But instead of griping about it, he made jokes, poked fun at himself. He had a highly developed sense of humor, especially for a Russian. He was like a laughing child with his toys—especially his newest ones, bright and shiny and oh so valuable. For Boris, his secrets were his toys.

"Boris," he whispered under his breath, "what are you trying to tell me?"

Sara knew she should rendezvous with Lev Bin, the agent in charge of the operation Mossad was mounting against Ivan Borz, but she didn't, for two reasons. First, she didn't like Bin, nor did she entirely trust him. Second, she could hardly believe he would welcome her with open arms.

Now there was a third, far more urgent reason: she had picked up a tail.

Not surprising given her father's intel that she had been made at Sheremetyevo. She thought it safe to assume that the police had turned over the double murder under the Bolshoy Kamenny Bridge to the FSB. Finding her on the airport CCTV would connect her, at least in theory, to the murders. They'd want her blood, no question.

Walking at a normal pace, she melted into a group of high-end tourists, with their own bodyguards.

"This city is a fucking disgrace," the newly minted Colonel Pankin said. He gestured at the uncontrolled shouting, honking, exhaust-pluming chaos that was Cairo. "It's a goddamned hellhole of heathens."

The newly minted General Korsolov raised an eyebrow. "Never having been out of the Federation can be a liability as well as a blessing."

"The Middle East," Pankin said with a whiff of disdain. "My field of expertise has always been Ukraine and the former Soviet States."

"Was," Korsolov said. "With your promotion comes new responsibilities. The Sovereign wants us both to broaden our horizons."

"There she is," Pankin said without pointing, and the two FSB officers moved off after the Kidon assassin they knew only as Rebeka.

"She's with a tour group," Korsolov said. "They're heading for the Mahmoud Mokhtar Museum."

"How d'you know about these things?" Pankin asked.

"Didn't you read the detailed tour guide supplied to us?"

"I was catching up on sleep."

"Don't fuck with me," Korsolov said with a growl of annoyance. "You were basking in the afterglow of your promotion, Colonel." He picked up their pace, as they passed between the monumental square columns of the entrance. "Keep your xenophobia on a tight leash, your eye on the prize. Otherwise, your promotion will be short-lived."

Inside the enormous anteroom was a hushed susurrus, as if swarms of insects rather than people had congregated in the galleries and stone corridors.

"Just so you know," Korsolov said, leading the way toward the periphery of the tour group, "Mokhtar was the father of modern Egyptian sculpture." He put his forefinger against his lips. "No Russian," he whispered. "From this point on only English, yes?"

Pankin nodded. "We should split up."

"Hammer and Tongs, eh?"

"Exactly."

Korsolov nodded his assent, and the two men moved to opposite sides of the tour cluster. Korsolov had spotted the guards right away, and, as a prophylactic against their suspicion, struck up a conversation with a young, affluent couple that looked as if they had just stepped out of a Ralph Lauren ad. Korsolov swallowed his disgust, put on a welcoming smile, and introduced himself as a professor of Egyptian art. He fed them just enough on Mokhtar for them to accept him as one of their own, and so he passed muster with the guard on his side of the group. They passed a large bas-relief hung on one wall, then two freestanding sculptures Korsolov recalled from his guide, spouted some nonsense that nevertheless fascinated the couple, before he passed on, insinuating himself deeper into the group within which Rebeka had cleverly embedded herself.

He could hear the tour guide now. Some of the group had donned wireless headsets to better hear the commentary, others preferred to listen on their own. Rebeka was one of the latter. Korsolov caught a glimpse of her in profile. He made a sudden move, a disturbance, though minor, that caused a ripple through the group, like a pebble thrown into a pond. Ever on the alert, Rebeka turned in his direction and saw him. This was the point. He was the Hammer; Pankin the Tongs. Rebeka, recognizing danger, began to edge away from him. He continued toward her, ensuring she would keep her distance, ensuring she would run right into Pankin and be caught in the closing jaws of the Tongs.

The knots of people swirled around him. The commentary had reached an end; the group was beginning to break up into family units or cliques, to move on, led by the guide. Korsolov saw Pankin, who was closing in on Rebeka with deadly intent.

Sara saw her tail—or at least part of it. She had spied two of them—one older, broader, one younger, hatchet-faced. They were FSB; there was no mistaking them. It was impossible for them to keep the swagger out of their gait, just as it was impossible for them to hide their discomfort at being in Cairo. She could tell immediately that these were no field agents. They were high-level officers, and the only reason why such as they would come after her themselves was their mistaken idea that she had killed their boss. They wanted to interrogate her here, in Cairo, then kill her. They had no intention of bringing her back to the Lubyanka.

She wormed her way through the group, as quickly as she was able, but in the back of her mind was the knowledge that there was a second officer. She didn't see him behind her, so he must be in front. They were trying to maneuver her into a pincer-prey trap, and with the swirls of people all around impeding her progress, let alone her escape routes, they had a good chance of succeeding.

27

WHAT IF SHE *knows there are two of us?* Colonel Pankin asked himself. He had just caught sight of Rebeka, the group commenced moving to the next exhibit, all was in flux, and he himself was in motion, rushing toward her.

But then he answered his own question: The group that had worked to her advantage was now a major liability, blocking any direct route of escape. They had her between Hammer and Tongs.

Beyond Rebeka, he caught sight of Korsolov, stuck in the corner of his eye like a fleck of soot. He knew no matter what he did now, how instrumental he was in the capture of a Kidon assassin—a monumental achievement—Korsolov would take all the credit. He knew it was the way of things, but he hated it nonetheless. Hammer and Tongs was his idea, and now here she came straight into his arms. He had only to scoop her up, manacle her wrists as Korsolov came up behind her. Then they would discreetly disengage themselves from the group, hustle her out of the museum into a car he would call. He was looking forward to pulling her apart, piece by piece, to her vomiting up all of Kidon's secrets, and then to slitting her throat as she had done to General Karpov.

She was almost upon him, almost close enough, and he began to reach out for her, his fingers stretching to encircle her wrist, when she abruptly lurched to her left, into the chest of one of the guards. She made a moaning sound, let her body go limp.

The guard caught her, rushed her over to a stone bench against one wall. His companion joined him. Pankin heard snatches of their conversation—"passed out . . . low blood sugar . . . mouth to mouth? Not necessary . . . hospital? See if she comes . . . and bring a car around, anyway . . ."—before the rest of the group gathered around, curious and concerned, a hubbub brewing louder.

The manufactured incident left Pankin and Korsolov helpless, standing pretty much with their dicks in their hands, effectively locked out of getting to her.

"Bitch!" Pankin said under his breath. "She thinks she's so clever."

"Our pursuit isn't over. It's just begun." Korsolov's eyes burned with hatred. "And when we do get her I will have my fun with her."

"I want a piece of that," Pankin said, but Korsolov was no longer listening.

The cipher Boris had left for Bourne was, properly enough, giving him fits. Even though he had been put through cipher training at Treadstone, even though he had been through advanced study on his own, he couldn't for the life of him figure out Boris's message. He sat hunched over in the Egyptian Museum of Antiquities' library, while at the other end of the vast room scholars and visitors came and went in hushed reserve. The inner life of ancient Egypt held an almost holy place among archeologists, architects, religious scholars, and mystics—not to mention grave robbers and tomb looters. Their pantheon of animal-headed deities were arbiters of both awe and fear.

No matter how he tried to interpret the cuneiform symbols he could not make of them even a single sentence. With the beginning of a headache deep behind his eyes, he rose, went to the window, looked out across the Giza Plateau toward the distant golden pyramids of Khufu, Khafre, and Menkaure. He'd been inside two of them—Menkaure had been closed for some time. He might have been inside, but he couldn't remember—and he'd been fascinated by the hieroglyphics, how they told a story in much the same way a modern rebus did: in pictogram/concept form.

And then, all at once, he swung away from the window, hurried back to his chair and began to look anew at Boris's cipher. Which, he thought excitedly, wasn't really a cipher at all: it was a rebus—Sumerian cuneiform, like Egyptian hieroglyphs, like Mayan pictograms, was a language particularly suited to writing in rebus.

Sara threw some money at the taxi driver and stepped onto the sidewalk. The guards had escorted her out of the museum and into a waiting taxi, giving instructions to the driver to take his passenger back to the hotel the tour was staying at. Traveling north up the wide Meret Basha Boulevard, Sara abandoned the taxi near the eastern edge of Gabalaya Park. She hurried across Wasim Hasan. Up ahead a pathetically shortened parade of tour buses passed Midan El-Tahreer, where the protest riots had become a symbol of what turned out to be a false and dispiriting Arab Spring. These days, no more than a handful of people were allowed into the square at one time by the military, whose presence was unmistakable. Beyond their myopic gaze rose the aquarium and the Museum of Antiquities.

In the low-key alarm caused by her medical "emergency" no one had bothered to ask her name or to verify that she was, in fact, part of the tour. The guide, who was her only potential enemy, was thankfully busy assuring the rest of the tour that everything was fine, herding their rising panic like a seasoned cattleman.

She held no illusions that she was safe from her FSB tails. What she had managed back at the Mokhtar Museum was simply a holding action. Sooner or later they would track her down and find her. She was not a runner; she had learned that fleeing a dangerous predator only got you pulled down from behind and eaten alive.

As she climbed the stairs to the aquarium, she did not even bother looking behind her. She knew her tails must be there; frankly, she would have been disappointed if she'd lost them so easily. More than that, she wouldn't have believed it. She'd had numerous field engagements with FSB agents, and had found them nothing less than competent, sometimes frighteningly so, especially the ones personally trained by General Karpov himself.

She paid the outrageous entrance fee, kicked away some of the garbage strewn in her path, and went through the filthy interior. The aquarium was one of those Cairo attractions that was so run-down and in need of attention it was a crime to see how the fish were suffering.

But it wasn't the fish she had come to see. She had been inside the aquarium once before, and she knew where she was headed.

"It's a miracle anything's left alive in here," Pankin said, craning his neck to peer through the dim fug of the aquarium's interior. "They have a fucking nerve charging to get into this pigsty."

"Even our pigs have it better than this," Korsolov said as they passed tanks with cracked glass, mossy green water, semiconscious fish hovering near the bottom, their gills struggling to suck in the oxygen-depleted water.

Pankin laughed. "At least until they're slaughtered."

"At least slaughtering is quick," Pankin said. "This is slow torture."

"Something we both know a bit about."

The two flitted from shadow to shadow. What little light there was came from the tanks, aqueous and sludgy. They were both tinting green, like zombies in a horror movie.

"Where the hell is she going?" Pankin said.

"Away from us. But this time there's no splitting up—she'll expect that."

The darkness continued to descend, as if from the twilight of evening into the black of night. As they entered the next chamber, the walls seemed to narrow, become rough-hewn, as though they had entered a cave. Plus, the rank smell of guano and urine assaulted them with an almost physical blow.

"*Kakógo chërta!*" Pankin said. What the hell! "Where the fuck are we?"

At that moment, something flew right into his face. He shouted, more in shock than anything else. Then, as he saw the red eyes, the wingspread, and the hideous face he screamed in fear.

"It's a bat!" Korsolov shouted.

"*Króme shútok!*" No kidding! Pankin drew his weapon and fired at the bat, which wheeled away.

"Stop it!" Korsolov shouted. "Someone will hear you!"

Then it seemed as if an entire bat colony was descending on them. Pankin was too busy batting them away to pay attention as a shadow detached itself from a larger one, thrown by the outcropping of the cave-like wall. It was only after the knife slipped between his third and fourth ribs, and just before the tip carved its name into his heart that he realized what had happened. And by then it was too late—too late for everything.

28

SVETLANA EXITED THE big Mercedes First Minister Savasin had provided to transport her to Sheremetyevo airport, telling the driver to wait. She plodded across the lawn, up the stone steps, used her key to unlock the door to the dacha.

How could she leave Moscow, how could she leave Boris without first saying good-bye to his beloved dacha? As she moved through the rooms she saw him in photos, smelled him, heard his rough, deep voice rolling up out of his barrel chest. She recalled his laugh most of all, a laugh that came from deep inside him, rumbled from his lower belly. *"Don't try to make me lose weight, Lana, my pet. Like the Japanese sumo, my strength lies in my lower belly."*

At first, she had thought he was joking, but after a while she had come to realize that he was perfectly serious, and she stopped trying to regulate his intake of food and vodka. And, oh, the man loved his vodka! Almost as much as he loved Tony Soprano. His most treasured gift was the complete DVD set given to him by Jason Bourne. Hard to credit it, but Boris adored that show. He identified with Tony—though God alone knew why. Could Boris really have been as big a monster as Tony? And yet Tony had loved that horse—what was its name?—Pie-O-My. What kind of a name was that for a racehorse? She shook her head, crying and smiling at the same time, as she touched all the possessions he'd loved—a fierce-looking plush bear she had given him, on which he had pinned several of his medals; his silver biathlon medal from his adolescence; the political cartoons he had painstakingly cut out of papers and magazines, some making fun of NATO, the EU, and America, but others laughing at the expense of Russia and, especially, the Sovereign. Beside a widely published photo of the Sovereign bare-chested, riding his horse, was one of a Russian citizen in a fur hat, looking morose. By his side is an open gift box, in front of him a line of nesting dolls, all in the Sovereign's image. "I want a refund," the citizen says.

Svetlana laughed, despite herself, but it quickly turned into a sob. At the open doorway to the master bedroom, she hesitated. Then she turned, retraced her steps. At the sidelights beside the front door, she peered through the curtains. The car was waiting for her, the driver, smoking, his head cocked back, clearly daydreaming. Even though she knew there was no one around, still she could not help looking. Some habits were so ingrained they never died.

Assured she and the driver were alone in the forest clearing, she shrank back into the shadows of the entryway, pulled out the burner phone she had purchased to contact Belov, the Ukrainian patriot and her contact. He had failed to check in. He was hours overdue. With a distinct foreboding, she dialed a local number, left a three-word message. She disconnected, waited the requisite amount of time, and dialed the number again. As before, the voice mail clicked on immediately, meaning Belov's mobile was off. Her sense of foreboding morphed into anxiety. What if Belov had been captured by the FSB? What if he had given her up? What if the first minister was just playing with her? What if this driver had orders other than to drive her to the airport?

She had one more shot left. She punched in the fallback number, to be used only in emergencies, if Belov's mobile burner somehow had been compromised. She listened, her hand sweaty and rigid. Dead air. Her anxiety grew into a kind of controlled panic.

Get hold of yourself, she admonished. *Everything will be all right*. She heard herself and had to laugh. How could anything be right now that Boris was dead? Belov, also, very possibly. She never should have…

With a convulsive motion, she hurled the burner into the stone fireplace, where it struck the carbonized back wall and shattered. Kneeling, she took the pieces, went into the kitchen, put them down the Disposall in the sink. Grinding them to powder, one by one, settled her a bit. Like washing dishes it was a task whose purpose was known, whose outcome was immediate.

Done, she thought with a furious mixture of emotions. Done and gone.

In the master bedroom, she sat on the bed in which she and Boris had often made love. That world seemed long ago and far away, like a dream of the adult world she'd had as a child. She stroked the bedspread she had bought him with the flat of her hand. It felt soft and wiry at the same time, like his hirsute chest. She looked at the plasma TV screen affixed to the wall opposite the bed, where, after their sweaty bouts of lovemaking they would watch episodes of *The Sopranos*, which left her deeply depressed, but which Boris absorbed in their entirety—every shot, every scene, every sequence. She thought he might have been a little bit in love with Dr. Melfi, but only because Tony had been. The shrink had been the only eligible woman in the show who hadn't wanted him.

With a heavy sigh, she rose. She was aware that the car was waiting for her, and yet she was reluctant to leave. She wanted to take something with her, something tangible, that would keep her close not only to Boris but to what they had had together. The bear, perhaps? But that had been something for him, and with the medals pinned to its furry chest, it was a reminder of the FSB.

It was then her eye fell on the boxed set of *The Sopranos* DVDs. Finding Boris's leather overnight bag in the closet she grabbed that, set it on the bed. She took the DVDs from the shelf below the DVD player, began to shovel them into the empty bag. But she was weeping in earnest now, her vision blurred and distorted by tears, and she fumbled the last one. It bounced off the bed, hit the floor, and she moaned. If the DVDs were damaged she'd never forgive herself. Each disc had suddenly become as precious to her as Boris's booming sumo laugh.

She knelt down, as if in prayer. The separate packs had spilled out of their case, and she found herself reverently opening each one to reassure herself that the discs remained unscratched. At precisely what point she discovered the micro SD flash memory card she could not, later, say. Perhaps it had been stashed beneath the last disc in the series, the one that contained the finale that they had debated about endlessly. She had maintained that Tony had been killed just after the shocking blackout. Boris was just as certain he remained alive. They both had arguments that seemed to prove their respective points of view. But at some juncture Svetlana told him she had changed her mind. She conceded she'd been wrong, that Boris was right, because it became clear to her that Tony being alive was important to him.

Ironic, isn't it? she asked herself as her palm cradled the microcard. *Now it's important to* me *that Tony survived, because it means that in some dimension close to me Boris has survived, is still alive and laughing.*

Secreting the microcard on her person, she quickly stuffed the packs into their case, stowed it in Boris's bag, and, grasping its handles, left the dacha without a backward glance.

Moments later, the Mercedes pulled away, growing smaller and smaller, until it turned onto the main road, and all that was left was a thin blue cloud of exhaust, quickly vanishing on the piney wind.

Bourne, working on the rebus Boris had created, was scarcely aware of time passing. He had parts of the message figured out, but not others. The difficulty with rebuses was that they were puzzles within puzzles.

It wasn't enough to decode the individual groups, you then had to work out what they meant when linked together.

After hours of brain-bending work he was fairly sure that what Boris had left him wasn't a message in the normal sense. The rebus was seeming to him more like a guide, or maybe even a map of coordinates important to what Boris was up to just before he was killed.

Since his mobile wasn't working inside the museum, he rose and, searching the stacks, pulled down a detailed atlas of the Middle East, brought it back to the table. When he opened it, he consulted the correct page for the first set of coordinates, but found them to be incorrect. Returning to the rebus, he saw now where he had made a mistake. The first glyph set seemed to refer not to letters but to numbers. Ten minutes of more brain-busting work led Bourne to the conclusion that the first glyph set was a date four days from today. That, in itself, sounded ominous.

He continued. The second glyph-set translated literally as "Red-leaf," "Hammer-on-toe." So what was he looking at? "Tea"? Surely not. "Tea" made no sense, even in the off-kilter logic of a rebus. Bourne crossed out "Tea" and wrote "Fall." Next he tackled "Hammer-on-toe." He wrote "injury," "pain." He wrote "blood," but immediately crossed it out. There were many better ways to depict "blood." He looked at his words: "Fall/Pain," and while they made sense as cause and effect that wasn't the logic the rebus maker used. Rebus words were never precisely what they looked like, but variations. Figuring out the impreciseness was the most maddening part of the puzzle.

Bourne looked away, cleared his mind of preconceptions, then studied the glyphs again. How about "Fall" and "Ow"? In rebus parlance: "Follow."

He wrote down that word, put lines through the others, then went on with his brain-twisting deciphering. Twenty minutes later, this was what he had: FOLLOW THE MONEY . . .

Follow the money where? What money? Something tickled on the edge of his consciousness, something he had seen or heard? He tried hard to find it in the palace of his eidetic memory, but it kept slipping away, like an eel. This was the flaw his amnesia had caused, like a fault line, a rift that occasionally opened up, swallowing what he needed to remember from before he was shot.

Back to work. From there on, the glyph forms switched from masculine to feminine, which required an entirely different mind-set. Bourne pressed fingers against his closed eyes, trying to massage away the ache building behind them. He opened them again. The entire glyph set was stretched out before him, as if it were a piece of contemporary art. And there was, he saw, a certain kind of beauty in the glyphs, sere slashes that looked like the desert that was their origin. Looking at them as a whole had made him realize how much danger he was in, now that he possessed Boris's message. Holding on to the original piece of art, beautiful as it was, was far too risky. He studied the whole in a different way, memorized the glyphs, their relationship to one another, then he rose, went out of the library, along the corridor to the men's room. There, in one of the stalls, he tore the message into bits, flushed them down the toilet. The message existed now only in his head.

Bats. The bats were everywhere. After having liberated them from their cave enclosure, Sara was as engulfed in their swooping, chirruping dives as was Korsolov. The difference was she had perpetrated the assault—a crucial distinction that had given her the edge with Colonel Pankin. But that edge had been used up. Korsolov was older, wiser, and had had time to recover from the shock of the colony on the loose. Further, he lacked Pankin's instinctive fear of bats.

Though he ignored them as best he could, Korsolov instinctively continued slapping them away when they swerved too close. Sensing her chance, Sara rushed at him through the chaotic darkness of the bat cave, moving inside his defensive perimeter, negating the threat of his Makarov pistol. She felt the weight of his body, the acrid odor of his sweat, as she twisted his right wrist, then chopped down on it with the edge of her other hand.

His fingers loosened, and she shook the Makarov away, kicking it across the cement floor. But in those few seconds, he was able to shift his concentration from shooting her to disabling her with a nerve pinch in the area of her carotid artery.

Sara felt her knees turn to jelly, her breath came hot and fast—too fast—she was losing oxygen as her lungs struggled to suck in air. She felt the weakness spreading through her arms, shoulders, into her upper torso. Soon she'd be completely helpless.

"You little bitch," Korsolov whispered in her ear. "Did you think I'd be as easy to kill as that wet-behind-the-ears Pankin? Why, he'd never left Russia before this. A pirogi out of the sauce." He laughed, his breath hot and biting as his words.

Sara struggled for purchase with her hands, forearms, and elbows, but the strength had been sucked out of her. Her head felt so heavy. It dropped onto his shoulder, and he laughed again, this time more loudly, more acidly as he bent his own head down as if to kiss her, as if they were lovers.

In that instant of forced intimacy, Sara gave a silent roar. Her jaws opened, her teeth bared, and Korsolov howled in pain and astonishment as she took a bite out of his cheek. Her teeth punctured skin and flesh, and he reared back instinctively, but she held on, her teeth driving deeper until they struck his own. Then she whipped her head back and forth, ripping the ragged pink flesh off him, spitting it out, lunging at him again, growling this time, her eyes wide and staring, fixed on his nose this time.

Her jaws snapped closed, just missing taking off the tip of his nose. Korsolov, bleeding profusely, eyes tearing, his breath sucked in fits and starts, had had enough. He broke away from her and stumbled away, running erratically through the whirling colony of bats, moaning as they struck his ragged wound, smelling blood, coming after him, bats out of hell.

Sara tried to go after him, but his terrible grip had enervated her for the moment. She looked out into a violent darkness, and thought, Let the bats do with him what they will.

The bats did what bats will do: they tunneled through the darkness of the cave, swirling, beating their wings, swooping en masse, driving through the filthy, sparsely attended aquarium building to the outside.

Bourne saw them darken the sky through the streaked windows of the library, and knew instinctively something was wrong. Bats at the time of day where there should be no bats. Rolling up his jeweler's kit, he left the library, exited the building, and made his way quickly toward the aquarium, knifing through the crowds of people either staring, dumbstruck, into the sky or, in the case of mothers, hustling their little children away from the area. Gripped by the human instinctive fear of bats.

His keen eye was forever on the lookout for the reasons for anomalies, and so he focused on the people pouring out of the aquarium building rather than watching the bats swirl and swoop in a dark, trailing cloud. That was how he saw General Korsolov—though Bourne was as yet unaware of his promotion from colonel. He had met him at Boris's wedding reception. Boris himself had introduced them, but in a way that had made Bourne wary of him, despite the fact that he was Boris's second-in-command. Boris had always been a student of Sun-Tzu, whose *Art of War* he considered one of his three professional bibles. *Keep your friends close,* Sun-Tzu had written. *Your enemies closer.* The manner in which Boris had introduced Korsolov had led Bourne to the conclusion that the colonel was one of the latter, not the former. In which case, Boris was telling him, he was a dangerous man who bore watching closely.

Now Bourne recognized him, running in a ragged line out of the building, oddly surrounded by a cloud of bats. Then, as Bourne came closer, he saw the blood leaking around the hand Korsolov had slapped against his cheek. He was bleeding profusely, and though many of the freed bats were fruit-eating, there were clearly some vampire bats that fed on the blood of small mammals. Korsolov could hardly be termed a small mammal—but despite his efforts to stanch the flow, there was plenty of fresh blood all over him.

Shielding himself with the people streaming past him, Bourne approached Korsolov with an almost obsessive resolve. There was only one reason an FSB colonel would be here in Cairo at this very moment—he was after Sara. Which meant she must be somewhere close, possibly even among the crowds on the plaza. But for the moment, at least, his attention was on Korsolov. Nearing him, Bourne could see the ragged hole in his cheek, knew it couldn't have been made by bats, but by a large predator, doubtless human. Sara. He had made contact and she had fought back. A stab of anxiety stabbed through him. Was she all right? Had Korsolov injured her—or worse? He refused to contemplate the idea; dwelling on it would do no good—worse, it would distract him from what he needed to do to Korsolov.

He was close now, and though up until now he had hidden himself well a sudden gap in the people exposed him to Korsolov's gaze as he looked wildly around for respite from the flock of bats that circled him like a black aura.

Korsolov's expression momentarily froze, then hardened. He recognized Bourne, and now he had a solid object on which to project his rage and frustration. He was a grotesque sight as he dropped his bloody hand, groped for a switchblade, which he snicked open, lunging at Bourne in almost the same motion.

Bourne, turning sideways, grasped Korsolov's extended wrist, pulling it forward and down, unbalancing the Russian, tipping him past his center of gravity. Bourne chopped down on Korsolov's neck with the edge of his hand. Korsolov coughed, shuddered, then drove his bent-over body into Bourne's side.

They both went down, rolled over amid those streaming past. No one seemed to give them a second look. The bats swooping and chittering kept their attention high above the pavement.

As Bourne hit the ground, his grip on Korsolov's wrist was dislodged, the switchblade came free and slashed across Bourne's throat. Blood flew from the blade, like droplets in the rain, but the blade had sliced a bat in half. Now Korsolov, still bedeviled by the flying beasts, reversed his grip on the knife, plunged it down toward Bourne's chest. Bourne twisted and the point of the blade pierced his shirt, missing his arm by inches. The bats closed in again, and Bourne, worming out from under, wrapped his left arm around Korsolov's neck, placed the base of his right palm against the side of the Russian's head, and gave a violent wrench. Korsolov's cervical vertebrae cracked, he gave a little sigh, his eyes rolled up into his head, and the bats settled onto his ruined face.

Bourne lay, panting. Beneath the flurry of leather wings, he could hear the wail of police and emergency vehicle sirens, and knew he had to vanish as quickly as possible. As he rose to his knees, a hand was extended, and he took it, looking up into Sara's smiling face.

"We all get what we deserve," she said, "in the end."

29

THERE WAS A private—and like everything government-related—secret exit from the east side of the Russian White House. It was an interior exit, invisible on the outside. Through three thick metal doors, resembling the flood-barrier watertight doors on a submarine, First Minister Timur Savasin and his new aide, Igor Malachev, the replacement for the late, lamented Lieutenant Avilov, trotted down three flights of steel stairs, into a subway station, as magnificent in appointments as it was deserted.

Timur Savasin's private train sat waiting for him, doors open. Savasin led the way into the first car, the doors closed, and the moment the first minister took his seat behind his desk, the train pulled silently out of the station. The train itself had been built entirely to Savasin's specifications. The interior had the appearance of a plush home. Paneled teak walls, marble floors over which were scattered expensive carpets, mullioned windows, one of which was of stained glass, upholstered furniture in the old European style, over which hung an ornate crystal chandelier. There was even a fireplace in which faux coals were heated by electricity. In the mantel were ornamental items small and large from the time of the czars, including an ormolu clock. The first car, in which the two men now sat, was a combination office and Pullman, with sofas and deep, upholstered chairs, as well as a Louis XVI desk and a pair of straight-backed chairs, in one of which Malachev sat, spine straight, one impeccably clad leg crossed over the other.

Unlike Avilov, who had been a military man, Malachev was a ranking Kremlin *silovik*, part of Timur Savasin's powerful coalition. Malachev was young, self-assured, and smart. He was also ambitious in a way that did not dismay his boss. Avilov's appetite for power had been animal; Malachev's was cerebral.

The second car contained the bedroom. Everything in it was oversize, as befitted Savasin's own appetites. Not many people had seen it—not even Savasin's wife, and certainly not his three children. But the first minister's parade of mistresses had. Rumor had it that more than one per night were often on tap as the train rolled back and forth on the private line between his office in the White House and his sprawling dacha in the piney forests outside Moscow.

As Malachev watched, the door to the bedroom opened and in walked a young woman, svelte, stylish, and very beautiful. She was sheathed in a pale-green dress that hugged her figure and complimented her skin tone. She wore high heels that set off her calves, butt, and breasts perfectly. In short, Malachev was entranced. She came across the parlor car and sat with a shivery sound of hosiery. She was not introduced; she said not a word, but studied the two men as a cat stares at a shadow upon a wall, with a curious and unknowable intensity.

Savasin lit a cigarette, steepled his fingertips on the desktop, and inhaled deeply. "Tweedle-Dum and Tweedle-Dee, Korsolov and his pet swine Pankin," he said on the exhale, "are never going to capture the Israeli agent Rebeka."

"With good luck, she will kill them in Cairo," Malachev said.

"That would be convenient. But who will terminate *her*?" Savasin tapped his fingers together contemplatively.

"There are any number of agents I can summon."

"No doubt. But this situation requires an outsider, someone so clever, so deadly—"

"I have just the right man." Malachev reached for his mobile. The train was equipped with Wi-Fi and uninterrupted cell service.

"Not him," the First Minister said with a dismissive wave of his hand. "After what he's done, he needs to lay low. Less exposure for him now is the wiser choice."

"Then who?"

"Who, indeed?" Savasin returned to tapping his fingertips together, as if he were listening to a melody only he could hear. He glanced over at the bookcase built into the teak paneling. There his eye rested on his two favorite novels. The phrase that Humbert Humbert repeats in *Lolita*—"Dolores, Lo, Lo-li-ta." A phrase with a decided lilt. "Curiouser and Curiouser," in *Alice's Adventures in Wonderland* also had a lilt. Both novels were steeped in childhood dreams, made dark and ominous by the looming shadow of adult pedophilia—and, in the case of *Lolita*, rape and murder. Leave it to a Russian to make explicit what a closeted Brit like Lewis Carroll could only sublimate through his writing. Still, Savasin found it odd that a Russian and an Englishman could have an obsession in common. He hated the English with a vibrant passion. Carroll wrote: "'It's a poor sort of memory that only works backwards,' says the White Queen to Alice." Whereas any good apparatchik knew it was the opposite: the best memory must work backward, in order to erase the inconveniences of history.

"First Minister?"

Hauled out of his contemplation, Timur Savasin's gaze returned to Malachev. There was a reason his thoughts had turned to Lo and Alice, two preternaturally clever girls. It would take a special sort of person to match them. As with Lo and Alice, so Rebeka. For just an instant, his gaze flickered to the woman who had emerged from his bedroom. Then, as if a mental door—a decision door—had closed, his heavy gaze fell once again upon Malachev. "I'm thinking of Zmeya," he said.

Malachev's eyes opened wide.

The first minister nodded. "The Serpent." No one knew his real name, not even Savasin. *Zmeya*, his operational name, was Russian for "serpent."

"He's meant to be the best in the business," Malachev said with some hesitation. "I hear he's also volatile, unpredictable, prone to changing plans on the fly."

"All traits that make him invaluable. Plus, crucially, he's close to the field of action." Savasin nodded. "Call him. Agree to all his terms, no matter how outlandish they may seem to you. He has a one hundred percent success rate with me. In the case of Rebeka that's all that matters."

Svetlana waited until the airplane took off, until dinner had been served and consumed, and the coffee and chocolates were in front of her. The first minister had been generous enough to seat her in first class, so there was no one sitting next to her. Still, she pulled up her privacy screen.

She stirred sugar and cream into her coffee with a tiny spoon. When she unwrapped the foil from the square of Belgian chocolate she found her fingers trembling. Popping the square into her mouth, she took out her mobile, opened the back, slipped out the 8 GB micro SD memory card in her phone, replaced it with the 64 GB card Boris had secreted inside the *Sopranos* DVD. Whatever was on there must be huge.

Fitting the back onto the mobile, she turned it over, fired it up in airplane mode. She had to put it on her tray table, her hands were shaking so badly. While she waited for it to boot up, she took a sip of coffee. She had to hold the cup in both hands to ensure she wouldn't spill any. Now she felt she was ready for whatever might come. The cup clattered a little as she set it in its saucer. Then she took up her mobile, navigated to the material on the SD card. There were three kinds of files: text, photos, and videos. No wonder he had needed 64 GB.

She started with the texts, which began with an overview of his mission. Right away she noticed something odd—the text was on plain sheets, not, as she would have expected, on FSB electronic docs. That was when she realized that Boris was running a rogue mission, outside the boundaries of FSB.

She read at a faster and faster clip, and, then, as she absorbed the monstrousness of what the Sovereign had put in play in all its Machiavellian deception, she felt her chest constrict, her stomach roil, and she pressed a napkin to her mouth to keep from vomiting.

But it was when she read past the overview, when she began to learn the true nature of Boris's black mission, that at long last the floodgates she had been holding in check since she had learned of his death let go. Tears rolled down her cheeks, she began to sob so deeply, so profoundly she was certain her heart must split asunder. A chill crept into her, seeping down into her very marrow, as it had when her father, looming big as God, rageful as an enemy, had punished her as a child. She began to shiver and shake. She could not stop crying. Her loss seemed monumental, overwhelming. She was inconsolable. Her world had been not only turned upside down but inside out. Everything she had known to be true was a lie. She had misjudged Boris's intentions entirely, and now even the thought of the plot she had almost mounted with him as an unknowing dupe made her want to plunge a knife into her soul, to carve out the blackness that must surely lie rotting at its core.

Zmeya did not yet know that his twin sister, Irina, was dead. When the call came in from Igor Malachev, he had, in fact, thought it was his sister calling. Not having bothered to look at his mobile's screen, he was surprised it was not Irina.

"Zmeya," Malachev said.

Only First Minister Savasin's people called him Serpent. It was their bit of skullduggery, their oh-so-secret conceit. Every time he heard the word he laughed inside.

"We have a commission for you."

A *commission*, like he was a traveling salesman. Well, he reflected, in a way he was—he sold death, a commodity no one wanted and everyone got, sooner or later. With him, it was always sooner.

"Sending now," Igor Malachev said.

He took the mobile away from his ear, put it on speaker, then clicked on the incoming email, which was textless. Instead it contained a .jpg photo file of a very beautiful young woman.

"This is Rebeka," Malachev said. "Kidon agent, currently in Cairo."

"Dossier?"

"She's Kidon, Zmeya. There is no file." Malachev took a breath. "Where are you?"

"Close enough." Then he told his interlocutor his terms and, because he had pissed him off with his tone, he doubled his price. The swift intake of breath mollified him somewhat.

"It will be wired to your account."

"One half immediately."

"Of course." Malachev cleared his throat. "The commission needs to be executed as soon as—"

"It will be executed in the time it takes, not a moment before or after." He rang off, then, annoyed all over again that this idiot had dared to give him a deadline. Didn't he know Zmeya's commissions were custom designed, depending on the target? Meticulous attention to detail was one of the many reasons he had never failed to execute a commission.

The day was still burning hot, dusty and dry. As he drove, he listened to a CD of The Doors, Jim Morrison singing "This is the end, my beautiful friend. This is the end."

He rode the highway west, toward Cairo, into the pure white glare of sunlight.

He missed Irina with all his heart and his soul. Like many twins he sensed the place inside him she inhabited, and it was now empty. This filled him with a rage beyond anything he had ever known. He had not heard from her, which was unusual, not to say unprecedented. They spoke at least once every day, unless, by prearrangement, they could not—when either of them was traveling, for instance. No such prearrangement had been made. He had no sure knowledge of her death, but that place inside him she inhabited no longer sang to her particular vibration. There was nothing. Nada. The Dead Sea, washed with the salt of unshed tears and nothing else.

He took out a little square wrapped in a branded bubble-gum wrapper, popped it in his mouth, let it dissolve. Then he counted backward from one hundred. By the time he got into the thirties the colors around him had begun to luminesce. The huge white sun was throbbing in time with his pulse. Jim Morrison's voice seemed suspended in the air, each word flitting across the windscreen as if written in Arabic script. He laughed out loud at the sight, wondered what Morrison would have made of it. Probably he would have loved it; certainly he would have understood how high the Serpent was, how far down the rabbit hole his homemade formula of lysergide had taken him. Doubtless Morrison would have gladly shared some with him. He would have understood it as a drug of his time. No one was dropping acid anymore. These days, it was heroin, coke, and X—or some near-lethal combo of cough medicine, nutmeg, drain cleaner, and God knew what else that street punks were always coming up with. Or the cheap-to-make Krokodil, the faddish, flesh-eating synthetic being fed to desperate Russian heroin addicts.

No, when it came to recreational drugs, the Serpent was strictly old-school, and making his own kept him safe. Safe to enable the vivid and meaningful flashbacks to his first real encounters with Irina. The end of childhood, the beginning of lust, obsession, wild, crazy love, and codependency. He was not so self-deluded that he could ignore that last, for he and his twin were certainly conjoined emotionally, if not physically. It was the acid that had made them so irrevocably crazy—he was certain of it. They had discovered this kernel of craziness during the third electrifying year of their illicit meetings in the woodshed, where he had one fateful day come upon Irina in the throes of self-ecstasy, where she had turned to him slyly and, as if she had known he had been watching all along, beckoned him on. The first time her lips closed around his almost painful erection remained the sweetest, most profound moment in his life.

Thereafter, they met for their trysts every day at dawn and dusk. He longed for more—as he imagined she did—but their fear of being found out stayed them. But this same fear steeped their lust for each other in the sweet pain of illicit hours.

They were thirteen when they started their sexual experimentation with each other. Three years later, Aleksandr had gotten his hands on a sheet of acid tabs, which launched their adventures into the furthest reaches of experimentation. It was the acid firing their systems during lovemaking that locked them together in a world of psychedelic color and exquisite, mind-altering sex, drawn out in tantric ecstasy for what seemed days on end. Unless it was all a fever dream, all a fantasy, all a product of their overactive libidos. Who could tell?

The drive into the heart of Cairo took just over three hours, though to the Serpent, wrapped in the arms of his lysergic flashback, time had ceased to exist. The long desert dusk was about to fall as he pulled into a filling station ten blocks from the apartment he maintained in the city. He got out of the car, felt the deep and abiding throb of Cairo as if it were his own heart. If Irina was gone, then where was Bourne—Bourne with the Roman coin that had been sent from Boris Karpov? The moment Irina had been told that General Karpov was running an off-the-books operation covert from both the FSB and the Kremlin, she knew that if they discovered what it was they would have power in the palms of their hands, power to use against everyone else—absolutely everyone.

The coin contained some kind of code that only Karpov's best friend, Jason Bourne, could decipher. The coin's secret was the lynchpin to what he and Irina were planning; without knowledge of Karpov's plan they knew they were dead in the water. Now, if Irina truly was gone, he would have to shoulder all of the load. Meanwhile, the world spun on, uncaring, indifferent, deeply troubled.

While his tank was filling with petrol, he breathed Cairo deeply into his lungs. He could taste it as well as scent it, his mind filled with memories of times here, with and without Irina. But now to work. He smiled as, feature by feature, he conjured Rebeka's face from the photo on his mobile. She was here; she was close.

"This is the end, my only friend. The end."

30

TWILIGHT WAS IN the city's grasp when Bourne led Sara back to his hotel room. They sat for a time, steeped in a long, trembling silence, side by side, their eyes filled with the sight of each other. They did not touch. For the moment what was happening was enough. It had been some time since they had seen each other, let alone been together in private. Bourne had stripped off his shirt, spattered with bat blood, but hadn't replaced it.

Outside, the city roared and groaned, Arabic voices rising and falling in a musical downpour. There was something comforting in the small conversations, the sharp arguments, the punctuation of brief laughter—the common language of commerce and friendship that for them normalized what had been a decidedly abnormal afternoon.

Decompressing from kneeling at the brink of death was no easy thing, no matter how long it had been a part of your life. Being together now, united in those moments of fear and adrenaline, when your wits, your strength, your cunning, and courage all were entwined, working at peak levels, made the aftermath sweet, rather than hollowed-out.

Bourne took out the gold star, blunted on one point, handed it to her.

Sara looked at him as she enclosed her beloved star in her fist. "Where did you find this?"

"Lodged inside the fatal wound across Boris Karpov's throat."

"I know he was your friend," she said. "I don't want to lie and say I'm sorry."

This was where her adamantine hardness came out. In many ways, she was tougher than her father, perhaps because she had had to be.

"In his day General Karpov ordered many Kidon killed, some of them close to me."

"And your father ordered many of his men killed, some of them close to him."

Now real sadness crept into her face. "This conversation has veered into the wrong lane."

Bourne nodded. He looked at her, said gently, "What was your star doing in Boris's throat, Sara?"

Her face clouded over. "You don't think I killed him."

"I already went through that possibility with your father. I think someone wanted the FSB to think you were responsible. Who knew you were in Moscow?"

"My father; Amir Ophir, head of Metsada; Dov Liron, my direct boss; and the people in the Scrivener Directorate who forged my legend."

"No one else?"

She shook her head.

Bourne considered this a moment. "How did you lose the star?"

"I don't really know." Sara frowned. "But, thinking back on my time in Moscow, maybe I do. A man bumped into me on the street. He had packages in his arms. The contents fell all over and I helped him pick them up. It was some time after that when I realized it was gone."

"Describe him."

"Slim, handsome, in his late thirties or early forties, I would say. Approximately six feet, one hundred and eighty pounds or so."

"Face."

"Let's see." Sara ran the tip of her tongue around her partly open lips.

"Dark, curly hair, long nose—an Arab nose, maybe. Sunken cheeks. An ascetic look—like a priest—a man who, at the very least, ate little and slept less."

"Speech?"

"He spoke to me in Russian, but that wasn't his native tongue. Beyond that I can't say."

"Ethnic background?"

"Burnished skin the color of tea with a bit of milk in it—an Arab, but not a Bedouin, and surely not Indian or Pakistani. A Turk, then, or an Armenian. Maybe Eastern European—there's a lot of Ottoman Empire blood still there."

"Chechen?"

She shook her head. "I don't think so. Why?"

He told her about Ivan Borz being in Moscow the same time she was.

For a long time she said nothing, but her features had whitened, as if she were under extreme duress.

Concerned, Bourne said, "What is it?"

She shook her head. "Nothing." But her voice came out strange, strangled. She looked at him. "You don't know for sure the man I ran into was Borz."

"Consider the chain of events. Borz was in Moscow when we were. A man bumps into you. Shortly thereafter you realize your Star of David is missing. You can't possibly think his bumping into you was a coincidence?"

"But we don't know what he really looks like, or even if Ivan Borz is his real name. He may only be posing as a Chechen."

"Whatever he is or isn't, Sara, one thing's clear. He knows who you are. He bumped into you on purpose, stole your Star of David to plant on Boris after he'd garroted him."

Silence fell like a deposit of ash, blown in through the window. A vendor called, over and over, like a dog barking. Vehicles slid past on the streets below.

At length, Sara said, "You haven't touched me."

Bourne slipped his hand into hers. He felt the soft burr of the star she clutched in the center of her palm.

She smiled sadly. “I'm not sure that's what I meant.”

“Tell me, then.”

“Your obsession with Borz.”

“You know the reasons.”

“Of course I do. It's just that . . .” She shook her head. “We're so much alike, Jason. I see me in you, I see how I would react—how I *have* reacted—when someone close to me dies.”

“I'm closer to finding Borz than ever before,” Bourne said. “I have work to do.”

She took her free hand, ran it through his hair, pushing it back from his forehead. “It's grown so long.”

“I haven't had time—”

“But, you see, that's my point. You haven't given yourself time.” Her fingers curled, grabbed his hair, pulled gently. “To remember Boris, to think about your time together, what great friends you two were. To acknowledge the terrible loss. We let so few people into our lives—really in, I mean. Boris was one of those few, wasn't he, Jason?”

“He was,” Bourne acknowledged with a suddenly heavy heart.

“Then you must make time to mourn him.”

“I can't. Where Borz is concerned there is no time.”

“No, my sweet. Where *you're* concerned there is no time.” She cocked her head. “What, do you think mourning your loss is a sign of weakness?”

Bourne studied her for a moment. “When I thought you were dead, I was on the verge of giving up—this work, this shadow world I live in—everything. Your father convinced me otherwise. He sent me on a mission to avenge your supposed death.”

“He saved you, in other words.”

“In a manner of speaking. He reawakened my appetite for revenge. He brought me back from the brink of despair.”

"And now," she said, pulling him to her with her hand in his hair, "it's high time I did the same."

When their lips met and Bourne felt hers open under his, tasted her, an alchemical reaction delivered him from what seemed to him so many days wandering in the desert of his rage and sorrow at Boris's demise. The tension that had gripped him from the moment he had seen Boris lying in a pool of his own blood, black in the FSB floodlights, as if oil ran through his veins and arteries instead of blood. Like a snake sheds its old skin in a ritual of rebirth, Sara's hands and mouth and naked body on him served to lift him up into yet another resurrection—the latest of so many in his life he had lost count. And yet this one seemed the most dramatic, the most profound, plumbing the deepest darkness from which he had emerged, saved from the bullet wound and the squally depths of the Mediterranean.

And when he entered her, when he heard the groan pulled out of her own depths, his head came down, his face pressed into the fragrant hollow of her shoulder. Hot tears filled that hollow to overflowing as his rage and sorrow broke like a tidal wave that could no longer be held back. There had been no one in his life like Boris, no man he admired so much, trusted implicitly and explicitly, a man who knew him, who saw through the unknown core that even he, Bourne, could not penetrate. Boris had been like an older brother—no, more than that, like the father Bourne could not recall no matter how hard he tried. He had been family, and now he was no more. Gone, but as Sara so rightly pointed out, not forgotten. Not forgotten at all.

In the aftermath of their hectic, bittersweet lovemaking, Sara held him, caressed him, kissed him tenderly, wordlessly, until, at last, his own tenderness was coaxed to the surface, and they made love again, slowly this time, lovingly, truthfully, washed in the purifying white-water rapids of dreams. And in so doing he fell into a state of grace: a kind of solace stole over him, an emotion with which he was unfamiliar, and yet, nevertheless, he instantly understood and for which he was profoundly grateful.

31

THE GOVERNMENT RESPONSE to the disturbance outside the aquarium culminating in the death of a foreign national would have been quicker and, doubtless, more vigorous had there not been a serious explosion outside the Egyptian Foreign Ministry at more or less the same time. A suicide bomber had blown himself up, killing two police guards and a junior minister on his way back from a meeting, and injuring a handful of army personnel. The generals who ran Egypt were far more concerned with their own dead and wounded than about the death of a foreign national. And when, finally, it was discovered that he was both Russian and, most probably, a spy, what investigation had been contemplated turned into a diplomatic accusation delivered forthwith to the Russian ambassador.

The athletic young man Bourne had met in the Meisterstuck Hotel in Frankfurt watched the aftermath of the bombing from the sidelines. Hands in pockets, he whistled a little fairy tale tune as if he were trying to soothe a crying infant. First Minister Savasin and *silovik* Malachev knew him as Zmeya. In truth Zmeya did not exist, but in his world truth did not exist, so never mind.

As the Serpent watched the military cleanup crews his sat phone buzzed. Melting back through the crowd, and then away where there was marginally less ambient noise, he thumbed the phone on, put it to his ear.

"She's dead, Aleksandr," Ivan Volkin said. "Irina is dead."

Aleksandr Vasilýev Volkin felt as though he could not breathe. The void inside him wasn't a figment of his imagination, just as it wasn't a manifestation of missing her with a lover's fervor.

"Aleksandr," Volkin said. "Are you there? Did you hear me?"

"How?" The Serpent could scarcely squeeze out the single word. His mouth felt as if it were filled with cotton wool, his tongue swollen to twice its size. As opposed to his mind, which seemed scalded by his grandfather's words, boiling with too many emotions for him to properly assimilate. "How?" he said again.

"She was uncharacteristically stupid," Volkin said with a growl. There seemed to be no sorrow in his voice, only a low-simmering anger typical of him at his lowest ebb. "She took Bourne to see Mik."

Aleksandr felt as if his eyeballs had been put to the fire. "He shot her?"

"He might as well have," Volkin said. "He blew up the warehouse. She was caught inside the blast radius."

"And Bourne?"

"Escaped," Volkin said. "As he always manages to do. The man's a full-on sorcerer."

"Where is he now, do you know?"

"Of course I know," Volkin said. "He's in Cairo. He's still after Ivan Borz."

"That's a good one." Aleksandr watched the bodies being carried away, the smears of blood, the twisted limbs left behind. He told his grandfather about his latest commission. "It looks like his luck is about to run out," he concluded.

"I find it instructive that Malachev called you," Volkin said. "I'd be surprised if Savasin wasn't grooming him to be the new head of FSB."

"Over Korsolov? He was Karpov's choice."

"What you don't know about Kremlin politics, Aleksandr. You're an outsider, after all. Boris Karpov, whom I loved like a brother and hated like my worst enemy, was wary of Korsolov. Boris locked Korsolov to him to keep him nearby—maybe he had other reasons, too. Knowing Boris as I did, that wouldn't surprise me, either. But whatever the case, Korsolov is going to be thrown to the dogs. Savasin has been wanting to grab control of FSB for years. Only Boris kept him at bay. Savasin feared Boris like no other."

"Why?"

"That, my brilliant grandson, is a mystery. And now that Boris is dead it will remain a mystery."

Which brought Aleksandr's thoughts full circle—to the Roman coin he had delivered into Jason Bourne's hand. But that just led him back to thoughts of Irina. Their grandfather never suspected the intimate relationship he enjoyed with Irina. *Had* enjoyed. *Dear God! Don't think about Irina now!* a silent shout that reverberated inside the raw wound in his skull, in a heart as black and shriveled as the ash of all hope.

"Why did she take Bourne to see Mik?" he asked.

"You know perfectly well why. Mik was *vosdushnik* for Borz, as well as for your father. He could have told Bourne where Borz is now."

"If Bourne somehow made Mik talk about Borz, he was sure to tell him about what my father and brother had been up to. Why would Irina take such a terrible risk?"

"I'm sorry," Volkin said, "my crystal ball is broken."

A terrible fury was once again building inside the Serpent. "It had to be Bourne."

"Very possibly. There was a definite rapport between them," Volkin said, for once the naïf. "On the other hand I cannot imagine Irina betraying us."

Aleksandr had another definition of "Irina betraying us," and it didn't include their grandfather. Always secretly the rebels, the two of them had been for years talking about forming their own business, but it wasn't until their father and brother were caught and executed by the FSB that their talk turned to action. What they planned was dangerous in and of itself, but combine that with the possibility of being found out by their supremely powerful grandfather and anyone else would have considered them insane. And possibly we were, Aleksandr thought now. Perhaps I still am. But, if so, what of it? Who in the shadows isn't a little bit insane? It was the crazies who got to run the asylum in the fringes of normal society; he only had to look at his grandfather as a prime example. Volkin was a different person to virtually everyone he came in contact with. His genius was in becoming what those people wanted him to be. Easy to change your spots when the reflection is already provided for you.

He and Irina both learned that particular feat of legerdemain, which was the probable explanation for why Irina had led Bourne to Mik. She gave him what he wanted from her—but either Mik or she herself ended things before Bourne could learn anything damaging to them.

"Aleksandr." His grandfather broke in on his ruminations. "I'm starting to worry about you."

"How d'you think I feel learning Irina is dead?" he said, a bit too defensively. "Twins have a special bond. I feel as if half of myself is gone."

"I never should have sanctioned your father's dealings with Ivan Borz. I should never have used him as a proxy, but he was the only one in this shithole of a world I could trust."

Aleksandr's ears pricked up. This was the first time he had ever heard his grandfather admit to making a mistake.

"Now look." His voice had turned mournful. "My son, two of my grandchildren are dead. That leaves only you, Aleksandr. The field has become too dangerous."

"I have my commission to execute."

"Forget what Savasin wants, Aleksandr. He's like all the rest. You already have your orders."

Suddenly he sounded like an old man to Aleksandr—not a grandfather, but someone who has seen too much of life, someone who was tired of the great game.

"I know what you're thinking," Volkin said. "You think I'm ready to roll over and die." He laughed. "Did I make you start, Aleksandr? I read your mind, didn't I?" He laughed again, the sound of leathery wings brushing against a cave's walls. "I'm pleased I can still surprise you. And here's another surprise. I know what you and Irina were up to. I know you wanted the coin's secret for yourselves."

"I don't—"

"Stop! Don't embarrass yourself further. You and Irina knew the coin held the location. Somehow, fucker." His voice had hardened to steel. "But I tell you this: consider crossing me and, grandson or no grandson, I won't hesitate to have you killed within the next three hours. Am I making myself clear?"

Aleksandr could hardly bring himself to make a noise, let alone speak. If his grandfather knew that he actually had had the coin in his possession . . . His mind recoiled from peering into that future.

"Answer me!" Volkin shouted through the ether.

"Y . . ." Aleksandr swallowed hard. His mouth was as dry as the desert outside Cairo. "I understand."

"Savasin is meaningless now. All that matters is the secret held in that coin. I wish you to find it."

"I need to find Bourne."

"That's right. Find Bourne, get the coin, discover the location. Once we have that, we have everything." The old man made a sound in the back of his throat that was open to interpretation. "I know you understand me, Aleksandr. You know what's at stake: everything. Absolutely everything."

32

WHEN SVETLANA ARRIVED at the dock in Amsterdam and took her first look at the cruise ship on which First Minister Savasin had booked her, she knew that if she sailed on it she would be killed. She knew this as surely as she knew she needed oxygen to breathe; it was something instinctual, buried deep in the most primitive part of her brain, the part connected irrevocably to survival. So she tore up her ticket, she turned on her heel, and strode away. With every step she took she felt freer, as if for the first time in her life.

The skies were a deep cerulean blue, the lights of the city had come on, glimmering in the waters of the canals. Bike riders flashed by her and, for a moment, she wished she were one of them. It took her some minutes to realize that she could be—that she could be anything she wanted to be. Surely Boris would have loved that; he was so un-Russian in his belief in her. He harbored a certainty that she would be successful in anything she put her mind to. Dear, dear Boris. To her dismay, she found herself brushing away tears again. And here she had been sure she had cried herself out during the flight from Moscow. Was it so very bad to cry? She knew she wasn't a weak person; her tears were a kind of memorial to a man she had loved, betrayed, then loved all the more—loved with all her heart and soul, and now, in the aftermath of his death both were broken, perhaps beyond repair.

She passed a bike shop, its cycles glowing in window lights against the sapphire twilight, and she stopped, deciding whether or not to join the cliques of cyclists speeding past, to become one of them, to lose herself in their carefree midst. But she made no move to enter the shop. Her feet were glued to the sidewalk, and she knew why. She knew it wouldn't matter if she bought a bike, sold or gave away the bulk of her clothes and possessions, went on the road, became a latter-day bohemian. There was no losing oneself, except in death. And there was certainly no losing her vertiginous sense of loss. Wherever she went, she knew it would be with her. You can't outrun life; it was foolish and counterproductive to try.

So what would be productive? she wondered as she crossed to a bridge, stood leaning against its wrought-iron railing. She stared down into the greenish-black water, purling against the curved wooden side of a passing boat. A young man in a woolen cap waved to her smiling. Reflexively, she waved back, but she could not muster even the ghost of a smile.

Then, as she shifted from one leg to the other, she felt the tiny weight of the micro-card move against her thigh. Instinctively, she put her hand into her pocket, felt it there, warm between her finger and thumb. Boris's operation, black as pitch, secret as a doge's mistress, and she had it all.

Pulling out her mobile, her forefinger hovered over the virtual keyboard for a long moment while the darkness closed in around her, while she listened to the accelerated rush of her heartbeat. Then she turned, hurried off the bridge. It took her fifteen minutes to find a mobile shop. It was just closing, but she managed to purchase a cheap pay-as-you-go phone that could not possibly be traced to her. She paid cash as added security.

Back out in the street, she dodged more cyclists until she made her way, Frogger style, to the relative calm of another bridge. On the opposite bank tourists were taking selfies and pictures of each other with their phone cameras, using the beautiful buildings of Amsterdam as background. Flashes lit up the evening, bright splotches against the stone and brick facades.

Leaning against the railing of the bridge, she punched in a series of eleven digits, tap-tap-tapping out the number Boris had made her memorize. With a trembling hand, she put the phone to her ear. It rang and rang. Instants before she lost her nerve and disconnected, a male voice answered.

"Yes?"

"This is Svetlana Karpova," she said in a rush. "Boris's wife—widow—I . . ."

"Are you all right?"

The terrible drumbeat in her ears. "Boris gave me your number. He said in an emergency I should—"

"Are you in danger?"

"We met at the reception," she said foolishly, because her head was suddenly in a muddle. "I don't know whether you remember—"

"Of course I remember you, Svetlana. I should have sought you out, but afterward I was very busy."

"Knowing what Boris told me about you, I can imagine." Another silence, and now she was truly afraid. Afraid to go forward. But she could not now go back. For better or for worse, she was committed. "Boris said I could trust you."

"You can, Svetlana. I promise you that."

She closed her eyes, heart in her throat. She could hear the cyclists whirring by her, busy on their appointed errands or in mindless enjoyment. Not that either meant anything to her; she was as walled off from them as Boris had been, as surely the man she was talking to was. They inhabited a different world entirely.

"Jason," she said.

"I'm here, Svetlana."

"Where are you?"

"Cairo."

"I have something . . ." It was decided then, all at once, like a searchlight switched on in the dark. "I need to see you. It's urgent."

"What is it you—?"

Then she told him the gist of what she had found in Boris's dacha—the dreadful plan hatched by the Sovereign. It was her worst nightmare come true—no, no, it was even worse.

"You have to stop it, Jason," she concluded.

"If what you're telling me is true—"

"It is. I have everything here with me."

"I don't see there's any way to stop it, Svetlana."

"But you must! Boris had found a way."

"What way?"

"I don't know!" she cried. "It's not on the material I found."

"Maybe it's the material itself. Does it contain incriminating evidence against the Sovereign?"

"I think so . . . Yes. There are official top secret papers containing his signature. There are e-mails. Even transcripts of phone conversations."

"This is good. Very good. You need to get them to me as quickly as possible."

"I'm in Amsterdam, but I'll book the first flight to Cairo."

She was at her wit's end. She had to do something. *My people, my people*, a voice inside her cried. "I'm coming as fast as I can. I'll call you as soon as I land."

She disconnected, threw the new mobile into the canal, as if it were radioactive. She was shaking so badly her teeth began to chatter.

33

WHEN SVETLANA CALLED, Bourne and Sara were on their way to Amira's. Amira had contacted him earlier to tell him that a man named Goga—a diminutive form of Georgi—was looking not for Feyd, Amira's father, but for Boris himself. Had Boris planned to come to Cairo? Bourne had asked Amira. If he had, she said, she had no knowledge of it. But she had met Goga once before when he had come to confer with her father not long before Feyd's death.

Amira, being highly intelligent and savvy, having been taught not only by her father but by Bourne himself, had not told Goga that Boris was dead, but instead was suspicious that he had not known. If he was part of Boris's group in Cairo, why wasn't he in touch with the FSB in Moscow? So she had him sit in her living room and, while she prepared mint tea and small cakes for him, called Bourne to ask what she should do.

"Perfect. You've done everything you should have done," Bourne had told her, a bolt of pride running through him. "Keep him occupied. I'll be there with a friend of mine as soon as I can."

When he knocked on her door, she opened it immediately. He could see the anxiety in her eyes, and smiled to reassure her as he introduced Sara by her field name, Rebeka.

The two women eyed each other warily—Sara because, as Bourne had told her on the way over, of Amira's father's connection with Boris, Amira because she was rightfully mistrustful of anyone new in her environment, even one brought by uncle Samson. There may have been, to Bourne's keen eye, a touch of jealousy on the part of Amira. She was now of an age to view her uncle Samson in a more adult light. Harboring a crush was certainly not out of the question.

Goga stood as Bourne and Sara entered. He had a tic in the muscle just beneath his right eye that made it water. He kept wiping it with the length of his forefinger, which was as filthy as a coal miner's or a car mechanic's.

"General Karpov," he said in a rough and gravelly voice. "I must talk with him, but I can't raise him."

He was speaking Russian, and Bourne answered him in kind: "I am the general's representative."

"He was supposed to come himself," Goga said doubtfully.

"It is my sad duty to inform you the general is dead," Bourne said, using the formal locutions of the Russian military.

Goga remained unmoving. "How," he said dully.

Bourne told him as much as he knew. Also that he believed Ivan Borz was responsible. "So," he said, sitting down at the table and inviting Goga to do the same, "what you had to say to the general you say to me."

Goga squinted at him as he sat. "You don't talk like FSB. You don't act like it, either."

"That's because I'm not," Bourne said. "I'm an outsider. That's the point. You understand the general's plan must keep going forward. It's even more imperative now that nothing stops us."

It was as if a lightbulb had switched on behind Goga's eyes. "Of course." He leaned forward, lowered his voice. "Tell me your name."

"Jason Bourne."

"Ah, the general told me that sooner or later you would come."

"And here I am."

Goga's eyes turned to slits. "You must present me with the parole."

"What parole?"

"The general said that Jason Bourne would know the parole—a private parole he used with Bourne."

Bourne knew the parole—of course he knew. For a moment, his mind sidetracked him. He had carefully put aside thoughts of his own acute sense of loneliness and grief at Boris's passing, but now they came rushing back at the thought of their old, private parole, the one they used as friends as well as compatriots when they worked outside the strict boundaries of their respective governments. No matter that he was a creature of the shadows at the fringes of the world, a loner, an outsider. Humans were not meant to live alone. When they did, they paid a terrible price. But there was no time for any of that now. For Bourne, it was always the present. The past was unknown, the future unthinkable.

Bourne gave the parole just as if it were Boris sitting across from him, not Goga.

Goga, grim-faced, called for vodka and two glasses. Silently, he poured the drinks and the two men toasted the fallen hero.

"To the general," Goga said.

"To Boris," Bourne replied.

They clinked glasses, downed the vodka in one gulp.

The necessary formalities dispensed with, Goga said, "The operation has reached a critical point."

Now the secrecy of the false Roman coin, the odd rebus Boris had secreted inside, began to have a probable context. Bourne knew that the rest of this conversation balanced on getting information from Goga without revealing that he had no knowledge of Boris's Cairo operation.

"Tell me," Bourne said. When confronted with the unknown simplicity and directness is always the best choice.

Goga shot the two women a glance. "Outside," he said softly.

The two men rose, Goga put away his Makarov, and they went out onto the houseboat's deck, kitted out in twinkling fairy lights, reflections glittering in the purling water like anemones.

"Ivan Borz is here in Cairo. He arrived here yesterday."

Goga was careful to stand with his back to the interior of the houseboat. He was well schooled in security. But of course he would be, being handpicked for this assignment by Boris himself.

"Have you found him?"

"Yes, and no." Goga was careful to keep his head and body still, to present an impenetrable facade to those watching from inside. "We believe he has a villa somewhere in Giza."

"What is he doing here?" Bourne said.

"Besides being watched by the Israelis? He's recruiting soldiers for ISIS and selling weapons to them. The ISIS high command has a huge amount of money, and they're willing to spend it to get what they want."

"What is the source of their money?"

"Banks they robbed in Syria."

"But they have more than what they stole, don't they? Where is it coming from? Borz?"

Goga shrugged.

Bourne's gaze flicked over Goga's shoulder to where Sara stood in the flickering candlelight of Amira's living room. "Does he know he's being watched by Mossad?"

"They are being more careful than usual," Goga said. It was clear from his expression that the movement of Bourne's eyes had not been lost on him. "And they are usually even more careful than we are."

"We need to capture him," Bourne said. "I'll direct the assault."

Goga's eyes clouded over. "What about the Israelis?"

"I'll take care of them," Bourne said. "Boris sent a Mossad agent with me for that very purpose."

Goga's eyebrows lifted briefly. "The agent you brought?"

"That's right."

"But she's a woman."

Bourne's countenance darkened. "What's your point?"

Goga's mouth opened and closed like a landed fish. He let out a loud exhale. More like a snort. "Just...Nothing. Except, the Israelis have a habit of deploying women for men's jobs. It's...not how we Russians would handle matters," he ended lamely.

When Bourne made no comment, he flicked his hand, as if to dispel his words. "I've heard there'd be a price on Amira's head if it wasn't for General Karpov. They're afraid of him here—the lot of them. I don't really know why, but whatever the reason I'm grateful for it."

"Nothing's going to happen to Amira," Bourne said.

Back inside, Bourne took Sara aside. "Has Lev located Borz yet?"

"Indications are he's somewhere in the Giza neighborhood."

"Unless he hasn't told you everything he knows." Bourne looked at her levelly. "Is that possible?"

"With Lev anything's possible," Sara said. "I've never trusted him."

"But your father does."

Sara was silent for some time. Then, "It occurs to me that perhaps he shares my distrust."

"Why do you say that? He entrusted Lev with this operation."

"Maybe he's thought better of it. Now I'm rethinking the scene in my father's office. Just after the operation dossier was delivered my father got a call and stepped out for a moment. Surely he'd know I'd take a peek at the dossier. Surely he was aware once I saw an operation mounted against Ivan Borz I'd insist on being involved."

"Why?"

"Ivan Borz and I have a history."

"Field history, you mean."

Sara nodded. "I cost him the arms deal of a lifetime. I got his clients, but missed him. Eli worried that I was blown in Cairo, so he had me recalled."

"You wanted another shot at Borz."

"You bet I did." Her eyes burned brightly. "And now I will have it."

When Bourne did not reply, she kissed him lightly, then broke away a little. "What did Goga have to tell you?"

"Not much," Bourne said. "They're still trying to pin down Borz's whereabouts in Giza."

"Then we can work together."

"Why don't you stay here with Amira." It wasn't a question. "From what Goga told me she's safe only so long as Boris is alive."

"You're making that up."

"Ask him."

Still she eyed him, but she couldn't hide from him that a good deal of her skepticism was gone. "There's no way you're going to go off and leave me here with—"

"It's for your own good, Sara."

"What d'you mean?" She had her back up now, which was entirely predictable. "How do you know what's for my own good?"

"By your own admission when it comes to Ivan Borz you're too close, too wrapped up in your shared history to—"

"He toyed with me in Moscow. He stole my Star of David." Her fingers closed around the new one she had bought. "He used it to implicate me in your friend's murder."

"What you were sent to do was professional. Don't you see, he made your relationship personal. He doesn't want you thinking clearly."

"That's bullshit. I'm thinking as clearly as ever. Nothing he can do will change that." She was speaking to him as if in an argument with her father. "Don't do this to me. Don't deny me my revenge."

"Just take a step back for a minute and you'll see that staying here is your best option."

"I won't. I can't. *You* stay here with the girl. You two have a shared history." She threw his words back at him as if they were gunshots.

Bourne shook his head. "Goga doesn't know—Goga won't accept you. For one thing you're Israeli; for another you're female. He'll only work with me. Amira needs to be protected."

"Fuck you!" She was furious with him for trapping her, but at the same time the longer the moment went on the more her Mossad training came to the fore, the more she recognized the truth of what he said. Still, she gave it one last shot: "What about you and Borz?"

"What about it? I've been following him for more than a year. I'm near to finding him. Is there more to it?"

"You know there is!" she burst out. "After what he's put you through."

"It's all on a professional level."

"Maybe from your side," she retorted. "When you do catch him ask him if what he's done is professional or personal."

"Does that mean we're in agreement?" He gave her a level look, was reassured by the high color on her neck and cheeks, the spit of her voice. He'd had to make sure that she was okay, that she had returned to the tough-as-nails Kidon fighter he knew her to be. With her armor back in place, he could leave Amira in her care without worry. "You'll stay here with Amira. I can't think of anyone better equipped to keep her alive. Come on, Sara. I need you to do this. If there is a price on her head, as Goga has heard, no matter where I send her she won't be safe. Only you can keep her out of harm's way."

Still angry as a threatened hornet, Sara remained silent, and her brand of silence spoke a thousand words.

"Feyd is murdered, then Boris; Borz was in Moscow, now he's here. No coincidence—none of it is. Cairo is now a hot zone. We've stepped into something as deep as it is dark. I want to make sure we all get out of it alive."

She stared at him for what seemed like an eternity but must have been less than a minute. Then she said, "Don't worry. Nothing will happen to Amira."

34

NOTHING EVER HAPPENS to me," Amira said mournfully.

"Be grateful," Sara said.

"It happens to everyone else," Amira said, ignoring Sara, "and I'm left to watch from the sidelines."

Bourne and Goga were gone, leaving the two women eyeing each other like two boxers sizing up their opponent at the start of a fifteen-rounder.

"Just what I need," Amira said now. "A babysitter."

"Do you think I want to be here? And, anyway, why are you pissed at me?"

All Amira did was glare at her. Then she turned on her heel, went out onto the deck.

"Going out there's not such a great idea," Sara said, following her.

"Fuck you. I don't listen to babysitters. I don't need a babysitter."

"But according to Uncle Samson you do."

They were both on the deck, Amira staring into the Monet reflections on the water. For her part, Sara was quartering the immediate environment, searching for glints of traveling lights off rifle barrels or binocular lenses.

"Do you feel confident ignoring him, Amira?" Sara shook her head. "I don't think you do. I know how you feel about him."

Amira's head snapped up, her dark eyes probing through the glittering darkness. "What do you mean?"

"It's just us women here," Sara said.

Amira looked away. "I don't know what you're talking about."

"I don't believe you." Sara took a step forward, leaned against the railing. Her eyes were still looking up and down the river for any anomalies, anything that did not belong or was lurking, patient, waiting, because now that Boris was gone those who had placed a price on Amira's head would feel free to collect the bounty. "You're too smart not to know what I'm talking about."

Amira's only response was to twitch her shoulders, as if shrugging off Sara's words.

"You don't like me simply because Jason brought me here. You see how we are with each other. You see me as a rival."

"Don't be stupid!" Amira snorted, but she kept her face averted.

Sara changed the pitch of her voice, softened it, made it more intimate, as she peered over the side. "Is that your motorboat?"

"It belongs to my neighbors."

"Which neighbors?" Sara asked, interested in the people surrounding Amira.

Amira pointed to the houseboat on their right. "Over there. I hate them." The houseboat was a mess. "They've gutted and are rebuilding from the water up."

A red flag waved in Sara's mind. "I bet there are a lot of workmen over there during the day."

"Crawling." A shy smile. "Sometimes I make them lunch the way I did for my father."

"You must miss him—your father."

Immediately, the smile was wiped off Amira's face. "I made him lunch and dinner because that's what he expected of me."

"Nothing else?"

"From his point of view there was nothing else."

"And your mother?"

"Gone, a long time ago."

"I'm sorry, is she dead?"

Amira shrugged her slender shoulders. "She left to be with cousins in the Gaza Strip. That was the last we heard of her."

"Why did she leave?"

Amira shrugged again. "My father."

"Why didn't she take you with her?"

Amira glared at her. "You know why. He said he'd kill her if she tried to abduct me. That's what he called it, even though I told him I wanted to go. I was severely punished for having an opinion."

Sara glanced over at the houseboat under repair, but she could make out no movement. Short of going over there with a flashlight—which, under the circumstances, was out of the question—she couldn't be sure it was deserted. The motorboat bobbed down below them. There were no small craft anywhere in the vicinity. She turned back to Amira.

"Look, it's really not safe out here."

Amira turned abruptly. "Is there really a price on my head?"

She's putting up a good front, Sara thought, but she's frightened. On the other hand, she could see no upside in lying to her. "Boris's influence was protecting you. Now that he's gone…" She shrugged. "I promised Jason I'd keep you safe." Smiling, she gestured to the open slider. "You don't want to make a liar out of me, do you?"

Amira hesitated for a moment, then stepped quickly back into her living room. Then turned to face Sara as she followed her. "If I'm to believe you, I'm not safe here—or maybe anywhere in Cairo."

"You're safe with me," Sara said.

At that moment, a hail of semiautomatic fire shredded the middle of the front door. In a blur of indistinct movement, the door burst open.

Aleksandr Volkin, he of so many aliases, had picked up Goga's trail with little difficulty. His grandfather had told him where General Karpov was headquartering his rogue Cairo unit. Now, as he sat in his rental car, waiting to see who emerged from the houseboat he knew had belonged to Karpov's man, Feyd, he could not halt his thoughts from marching backward, could not stop himself from feeling Irina's breath in his ear, her whispered voice sending electric shocks through his thighs and groin. He knew psychology as well as anyone, he knew how susceptible teenagers were to outside influence, and how sexual tendencies are imprinted so deeply on their psyches at that vulnerable age they never stray from them. Because of their teenage intimacies he could never get over Irina; he had never wanted to. She was all he wanted—always and forever.

Now she was gone. Now the void inside him, the lethal blackness, was expanding, taking control. Without her was life worth living? He had asked himself that question innumerable times since his grandfather had confirmed his twin's premonition.

The worst thing was waiting. No, the very worst thing was remaining still. His mind, his body buzzed as if he had plugged himself into a power grid. Too much of him was being pushed to the outer edges by the void's ghastly expansion, doubling and redoubling.

At one point he thought he saw movement in the houseboat under construction to the right of his target area. The movement, caught like a gnat in the periphery of his vision, flickered and was gone so quickly he was unsure he had seen it at all.

He returned to his surveillance of Feyd's houseboat and, long moments later, was rewarded by Goga emerging, crossing to his vehicle. Then Aleksandr went rigid. His chest barely moved as his breathing virtually ceased for the amount of time it took Jason Bourne to step to Goga's car and get in.

35

AMIRA SHOT THE first man who came through the door. Her aim was very good; someone—possibly Bourne—had taught her how to shoot. But they came so fast, and used the man she had shot as a shield, she missed the other two men who had burst through.

By that time, Sara had upended the table. Now she pulled Amira down behind it as a hail of bullets were fired at them. They struck the table, making it shudder and jump, as if alive. She poked her CZ 75 SP-01 9mm around the side, squeezed off two impeccable shots that stopped the remaining intruders in their tracks.

She expected more men, a second salvo, more withering this time, but when none came she stuck her head around the side. Three men dead; no sign of more.

"We scared them away!" Amira said from over her shoulder as she surveyed the scene. "They're gone."

They were gone. Now why would that be? Sara wondered. Then as Amira stood up, the short hairs at the nape of her neck stirred, and she knew.

"Come on!" she shouted, grabbing Amira by the hand.

"What? What are you—?"

Sara pushed her urgently through the slider, out onto the deck, bringing them both to the railing where the fairy lights still winked on and off in their gay semaphore.

"Now jump!"

"What?"

Clutching her, Sara lifted her over the rail, let go. As Amira landed on the aft section of the motorboat, she threw herself over the side.

"Keys?"

Amira reached under the console. Sara grabbed the key out of Amira's outstretched hand, started the engine—and thank God it was gassed up and ready to go. In the meantime Amira untied the boat. Sara slammed the engine full out, heading into the center of the river.

"Get down!" she shouted an instant before the houseboat exploded into an vicious fireball, oily black smoke rising from the flames that engulfed what moments before had been Amira's home.

The boat bucked and rocked; the violent thrashing almost dislodged them. Water sloshed over the sides as Sara struggled to keep the boat on course, away from the wreckage. She thought of her times on board her father's sailboat, helping him when a sudden squall overtook them, the sky as black with angry clouds as it was now with choking smoke. The first lesson her father taught her was not to panic, the second to go about securing the boat—keeping the storm directly aft so the boat wouldn't be broadsided as he reefed the sails. Those lessons were key now, because blind instinct would have caused her to steer the boat in a broad arc, and they would have been broadsided by the aftermath. Instead, she put the explosion site directly aft and put the engine full out.

Debris fell like sleet. She felt an intense burning in the center of her back. Then Amira was beating the flames out with her bare hands, scrubbing her palms around in a circle, then ripping away the blackened material so she could stamp out the last embers with the sole of her shoe.

"Amira," Sara said, "are you okay?"

"Physically fine," Amira said breathlessly. "As for the rest, ask me tomorrow or the next day."

Something in her voice caused Sara to turn. That was when she saw the blood.

The Cairo area west of the Nile is actually Giza. It includes Imbaba, the upscale Mohandiseen, Agouza, and Dokki. Historically, it was centered around Memphis, Egypt's ancient capital, when the Giza area was maintained as sacred pharaonic burial grounds. Nasser's great urban achievement in Giza was to turn the west bank of the Nile into a modern hell of brutish concrete tower blocks, multilane flyovers, and massive shopping centers.

Mohandiseen, the upscale neighborhood, had originally been built for engineers, and was now a mecca for tourists, foreign embassies, as well as duplex apartments of pharaonic scale. This is where Goga drove Bourne.

Beneath a patchwork sky appearing in the first tiny glimmerings of dawn, Goga drove down Gam'et el Duwal el Arabya, known in English as Arab League Boulevard. Ugly high-rises loomed on either side of them. Goga's Jeep was equipped with what appeared to be an outsize radio. From it emanated sporadic bursts of Arabic, chopped into slaw by waves of static.

"We've been monitoring Ivan Borz's intermittent electronic traffic," Goga said. "It's coming from somewhere here in Mohandiseen. We keep vectoring, closing in on the area. We have it down to a radius of six square blocks. Still a lot of buildings to canvas. But we continue to make progress."

None of this was helpful to Bourne's pursuit of Borz.

"Do you know where the Israelis are stationed?" he asked.

"They know where we are, we know where they are. It's a kind of détente; sometimes that happens when we both find ourselves in enemy territory at the same time."

"I want to know where they are." He could have called Sara, of course, but he didn't want to give her more fuel to feed her obsession with Borz. "No," he said, "don't drive me there. Give me directions. I'll go on foot."

"It isn't safe here," Goga protested.

"Alone." Bourne got out of the Jeep the instant Goga pulled over. It was still moving, and he ran a few feet to regain his equilibrium. Then he set off toward the apartment complex where Lev Bin was running the Mossad operation against Borz. He remembered Lev from his previous dealings with Mossad, but he did not know him, so he had only Sara's warning about the agent to go by.

A half hour later, taking a circuitous route along the smoggy canyons of Mohandiseen's streets, he arrived at the building. According to Goga, the Mossad had set up in an apartment on the top floor. Heading around to the rear of the building, he picked the lock on the service entrance door, let himself into the building. In the lobby, he took the elevator up to the top floor, went down the hall to the fire stairs, pushed through the door, and turned, watching the hallway through the wire-mesh glass panel at head height.

He waited, calm, still, patient. He was so fiercely concentrated on his view of the hallway and the elevator door he almost missed the sound. It caught at the very edge of hearing, could almost have been mistaken for one of the multiple noises every building exhales, from foundations shifting in sandy soil to the HVAC recirculating, resetting itself. But it wasn't any of those—it was neither geological nor mechanical in nature.

It was man-made.

Bourne whirled in time to receive a powerful blow to the jaw. As he was slammed back against the fire door, his assailant jabbed with his left hand. Between two curled fingers a wicked-looking push-dagger blade extended like the claw of a tiger.

Bourne allowed the lunge. Rather than shrinking back he stepped into the attack. As the blade of the push-dagger slid past his right side, he struck his assailant in the throat with the heel of his hand, disarmed him as he went down to one knee.

Then he hauled him up, and said in Hebrew: "Tell Lev Bin Jason Bourne is here to see him."

"How did you know he was one of mine?"

"I've worked with Mossad before," Bourne said. "Standard operating procedure."

"It's depressing when we become predictable," Lev said.

He had wrinkled his nose in disgust when his man had brought Bourne through the door to their quarters. His disgust had made him pugnacious. Or maybe, Bourne thought, that was simply his nature.

"Dangerous, too," he said.

"Don't tell me my business." Lev stood with his hands on his hips. Behind him, three men were hunched over laptops, shortwave receivers, and broadband interceptors. The stink of warm metal and multitasking electronics imprinted the air with the signature of the modern world racing at hyperspeed. The distant buzz of static and the echoes of dismembered words circled over their heads like malcontent spirits.

Lev moved so that he blocked Bourne's view of his people at work. "We should speak in the back room."

"Here will be fine," Bourne said, and when Lev, being contrary, took a step toward the rear of the apartment, told him: "The Russian team knows where you live."

Lev halted, turned back, but with a slight curl to his upper lip, said: "I don't care. I can handle the Russians. All of them are idiots."

"Not these," Bourne said. "They were handpicked by General Karpov himself. They're working a rogue operation, completely off the books."

Lev sniffed, puffed up with his sense of self-superiority. "Only the Americans work that way, not the Russians."

"Boris Karpov doesn't work the way other Russian operatives do."

"Perhaps that's why he's dead."

Now Bourne knew that even Lev, stuck here half a world away, was being kept well informed. That bit of intel was vital to how he would proceed. "Doesn't matter," he said. "The operation was designed to continue with or without the General's leadership. The directives have all been baked in."

Lev shook his head. "And you know this how?"

"Through the Director."

Lev laughed. "*Our* Director?"

"Eli, yes." Bourne stood his ground. He had dealt with men like Lev Bin before. They subsisted on the slightest sign of hesitation, which they interpreted as fear—in other words, weakness.

"I don't believe you."

"You would say that."

Lev drew out his mobile. "I'll just call him and find out the truth of the matter."

"By all means call him, Lev. But I can guarantee you Eli will not tell you the truth."

Skepticism ruled Lev's face, along with a kind of bewildered amusement. "And why would that be?"

"He's lost confidence in you."

Lev let out a short bark of a laugh, but his mouth had formed into a rictus, tension whitening the corners of his lips. "Ridiculous. He put me in charge of the operation."

"No," Bourne said with a deadly quiet. "He put you in charge of *an* operation. A decoy for Ivan Borz and the Russians. While he's watching out for you and Karpov's people, Rebeka and I head the real mission."

"Rebeka is in Jerusalem."

"No," Bourne said, relentless. "She's here, with me."

"I would know if she was. As head of the operation it's my right to know."

"Nevertheless, she's here."

Bourne said this with such absolute conviction that, for the first time, he saw fear flicker behind Lev's eyes.

"If what you say is true..." He took a moment, apparently needing a small time-out. "Why are you telling me this?" His tone had altered subtly, concern slipping in front of arrogance.

"I want to get to Ivan Borz before Karpov's people do." Bourne knew he had hooked Lev. What was left was to reel him in slowly and delicately so that he wouldn't escape the hook. "I've talked with Goga—their head of ops. He's the one who drove me into Giza. He would have driven me to your building if I hadn't stopped him."

Lev nodded slowly. "I suppose I owe you a vote of thanks for that."

"Worse for us, Goga's closer to finding Borz than you are. When he gets within shouting distance of Borz he'll kill him on the spot. Eli sent me to prevent that. He wants me to interrogate Borz."

"Why? The fucker deserves to die."

"No question," Bourne said. "But not before he gives up all his identities, all his contacts, all his secrets."

"And you came to me...?"

"I'm asking for your help. This is something only you can do." This appeal was the essence of the con game. You give your mark your confidence. In return, he gives you precisely what you want.

"Explain, please."

"I see your operation here. I have more confidence in you than Eli does. He doesn't have eyes on the ground."

Lev considered a moment. "We still don't know precisely where Borz is."

"There I can help," Bourne said. "Borz has a thing for anal sex—girls or boys, it doesn't seem to matter to him."

Lev's face lit up. "That's something I can work with. The military clamps down hard on any form of sex it deems unnatural. There's an underground electronic bulletin board in Cairo. It's on the Dark Web, where all the bottom-fishers reside."

Bourne thought this comment amusing considering Borz's sexual predilections, but Lev evidently missed the humor. Lev was too busy being reenergized at the thought of redeeming himself in the Director's eyes. He turned to one of the men operating the electronic equipment, delivered a series of rapid-fire orders in Hebrew. Then he turned back to Bourne.

"The bulletin board is quite specific."

Bourne didn't bother asking him how he knew that; frankly, he didn't care.

"Let's see what happens. My man is following the current electronic conversations on the bulletin board, following them backward in time to see if—"

At a prompt from his IT man, he turned back, hunched over his laptop screen, engaging in a short whispered conversation. When he stood up, his smarter-than-thou smirk was back on his face. "A woman named Meira has been in communication with someone using a different burner phone with each conversation, no matter how terse. She's got another handle on the bulletin board, of course, but we traced her IP address. She works for one of the tour companies that takes people out to the Pyramids in the morning. Hold on." He raised a forefinger, got the number he was looking for from his man, punched it in on his mobile. The subsequent conversation was brief and to the point.

He disconnected, said to Bourne, "Meira's out at the Pyramids. We're in luck. She'll be off work in forty minutes. She asked for a sub so she could take the rest of the day off."

"Borz," Bourne said.

Lev shrugged. "It's a better shot than we have anywhere else." He grabbed his handgun out of a desk drawer, shoved it into a shoulder holster. "Let's go."

36

THE REDDISH SUN—permanently stained by the modern city's caustic pollution—streamed across the desert, interrupted only by shivering palms and vehicular traffic that raised the temperature five degrees, turning early morning into noontime.

By comparison to the modern city, the Great Sphinx and the Pyramids were structures timeless in their beauty, design, and manufacture. The pyramid of Menkaure, the pyramid of Khafre and the Great Pyramid of Khufu are precisely aligned with the Constellation of Orion. The King's Chamber in the Great Pyramid points to Al Nitak, an important star in Orion, constellation of the ancient Egyptian god, Osiris. The Great Pyramid is located at the center of the land mass of the earth. The east/west parallel that crosses the most land and the north/south meridian that crosses the most land intersect in two places on the earth, one in the ocean and the other at the Great Pyramid. The curvature designed into the faces of the pyramid exactly matches the radius of the earth. The pyramid had built into it a swivel door, weighing some twenty tons, so perfectly balanced that it could be opened by pushing out from the inside with only minimal force, but when closed, was so perfect a fit that from the outside it could scarcely be detected. It was originally sheathed in highly polished limestone, which reflected the sun's light and made the pyramid shine like a jewel. The original pyramid acted like a gigantic mirror, reflecting light so powerful that it would be visible from the moon as a shining star on earth. Appropriately, the ancient Egyptians called the Great Pyramid *Ikhet*, meaning "Glorious Light."

These facts and more, Bourne and Lev learned from the latter part of the lecture Meira gave the ten or so intrepid visitors on her tour, as their bus cowered in the heat, its air-conditioning unit panting, unlike the nearby Sphinx, stolid and inscrutable.

They stood apart in the young morning, beyond the last curved row of intently listening tourists, as innocent bystanders, blending in, posing as just two more visitors to the Great Pyramid. Behind them were the legions of touts selling tacky souvenirs and camel and horseback rides for exorbitant fees; kids with huge eyes and ribs protruding who claimed to be guides, dusty, red-eyed yellow dogs snapping at their heels. And, of course, the military guards, as well as the private ones at either end of the semicircle of Meira's clients.

And now Bourne knew without a shadow of a doubt they had Borz. Meira was pretty, slight, appeared far younger than she must be. Tracing the line of demarcation from Sara's devastating attack on Ivan Borz's business to his deliberately bumping into her on a Moscow street, it seemed clear Sara was right: he was toying with her, trying to frighten her, intimidate her. Bourne knew the danger to Sara was acute. For this alone he deserved the dreadful fate Bourne would wreak upon him.

Five or six of Meira's group were lining up at the ticket office to pay the tariff for entrance. Bourne looked at his watch. Almost time for Meira to be relieved. Was it also time for Ivan Borz to show up? He looked around, quartering the area, while Lev climbed back into his car in order to take a mobile phone call. Bourne was not only on guard, he was also on the lookout for Sara. He wouldn't put it past her to have found a place to stash Amira temporarily so she could come after Borz. Possibly no one better than him understood her need to resolve the incident with Borz, to cleanse herself with his blood. But he knew Borz better than she did. He could stand back, ensuring he would not underestimate the man. Sara thought of Borz as a monster—which he was, in every way imaginable. The problem was humans tended to equate monsters with lowered intelligence, which, in Borz's case, at least, was a delusion. Bourne did not want that to become a fatal delusion for Sara.

The sun beat down mercilessly. The city itself might be swaddled in the particulate smog of civilization, but out here on the desert plateau the sky was a dazzling blue. Bourne ducked down, poking his head through the car's open shotgun seat window. The car was old, beaten up, the better to blend in with the junk on Cairo's streets. What air-conditioning it might once have had was long dead and buried in rust. As a consequence Lev had all the windows cranked down.

Bourne was reaching for a bottle of water when he realized that Lev was leaning to one side. He grabbed the Mossad agent's shoulder, felt the dead weight of his torso. Turning him slightly, he saw the back end of a tiny dart that had been shot into the side of Lev's neck. The dart must have been coated with some form of fast-acting poison. Fingers on Lev's carotid, beneath his nostrils, confirmed he was already dead.

Immediately, Bourne searched inside the glove compartment, grabbed a pen flashlight, a Glock 9mm, a noise suppressor he could screw on the muzzle. He withdrew from the car's interior, stepped back into the blinding sunlight, where the touts shouted and waved at him, the kids and their dogs circled him, hollering, begging. Bourne distanced himself from the car and its corpse. Keeping to the open would save him now. No one would attempt to kill him here under the vigilant gaze of multiple security guards. No one would attempt to kill him as long as he possessed the coin. Of these two things, and these two things only, was he was certain.

But the coin was no longer the coin; it was merely dead weight, a reproduction that Bourne had stripped of its purpose and design. But only he knew that. He continued to monitor the environment, as he moved farther away from the pyramid of Khufu, toward the smaller and, in some ways, even more mysterious pyramid of Menkaure. No one knew much about this pharaoh, even precisely when he lived. Only legends remained, most, in the manner of myths, either contradictory or implausible. It was the only one of the three Pyramids whose interior was still closed to the public, and so seemed the best bet for what he had in mind.

Bourne was under no illusions. He knew Lev had been killed for a reason. He was being cut off from his resources—isolated, so as to be more easily taken prisoner. As in all warfare, the trick was to turn that strategy on its head, make it work for him, rather than against him. The success or failure of that would determine the outcome. Either way, to give himself a chance, he had to find home territory in a hostile environment. His only choice was this: utter darkness, a place where, having entered first, he might yet gain the figurative higher ground, and thus the upper hand.

Approximately a third of the way up the north face of the stepped pyramid was a long vertical slash, remnant of the time when the structure had been set to be demolished. But the pyramid had defeated those who sought to ruin the monument. That would, of course, be the easiest way in, but he was certain to be seen and stopped by the guards before he was halfway up.

Bourne moved closer to the pyramid, to where sawhorses roped off the entrance that had been used by the archaeologists before their various institutions deemed their presence in Cairo too expensive due to the volatile situation. It was currently off-limits to tourists. The area was deserted; not even a guard stood watch outside. A thick wooden door on oversize iron hinges had been fashioned to block the entrance, the planks joined by heavy iron bands. It was secured by a padlock that revealed its secret to Bourne in under twenty seconds. He ducked inside.

Five steps from the entrance the interior became black as pitch. He switched on the penlight, played the beam around. He found himself in a claustrophobically narrow shaft that sloped downward, the ceiling so low he was obliged to hunch over in order to make his way through it. It was dusty, dry, and oven hot. Electric lights had been placed along the way, but now they were inoperative. The floor of the shaft had been overlaid with sheets of wood to which had been affixed horizontal slats at eight-inch intervals, along with rough wooden handrails to help people in their descent into the Egyptian tomb. The weight of ages pressed down on him, tons of limestone flexed their muscles above him. He began to wonder whether he had made a mistake, but what choice did he have? He could not have successfully escaped in the car, not with Lev's corpse sprawled on the seat. Besides, he had to flush out whoever had come after him. It would be easy to assume it was Borz, even easier, in fact, to assume that Borz had laid an electronic trap to lead the FSB or Mossad to Meira so he could eliminate them.

Of course, Borz could simply wait outside for Bourne to exit the pyramid, but it was no sure thing he'd do that through the archeologist's entrance, and under cover of night, Bourne could easily slip away. No, Borz would come after him, Bourne was certain of it.

Abruptly, the floor evened out. By the narrow beam of his penlight, Bourne saw that he had reached an antechamber—the first, if his knowledge of the burial chambers of other Egyptian pharaohs held true here, of a number, all connected by narrow passageways that would finally lead to the heart of the interior: the room that held the pharaoh's sarcophagus, or would have before the pyramid had been looted by grave robbers and archeologists alike.

In the paneled anteroom, Bourne paused to listen. It was even hotter here than in the downward sloping passage, if that were possible. The air was thicker, drier, dustier, and somehow heavy, as if existing here unbreathed since the dawn of Egypt's pharaonic age had somehow compressed it into an alien atmosphere.

Above him, the immense structure rose in blind witness to the passing of centuries. The utter silence was like a living thing, gobbling up the darkness, turning it into a stew of stone, plaster, and wood, so there was no place left to hold air to breathe.

But suddenly, sound. He heard one—just one. Then the silence closed in again. He stood immobile facing the way he had come, until he could make out a dim penumbra of darkness—the faintest lightening, bobbing in time to the gait of an adult human being. It was enough to assure him that, indeed, someone was coming after him.

He left the antechamber, passing through three portcullis blocks, along another passage, shorter this time, that opened out into the second antechamber. This one was much larger and, as such, hotter still. The baking air felt fiery in his nostrils and throat.

Dead ahead was a stepped passage that continued downward. He played the beam of his flash past it, saw a smaller chamber attached to the larger one. If other pyramid interiors were any guide this would be the way down to the pharaoh's burial chamber. Though from this distance the rear wall projected as blank, Bourne knew there must be a secret door hidden flush with the stone wall. Bypassing the stairs down, he moved into the small chamber, ran his hand over the stones. Not surprisingly, he could feel no nook, no crevice that would mark out the door.

Moving to one side, he played the flash in a raking beam across the wall, moving it slowly, even when he heard multiple sounds in the passageway leading to the second anteroom. This procedure could not be hurried. Abruptly, he held the beam absolutely still. The raking light—the acute angle to the wall—revealed the seams of the door, minute though they were. He pressed on one side, then the other. With the soft shriek of a ravenous vulture, the secret door swung inward. It led to a less steeply declined passage. There was an altogether different scent as Bourne stepped through the portal. He closed the stone door behind him, but not all the way, leaving the smallest opening, which was not only for himself.

There was no flight of stairs here, no wood planking, no guardrail, just stone, gritty with age. It was easier going down, he knew, than when he would need to go back up. The scent continued to build as he made his way along the passage, which was wider than any other he had come through. Parts of Egyptian murals lined the walls, depicting scenes of the pharaoh in life on one side, overseen by the goddess Isis, and the descent of his sarcophagus into the netherworld, guided by the gods Horus and Osiris, on the other. Above the thick lintel of the doorway was the inscription: *Anet aledy tedkhel hena hedar*. You who enter here beware.

Those ancient Egyptians, Bourne thought, had a flair for the dramatic. Only in this case they might be right.

He remained still, waiting, listening, hearing nothing. He saw the hieroglyphics, and immediately Boris's rebus scrolled across the screen of his mind. Switching from masculine to feminine Sumerian, he continued the deciphering. What he came up with was: *ALBEDO*.

An almost silent pad of feet, a soft *phut*, and something glanced off the stone near Bourne's left cheek: a dart, identical to the one that had killed Lev. He doused the penlight, duck-walked the rest of the way into the pharaoh's burial chamber. The sarcophagus was, of course, long gone, but the massive stones on which it had rested for ages still hunkered against the right-hand wall. Bourne could feel their twin presence as if they were people. Skirting them, he progressed along the wall, carefully feeling his way. Now was not the time to miss even the smallest detail of the chamber. The left-hand wall was as smooth as the others before it had been, as well the one at the rear, save for a semicircular cutout in its center, but the right-hand wall was a different matter. It was composed of a series of vertical niches, rising from floor to ceiling. It was unclear what they had been for, though Bourne thought it likely they had once held immense funerary urns in which the pharaoh's possessions had been stored, for use once he arrived in the netherworld. These, too, were long gone. Lucky for Bourne. He made use of the niche closest to the entrance opening, flattened himself into the narrow space with his left shoulder jammed up against the niche's near wall. Even if his pursuer emerged with a bright light, the shadow cast by the niche would hide Bourne from view, giving him time enough to—

A figure was framed by the doorway. He was bathed in a weird blue light, lit from below like a ghoul in a horror film. Then Bourne saw the

LED anklets, spreading the heatless light. The aurora distorted his features, but not enough. Bourne saw that his pursuer was the man who had claimed to be Captain Vanov. Another piece of the puzzle fell into place. This man—whoever he really was—had known about the coin—just as Irina had known about the coin. In fact, it was this very man who had directed him to Irina, claiming that Boris had wanted her to serve as Bourne's partner at the wedding. Another lie. He hadn't had the time to ask Boris about her, which was a stroke of luck for Irina—the last bit of luck her life had held.

Yet another piece of the puzzle clicked in. This man and Irina had been working in concert. Irina had taken Bourne to Mik, Borz's *vosdushnik*, his moneyman. Her motivation for doing so was still unclear.

"Bourne," the false Vanov called, "I have you trapped." His dart pistol glimmered eerily in the LEDs. "There's no escape for you." The muzzle tracked from one side of the chamber to the other. "I know you must have figured out the coin's secret by now. Just tell me what it is and I'll leave you in peace. Or you can take the dart I shoot into you. Unlike the one I used on the Israeli, this one will only paralyze you. Then I'll go to work on you. I'm sure you don't want that. Hell, *I* don't want that." The pistol's muzzle kept tracking back and forth in metronomic fashion. "No? Tell you what, give me what I want and I'll even leave the girl—Amira—in peace." He chuckled. "That should make your day."

Bourne had the sound-suppressed Glock held against his leg. He raised it now and put three shots into the false Vanov's chest. The man was flung backward into the passage. The doorway was clear.

37

BOURNE, LISTENING, HEARING nothing, moved silently out of his niche, toward the doorway that led back out and up into the Cairo sunlight, which now seemed but a distant memory. He approached the doorway with extreme caution even though he knew precisely where each bullet would have penetrated the false Vanov's chest: lung, lung, heart. No chance of him still being alive; he was dead before he hit the floor.

And yet as Bourne passed through the doorway, there he was on his knees, very much alive. The bullets had shredded a section of his shirt-front, revealing the Kevlar vest underneath.

As Bourne raised the Glock, he heard another *phut!* and put his left hand up just in time to take the dart in the back of it, instead of in his throat. He pulled the dart out, then squeezed the Glock's trigger. The bullet went wide of its mark. Bourne aimed again, but found his vision clouded, as if a net had been thrown over him. The figure in front of him morphed into two, then three, he squeezed off more shots until the magazine was empty.

Grinning, the false Vanov aimed the dart pistol lower. "One in the hand just isn't going to do it fast enough for me," he said, just before his forehead exploded in a geyser of blood, brains, and skull fragments. He pitched forward, onto what was left of his face, twitched once, and lay still.

Behind him, barely visible in the blue glow, was a tall, slim man with the ascetic face of a priest. Bourne had encountered him before through Sara's vivid description of the person who had stolen her Star of David in Moscow.

Ivan Borz, in the flesh, at last.

Bourne threw the useless Glock at Borz, but it went wide of the mark, his aim unaccountably off until he remembered the dart in the back of his hand. A wave of vertigo lapped at the edges of his consciousness, and he reeled backward into the darkness. A shot rang out, filling the death chamber with noise without end. At any other time, Bourne would have rushed Borz, would have taken him head-on, but he could no longer rely on his reflexes or his breathing. His only recourse was to find an avenue of escape.

"That shot would have struck you if I'd wanted it to," Borz said in Arabic.

Stumbling backward, Bourne ran into the rear wall before he knew it. Behind him, he heard Borz step into the burial chamber.

"It's been a long time," Borz said in Russian. Then, switching to English, "But I don't suppose you remember our previous shared experience."

Bourne was hunched down in the semicircular cutout, his hands pressed against the stone floor to support himself. There was a buzzing in his ears that matched the fizzing in his veins as the paralytic spread through his system. He knew that if the dart had found its mark he would be completely helpless by now, unable to move or even to think clearly until given the antidote or the effects wore off.

"I've had it on unimpeachable authority that your memory isn't working the way it should," Borz went on, "that it's a blank past a certain date in time when you were shot in Marseilles. I was so sure you'd been killed, Bourne. How you disappointed me!"

Bourne's fingers—at least the ones on his right hand, which still felt normal, had encountered one of those clever flush ball-and-socket features so beloved of ancient Egyptian architects, who had outfitted the pyramid interiors with a system of secret chutes and ladders—shortcuts they used when ensuring their designs were being followed to the letter.

"By guile or good fortune, you somehow made it out of the Mediterranean. But pressing matters necessitate I stop throwing doppelgangers at you; the game is at an end. Your miraculous rebirth is just one of the things you'll tell me now that Aleksandr Volkin's toxin has tamed you."

At the sound of the name Bourne froze for a moment, and his straining heart seemed to skip a beat. "Aleksandr—"

"Volkin," Borz provided helpfully. "I knew that would focus your attention." He was in the chamber now, silhouetted by the blue glow that seemed fainter and fainter by the second, as if with Aleksandr dead, the LEDs too were dying. "That's right, Aleksandr is—excuse me, was—old man Volkin's last remaining grandchild. He was Irina's twin brother. I bet you didn't know that, either."

Bourne, of course, hadn't, but at the moment he had bigger problems to occupy his mind. The first was getting out of this locked burial chamber. The second was how to stave off the effects of the paralytic. First things first.

Lifting the ball out of the socket, he turned it forty-five degrees, and was rewarded with the bottom of the cutout swinging down. He fell from darkness to darkness, landing painfully on his right hip because his legs would no longer fully support the weight of his head and torso.

"Where have you gone, Bourne?" From the sound of Borz's voice, speaking in dulcet upper-class British tones, he seemed to be crouched over the void in the floor. "Down the rabbit hole, I expect." He chuckled. "No escape for you, down there, however. Not with those unsteady pins of yours. The toxin must be speeding its way to your autonomous nervous system by now, and, ironically, the faster you move, the more quickly you're pushing it along."

Bourne, ignoring the taunts, began to pull himself away from the wall, away from the chute down which he had plummeted. He could feel his heartbeat as if it was in his throat, but it was slowing, slowing. He could no longer feel his left hand, and half of that arm was tingling as it verged on numbness. Only moments left, he knew, so he continued on, like a snail trying to get across a nighttime garden. He had lost his penlight in the fall. He was in a chamber even lower than the pharaonic burial chamber with no idea what it was used for, no idea whether it held anything he could use as a weapon. He had only one hand with which to grope forward, seeking something—anything—that would help him defend himself.

From behind him he heard the sound of boots landing on the ground, the soft grunt as bent legs absorbed the fall.

"The thing of it is, Bourne, I don't even need to see you," Borz said in Hebrew. "I know where you are: dead ahead of me. I know where you're going: nowhere. I'm thinking you can scarcely move at this point." He strode toward where Bourne lay, unable to go on, helpless. "But that's all right, my friend. Don't concern yourself about how you'll escape. You can't. You won't."

Bending over, he slammed the back of Bourne's head with the butt of his handgun.

Bourne's last thought was: How fitting to die in a tomb.

Then all was silence.

Part Three

Modern empires rise and fall not on armies, ideology, or violence,
but on the instantaneous flow of capital.

—Boris Karpov

38

SHE'S GOING TO be all right," Dr. McGuire said.

Sara looked down at Amira, lying on Dr. McGuire's home-surgery table. "She's as white as the moon."

Dr. McGuire nodded, the powerful overhead lights flicking off the thick owlish lenses of her wire-rimmed spectacles. "She's lost a lot of blood. It's fortunate that she had you, my dear Rebeka. Otherwise..." Her spectral voice trailed off. She looked down at her patient and smiled, her very white teeth shining from out of her wide, open face, the kind of face everyone liked, believed in, trusted. No one would suspect that Martha McGuire was anything but a first-class surgeon. "Not to worry, my dear. You're going to be right as rain in no time." She had the habit of using old British phrases, especially with her younger patients. She claimed it helped allay their anxiety.

"How is that going to happen?" Sara wanted to move the doctor away to the other side of the surgery in order to talk to her in private, but Amira's hand was clutching hers with such desperation that she could not bring herself to leave her. "She needs blood."

"And she shall have blood!" Dr. McGuire's face now split into a grin.

"Happily Amira has AB-positive, the universal recipient blood type. My assistant has kindly consented to donate."

Martha McGuire's assistant, who had just finished treating the burns on Sara's back, was a roly-poly Egyptian with a constant smile on her face, even when she was working hard at cooking or cleaning. Dr. McGuire sat her in a chair beside the table. Her right arm was already bared. Clearly she had done this before.

A shard of wood, turned by the explosion into a spear, had pierced Amira's side, in the soft area below the rib cage and above the kidney. So it could have been worse, but there was serious bleeding. While navigating the boat downriver, Sara had called Martha McGuire—the field name of Mossad's surgeon in Cairo—and described the injury in detail. Long experience in the field guided her; she knew what was important to a surgeon and what could wait until she saw Amira in person.

Now Dr. McGuire inserted the needle, was in the process of connecting the two women, setting the apparatus in motion. Sara, keeping hold of the young woman's hand, stared down into her large, liquid eyes.

All at once they rolled up in her head and she lay deathly still.

Svetlana arrived in Cairo and immediately felt overwhelmed by the stifling heat, the densely packed area outside arrivals, the shoving, the chaos of shouts, crying babies, and imprecations from touts and hideously disfigured beggars.

She stood, suitcase in hand, momentarily paralyzed by the whirlwind, buffeted on all sides like an underpowered boat in an increasingly choppy sea. It was about then, as she was looking around for someone to help her navigate the chaos, when she saw a man she thought she recognized. A terrible chill seemed to fracture her bones; the suitcase slipped out of her nerveless hand. The man was Russian, the man was

FSB, the man was watching her the way, she was sure, a hawk watches a baby rabbit.

Svetlana had never wanted for bravery, had never been cowed or intimidated by men. That was one of her traits Boris liked best. She had learned that in order to stay on top of situations, she had to take the initiative. Waiting—indecision—meant slavery. Acting on a decision—even if turned out to be the wrong one—was better than doing nothing.

But that was in Moscow, which she knew with the intimacy of a longtime lover. Only this lover she never tired of. But now she was here in Cairo, a city totally alien to her, with Arabic flying every which way toward her and around her like hand-tossed missiles. I am Russo-Ukrainian, she thought. And I am lost.

Not only lost, but on the cusp of being hunted down and terminated. She had felt it when Savasin had insisted she take the sea cruise. She had felt it more strongly when she had reached the pier where the liner was docked. She had changed her plans without telling anyone, except Boris's friend, Jason Bourne, and now her past was hanging on to her like a street cur whose jaws were clamped to her trouser cuff. Watching this man watching her clarified what she had suspected all along: that Savasin had attached someone to her to see her onto the ship, and then to dispatch her during the cruise. Pushed overboard on a romantic cruise—a novel way for her to die, she had to give him that.

But what to do now? The FSB agent, blue stubble and all, was making his way through the thickening cross-currents toward her. Instinctively, she backed away, then remembered her suitcase, took a step toward it, and saw an emaciated teenager snatch it up and vanish into the crowd before she could even sound an alarm. Anyway, in this maelstrom what would constitute an alarm that would make people stop and take notice? How loud would she have had to scream, and for how long?

Thinking that the kid needed what was inside more than she did, she continued backing away. But she was having more difficulty than the FSB man was. He seemed at ease eeling his way through the currents with the least amount of pushback, while she seemed enmeshed in the tentacles of an octopus that kept slowing her, impeding her progress.

She felt her breath coming more quickly, more shallowly. The short breaths only increased her anxiety. Dimly, she was aware that her state of mind was heading in the wrong direction. The more anxious she was the worse her decision making would be. And yet as Blue-Stubble continued to gain ground on her, she could not help herself. Not for the first time since her dreadful wedding night she wished Boris was with her. She wished she had confided in him, instead of seeking to play him. She wished she had told him she loved him more. Above all, she wished she had taken the time to appreciate him. But she had done none of those things, and now tears clouded her eyes, and she thought, Dear God, what next?

What was next froze her. Continuing to back up, she ran right into a stone wall—or, in this case, a man's rock-solid chest. At once, she flinched away, but she was too late. His powerful arms clamped around her torso.

"*Zdravstvuyte*, Svetlana," an unknown male voice said in her ear. "*Dobro pozhalovaty v vash nova dom.*" Hello, Svetlana. Welcome to your new home.

"Stand back!" Dr. McGuire said.

Reluctantly, Sara let go of Amira's hand. The girl's lips had turned blue. She did not look as if she was breathing.

"Martha, what's happening?" Sara said.

"Vasovagal syncope," the surgeon said. She appeared unperturbed. "It's quite common, you know. Fainting at the sight of blood or a needle and such. The body overreacts to certain triggers. Heart rate and blood pressure drop precipitously."

"Do something," Sara said anxiously.

Dr. McGuire smiled. "There's nothing to do. She'll come out of it on her own." She gestured as Amira's chest heaved and she began to stir. "You see. It's as I said."

Amira's eyes fluttered open. Sara smiled at her. "You're fine. Don't worry. You're fine."

"Keep talking to her while I start the transfusion," Dr. McGuire said. "The sooner she gets the blood the better."

Amira lifted her forearm off the bed and Sara took her hand. At once, Amira's fingers clamped around hers. They were damp and clammy. Leaning over, Sara wiped the sweat off her forehead.

"What happened?" Amira asked.

"You passed out." Sara broadened her smile, masking her concern. Was Amira out of the woods? Was Martha telling the truth? She would just have to trust the surgeon. "It's a common thing," she said, echoing what Martha had told her.

All hooked up, the blood began to flow from the assistant into Amira's arm. The surgeon's face relaxed as she monitored the flow. Sara took that as a good sign, and she, too, relaxed somewhat.

But now Amira's expression had clouded over and, worried again, Sara said, "What is it? Are you in pain?"

Amira shook her head. "Come closer," she whispered.

Sara sat on the edge of the table, her face close to that of the young woman. An entire world seemed to swim in her large, dark eyes. Questions, answers, unknowns, solutions, and, above all, disappointments. Her father, Sara thought.

"Rebeka," Amira husked, "I've done a terrible thing."

"Then you must forgive yourself, Amira."

"I can't, I . . ." Tears leaked from the corners of her eyes.

"Rebeka, her blood pressure is spiking," Dr. McGuire called from the other side of the table. "Please keep her calm."

Sara, wiping away the girl's tears, said, "Have you killed someone?"

"No," Amira said in a weak voice.

"Well, I have, and I've found a way to forgive myself." Sara kissed her cheek. "So you must find the strength inside yourself to do the same."

"But I lied to Uncle Samson." She meant Bourne.

Something formed in the pit of Sara's belly, but she showed none of this sudden inner turmoil, only smiled. "It can't be so bad."

"But it is."

Amira began to struggle against the tubes and needles, as if she wanted to rise up and flee the surgery, flee her own treachery. Placing her hands firmly on the girl's shoulders, Sara held her down.

"Why would you lie to Uncle Samson?"

"I was afraid, Rebeka."

"Of what?"

"I was afraid Uncle Samson would hate me."

"That would be impossible. You know that, don't you? Uncle Samson loves you unconditionally."

This brought more tears. "I'm so ashamed."

"Shhh," Sara crooned, pressed her lips briefly to the girl's forehead. "Calm yourself, Amira."

"I can't!" the girl wailed.

"Then tell *me* the truth. Tell me what you couldn't tell Uncle Samson."

Amira stared up at her. Color was already returning to her face. "You won't hate me?"

"I *can't* hate you," Sara said, grinning. "I don't know you well enough."

A bubble of laughter escaped Amira's mouth. For a moment, the two women were joined in the unrestrained joy that was the main gift of humor. Then the bubble—like all bubbles—burst, leaving the terror of what, until now, Amira had left unsaid.

"Rebeka," she said, "I told Uncle Samson my brother, El-Amir, worked at CloudNet sat TV."

"And he doesn't? So what? I don't understand."

Amira stared up at Sara, her eyes pleading. "He *did* work there. He learned a great deal, worked his way up the ladder. All that's true enough. But…but he's not working there anymore." She swallowed hard, almost choking until Sara lifted her head a little. She took a breath, gathering herself. "Last year, he disappeared. Without a word, he left his job, his wife, everyone. No one could find out what had happened to him. Until, a week before his murder, my father discovered that El-Amir had been secretly attending a mosque in the suburbs of Brighton, where over the course of months he was radicalized."

She stopped, seemingly exhausted. When she began again, she appeared to be talking as much to herself as to Sara. "How? How could this happen? El-Amir is so smart, so clever. How could he let . . . ?" Her eyes closed momentarily. "The shame of it, Rebeka. I can't bear it." Her breathing had become so labored that Dr. McGuire, shooing Sara away, took her blood pressure, her pulse, listened to her heartbeat, her tongue clucking rhythmically against the roof of her mouth.

"You must leave now," she said. "My patient needs more than rest—she needs sleep. I am going to introduce a mild sedative."

"No!" Amira cried. "Wait! Please!"

With the drug drawn into a syringe, Dr. McGuire looked at her askance. "You are under my care. Therefore—"

"Just a minute," Amira pleaded.

"Martha," Sara said. Her heart went out to this girl. "One minute."

Dr. McGuire made a show of pulling her cuff back to reveal her wristwatch. "Begin," she said.

Amira returned her attention to Sara. "Listen to me. I think the real reason my father was killed was because he discovered that El-Amir had joined Ivan Borz. That he was directing all the videos, using the techniques he'd learned at school and at CloudNet."

"How did Feyd find out?"

"He traced the money El-Amir was sending us back to a man named Mik, in Moscow. Mik is a middleman, a—my father told me the Russian word—*vos*-something."

Sara could see the great money circle forming as if it were a tantric wheel. "A *vosdushnik*," she said, her heart beating fast. Amira's truth was important. More important than the girl could know. "A man who makes dirty money disappear into thin air."

"Yes, that's it. Through Boris, my father found out that this Mik is tied to Ivan Borz. That's the last thing my father found out. Three days later, he was killed." She swallowed. "And there's something else."

"Time," Dr. McGuire looked up, but Sara stopped her from injecting the sedative into Amira's bloodstream.

"Please, Martha."

Dr. McGuire sighed and stood back, but watched her patient with a sternness that was crystal clear.

Sara knew she was on borrowed time. She leaned closer, her ear almost touching the shell of the girl's ear. "What? Amira, what else do you want to tell me?"

Amira stared up at her with frightened eyes, whispered, "My father betrayed General Karpov." The tip of her tongue swiped across her dry lips. "We had money trouble, as I told you. The houseboat. General Karpov set up a note for us to pay off over time, at a non-Sharia bank. But our neighbors next door bought the note. They wanted both slips. They threatened to kick us out if we didn't pay in full within the month. My father found another paymaster."

"Who, Amira? Who was he?"

"I . . . I don't know." Her eyes began to lose focus.

"Enough." Dr. McGuire, normally a mild enough woman, shouldered Sara away, injected Amira with a powerful sedative.

"Amira," Sara said, "are you sure you don't know the paymaster's name?"

"I swear, Rebeka. Please believe me."

"I do, sweetheart. You rest now."

Amira shook her head, but it seemed as if her thoughts had lost their edge, as she was drawn under by the tide of the sedative. Then, abruptly, they snapped back to life. "Please, oh, please promise me you won't let any harm come to my brother." Her eyes were losing focus, but she was still agitated, struggling against the sedative's increasingly powerful current. "Rebeka, promise me!"

"I promise," Sara whispered.

Amira sighed deeply, her eyes fluttered closed, and her breathing turned deep and slow. Sara watched her for some time. The peacefulness in her expression was profound. After a short while, she tiptoed out.

39

BOURNE, HIS MIND rising slowly and drunkenly into consciousness from the abyss into which it had plummeted, felt as if his head was stuffed with congealing cement. Thinking was difficult, putting words together to form a sentence impossible.

He was lying down; that was as much as his twilit senses told him at the moment. He turned his head, saw a very fit man dressed in a khaki outfit that looked vaguely military. He sat back on a tilting chair that from time to time creaked as he moved, his long legs extended, ankles crossed one over the other, the heels of his boots resting on a metal desktop.

To his utter astonishment, he saw his own face watching him, a half smile on his slightly curved lips.

"Surprise, Jason! Arise to meet yourself!" the man said in an uncannily accurate imitation of Bourne's voice.

The lips, though, Bourne realized, those lips were not his—they were a bit too thin. A subtle difference, not likely to be detected by anyone who didn't know him intimately, a minute pool. Nevertheless, theatrical makeup made them precisely the same color; they would pass muster at a cursory glance or with someone who didn't know him well. Now, as his vision cleared further, he saw the man was wearing prosthetics to alter the shapes of his nose and cheeks, colored contact lenses in order to mimic Bourne's own eye color. Again, they would do for everything but close-up scrutiny.

"But now I'm getting ahead of myself." The man—who could only be Ivan Borz—folded his legs, scooted his chair across the floor to where Bourne lay.

"Where am I?" Bourne croaked.

"A question for another day." Borz smiled down with the strange benevolence a hunter shows a hare caught in his trap. "After you have answered all of mine."

Bourne's mouth was horribly dry. Borz appeared to notice this, but didn't offer anything to drink. In fact, he poured himself a glass of ice water from a pitcher on a small, square table beside his left hand, drained it slowly. He put the empty cup down, smacked his lips.

"Okay, now. I just have to indulge my curiosity. How badly are you hurting? General Karpov was a friend of yours. A good friend, I'm given to understand by multiple contacts. What are the odds, eh?" His smile widened, showing large, vulpine teeth. "Gone but not forgotten. At least not by me. His death set you on this road, his death brought you to me."

His eyes flicked over to Bourne. "My men have determined you're not carrying any concealed weapons. Having hurled your Glock and its noise suppressor at me, not very accurately, I'd say you've got nothing." He chuckled. "But I digress."

With a wicked half smile, he watched Bourne start to thrash around on the trestle table. "Getting your motor skills back, I see. Admirable recovery time, I must say." He nodded. "Your attempts to get up are useless, however. You're quite steadfastly bound to the mast—like Odysseus, yes?" He sighed. "Sometimes, it's all about the classics. Which is a shame, because these days there's so little time to read."

Tilting his head, he said, "But again, I digress." His smile was re-strained and yet, in a purely theatrical manner, seemed to consume the space around him. "I've heard so much about your eidetic memory, even seen it at work." He crossed his burly arms across his chest. "But you don't remember a bit of it, do you, Jason? Where was it? you're asking yourself right about now. Where did I meet this man—a man I can't remember for the life of me?

"In the end, it might come to that." He crossed his arms over his chest. "But first let me see if I can help you. We met in a city. But which one? A place where you felt a strong sense of déjà vu upon arrival: Paris, Zurich, London, Budapest, Cambridge, Beijing? Or might it have been a city in the Middle East—Doha, for instance? Beirut, Damascus, Jerusalem. Or maybe—maybe even Moscow. Moscow would be ironic, wouldn't it? Any of them ringing a bell?" He grunted. "I didn't think so."

He tapped his cheek. "Wherever it was, you taught me the basics of becoming a human chameleon, not only through theatrical makeup and prosthetics, but altering voice pitch, speech patterns, gait, and the incline of the torso standing or sitting. 'Mannerisms, Bobby'—you used to call me Bobby, remember? But of course you don't. When it comes to memory you're as useless as a store window mannequin. I hated when you called me Bobby; I much preferred Rob.

"In any event, you'd teach me: 'Mannerisms, Bobby, will make you or break you when you're out in the field. Someone from the opposition might find your eyes, nose, or mouth familiar, but if your mannerisms don't match, he'll pass you by, forget you in an instant. When the opposition is looking for you, Bobby, mannerisms become a matter of life and death.'"

Borz poured himself another glass of water, drank it more slowly, as tantalizing droplets of condensation slithered down the sides. During this deliberate act of withholding he never took his color-corrected eyes from Bourne's. "So," he said at length, "do you remember even a phrase of that particular lesson?"

Bourne said nothing, understanding that Borz not only reveled in the sound of his own voice, but felt compelled to answer his own questions.

The more Bourne lengthened his verbal leash the more accurate his psychological assessment would be. Understanding the enemy was the first step in the steep climb to defeating him. But, of course, there was another reason for his silence. He was desperately trying to fit something about Borz into the picture the terrorist was painting for him. He had received his undergraduate degree in hiding in plain sight during his rigorous Treadstone training, but the rest—the graduate and postgrad diplomas—he earned on his own, after his violent break with Treadstone. He had no memory of this man or of teaching him—or anyone—the techniques of being a human chameleon. Even more baffling, he couldn't think of a reason why he would have.

Borz's grin was as awful to look at as a slab of bloody meat. "No? I didn't think so." He shrugged, a deliberately theatrical gesture. "I'd say it's a pity, but your ignorance provides an opportunity to open up the box of this episode in your past and show you what's inside."

It had taken Bourne this long to make sense of his surroundings: a long, narrow room, whitewashed and nearly barren. Across from him was an old-fashioned, leaded-paned window. But beyond there was nothing of value: just the wood-plank wall of an adjacent structure. No tree, no patch of sky, not even a leaf was visible. The air didn't stink of antiseptic or disinfectant, so he could rule out a hospital or a clinic. In fact, it had nothing about it of a municipal building. On the contrary, he picked up the scents of sandalwood, sandy earth, the ubiquitous dust of a barren landscape. No animal smells whatsoever, so rule out a farm. Likewise, the subtle scents of the desert were nowhere in evidence.

Wherever he was, it didn't seem like anywhere in or near Cairo. Not knowing how long he had been unconscious, he could be virtually anywhere on earth, save the Poles.

Borz suddenly hunched forward. "I can feel that brain of yours working up a sweat, Jason, as if it were a nuclear reactor nearing critical mass." He laced his fingers together as he rested his wrists on his knees. "So. Where did we meet? Was it any of those cities I mentioned, or none of them? Does it even matter? Rob and Jason. Yes, those were the days." His eyes grew hard. "At least they were until you betrayed me."

His fist slammed hard into Bourne's cheek.

Svetlana, in the grip of the unknown, unseen man, had never felt so alone and helpless. Without ceremony, she was jerked away into the crowd, but not before she caught a quick glimpse of a man approaching the FSB agent from the side. Did the FSB agent crumple? The image was lost in the riotous throng. She was hustled into the back of a nondescript car. The man holding her let go and seated himself next to her. He slammed the door shut and the driver began to wend his way through the traffic-snarled exit from the airport.

"My apologies for the roughness of your arrival," the man said with a smile that seemed just as rough around the edges. "My name is Goga. Your husband handpicked me to head his personal mission here. You're among friends, Svetlana."

Svetlana, who had been sweating profusely through her clothes, felt the perspiration congealing as she began to calm down. "How... how did you know I was coming?"

"Jason Bourne."

Of course. Had she not been so freaked out she would have arrived at the same conclusion. "And that man?" She tossed her head in the direction from which they had come.

"With the general's death you have become a liability to some within the Kremlin."

"Savasin."

Goga nodded. "There can be little doubt."

She looked out the side windows, which were heavily smoked. "Where are you taking me?"

"Somewhere safe." Goga grunted. "All of a sudden Cairo has become a hornet's nest of conspiring and conflicting interests." He smiled. "Not to worry. We'll take good care of you."

Then he pulled out a Makarov, said, "Greetings from First Minister Savasin," and shot her point-blank in the side of the head.

"Poor thing," the driver commented, as he ducked out of traffic and pulled into the curb. Immediately, the kid who had snatched Svetlana's suitcase with Boris's incriminating material opened the shotgun door, tossed the suitcase in. The driver leaned over, held out a wad of bills, which the kid snatched out of his hand before running off.

As the car returned to the endless flow of vehicles, Goga said with a shrug, "Poor thing maybe, but politics is politics. We all have to make a living."

40

THE FIRST OF the bombardments interrupted Borz's history lesson. The walls shook, the floor shuddered, the windowpanes rattled, the water jug crashed to the floor, shattered.

An active war zone, Bourne thought. That narrowed it down. He had been transshipped out of Egypt. He looked around. His viewing angle had changed dramatically. He was now strapped to a chair, which was pulled up to a trestle table that looked to have come straight of out a priory refectory—heavy, dark wood, carved apron. Where was the spot where he'd been lying? Had he blacked out again or had Borz injected him with a sedative? It must have been the latter; his head felt heavy, his thoughts muzzy.

Borz, still looking like Bourne's identical twin, sat at the head of the table. Bourne was at his right elbow. A meal was being served: two place settings, one in front of Borz, the other at a spot directly opposite Bourne. Dishes were brought: Moroccan pigeon-and-date bastilla, dusted with powdered sugar, a savory lamb tagine with preserved lemons, and bowls piled high with pale yellow couscous.

Borz began to help himself as soon as the dishes were laid down. "I don't know about you, but I'm famished. Plane rides tend to pique my hunger. You?"

"Why did you murder Boris?"

Borz looked up, clearly astonished. "But my dear Jason, you know why I killed General Karpov. It was the same reason why I garroted him and arranged him in that Christ-like position." He cocked his head. "Still can't guess? It was all because of you. I wanted to draw you to me by engaging first your need for revenge and second your insatiable curiosity. I made the murder of your friend so outré, so outrageous that you could not fail to become involved. Besides which, your friend was a fucking atheist, a godless Russian." He spread his arms wide. "And now here we are, proving how very right I was."

Having delivered this pleasing oration, he returned to the study of food, which he shoveled into his mouth with evident delight.

"The businessman, such as yourself," Bourne said slowly and deliberately, "is without both God and conscience."

Borz looked up, his lips grease-rimmed, and smiled. "That's what I like best about you, Bourne. Your quick wit." He recommenced eating.

"Aren't you going to wait for your guest?" Bourne said.

"The guest would be you," a tall handsome Arab, a decade younger than Borz, said as he entered the room. He spoke English like a Brit, his voice plummy with an upper-crust London accent. He nodded to Borz, an acknowledgement of some kind, before sitting down at his appointed place. "As for myself, I'm a part of the family."

Borz smiled, ignoring the next round of shelling, which was, in any event, detonating farther away. As the Arab began to help himself, Borz turned to Bourne and, wiping grease from his lips, said with a smile just shy of being a smirk, "Jason, meet El-Amir, Feyd's son, Amira's brother."

Bourne took a deep breath, let it out slowly as he studied El-Amir while he tried to quell the growling of his empty stomach. Keeping his expression carefully neutral, he saw some of Feyd's features, remolded by the familial genetic stew. Feyd's wife had been long gone by the time Bourne came on the scene, but Bourne had seen photos of her. She had been a beautiful woman—dusky, exotic, with the large, flashing eyes of a film star. Amira had inherited much of her good looks, wild and natural; she was still very much a part of the Third World. El-Amir's, on the other hand, was altogether different: polished and manicured in the First World manner. His pitch-black hair was expertly cut, rippling back off his diamond-shaped face to cover the tops of his ears, thick at the nape of his neck. His sharp desert features combined with a highly-polished Western demeanor to give him the aspect of a Hollywood mogul.

Why was he here? Why wasn't he in London? "And as part of Bobby's family, what is it you do?"

El-Amir frowned. "Bobby?"

"Yes. Ivan's real name is Bobby." Bourne saw Borz wrinkle his nose as if he'd just smelled a dead rat. He smiled. "Didn't he tell you? Or aren't you in the inner part of the family circle, like me?"

El-Amir turned to Borz. "What's he raving about?"

Borz, in the midst of taking up some tagine in a triangle of flatbread, said, "A joke, nothing more."

"A *family* joke." Bourne, doing his best to put aside his growing hunger, watched how El-Amir reacted to the taunt, then turned back to Borz. "I assume I've been out—"

"Less than twenty-hour hours, more than eight." Borz popped the food into his mouth, chewed slowly, relishing the tastes. "Not that it matters to you."

"But it matters to *you*, Bobby. In two days something cataclysmic is going to happen. Boris knew it and now I know it. What is it?"

A curious expression flitted across Borz's face before vanishing into the vault protecting his reactions. And now Bourne felt a surge of both elation and bafflement. Borz was not, as Bourne had assumed, the instigator.

Borz wiped his right hand, with which he had been eating, Bedouin style. "The one thing I'm short of information on is just what the hell Karpov was doing behind the Sovereign's back. He was playing a dangerous game, but then I don't have to tell you that. There's something afoot inside the Kremlin. Some kind of internecine warfare, is it? Whatever it is, it's big—very big."

"And you want in on it."

"I want to be on the winning side. And it seems to me that a lot of people besides Karpov have had their flames snuffed out of late. Not the least of them being Ivan Volkin's progeny." Borz switched to Russian. "Irina and Aleksandr, what a pair! Poor Ivan, he never knew how to control them. Well, it couldn't happen to a shittier *zvezdá*," *Zvezdá* was Russian for "a celebrity," but Borz was using the term sarcastically. He sniffed. "But I suppose that is the inevitable result of them working for their grandfather."

But that couldn't be right, Bourne thought.

"I suppose it was lucky for you Mik blew up his Moscow operation before I got a look at what he was doing for you."

"Not just me," Borz said sourly. "Old man Volkin as well."

Bourne was shaken. If they had been working for their grandfather, why would Irina have led him right to Mik, Borz and Volkin's money launderer? Why had she tried to keep Mik from blowing himself and his electronic files up? Something didn't track, unless... Unless Irina and Aleksandr had gone into business for themselves. It was a logical assumption based on the new facts. Irina had led him to Mik as a favor to him. She had wanted to prove to him that she was a friend, one who went to extraordinary lengths to get him what he wanted most: access to Borz. And what did she and her twin want most? The coin and whatever was inside. She had hoped to trade on Bourne's gratitude.

All the while they spoke, El-Amir remained in Bourne's field of vision. He was eating his meal, observing but not interjecting, not wanting to interfere with the flow of the dialogue. Amira was right about him: he was both smart and clever. Observing was learning, in whatever field you were in, especially the shadow world of spies and terrorists, oligarchs and *siloviki*.

"Bourne, what was your friend, Boris, up to? What did he find so fascinating in Cairo?"

"You, Bobby. He wanted to nail you as badly as I do."

"Again with the Bobby," El-Amir murmured as if to himself.

Borz pointedly ignored him, his basilisk gaze fixed on Bourne. "What a fucked-up life you must lead, Jason." His head waggled from side to side. "You're like a man with one leg and no crutch. How do you manage?"

"I've developed a highly refined knack for adaptation."

Borz made a sound in the back of his throat. "I'll just bet you have."

"We met in a city. You were saying..."

Borz stared at him for a long time without so much as a blink of his eyes. "You'd like that, wouldn't you? For men like us information is everything; without it we wither and die." He pushed his plate away. "Hungry?"

Bourne tried to move his arms. "I couldn't eat even if I was."

The shelling had ceased for the moment, replaced by a deathly silence that reverberated like a bell with a phantom clapper.

"Maybe there's a way out of this," Bourne said after a time.

"Oh, there is," Borz said cheerfully. "And I'm about to show it to you."

"A compromise. We both get what we want."

He cocked his head. "Sounds so good, the way you put it." He produced a rueful smile from his deep bag of tricks. "You see, Jason, the trouble is we're both scorpions. We'll sting each other as soon as we get close enough."

Borz's sigh was strictly for the invisible balcony. "The truth is, trust has no provenance here." He stood. "Which is why I have devised a plan to compel you to tell me what I want to know."

"If you intend to have me interrogated, you'll be sadly disappointed," Bourne said. "There's nothing you can do to me." His face darkened. "You've already tried everything, including kidnapping friends of mine and holding them hostage. How did that work out for you?"

Borz's face turned stormy. "Don't take me for a fool, Jason," he snapped. He gripped the back of his chair, as if seeking to regain his emotional equilibrium. "But all men can be persuaded. The craft lies in determining the nature of the inducement." He paused for a moment, another smile played cruelly around lips that were not quite Bourne's. "Another lesson you taught me."

He gestured toward El-Amir, who stood also despite not having finished his meal. He looked like the type who had become used to snapping to. "I assume Amira told you what El-Amir does."

"He works for CloudNet TV," Bourne said.

Borz's grin went coast-to-coast. "Oh, she's been a naughty girl."

El-Amir, frowning, said, "Maybe she doesn't know."

Borz snorted. "As you would say, Don't be daft, old man. Your father found out you're working for me; a smart girl like your sister, it's altogether likely that she knows. The interesting thing is that she didn't tell Jason."

"She's ashamed of me," El-Amir said.

"Maybe," Borz allowed.

"Trust me. I know her."

Borz tossed his head like a wild horse. "Be that as it may, I think it's time we showed Jason what's in store for him." He nodded, and a man who Bourne hadn't seen before stepped up and cut his bonds, stuck the point of the knife into the flesh just above his kidney, and frog-marched him briefly outside and into the building next door that Bourne had glimpsed through the window.

Inside was a different world altogether. Camera, snaking cables, boom mikes, a massive array of lights high up, follow-spots, key lights, even a teleprompter. A thick pane of clear plastic had been jury-rigged to wall off the banks of monitors. He might have been on a Hollywood soundstage.

Bourne saw the green screen first. "What's being projected onto that?" he asked.

"Check the monitor," Borz said as he came up beside Bourne. The man holding Bourne jerked him around to the left, behind the plastic wall, sat him down in a director's chair in front of the monitors, to which he then bound him hand and foot. Nearby, El-Amir, bent over, spoke in low tones to one of the seated engineers. A moment later, a desert scene bloomed on the monitors.

"Righto, we're all set with lights and sound," El-Amir said, taking a seat. And turning to Borz, "Are you ready for your close-up?"

Bourne watched himself climb onto the soundstage. On the monitors, he was in the desert, not in an ad-hoc video studio.

"Places, everyone!" El-Amir said into the mic built into the console in front of him. He sat. He lifted an arm, then let it fall like an ax blade. "And, we're rolling!"

That was when two hooded men brought out a prisoner. He looked like he'd been through the seven levels of hell. They brought him in front of Bourne/Borz, pushed him to his knees. One of the men handed Bourne/Borz a knife with a long, scimitar-shaped blade. Bourne/Borz grabbed a handful of hair, yanked the prisoner's head back, exposing his throat. He laid the blade against it, grinned at the camera as a thin line of blood oozed out, dripped onto the boards of the stage.

El-Amir scooted over to where Bourne sat. "Here's where it really gets good," he whispered in Bourne's ear. He gestured toward the bank of monitors, where the engineer had put up Bourne's name, the name and rank of the prisoner, and a brief exhortation to jihad. The words scrolled across the bottom screen, in an endless loop, American TV style.

"Don't look so glum, chum. You're about to be reborn as an international star." El-Amir gave the back of Bourne's head an affectionate pat. "The entire world is going to watch as Jason Bourne beheads a British liaison officer."

41

WHEN HE WAS a fresh-faced young man, Roy Michael Tambourine couldn't wait to get to Cairo. After all, Cairo was the epicenter of the great Egyptian Pharaonic Empire that had fascinated him all his life. He had studied its mysteries in college, had learned to speak the guttural Egyptian Arabic, and, when, at length, he had first arrived he could scarcely contain his excitement.

That was almost forty years ago. He had for decades been teaching at Cairo University as a more or less permanent visiting professor. He had borne witness to regimes coming and going, to revolutions, counterrevolutions, the so-called Arab Spring, which was nothing more than a catchy tagline for Western mass media outlets. It astonished him that in the end, the more things changed the more they stayed the same. Egypt was embedded in amber, ossified as expertly as the mummies and artifacts in the Archeological Museum, in whose dusty recesses he still spent the bulk of his free time.

Today was just like every other day in the last forty years: Professor Tambourine awoke in his small apartment, showered, shaved, pomaded his hair, dressed in one of his three tropic-weight suits. In his tiny kitchen he ate two pieces of toast—just this side of burned—with butter and marmalade, drank a cup of Earl Grey tea with a spot of milk, and, after cleaning up, braved the chaos of crosstown traffic to his dimly lit office at the university.

For the first forty minutes of the morning, he sat at his wide desk, a remnant of Britain's Colonial hold on the country, grading papers. It wasn't long, however, before he realized that his mind was wandering. He looked up, peering over his spectacles at the portrait of Zahl Hawass, the most famous Egyptian archeologist. The young man stared back at Tambourine, completely unaware of the ignominious downfall in his future, exiled for agreeing to concession contracts at the Egyptian Museum. In fact, Dr. Zahl's real crime was vigorously backing Hosni Mubarak, even during the mass protests of the Arab Spring.

Tambourine had hung the portrait not because he venerated Dr. Zahl, but as an object lesson in the consequences of becoming embroiled in the treacherously shifting sands of Egyptian politics—even for visiting professors.

Dr. Zahl's familiar face blurred before Tambourine's eyes, as his mind continued to wander. He realized, somewhat belatedly, that he was bored, that he'd been bored for years. The tedium of academic life had seeped into his pores like desert sand, graying him out. He was old, and what had he done with his life? All the secrets of ancient Egypt had either been found or were missing, never to return. His field of expertise had turned into a dead end.

He sighed deeply, saddened in the way only the British can get when they've been away from home for too long. He was just about to make himself a cup of tea, when his private mobile buzzed. At once, his heart-rate began to gallop. He fumbled for his phone, almost dropped it in his haste and excitement, flipped it open.

There on the screen was a text message: IS THE BAKERY OPEN?

It's true, he thought. God does love Englishmen!

With a rock-steady forefinger, he typed FORTY MINUTES, then hit Send.

He told his secretary to cancel his morning classes, he had been taken ill. On the way down the hall, he began to whistle his favorite melody from *Mary Poppins*.

The slender minarets of the city rose, silhouetted with their many close-waist balconies beyond the treetops of Al-Azhar Park. Precisely forty minutes after he had left the university, Professor Tambourine, a tall, pear-shaped man with the small, delicate feet of a ballet dancer and the soft hands of an academic, stood in the shadow of the southwest corner of the pavilion closest to the unearthed Ayyubid wall. The pavilion was newly constructed of fragrant cedar, aged with stain, and arabesqued in a design proper to this historical district.

He had bought a small paper bag of pistachios from a vendor, and was now eating them, slowly and methodically, as he gazed at the skyline that still seemed as alien as it was familiar. It was a fine morning, the haze having for the moment lifted, revealing the piercing blue sky overhead. The desert breeze was already heating up the sunlit sections of the park.

Tambourine wasn't aware of her approach, but then he hadn't expected to be. One minute he was standing alone, amid the families, running children, young couples holding hands, and milling groups of tourists with their cameras, mobiles, and iPads, indiscriminately taking photos of everything, the next she was right beside him, head-wrapped in a cream-colored hijab.

"I'm not really a big fan of pastries," she said.

"Nor am I," Tambourine replied. "But we all have to make a living."

Having gotten through the preliminaries, the two of them began to stroll along the packed pathways. He offered her pistachios, and she took a handful.

"I need passage out of Egypt right away," she said without looking at him.

She was quite beautiful. He had known who she was at first sight, having memorized all of the Kidon personnel. This one—Rebeka—was part of the Caesarea unit. He felt honored.

"Destination?" he said.

When she told him, he was so astonished he broke protocol, turned to her, and said, "You're joking."

"I only wish I was," Rebeka said. "Ivan Borz flew out on his private jet ten hours ago. Even flexing my muscles it took me that long to find out he'd left and to obtain his flight plan."

"But you're asking me to send you into the heart of a war zone."

"And?"

"Does the Director—?"

"Is this assignment too difficult for you?" Her voice had the force of a fist striking flesh.

Professor Tambourine laughed. "Hardly." He lengthened his stride, his pace quickening with his pulse. "Come with me. There's no time to lose."

"Wait!" Bourne shouted.

"I'm afraid he can't hear you," El-Amir said.

"I'll give him what he wants."

"In his current frame of mind he won't believe you."

"Tell him!"

El-Amir shrugged. "Cut!" he said into the mic. "Ivan, our guest seems to have had a change of heart."

"I don't make deals with terrorists," Bourne said when Borz, stepping off the killing stage, came back behind the plastic screen.

"I'm not a terrorist," Borz said. "I'm a high-functioning sociopath."

Bourne looked up at him. "Then we have our starting point."

"Cheeky bastard, isn't he?" El-Amir said.

"Go take your pal for tea and crumpets," Borz said without looking at him.

Without a word of protest, Amira's brother rose and left the building, the engineer following. Borz took his seat. The shelling began again, muffled by what Bourne suspected were the double walls and insulation of the field studio.

"So, Jason, you've changed since we last met."

"Where was that again?"

Borz grinned. "Like ill-fated lovers, our paths first crossed in Istanbul, the city where East meets West. A fitting place for us, don't you think?"

"Istanbul," Bourne said, sensing Borz needed a push to get him to make the jump into the past. "One of my favorite cities."

"Mine, as well," Borz said. "You'd know that if you still had your memory." His hands were steepled as if he were a bishop at prayer. "Since that time I see you've grown a sense of humor. I commend you. In a world where cynicism is king, a sense of humor is required to maintain perspective, don't you think?"

"I do," Bourne said, thinking the time had come to become verbal.

Borz nodded. "Then, as one high-functioning sociopath to another, let's begin. You said you would tell me what mischief Boris Karpov was up to."

"First, have your men take the prisoner away. He looks like he could use a place to lie down."

Borz stared at Bourne, seeming to examine every feature of the face he had come to know so well. "It's like looking into a mirror, isn't it?"

"A fun house mirror."

Borz's lips flickered in the semblance of a smile. He swiveled, spoke into the console mic. His men picked the SAS officer off his knees, carted him away. He seemed barely alive.

"Get him some medical attention, will you?"

"Waste of resources," Borz said. "He doesn't have long to live anyway."

"Give him at least a modicum of relief, then."

Borz tapped a forefinger against his lips. "You know, I'm beginning to think you may not be a sociopath after all. Then what would you be? A high-functioning what, do you suppose?"

"We are what we are, Bobby. Nothing can change that."

"True enough. Take me, for instance. I'm a businessman by nature. Violence is not my instinctive métier. In fact, I rather hate it. But what can you do? I had to learn violence from the ground up—with my head held underwater, metaphorically speaking. It was an agonizing experience, believe me."

Borz's voice seemed to be honing a double edge. The second edge, keener, darker than the first, riding just below the surface, was the one that interested Bourne the most. He had the uncomfortable feeling that Borz was speaking not in the abstract but in the particular, not in the objective but in the personal, and more than ever, he wondered what had happened in Istanbul. He could sense how badly Borz wanted Boris's information. But he was also keenly aware of how much he himself wanted to retrieve a piece of his lost past—and at the same time solve the enigma of who Borz really was.

"Tell me," was all Borz said now.

"Tell me," Bourne replied.

Two mirror images tossing words back in each other's face.

"Your good friend, the late Boris."

"Istanbul. Our ill-fated affair."

"This was your idea," Borz said.

There was no help for it, Bourne knew. As Borz himself had said, trust had no provenance here among the scorpions. But if there was a chance to save the SAS officer, if there was, moreover, a chance to regain even a sliver of his maddeningly forgotten past, he had to take it.

"Boris discovered a plot hatched by the president."

"You mean the Kremlin."

"Not quite." Bourne was homed in on Borz's eyes. This close up, he could see the irises beneath the colored contacts. "None of the inner-circle oligarchs and very few of the *siloviki* know."

"Continue."

Understanding that he had acquired Borz's complete attention, he continued with the information Svetlana had relayed to him from Amsterdam. "In two days' time, the president intends to order his troops massed along the border to engage in a full-scale invasion of Ukraine."

Borz looked at Bourne incredulously. "This is your story? This is why I shouldn't behead that officer?" He shook his head as he rose to his feet. "You disappoint me, Jason. Deeply and completely."

"You haven't heard the rest."

"Why should I listen to the rest when the first part is so patently absurd?"

"The current Russian pact with Ukraine for natural gas is a ruse. A means to allay Western fears."

"And all the while the Sovereign is thinking war that will rain fire down on him and his country," Borz said with a derisive snort.

"Yes." Bourne had worked out the larger pattern, extrapolating from what Svetlana had told him. "Let me pose a question: Where do you think all the money ISIS has is coming from?"

"Why guess when it's clear you're going to tell me."

"It's you, Bobby. The money is coming from you."

42

GOGA STOOD IN the living room of Ivan Borz's villa in Giza. Through the glass sliders he watched the sun spark off the slanted sides of the Pyramids. The Great Sphinx returned his gaze with the stored wisdom of the ages.

Goga shook out a cigarette, lighted it, inhaled deeply. The general was gone, Borz was gone, Bourne was gone, Amira was gone. Everyone, even the Mossad unit—taking their dead leader—had slunk back to Jerusalem, tails between their legs. Well, Goga didn't mind that, at least.

He was alone in Cairo with nowhere to go and nothing to do. He glanced down at Svetlana's open suitcase. He had opened it, taken a photo of the contents, so he could put every article of clothing and cosmetics back precisely as she had packed them.

He had orders from First Minister Savasin to send Svetlana's effects back intact. Savasin had made the order very clear. Goga hated Savasin, but the general's death had cast him adrift. He needed a rabbi, as the Jews said, otherwise, as one of Karpov's most trusted agents, he would certainly drown in the rising tide. So he had called Savasin, who gave him assurances of safe haven in exchange for terminating the general's widow and returning her effects.

He had had every intention of pawing through Svetlana's clothes, digging for whatever it was the first minister was so intent on retrieving. But as of yet he hadn't made a move. He inhaled the smoke, seeking to calm himself, soothe an inner part of him. He expelled the smoke too fast; he would not be soothed, thinking about how Savasin had so quickly disposed of Svetlana. He smelled a purge—the air was rank with it, even here in Cairo. He strongly suspected that the moment he returned to Moscow he would be met by Savasin's people, who would throw him into the Lubyanka—or someplace more remote, more bestial—and interrogate him until he vomited up every secret of his life and of the general's. This he would do, he had no doubt whatsoever. He was far too familiar with the rendition procedures to delude himself. Eventually, he would tell them everything they wanted to know, and more.

He could not go back. He could not let that happen. He was already racked with guilt. His instinctual fear of the implacable Federation system had led him to reach out to the first minister, and Savasin had taken full advantage of Goga's fear. He was revolted at his own weakness, sick to his soul at his betrayal. Shooting the general's widow, at the time seeming such a practical solution to his altered situation, now revealed itself as the basest of crimes. Unforgivable.

Now to ransack the suitcase of the general's widow—all that was left of her—was totally beyond him, a violation too far.

Sunlight moved through the room, silent as the great necropolis across the desert plateau. Abruptly, Goga dropped his lit cigarette onto the top layer of clothes. When that didn't get a fire going fast enough, he flicked the flame on his lighter, tossed it in.

A *whoosh* went up as flames brought an acrid stench to the room.

Stepping around the rising fire, he opened the glass slider, stepped out onto the balcony. He looked out at the Sphinx, wished once again that it would speak to him, give up its secrets, because for him there was no solution.

Silence. Always silence from those with the most wisdom. At least he could do something honorable for his General.

As he inserted the muzzle of his Makarov into his mouth, he tilted his head back, stared up into the sky: blue and white and then…

Nothingness. Peace, at last.

For a moment Borz stood stock-still, then, slowly and methodically, he refolded himself into the chair opposite Bourne.

"Explain yourself."

Bourne shook his head. "I don't think so. First, I want to hear about Istanbul."

"Jason, Jason, you're in no position to negotiate."

"I gave you a sliver of trust."

"That's your problem." Borz turned to the mic, spoke into it. "Bring the prisoner back."

"Don't do that," Bourne said. "You need me."

"Really?" Borz looked at him askance.

"You claim to be a businessman, not a terrorist."

Borz watched two of his men drag the SAS officer back onto the killing stage. "I stand by that statement."

"Without me, you'll never get your money back."

Borz turned slowly toward him. "What money?"

"You really want to hear this?"

Borz sat down opposite Bourne. "I'm listening."

"It's getting more difficult to speak, bound like this."

Borz hesitated only a moment. Then he took out a stiletto, cut through the plastic ties binding Bourne to the director's chair. Then he sat back.

"The SAS officer is waiting, Jason."

Bourne rubbed circulation back into his wrists and ankles. "I kept wondering why Irina would willingly bring me to Mik, your *vosdushnik*. He also made her grandfather's money disappear from one place and appear in another." This was the meaning of the second part of Boris's rebus: *Follow the money*. "But what no one knew, what Boris discovered, was that Mik was also the sole conduit for the president."

"How could that be?" Borz said. "There would be no plausible deniability."

"There would be if Vasily, Irina's father, was his cutout."

"This is pure fancy. Vasily was killed on orders by the president."

"I think Vasily—and his older son—got greedy. They were skimming."

"There are records in there you need to see," Irina had said outside Mik's. *"Something terrible has been going on. What I'll make Mik show you will explain everything."* This was the shard of memory he had been trying to pull out of the darkness of the rift in his mind. Irina knew her father's real work and, he surmised, so did his wife. That knowledge and the fact that he wouldn't stop had driven her mad. Of course she believed she was possessed by the devil. In her mind Vasily was the devil. "Irina wanted me to see the proof because then I could connect the Sovereign to the scheme he had hatched."

"What has all this got to do with me?"

"Patience, Bobby. The president was using Vasily and Mik to move money around—it became an immense shell game. The money you deposited with Mik was halved—probably halved, anyway—and sent—"

"And you really think I wouldn't know?"

"It's Madoff accounting—voodoo economics. Your money *seems* to be there, but if you had ever asked Mik for all of it . . ." Bourne allowed the unspoken end of the sentence to hang in the air, giving the treachery far more weight than if he had voiced it.

Without a word, Borz rose, strode over to a sturdy metal briefcase, opened it, took out a military-grade laptop. He brought it back, opened it, fired it up. The top prevented Bourne from seeing what he was doing. It didn't matter; Bourne knew that Borz was accessing his account.

"There," he said, with a distinct note of triumph in his voice. "It's all there." He looked up. "I knew you were full of shit."

"You must have other accounts elsewhere, Bobby. Transfer that money into one of them."

Borz frowned. "This is a trick of some kind."

"I'm trying to help you, Bobby. Trust me."

"Trust."

"Even though it's not a word in your vocabulary."

Borz considered for a moment, trying to work all the angles, trying and failing to see how Bourne could trick him. His fingers began to dance over the keyboard. "I'm in," he said, almost to himself. "Transfer complete." For long minutes afterward he sat staring at the screen, so still the instant of transfer might have been frozen in time. At length, he sucked in a deep breath, let it out in a hiss. "Half," he said. "It's half of what it should be.

"Fuck!" Borz seemed ready to smash his laptop to pieces. His gaze locked onto Bourne. "Where the *fuck* did my money go?"

"You know, Bobby. The question has already been asked."

"What question?" And then it dawned on him. "You can't mean that ISIS—"

"Is being funded by the Sovereign with your money. Yes."

Borz jumped up. "This is crazy." He paced back and forth, as if caged, which, in a way, he was. "Why would he do such a thing?"

"It's all part of the shell game," Bourne said. "Misdirection. Make the world look one way—force it to concentrate on ISIS—"

"—while the Russians overwhelm Ukraine, before the West can act."

"The Western powers make decisions about as quickly as the *Queen Mary* turns around," Bourne said drily. "And, so, two days from now, the first stage of the president's goal of retrieving the territory lost to Russia at the fall of the Soviet Union will be complete."

"At no cost to him." Borz glanced down at his laptop screen as if hoping the figures would have somehow magically changed. Then his eyes flicked back up. "And you can get my money back? How?"

"Bobby, Bobby," Bourne said, "be kind enough to tell me about what happened in Istanbul."

"Kindness doesn't enter into it," Borz replied, slamming down the lid of his laptop.

43

THERE WILL BE consequences when you get home," Professor Tambourine said.

Sara shrugged. "There always are."

Tambourine was getting her settled in the cockpit of the humanitarian freight flight outward bound to Kobanî, the Syrian city on the Turkish border that was under siege by ISIS. The flight was being sent to drop supplies to the embattled Kurds. Tambourine had arranged for Sara to parachute in with the crates, without anyone aboard giving her a second thought.

"I'm afraid this time it's different." The professor looked rueful. "I received a call from the Director wanting to know why you hadn't arrived home with the cadre."

Sara's eyes flashed. "And what did you tell him?"

"Before I had a chance to say anything, he told me he was sending—"

"Don't tell me," Sara said, strapping herself in as the pilot and navigator in the row in front of her went through their final checklist. "He's sending my boss, Dov Liron, to fetch me." She shrugged. "That's been done before."

"It isn't Liron he's sending, Rebeka. It's Ophir."

"Oh dear." Amir Ophir was the head of Metsada, Mossad's Special Branch Ops. Ophir was second-in-command under her father. "That's unfortunate."

"Well, it would have been," Professor Tambourine said with a twinkle in his eye, "if he knew where you were headed."

"Why? What did you tell the Director?"

"That you were no longer in Cairo. That you'd gone to Tunis."

"Tunis? What on earth would I be doing there?"

Tambourine shrugged. "I'm sure I have no idea." He grinned. "I'm just a stringer on this bus."

"From the bottom of my heart, Professor, thank you."

"You're welcome. But when this adventure finally shakes out, I fear it may be the end for the both of us."

Sara winked at him. "I wouldn't count on it."

He gave her a nod of approval. "I have weaponized you to your satisfaction?"

"Completely. You're a whiz, Professor."

"I do what I can."

"Ready," the pilot said. "You'd better leave, R. M. We only have one extra chute, and that's for the young lady."

Professor Tambourine laughed. "Drinks and dinner at Cairo's finest for you and the crew when you return, Richard." Then, rubbing his hands together in his best professorial fashion, he addressed Sara. "Righto. Luck and a stalwart heart, my brava." He gave her the V-for-victory sign just before he left the cockpit and deplaned.

She watched him stride across the tarmac, head held up, back ramrod straight, ready for whatever else the day might bring. There was a spring in his step she hadn't seen before. She promised herself that when she returned to Jerusalem, whatever else happened, she would keep him safe from harm.

Moments later, the tarmac clear, Richard revved the engines to full power. The ailerons were at full lift as the plane taxied down the runway, and, with a great leap upward, punched its way into the burning sky.

"In those days, I was running guns out of Istanbul," Borz said. "In those days, before the Islamic voice of Turkey rose up, you could run guns with impunity."

"You can still run guns out of Istanbul with impunity," Bourne said. "It's only the officials who've changed, not the policies." He regarded Borz for a moment. It was still disconcerting to be talking to someone who looked like himself. That was the point, he assumed. Borz had demonstrated a keen grasp on human psychology. "So either you weren't running guns or running them was a front for something else."

Borz sat stock-still. Only a piteous moan from the British SAS officer broke the silence that had overlaid the ubiquitous thrum of the electronics. Bourne assumed there must be an immense generator somewhere nearby to power all the equipment. Electricity in a war zone was inconstant at best.

"I can't stand that sniveling," Borz snapped. He pointed to Bourne. "With me."

An armed guard accompanied them for the short walk back to the first building. All the dishes in the center of the table had been cleared.

"Here," Borz said, indicating the chair where El-Amir had sat. "He never did finish his food—so sit. Eat."

Bourne did nothing of the sort. Instead, he sat back, arms folded across his chest, studied Borz through half-closed eyes. "What sort of trade would appeal to a man like you, Bobby? A businessman and a self-professed sociopath."

Borz's fingers gripped the back of the chair opposite Bourne. "*High-functioning* sociopath."

"Yes, of course." Bourne stared up at the ceiling, then back down to Borz. "You were transshipping young girls."

"How d'you come to that?"

"One, the white slave trade is the most lucrative of all criminal activities. Two—"

"Wait a minute. Why not drugs?"

"You have to be well connected to be in the drug trade in a place like Istanbul, and you were too young for that. Besides, as I was about to say, Istanbul is perfectly situated geographically to transship girls from Eastern Europe into the West, where you'd get top dollar. Plus, being a sociopath, trading in human beings wouldn't bother your conscience in the least. You don't have a conscience."

"Perhaps you should tell this story," Borz said testily. When Bourne made no reply, he continued in an altogether different tone of voice. "You had been inserted into Istanbul to terminate—does the name Dolman strike a spark? No? Well, he was your target, Dolman. I found this out only much later. Too late, I would say.

"I had worked for Dolman briefly before breaking away. Going out on my own wasn't easy. A lot of people died, even more blood was shed before an uneasy détente was established.

"Afterward, I figured out that you had been provided with intel indicating I knew Dolman's operation inside and out. I was impressed from the first time we met by how much of the underground workings of Istanbul you knew."

"And what was your name then, Bobby? Your full name?"

Borz bared his teeth. "The story, Jason. The story is what matters here." He slipped into the chair opposite Bourne. "Not hungry? Well, this story won't help your appetite, this I can guarantee."

"Back to Dolman."

"No. Dolman was only a minor player in this particular drama. Back to you and me. Because that's what it became, back then in Istanbul. You made yourself useful to me, then indispensable. You have that knack."

"What knack?"

"Of being able to insinuate yourself into any situation."

"It's a gift."

"Right." Borz laughed, but it was a sound devoid of pleasure. He leaned forward, placed his elbows on the table. "So the two of us, all those days ago—we became inseparable. My business was never better—the military-grade weapons, anyway. You didn't find out about the . . . girls . . . until near the end. That's what I thought, anyway. There came a time, however, when I realized that I was wrong, that you knew about the girls right from the get-go. Your fucking intel was so good."

Borz seemed lost in thought for a moment. Then he went on: "So. There came a time when you had insinuated yourself so deeply into my regime that you felt comfortable bringing up the topic of Dolman. He was my main rival—older than me, more connected, more powerful. I wanted to be like him, and he knew it. He could feel me breathing down his neck. So did you.

"You offered to take him out for me, but, of course, you needed the intel only someone who had been inside his organization could give you. Me. So I gave you everything I had learned while I was working for Dolman: his organizational structure, the people close to him, the ones he trusted, the ones he didn't. Most important of all, I drew a map of the inside of his compound, gave you his schedule. Dolman was a man of habit; those things never change. And armed with all this knowledge, you infiltrated his compound, found him, and killed him."

Borz rose, restless again, came around the table to stand behind Bourne's chair, his hands resting lightly on the top slat, so that Bourne could feel his knuckles across the middle of his shoulders.

His voice grew tight. "What I had never imagined, what you did to me, Jason, was make me the prime suspect in Dolman's murder. You stole my stiletto—a knife that was special to me; Dolman had presented it to me. Everyone knew that knife—they'd all seen it. And you sliced it across Dolman's throat."

Bourne had just enough time to think, *The way you sliced open Boris's throat*, before Borz coiled his arm around Bourne's own throat, locked him in the hold with the heel of his hand against the nape of Bourne's neck with such force he lifted Bourne out of his seat.

"I . . . want . . . my . . . money . . . fucker," Borz rasped in his ear.

Instead of resisting, Bourne went with the pull and lift, drawing his knees up to his chest, and somersaulted back over Borz's head. His own head was still locked; worse, the bones of Borz's forearm were virtually crushing his windpipe, cutting off all air.

On the other hand, he was now behind Borz, he had Borz in an awkward and indefensible position, and when he drove his knee into Borz's kidney, Borz grunted, had no choice but to let his grip slip. Bourne drew his fist back to deliver a blow that would crack Borz's lower ribs, but he was held back by Borz's gunman, who put the muzzle of a handgun to the side of his head.

That was a mistake. Bourne slammed into him while, at the same time, his hand shoved the barrel away so that when the gunman fired he almost took the top of Borz's head off. Borz ducked down. His harsh shout of alarm and momentary fear caused his gunman to freeze, not knowing what to do. That was all the opening Bourne required. Driving the edge of his hand into the place between the gunman's neck and shoulder, he ripped the weapon out of his hand, smashed the butt into the back of the man's head. The gunman fell beside Borz, who was trying to rouse himself from his close encounter with the bullet.

Bourne bent, grabbed Borz, hauled him up, struck him a blow on the point of his chin. Borz staggered back, regained his footing, struck back. The blows came so thick and fast they were mere blurs, difficult to defend against. Then Bourne struck Borz with such force that he was sent reeling across the room. From down on one knee, Borz rose, grabbed a chair, smashed it against the wall. One thick leg remained in his first, transformed into a cudgel. He was in the process of launching himself toward Bourne when a mortar shell struck the side of the building, sending everyone and everything flying.

44

SARA AWOKE FROM a deep sleep to find ten more messages from her father on her mobile. That made twenty-five. Professor Tambourine had been right; she was going to be in real trouble when she returned to Jerusalem.

"Miss?" Richard, the pilot, had turned in his seat to address her. "Shelling has recommenced over Kobanî. We can't get down as low as we'd like. Can you skydive?"

Sara smiled. "I've done it once or twice before."

Richard looked dubious. "I'm afraid this is going to take the skills of an expert."

Sara was up, shrugging on her parachute. "I'll be fine. I was just kidding."

"You'd better be," Richard said, facing forward again. "Otherwise you'll be dead before you hit the ground."

Flung through a gaping hole in the wall, Bourne found himself outside. His ears were ringing and his head ached fiercely, but he was otherwise unhurt. Bodies were sprawled on the ground, some bleeding, others dead. Scooping up a fallen semiautomatic weapon, he went back inside the building, but there was no sign of Borz. He wanted to search every room, but all was chaos. Outside, the bombardment had intensified. Another shell could hit the building at any time.

Bourne once again stepped through the ragged opening. One look at the terrain, a glimpse of Kurdish fighters, and his mind, sifting at lightning speed through the possible world's hot spots, realized he was in Kobanî, Syria, just beyond the western Turkish border.

More mortar shells were falling as ISIS troops recommenced their attack. The ground rumbled and shook, the air swirled thick with smoke and burning debris. Men were running for cover. He looked up, saw a plane high up, headed more or less toward the compound. It looked like one of the small relief corps bringing in supplies to the embattled Kurds.

No more than a hundred yards away he saw a helo standing alone, a single guard in front of the access. Firing started up behind Bourne, bullets chipping away at the corner of the building against which he was pressed. The guard came to alert, and his semiautomatic weapon swung down, its muzzle at the ready.

Caught between a rock and a hard place, Bourne reached down, hefted a rock in his hand. He threw it to the side of the guard. As he whirled, Bourne detached himself from the cover of the building, ran directly toward the helo, praying that it wouldn't be blown to smithereens by a mortar shell.

The guard saw him coming, swung around, fired without aiming. Bourne shot him in the chest, tossed him aside, and climbed into the helo. In war zones, vehicles were always on standby, ready to be used at a moment's notice. The helo was no exception. He fired the ignition, started the rotors going just as three of Borz's men rounded the corner where Bourne had been concealing himself. They saw the guard on the ground, pointed, and began running toward the helo. They didn't dare shoot, lest they cripple a vital piece of multi-million-dollar equipment.

He heard the signal noise of a mortar shell nearing, ground the sticks, and got the helo into the air just before the explosion took out one of the men and maimed another. The third scuttled back into the building.

He brought the helo around, wheeling through the smoke and debris screen. He was high enough now, as he came out of the thick fug, to see the black-garbed ISIS fighter units assembled to the southwest. The moment they spotted him, semiautomatic fire started up, and he lifted the helo higher, getting a right reading on the compass. He turned toward the Turkish border and had started out for it when he saw two ISIS terrorists, one with a shoulder missile launcher, the other with the missile. They loaded up the weapon and began to track the incoming plane Bourne had seen before. With a tricky twisting maneuver he swooped lower, gaining their attention. The man in back tapped his partner on the shoulder. Bourne was low enough to see the firer's lips turn up into a grim smile.

He put on speed, heading up, up, and away as the firer swiveled the helo into his sights. Bourne knew he knew he couldn't outrun a missile. His one hope was that it was an old one, that its guidance system wasn't working properly. A moment later he saw the contrail of the missile as it shot up toward him. At least now the incoming supply plane had a chance.

Now the missile was directly behind him, and he commenced evasive maneuvers, pulling the helo to the left and right, dipping it down, lifting it steeply upward. The missile kept homing in on him. So much for a faulty guidance system. The continuing barrage buffeted the helo, and he struggled to keep it on course toward Turkey. The helo whirred through thick clots of black smoke. He was leaving behind an inferno of fiery debris, maimed bodies, lost causes.

The helo had far less maneuverability than a fighter jet, to say nothing of its comparative lack of speed. No matter what he did, he couldn't shake the missile. It continued to gain on him as the border loomed ever closer. Now he put the helo into the steepest climb it could handle. He calculated he had less than a minute to make the definitive maneuver that would save him.

Up ahead, at more or less due north, he could see the border, and beyond it, Turkey. There wasn't much difference in the terrain—dry brown earth, clotted with roots exposed by gunfire and explosive ordinance, low hills, brown again, in the distance. Not a tree or leaf in sight. But there were clusters of ragtag Kurdish fighters, weapons raised, watching the missile close on him. He put the helo on autopilot—a dangerous, possibly lethal, decision—but he had no other choice. He ranged through the interior, searching for anything that could help him.

Forty seconds later, the missile struck aft in a blinding burst of propellant, warhead, fuel, molten plastic, and twisted metal. The stricken helo spun around twice before the entire fuselage combusted, sending whatever remained of it cartwheeling onto Turkish soil.

45

HEAD DOWN, FALLING like a rocket, Sara felt like a missile. It was not yet time to pull the cord, to deploy the chute. A million thoughts ripped through her brain, none of them helpful, all of them tinged with fear. The fear was, of course, mixed with exhilaration, but the important thing—the only thing—to remember was to keep her mind clear, to begin the countdown to deployment, to remember what she had to do afterward to compensate, not only for the prevailing wind, which Richard had called out to her along with the altitude just before she jumped, but also for the violent air pockets caused by the detonating ordnance. She was jumping into the midst of an all-out assault on Kobanî.

Because of the smoke and explosions, she had no visual she could count on. She needed to rely entirely on her countdown to deploy at the proper altitude: too soon and the upper level winds would take her too far from her drop zone; too late and she would cripple herself, or worse, when she landed at shocking speed.

There came the moment when she held her life in her right hand, pulled the rip cord. An instant of blackout, then momentary disorientation as her brain adjusted to the humane rate of descent. She was passing through clouds of choking smoke and cinders that made her eyes water, the inside of her nostrils sting. She was in the process of orienting herself when, off in the distance, toward the border with Turkey, she saw a midair explosion, saw for just an instant part of a helo's fuselage spinning around before, it, too, vanished in a ghastly fireball.

Then she was jerked off course by a detonation on the ground, and for the next twenty seconds, she was so busy with her waylines, course correcting, all thought of the exploded helo was wiped from her consciousness.

She was almost down when another explosion hit close enough to her to send a chunk of a building hurtling through the canopy above her. At once, the chute canted over, and she began to fall much faster than was safe.

The uneven, deeply pitted ground came up in a fiery blur. She jerked free of her harness, climbed the waylines, pulled the rapidly deflating canopy around her. She hit the ground with much of the chute under her curled-up body, and rolled into one of the mortar craters, whose concave surface further cushioned her landing.

For a moment, she lay faceup, trying to catch her breath. Then she used her knife to cut through the silk draped over her like a shroud. Her lower back and hips felt as if she had gone fifteen rounds in a boxing ring. Her heart was thudding hard in her chest, and she was assailed by the stench of war: blood, burned flesh, human feces, charcoaled plastic, and superhot metal. None of these smells were alien to her—they were, sadly, far too familiar. Pulling herself together, she stuck her head out of her impromptu foxhole in order to get her bearings. She was somewhere southeast of the town, in an encampment of some kind. She saw three buildings—or parts of them, anyway.

Men were strewn everywhere, looking like rag dolls pulled apart by vicious dogs. They interested Sara inasmuch as they were dressed neither as ISIS terrorists nor Kurdish irregulars. Whose compound was this? Could it be Ivan Borz's? If so, what was he doing setting up shop between ISIS and the Kurds of Turkey?

A lull in the bombardment gave her a chance to scramble out of her foxhole. She snatched up a semiautomatic rifle on the run. She was heading toward two adjacent buildings, one of which was half bombed out—and recently, by the looks of things. As she ran she passed over what could only be a helipad, complete with a ring of purple lights and a luminescent cross at its center to guide pilots in. She remembered the helo being destroyed in midair—most likely from a ground-to-air missile. It must have taken off from here. Had it been carrying Borz to safety? Then where was Jason?

Heart in her throat, she entered the burst building through the jagged hole in its side. A man lay dead on the floor, a table had been knocked over on its side, chairs splintered near it. A dish of food was sprayed across the floor. The other rooms were deserted. She left, crossed outside, and ducked into the second building.

That was when she saw the stage set, the boom mics, the arrays of lights overhead, the makeshift control room. Lights were dimmed, as if not getting enough power. Some were off altogether, their bulbs burst apart, useless filaments dangling, and off to one side, a snaking electrical cable, ripped loose from its mooring, sparked and sizzled on the floor. She stood for a moment, stunned. Then she walked slowly up onto the stage. The area center front was stained so dark it seemed to be the opening to a bottomless pit. Squatting down, she put a fingertip down, then drew it back quickly. She didn't have to touch it; the stench of it filled her, caused her to rear back. The floor here was covered with many layers of human blood, some of it fairly fresh. It had seeped into the wooden boards, soaking through the grain. She was certain if she sawed one of these boards in half it would be black and bloody all the way through.

She was about to stand up when a voice said, "Rebeka, it's really you. How did you get here?"

She turned slowly, the voice making her tremble. "Jason!" She rose and rushed into his arms.

46

FIRST THERE WAS only a dun-colored blur and the wind rushing through his ears. Then the second explosion blew him sideways, farther over the border. The canopy billowed out, almost collapsing from being on its side. He pulled on the lines, compensating as best he could. A hail of melted plastic bits struck him, burning briefly before spiraling away. He ducked several chunks of metal, twisted and charred beyond recognition. He was swung around so that, for several moments, he was looking back toward Borz's compound. He thought he saw another parachute, its canopy swinging back and forth, shoved this way and that by the wind currents. Then a shell exploded below, something tore through the canopy, and the chutist began to fall. The figure seemed too small to be a man, but he was too far away to know for certain. Then he was twisted around again, and he lost sight of the falling chutist. He struggled briefly to turn around, to see what had happened, but his own chute was caught by the crosswinds, and in any event, he was almost down.

Here came the Kurds, surrounding Bourne, stripping him of his harness, lifting him up, pressing him with barrage after barrage of questions for which he had no answers.

Three times a week, Abdul Aziz took the long, meandering walk through the crooked streets, bustling markets, and back alleys of his beloved Istanbul. Three times a week, he looked forward to getting away from the hectic pace of his import-export business, the incessant yammering of his two sons, who seemed to constantly be coming up with postmodern upgrades, making his mind swarm like a beehive. Without being able to take his pleasure at his favorite Istanbul hammam, he was quite certain he would have had a breakdown years ago.

Not that he didn't love his sons—they were smart, maybe too smart for their own good. The week after they moved the company's telecom to an Internet company, he had come back to the office on Monday to find that $50,000 of overseas calls had been made from his numbers but by no one in the organization. Kazakh hackers had rerouted the numbers to high-toll call sites from which they took a percentage. "This never would have happened if we'd stayed with our over-the-air carrier," he'd told his chagrined progeny. Worse, the Internet telco refused to reimburse them for the fraud. Aziz promptly switched the lines back and, to teach them the hard lesson, took the fifty thousand out of his sons' salaries month by month. Praise Allah that he'd stopped them from moving the company's most sensitive material online, where some clever hacker could have gotten to it. Slowly but surely they were learning that in the business they were in going postmodern cyber wasn't always wise. When it came to security, it was often true that old-school methodology was the best way.

He was just entering the hammam's front door when his mobile buzzed. Ignoring it, he passed into the cool, dim interior. He was immediately greeted as a preferred customer, as though he were part of the family that had run the hammam for almost a century.

As he was beginning to disrobe in the locker room, his mobile buzzed again, seemingly angrily this time, though he knew that to be impossible. Just as angrily, he took it up, was about to turn it off, when he saw who the call was from.

"*As-salamu alaykum*, my friend," he said.

"*Wa alaykum as-salam*," Bourne replied at the other end of the connection.

Aziz, who had worked with Bourne before, possessed a kind of sixth sense when it came to his friend. "How serious are your difficulties?"

"I'm on the other side of the border from Kobani."

"*Hayyak Allah!*" May Allah grant you life! Aziz cried. He knew better than to ask why Bourne was on the border between Syria and his country. The truth was he didn't want to know, not unless Jason needed him to, though he fervently hoped that was not the case. He was all too familiar with the horror hanging over Turkey at its border with Syria—disruptions in his shipments was the least of his woes. "You are injured?'

"I'm fine," Bourne said.

"You would say that even if you were bleeding to death. Please tell me."

"I'm okay, Abdul. I swear," Bourne said.

"On the lives of those you love?"

"Yes."

"All right then," Aziz said, mollified. You never knew with Jason.

"I need your help," Bourne said.

"Anything, my friend," Aziz said, thinking, There goes my afternoon's peace.

"A plane would make things right—as right as is possible at the moment."

"Give me your GPS coordinates." Aziz copied them down on a pad he withdrew from the inside pocket of his suit jacket. "Good, there's a new military airfield not far away just outside Suruc. I'm sure you can commandeer ground transport from your current location."

"No need. Since I've given the coordinates of the ISIS units assaulting Kobanî I've got hordes here who will be happy to take me."

"I'll need twenty minutes for the fueling and fifty more to get to you."

"Thanks, Abdul. I'll be waiting."

"Until then," Aziz said, "*fi Aman Allah*." Allah protect you.

Bourne spent the time until Aziz's plane arrived to work on the meaning of the word *albedo*, the third cluster of Sumerian glyphs in Boris's rebus. The scientific definition of *albedo* was "the light or solar radiation reflected off the surface of a planet, such as Earth, or a moon," but Bourne was reasonably certain science had no role to play in Boris's message.

What else could *albedo* be or stand for? For several moments he grew concerned that radiation was the answer, but the thought of the Russian president using nuclear weapons in his invasion made no sense—even for a madman. There would be nothing left of the country he wished to bring back into the Federation fold, not to mention nothing left of the Federation itself when the Western allies retaliated, as they were sure to do.

He pictured the entire rebus—the four sets of glyphs: the first was the date, thirty-three hours away, the second, *Follow the money*, the third, *albedo*. Or was it? With a jolt Bourne realized that he had mistranslated the word after he had deciphered it from the female Sumerian. The third group wasn't *albedo*; it was *tewahedo*, a Ge'ez word meaning "One United Nature" as in the Eritrean Orthodox Tewahedo Church, one of the breakaway Oriental Catholic religions. *Tewahedo*.

Bourne knew the High Eritrean Orthodox Tewahedo Church was in Asmara, the capital of Eritrea. That was where he was headed next. The vehicle had stopped at the airfield's gates, where a rapid-fire conversation ensued between one of the Kurds who had taken Bourne under their wing and the guard. Bourne thought they might have been cousins. They were talking about an upcoming party of some kind. Eventually, they were waved through with a nod and a smile.

Above him, he could hear the drone of Abdul's private jet, a silver bullet streaking through the sky. The Jeep slowed, then stopped beside the runway.

Here comes my ride, Bourne thought, his hair caught in the mighty downdraft.

47

SARA PUT HER forehead against Bourne's chest. It was then she knew something was seriously amiss. With a lover's unerring instinct, nothing felt right—not the muscles, not the heartbeat, and certainly not the smell.

"What—?"

But it was too late. The needle slid into the side of her neck, and everything around her began to melt. She tried to push herself away from the imposter with Jason's face, but she seemed to have lost the ability to move her limbs. She was caught as her legs gave out, and laid gently down on the blood-smeared stage floor.

She stared up at Bourne's face. It wasn't Bourne, but the uncanny resemblance dizzied her. She was fully conscious, but she was paralyzed. He's shot me up with Rohypnol, one of the prime predator drugs, Sara thought as if from a shadowed place where she was drowsing.

As he straddled her, he said, "How does it feel now, to be utterly helpless?"

She was aware of the silence around them as a physical thing out of which his voice loomed over her like a stone tower. The shelling had ceased, at least for the moment. But paralyzed as she was, this interruption in the war was in its way worse than the assaults themselves; it forced her to feel the fear flooding through her, growing into a beast beyond her control.

"I allowed Bourne to slip through my fingers. He was here and now he's gone. But not to worry, I'll pick up his trail soon enough." He bent close enough for her to smell his breath, rank as a flesh-eating animal's. "But now I have my consolation prize; one beyond measure. You're here with me now, dearest Rebeka. We're together."

He reached up and, one by one, removed the prosthetics, the colored lenses, wiped his face of the theatrical paint that had helped maintain the illusion of Jason Bourne's features rather than his.

"And now here I am, revealed to you at last."

Revealed as the man who had bumped into her in Moscow, the man who had pilfered her gold Star of David on its chain, had buried it in the bloody mess he had made of Boris Karpov's throat.

Ivan Borz. But even that wasn't his real name—not by a long shot. He had more legends than she did. She wanted to ask him, but her lips were beyond her control.

As if he had heard her, as if he had crept inside her brain, he leaned over and whispered, "Not Ivan, not Borz. You and only you, dearest Rebeka, will know me by my real name, Radu Ozer, birthplace unknown, likewise parents. An orphan in the storm, in other words. I count myself lucky, not having parents. I have no wish to see people grow old, feeble, and die."

He began to unbutton his shirt. "Homeless and homicidal, that was me, burned my foster family's house down with them in it. That was in Carpathian Romania. You know those stories you heard about Romanian mothers? They're all true. Not a drop of compassion; not an instant touching or holding. Romanians bite, though, at least my older brother did until I burned him to a crisp. I stood outside and listened while they screamed. My mother tried to burst through the front door. I poked her back inside with her own broom, a flaming torch she recoiled from, rushing back inside to her doom.

"There was never any danger to me. Any lawyer worth his thousand dollars an hour would trot out all the atrocities visited on me. He would tell the jury that I was justified in what I did, and he'd probably convince them. People are such sheep, don't you think? The truth is I enjoyed every minute, watching that house burn, knowing they were in there, flesh curling back from sinew and muscle, fat turning to liquid while the rest blackened was for me a kind of ecstasy. And when I forced my foster mother back inside that burning hell I nearly orgasmed."

He threw his shirt to one side, baring his chest. It was dark as an Arab's, covered with a crisscrossed welter of raised scars, white and pink as a little girl's dollhouse. "Like the Arabesque? It was built up over time and space. Think of it as a map of this pilgrim's progress, business deals stretching across the globe in a network like a spider's web.

"My killing sprees stopped abruptly when I stole and embezzled enough money to start my own business. That was the beginning, the metamorphosis from maniacal caterpillar to cutthroat moth. But only the beginning."

Suddenly, there was a knife in his hand. He tapped the valley between her breasts with its sharp point. "I know you'd cringe were you able. But why, dearest Rebeka? Bourne and I are virtually the same: we're both high-functioning sociopaths. Not too many of us on this rarified level, and you're drawn to us both."

He laid a stroking finger against her jaw. "What does that say about you? You're as homicidal as the rest of us. You murder on command. If I hadn't stepped in, speeding the demise of General Karpov, you would have been given the order. Sooner or later, your paths would have crossed, and he would be dead. So we're all in this sandbox together. We all have the same expertise, we all play with the same toys. We know how to take a life and go on with our lives until the next savage bloodletting."

His grin grew broader. "You know I'm right, even if at the present time you can't say so. But in the end, we're told time and again, we will all admit to our sins. The grossest of lies. I have committed no sins. Like you, like Bourne, I have lived! That's the sum and substance of it. I live; others die. Isn't that how life works? Of course it is.

"I had expected you sooner because recently wherever Jason shows up, sooner or later so do you. That was the sole purpose of Karpov's murder. Bourne would follow the breadcrumbs, as he always so cleverly does, and you—you, my dear, would be right on his heels, yes? Of course you would! I stole something precious to you, I used that thing to turn you into the murderer you are." His laugh sounded sharp-edged, metallic. Weaponized. "I mean, who's the terrorist here, me or you?" He spat sideways. "I could have killed you there in the streets of Moscow, Kidon, but that would have been too easy. You wouldn't have suffered, and, after all, suffering is what this thing between you and me is all about." His nostrils flared, as if catching her scent. "I waited for you in Cairo, but you didn't come. I had almost lost hope. When I saw you descending through the clouds and smoke I couldn't believe the lengths you had gone to find him."

His smile had about it a bone-chilling tenderness. Like a psychopath feigning compassion the sight was incongruous, dislocating. "Which brings us to the main event: the two of us. Many things I can forgive, *yakirati*." She shivered internally at his use of the Hebrew endearment. "But you made an unforgiveable transgression—you cost me money. A great deal of money. You made me look bad. As a consequence of your meddling my business suffered. It took me some time to regain the full trust of my clients."

Sara seemed submerged in a tub of ice water. She was so cold her bones seemed brittle, about to snap with any harsh treatment. She had no choice but to stare up into the face of the man she had almost killed, whom she had subsequently encountered on the crowded Moscow streets, when he had deliberately run into her, when he had stolen from her that which was most precious. The thought of her beloved star in his possession was like a twist of a knife in her side, in a place she could not reach to pull it out.

He ripped open her shirt, placed a knife blade between her breasts. There must be a way out of here, said the joker to the priest. She was sure Bob Dylan never envisioned this literal iteration of his metaphysical lyrics, but here she was, the joker talking in her mind to the priest looming over her.

"There's no hope for you," he said. "You'll never leave here alive."

48

ROHYPNOL, LIKE ALL predator drugs, was a central nervous system inhibitor. Its main antagonist, outside of a countervailing drug, which was unavailable to Sara, was adrenaline. Part of her Kidon training included methods of hyperadrenalizing her body in preparation for a termination and/or escape. Hyperadrenalizing was not without risks. It could, for instance, lead to bleeding out, which almost happened to her in Mexico City when Bourne felt sure she had died. Still, it was either risk a brush with death or allow herself to submit to whatever atrocities Radu Ozer had in store for her. In any case, she did not know whether the metamorphosis could be actuated with the Rohypnol in her system.

And so, as Ozer slit her skin, dipped the tip of the blade into her blood, she began. The transformation commenced deep inside herself, in the medulla of the adrenal glands. Adrenaline was, among other things, a neurotransmitter, firing the ends of sympathetic nerve fibers, stimulating and increasing the speed of nerve impulses.

Unable to close her eyes, she was forced to watch the blade score a line in her flesh.

"What shall it be, hmm?" Ozer said. "Shall I imprint you with the cross of Jesus?"

She withdrew to the part of her that was still and serene, her limbic system, the brain's most primitive and highly defended area. A place that was always and forever her own. Once in her fortress, she gathered herself in a form of deep aggressor meditation, which seemed counterintuitive, almost oxymoronic, until her teachers had proved to her its efficacy. Venturing outward, she made her way, carefully skirting the sections of her system already taken hostage by the Rohypnol molecules. Her adrenals began their pumping. She had some difficulty pushing them into overdrive as they had already been invaded, and were sluggish. But once she got them going they responded.

"Or with the Star of David, branding you the Jewess that you are."

Ignoring his taunts and the mounting pain, she felt the first faint glimmerings of movement in her fingertips. She blinked—her lids responding to her commands. She felt the epinephrine's warmth seep into her bones, and then into her muscles and soft tissues. She felt the epic battle raging inside her between the epinephrine and the Rohypnol for control of her central nervous system. All at once, her lips curved up into a half smile. Ozer was too busy watching her blood run red to notice.

"Blessing for you. I would take you now by force as I've done with so many others. But I would not sully myself, Jewess. You're an animal."

She could not feel the pain; she felt only the river of heat running through her, the accelerated pulse, the galloping of her heart, seeming to ragefully hurl itself against the cage of her ribs. But it was a cool rage, one where her mind was perfectly lucid, where now one thought connected to another in a gossamer skein that lit up her mind in glittering strands.

When Ozer's head came down the better to incise her, she reared her head up and bit him. Once her teeth had sunk into his lower lip she shook her head violently, tearing away skin, flesh, and nerves.

Ozer was so stunned that his own blood had filled his mouth before he was released from the stasis of shock. By that time, Sara had jammed a thumb into his left eye, pushing hard through the jelly, popping the eyeball, destroying the retina, her nail digging into the tender flesh behind, the membranes that separated the eyeball from the brain.

An eerie screaming arose, as of a nocturnal beast in the agony of rutting, which, in some, was a form of ecstasy. Not here, not now. Not with Radu Ozer. His agony was unadulterated as he reflexively swung the knife, but she snatched it from his grip. She could have plunged the blade in, blinded him in both eyes, but that would have defeated her purpose.

As he spasmed and tremored with the onset of real physical shock, Sara flipped him over on his back, straddled his hips. She brandished the knife still running with her blood.

"Perfect for slicing, Radu," she said with a grim smile. "I know your history with women, I know who's the animal here. So come here, animal. This is where *I* fuck *you*."

Turning, she pushed the tip of the blade through his trousers' crotch, widening the opening, then drew the blade lengthwise across his member with agonizing slowness.

Ozer howled, did his best to crawl away from her, but he was finding it difficult to move, let alone move quickly. He left a bright trail of blood behind him as he inched his way across the floor.

She watched him for a moment, as if he were a particularly loathsome insect, then she went after him. Taking a handful of his hair, wet and greasy with his sweat, she brought his excruciating slither to a halt.

"It hurts, Radu, doesn't it?" She held his member up in front of him. "But, you know, I think with all the mayhem this has caused over the years, you're better off without it."

She studied the elements of his face, twisted in agony or slack in shock. "Cry havoc and loose the dogs of war." She tossed the pink and red thing aside. "That's what you've done, Radu." Her fingers in his hair turned to a fist, and she shook his head violently. "No, no, no sleep for you." She slapped his cheek, bringing back the color shock had drained from it. "Keep your good eye open, Radu."

She inched closer to him. He tried to slither away, but she held him fast. "Your good eye needs to fix on me, Radu. I am the dog of war your actions have loosed. You see me and you see your own end."

Holding up the knife, she said, "Now it's your blood running down its edge, and there will be more before I'm finished with you."

His lips twisted in a horrific parody of a smile that was more a grimace of escalating pain, now that the pain-inhibiting endorphins released at the trauma site were fading. "*You're* going to interrogate *me*?" He tried to laugh, almost choked on a clot of blood before he managed to spit it out. It lay on the floor between them, a symbol of the end of days.

Sara rose, brought the knife down, piercing his boot and instep to the hilt, pinning him securely to the floor.

She buttoned her shirt as she strode toward one of the video cameras. Her chest was sore and blood streaked. Dark imprints were beginning to sprout on the fabric, shadows pushing aside the sunlight.

Positioning herself behind the center camera, she switched it on. She watched through the viewfinder as what was left of Ozer tried and failed to wrench the blade out of his foot. He was impaled, sure enough, an insect in an entomologist's lab.

Satisfied, she started recording. Then she went behind the plastic barrier to the control room. Twenty seconds of scanning the equipment gave her full access to the control boards. She had seen them before, even worked them when she was a teenager.

She hit the Live Feed button. From this moment on, whatever Ozer said or did would be streamed out to the YouTube stations this facility was connected to. Then she went back to the stage, bringing a chair with her, sat just out of the range of the live video camera, but in range of the boom mic, which she positioned midway between where she sat and where Ozer lay.

"Welcome, viewers. Here lies Ivan Borz—the real Ivan Borz, not one of his fakes. He has admitted to his real name: Radu Ozer, but who really knows. A liar falls so deeply in love with his lies they become the truth. Human beings are experts at self-delusion; they rarely do anything better."

She was about to continue, but a tall, slender man appeared in the doorway, "*Subhanallah*, I finally convinced ISIS to stop the shelling, but I—"

He stopped in midsentence as he took in the bloodily macabre scene. He advanced into the studio section, killing the On-Air switch on the camera. "What is going on here?"

"El-Amir," Ozer said, but then could not find the strength to go on.

Sara rose, turned to El-Amir. "*As-salamu Alaykum.*"

"*Wa alaykum as-salam.*" He nodded curtly. "What have you done to Ivan?"

Sara smiled, holding her ground. "You're Amira's brother, aren't you?"

"And who are you?"

"Rebeka."

"She's the worst of Mossad," Ozer managed. "Kidon."

El-Amir's eyebrows lifted. "Is this true?"

"What I am," Sara said seriously, "is a woman the man you call Ivan Borz tried to kill."

"Don't listen to her," Ozer said. "She's insane. She has me confused with someone else."

El-Amir hesitated, clearly caught on the horns of a dilemma.

"Who to trust, El-Amir? The predator or the prey?" She turned so he could see the needle mark on the side of her neck. "He injected me with Rohypnol."

"Then how are you standing? How are you talking?" His arm swept out. "How did you do—*that*—to him?"

"She's a witch, that's how." Too late, Ozer realized he'd given the game away.

El-Amir turned. He had a sidearm Sara had not seen before, and she tensed. He removed the Walther PPK, stepped up onto the stage, and shot Ozer in the head at close range.

Then he beckoned to Sara. "Walk with me."

He led her out of the studio and into the first building she had explored. Too hastily, it turned out. He threw back the corner of a threadbare carpet, revealing a trapdoor.

"How is Amira?" El-Amir asked. "She must be having a difficult time without Father."

Sara was unsure at this point whether to tell him that his sister was injured. "She told me the monthly money you send makes a difference."

"Good, good." He nodded. "I'm pleased." Then he frowned. "But you're bleeding through your shirt."

"It's nothing."

"Here, let me." He carefully unbuttoned her shirt. "Allah, this isn't nothing. Stay there a moment." He crossed to a line of shelves, took down several items. With them, he disinfected the cuts, slathered on some antibacterial cream, then bandaged the area.

"Thank you," Sara said, rebuttoning her blouse.

Waving away her thanks, he lifted the trapdoor by pulling on a heavy iron ring, led her down a short flight of wooden stairs, into a basement of sorts.

"She misses you terribly," Sara said. "She wishes you would return home to Cairo."

"Ah, one day," El-Amir said with a wistful smile. "And, if Allah wills it, may that day be soon."

"You'll make her very happy."

"Little Amira. She deserves that."

A tamped-down dirt floor was almost a quarter sand, shifting under her feet as she followed El-Amir across the space to a prison cage.

"I need your help here, Rebeka. A woman's touch, yes?"

Inside she saw a man, hunched over, emaciated, his tangled hair and beard overgrown. He was filthy and he stank, but the uniform he wore was still recognizable.

"British SAS," Sara said.

"A liaison officer." El-Amir nodded as he opened the cell door. "The planned next in a long line of televised beheadings." He lifted an arm. "See what you can do for him."

"You first."

El-Amir shrugged, stepped inside. Sara followed him warily. The prisoner's head came up, his rheumy eyes focused.

"No," he said in a cracked voice.

The hairs along Sara's forearms stirred uneasily, and she turned too late. El-Amir struck her a dizzying blow to the side of the head, knocking her down.

A moment later, El-Amir was outside and the self-locking cell door slammed shut in her face.

49

THE FIRST PART of the flight out of the Turkish air base was exceedingly difficult. A great deal of expert maneuvering by Abdul's private pilot was required to ensure their continued safe travel. They were shot at, tracked by hostile radar, and even, once, made the target of a missile launch, which failed, killing the two men at the launch site when the warhead exploded in the launcher.

Bourne was impressed by both the pilot's skill and his nerve under fire, and did not hesitate to tell him so. Following the first forty or so hairy minutes, the flight proceeded without incident, giving Bourne time to fill Abdul Aziz in on the increasingly dire situation: In thirty hours the Sovereign of the Russian Federation would order the full-scale invasion of Ukraine, possibly provoking a third World War. Boris had discovered the plan, which featured the secret arming of ISIS as a distraction for the Western powers, to keep their military eye away from Ukraine. Further, the Sovereign had been utilizing the criminal monies amassed by Ivan Borz to clandestinely fund ISIS. Which meant that Borz and the Sovereign had formed some sort of relationship. And why not? The Sovereign could hardly entrust the recruiting for ISIS to anyone in FSB—particularly Boris, who would have flat-out refused. How many others might have done the same? Far better to go outside the Federation political structure altogether. Who better than Ivan Borz, who doubtless had been arming ISIS for a fat fee? Following that logic path, Borz would already have a secure relationship with ISIS's upper echelon. They would trust him. But what had the Sovereign offered Borz that would attract him? Money? The Sovereign didn't have any to offer. What else would Borz find attractive? Something more valuable than money? But, of course, the promise to allow him free reign in his other dealings, even when they entailed Russian armaments. And all the while the Sovereign was slipping millions out of Borz's pocket via Mik. Bourne's lips curled into a smile.

Abdul was in shock, as well he might be. At length, he said, "It's interesting that the Sovereign would resort to skimming money, rather than using the Kremlin oil dollars," he said. "It must mean that the Kremlin's cash hoard has been compromised more severely than is publicly thought."

"True," Bourne replied. "The Sovereign is out of money. He had no other choice. The Federation is skating on thin fiscal ice, the expansion into Ukraine and, from there, the Baltic States is a desperate attempt to refill those coffers, to put the Federation on stable financial footing."

Abdul nodded. "Makes sense. For a decade or more the Sovereign has milked the oil trade and raked in billions. Now that's all slipping away at breathtaking speed."

"Now that the price of oil has plummeted by almost more than fifty percent, something drastic had to be done. Money had to be extracted from all the dirty crevasses the Sovereign had heretofore ignored."

"He stole and stole big from one of his main moneymen." Abdul tapped his forefinger against his armrest. "That would mean the involvement of Bank Rossiya. Do you know of it?"

Bourne shrugged.

"You're in the majority there, Jason, almost no one does. I know a bit—just the tip of the iceberg because I dealt with one of the

Sovereign's cronies. I was paid through Bank Rossiya. It happens to be the Sovereign's personal bank, that's all I know. That's all anyone outside that tight circle knows."

"Maybe not. You have a sat phone?"

"Of course." Abdul reached into the side pocket of his seat, handed over the phone. "Should I go up front?"

Bourne waved away his words as he punched in a number.

"It's Bourne," he said when Volkin answered.

"Not now, Jason. I'm on my way to Sheremetyevo to pick up Aleksandr's body."

"My sincere condolence, Ivan, but I need your help and time is of the essence."

Bourne could hear the sigh even through the sketchy sat phone connection. "All right then."

"I need information on Bank Rossiya."

"You're speaking of the Sovereign's personal bank as well as that of his despicable Kremlin inner circle." Just like Volkin not to ask questions he knew Bourne wasn't going to answer. "It was built during the Sovereign's early days in St. Petersburg, when he was KGB. Even then he had friends and cronies in high places. I know; I was there. I saw it all unfold. I saw how they were gaming the system. No, no, they were rewriting the system itself. That was the genesis of my life in the underworld." He made a noise that sounding like spitting. "In any event, this cabal built Bank Rossiya, and they run it currently."

"Where is it? St. Petersburg?"

"This I don't know. No one does outside of the Sovereign and his circle."

"Come on, Ivan. A bank—a bank with international ties—can't be hidden."

"This one is." Volkin sighed again, more deeply this time. "You know, it's Russia, Jason. Anything's possible, especially when it comes to the secretion of money."

"Thanks, Ivan. Now go take possession of your grandson."

"One other thing, Jason. It's just a rumor, so take it . . . Well, you know what rumors are like here."

"Tell me anyway, Ivan."

"The rumor says that Bank Rossiya is low on capital."

"How low?"

He could almost hear Volkin shrug. "Who can say? And, anyway, maybe the rumor's false."

"Anything?" Abdul asked as Bourne gave him back the phone.

"Not much," Bourne said. He told his friend what little Ivan Volkin knew about Bank Rossiya.

"No help. If we can't find it . . ." He let the sentence peter out. No use saying the obvious. Taking a judicious look at his friend, he rose, said, "I'm going to congratulate the pilot. His wife just had a baby boy."

Bourne nodded absently as Abdul went up the aisle to the front of the jet. He was thinking about what Volkin had let slip. If the rumors were true, if Bank Rossiya was low on capital, then they were barking up the wrong bank. With that possibility in mind, he sank back into the quiet space where he could once again concentrate on Boris's rebus.

The Sovereign had put an end to Ivan Borz's luck. Bourne could do the same to the Sovereign's, if he could decipher the entire rebus. *Follow the money*. There was only one way to stop the invasion: Turn off the money spigot at the source. Find the bank, access the account. Bourne was certain he knew where the bank was. Now to decipher the fourth and final group of cuneiform glyphs, which must be a number combination that gave access to the account itself.

The bank the Sovereign was using to fund his dirty asymmetric war couldn't be Bank Rossiya itself—that would be too direct. Plus, if the rumor Ivan had passed on was true, the Sovereign wouldn't want it to be associated with these particular monies. The more Bourne considered the situation as the Sovereign might have done, the more certain he became that the absolute secrecy of the plan required a secure cutout bank. It needed to be an obscure one, with an appetite for the Sovereign's business. It also needed to be located in an obscure place where no one would think to look. And there was *Tewahedo*, the third glyph of Boris's rebus. The High Eritrean Orthodox Tewahedo Church in Asmara, the capital of Eritrea. The perfect obscure place.

"Businessmen," El-Amir said with contempt. "In the end, they're all alike: soulless and greedy. You have done me a great service, softening him up for the kill. I fully agree with you that Borz got what he deserved."

"Radu Ozer," Sara said, gripping the bars. "That's his real name."

"So I've heard." El-Amir shrugged. "Shit by any name stinks just as badly." Eyeing her closely, he frowned. "Are you all right? You look a bit shaky? Yes? Okay, then. Onward.

"I had been racking my brains as to how to get rid of Borz. The ISIS bombardment was what I came up with; always use someone else to do your dirty work. That's the way we work in the TV and film biz, eh? But in retrospect the bombardment was like using a shotgun to kill a mouse: brutal but inaccurate. Now, because of your—and I must say magnificent—work, all it took from me was a bullet to the head."

"A hunter stalks its prey and then kills it. A coward traps his prey, and as it tries to gnaw its paw off to free itself, stands over it and puts a bullet in its head."

"Either way, the prey dies," El-Amir said, the insult seeming to slide off his reptilian hide. "The prey doesn't care which one ends its life—hunter or coward. The result is the same."

"But the coward knows who and what he is," Sara said. "The result for the living—"

"Is life," El-Amir finished for her. "And that, my dear Rebeka, is the point." The smile that gradually appeared on his face was dreamy, sugarplums already dancing in his head. "Allow me to enumerate what killing Borz has given my life, now that I am alive and Borz is dead. I now have command of eight battalions of troops fully committed to Allah, their numbers growing by leaps and bounds every week thanks to my many-pronged social media recruitment campaign. I have control of international arms shipments, of skids of American weapons drop-shipped to the Kurdish rebels, a flow of American dollars, along with connections to the Mexican cartels, the Albanian mafia, and the opium khans of the Golden Triangle. And oil—let's not forget the oil fields we now control."

He threw his arms open wide. "All this is mine now. Because of you."

"You don't want this life, El-Amir," Sara said. "Why would you embrace this gross distortion of Allah's teachings?"

"I am being lectured on the precepts of Allah by an *Israeli*? Really?"

"Israelis and Arabs are not so very different, El-Amir. We're all Semites, after all."

"With very different views on the future of the Middle East."

"What will Amira say?"

"My sister is an idiot."

With that flat statement, Sara understood the depths of the brainwashing El-Amir had been subjected to. She understood that wherever he was—standing out on a windy precipice—he was never coming back. What had to happen now was a catastrophe. It would surely break Amira's heart. But it could not be helped. You cannot reason with faith—or the semblance of faith, which by definition was a stranger to reason.

"Bourne," she said. "He was here."

"He was," El-Amir said. "I was going to broadcast his beheading all across the world."

Sara's breath caught in her throat. "But you didn't."

"Sadly, no. Other circumstances intervened."

"Where is he now?"

"Bourne? Flown away. He stole our helicopter."

Seeing in her mind's eye the helo hit by the ground-to-air missile, she felt a sick feeling come over her. No, no, no, she thought. There's still a chance . . . "Which way did he go? Did you see?"

"North. Toward the border with Turkey."

Sara gripped the bars with white knuckles to keep herself from collapsing in despair. Jason gone. It couldn't be, it just couldn't. Maybe it was another helo she had seen explode, but she knew there were few of them in this area, and in her heart she knew he was piloting it when it was hit. *Dear God, please save me.*

He peered in at her, mistaking the origin of her sorrow. "Rebeka, Rebeka. Did you really think I would go back with you to Cairo?"

With a Herculean effort she gathered herself, pushed her intense grief into the background. She still had work to do here. "There was a time—only minutes ago, when I thought you were still Amira's brother—when I hoped you would."

"But you see now that could never happen." His laugh sounded like nails on a blackboard. "I'm a true believer, Rebeka—or whatever your real name is. *Tawakkaltu 'ala Allah.*" I have put my trust in Allah. "When I do return to Cairo it will be in the company of my brothers in arms who have swept away all trace of Western corruption. All will be as it was before the first invasion of infidels. We will return to Allah that which belongs to Allah. This time, the sea will not part when we drive the Israeli terrorist nation into it. You will all drown as we curse your name. *La hawla wa la quwwata illah billah.*" There is no strength or power except Allah.

It was at that point that Sara's eyes rolled up in her head, and she collapsed like a marionette whose strings have been cruelly cut.

50

IT WAS THE fourth and final group of glyphs that was giving Bourne fits. He knew it must be a string of numbers. Could it be SWIFT coding? SWIFT coding, used by all banks worldwide, secured money transfers across international borders.

As he showered and shaved in the jet's compact but lavishly equipped bathroom, he continued to dissect the problem. But he kept circling back to one inescapable fact: the glyphs made no sense as numbers. In fact, as Bourne had painstakingly translated them, he could make no sense of them at all. And now his time had run out. Abdul's plane was descending, making ready to land at one of the two runways at tiny Yohannes IV International Airport, shared with the equally tiny Eritrean air force.

Back in his seat, clad in an expensive suit and Italian loafers his friend had thoughtfully brought, he fastened his seat belt, closed his eyes, and allowed his mind to rest, hoping his subconscious would work out the solution as they landed, taxied along the runway, and came to a stop. Abdul, who was staying onboard, working from his mobile office, knew people at customs and immigration—as he did in nearly all countries with which he did business—and had arranged for Bourne's swift and unimpeded passage through the arrivals terminal. After changing some money into Nakfa, the local currency, and purchasing a beautiful and costly Italian leather briefcase at the one upscale concourse shop, Bourne emerged into Asmara's mild Steppe-like afternoon. Bronze sunlight fell over the Art Deco and Italian Modernist buildings of the old city, remnants of several wartime Italian occupations.

On the rattling taxi ride into the city, the glyphs kept forming and re-forming in Bourne's head. One of the words must surely be *communicate* or *communication*, which could mean anything. On the other hand, the definitive translation still eluded him. Until, that is, the taxi passed the fortresslike facade of the Caserma Commerce Bank of Eritrea, and he had the driver pull over. After paying him, he retraced the taxi's route until he stood in front of the entrance to the Caserma Commerce Bank. The building was immense, the architectural design making it look innately heavily defended. It seemed like a place for spooks, like the headquarters of the NSA.

He trotted up the limestone steps, went through the glass doors, into the marble-clad interior that must have been dreamed up by some Italian madman, all swirls and curlicues.

A dark-skinned young man in an impeccably tailored suit stood up from behind a console, stepped over to where he was standing.

"How may we assist you, sir?" he said in British-accented English.

Bourne handed him a business card identifying him as Fyodor Ilianovich Popov, second vice president of Gazprom, the Russian state energy company. "I am seeking a word with your director. What is his name again?"

The functionary could not help but risk a glance at the briefcase Bourne was carrying, and, being well trained, instantly assessing its worth and, thus, the worth of this prospective client, said, "Mr. Gebre Tesfey, sir."

Bourne snapped his fingers. "Just the one I was told to see by First Minister Savasin."

That name spoken caused the functionary's eyes to light up like a Hollywood premier. Still, he could not help inquiring, "May I ask the nature of your request?"

"Surely," Bourne said. "On behalf of Gazprom, I wish to establish an account of a sizable amount."

This answer fulfilled the incipient smile on the functionary's face, as well as his hopes that this rather boring day would turn into a stellar one. "But of course, sir! I will contact Mr. Tesfey at once. We here at the Caserma Commerce Bank are determined to meet and exceed all your banking needs. And allow me to add to that end we have direct linkage with both Citibank and Deutsche Bank worldwide."

Briefly, he returned to his console, punched in a four-digit extension on his phone. A short conversation ensued, after which the functionary hung up and, raising an arm to indicate Bourne should follow him, said, "I am directed to escort you to Mr. Tesfey's offices forthwith."

Forthwith, Bourne thought. These people were caught in a time warp.

As he ascended in the private elevator in the far left corner of the bank, he thought again of the fourth glyph grouping. The translation that had eluded him was neither "communicate" nor "communication." It was "commerce."

"What is this?" El-Amir said.

The British SAS officer rose and, on shaky legs, went over to where Sara lay, examining her. "There's a new puncture mark on the side of her neck."

"Borz shot her up with Rohypnol."

The officer looked up at El-Amir. "Then how was she standing on her feet, let alone talking coherently?"

"Borz said it was witchcraft."

The officer grunted. "Well, whatever she's done to herself has caught up with her."

Sara began to spasm, her back arching up, foam riming her half-open lips.

"Well don't just stand there," the officer said. "For God's sake help her."

"You'll be dead in an hour," El-Amir said. "What do you care?"

"I care because I'm a human being," the officer snapped. "What the hell are you?"

El-Amir glared at him for a moment. "Get back," he ordered, and the British officer crept to the rear of the cell. El-Amir opened the cell door, stood staring down at Sara, still convulsing, said, "She's going to die. It must be only a matter of minutes now."

"What inhuman form of life *are* you?" the officer said.

El-Amir fastidiously hitched up his trouser legs, squatted down beside Sara.

"Good God, man!" the officer cried. "Do something, otherwise she'll choke on her own tongue!"

"For a Kidon agent," El-Amir said, "that sounds appealing."

Sara's eyes snapped open. She drove her stiffened fingers in under his sternum and, as he rocked back, breathless, she kicked his legs out from under him. At once, she was atop him.

Her right arm drew back, she thought of Amira, of her promise. But then she thought of Jason, ripped away from her, she thought of this man's heinous beliefs, the dreadful acts he had committed in the name of Allah, and, like a piston, her fist hammered directly down into his sternum, fracturing it. The second blow drove the bone fragments into his lungs.

He stared up at her, wide-eyed. His mouth opened and closed with only a distant, strangled croak audible.

"Drowned in your own blood," she said. "In death as well as life, faithful as a dog, you have followed Ozer."

"Good afternoon!" Mr. Gebre Tesfey said, coming around from behind his supersize polished wood desk. "Gospodin Popov, is it?" He spoke with the overpolished heartiness of a cruise director.

"Fyodor Ilianovich."

"Indeed, indeed!" Mr. Tesfey agreed. "Thank you kindly!"

"My pleasure."

The two men shook hands as if they were old school chums. Mr. Tesfey gestured to a sitting area on the other side of his football-size office. "Please." He brought over with him a buff-colored file. The two men sat, Bourne on an ultramodern Italian leather chair, the bank director on a matching sofa. They were served coffee so dark it was almost black, and small, flat almond cakes.

Mr. Tesfey waited until he had poured them both coffee and offered Bourne the plate of cakes before he said, with hands reverently placed on the folder that he expected would mark the beginning of a long and lucrative relationship, "It is my privilege to personally serve clients such as yourself, Fyodor Ilianovich." He presented the cruise director's microengineered smile. "Tell me how I can be of service to you, your company, and the Federation."

Bourne tapped the empty briefcase at his side. "We wish to establish an initial deposit of fifty million dollars, American."

With some amusement, he watched the blood drain out of Mr. Tesfey's ascetic face, then, moments later, rush back up in profusion.

"My dear Fyodor Ilianovich." He opened the file on his lap. "It would be our pleasure to open an account in the name of Gazprom." Unscrewing the cap of a Montblanc fountain pen, he began to fill in the uptake form as quickly as he could, as if he expected this fantastic windfall to vanish at any moment. "With the ruble losing value twenty straight weeks in a row it certainly makes sense for Gazprom to open a sizable account here in American dollars."

"The account won't be in the company name," Bourne said.

Mr. Tesfey's writing hand paused, pen coming off the form as he looked up. "I beg your pardon. In the name of what entity shall we open the account?"

"The entity, as you put it, Mr. Tesfey, is not a what—it's a who."

"What?" Mr. Tesfey swallowed. "Please forgive me, but your desire is for an individual to open an account here in the amount of fifty million American dollars?"

"Now you have it," Bourne said with a wide smile, as if he were pleased with the director's quickness.

The director nodded. "I assume this person is you, Fyodor Ilianovich."

"Hardly. You will open the account in the name of Llewellyn Beers."

Mr. Tesfey scarcely seemed to be breathing. "And who might this gentleman be? Is he perhaps still downstairs?"

"I wouldn't think so," Bourne said. "Llewellyn Beers does not exist."

The director sat back, frowning. Bourne could see the fear in his eyes that the windfall so recently his was beginning to slip through his fingers.

"Fyodor Ilianovich, I confess I do not understand your rather, ah, unorthodox request."

"Unorthodox it may be," Bourne said, "but surely it isn't unprecedented."

"I don't—" Mr. Tesfey's frown deepened. "I'm not sure I understand your meaning."

"Let's stop beating around the bush, Mr. Tesfey. I know I'm not the first Russian national who has opened—how shall I put it?—a black account."

"But you are. I have been director of this bank for more than seven years, Fyodor Ilianovich, and I can assure you without fear of contradiction you are the first and only individual of any nationality who has made this request."

Bourne, who had the director's number from the moment they sat down, knew he wasn't lying. This wasn't the cutout bank the Sovereign was using. How had Boris's rebus steered him wrong? Either his deciphering of the Sumerian glyphs had failed, which was unlikely since he had been accurate with the first three groups, or he had incorrectly interpreted the rebus. Either way, he was at the wrong place at the wrong time.

Dead end with less than twenty-eight hours left until Russia invaded Ukraine.

51

YOU DON'T LOOK good, if you don't mind me saying so," Lieutenant Jock Southern said.

"That's a good one." Sara laughed heartily just before she passed out on top of El-Amir's corpse.

Ignoring his all-body pain, Southern went to her, his knees cracking as he knelt. Two fingers on her carotid confirmed she was still alive. Her pulse was slow but strong enough. But he had no strength to lift her up. Rolling her off the corpse, he tried to drag her back to the wooden slab on which he had tried to sleep for four nights. Too soon he was out of breath, and for a moment he hunkered down, trying to gather himself both physically and mentally. One step at a time and first things first, as his mum used to say.

Stepping over the bodies, he exited the cell, went up the stairs, into the house proper. Bars of sunlight slanting in through glassless windows and the huge rent in one wall made him half-close his eyes. He felt a headache start up like a faulty engine. Foraging in the kitchen, he found water and a tin of tea. He brewed himself a cup and, while it was steeping, removed food from the refrigerator. Then he sat at the oval table, spooned a lot of sugar into his tea, drank it while he ate a bit of cold couscous and congealed bastilla. He did so slowly and sparingly. Apart from some water with a fistful of dead mosquitoes floating on its surface, he hadn't had much in the way of sustenance in more than four days by his possibly inaccurate accounting, and his stomach must be seriously shrunken.

When he felt energy flooding back into his system, he drank some more, took some sweets in his mouth, letting them dissolve. Then he rose and returned to the basement cell. Sara was still unconscious, but her breathing was steady. Bending, he picked her up off the floor and, carrying her in his arms, slowly and painfully brought her up out of the subterranean cavern and into the half-ruined building. He found a piece of furniture to lay her down on, then took pillows off the floor, shaking them free of glass shards, and propped her head up on them. Overcome with a wave of vertigo, he perched himself on the edge of the cushion. His heartbeat was elevated; he needed to slow his system down. He did this by staring at her face, concentrating on each feature one at a time, describing them to himself in the most detailed terms.

After several deep breaths, he felt at least a semblance of calmness. His vertigo faded and, at length, vanished. He tried to feed her the sweetened tea, first wetting her lips with a fingertip he dipped into it, then, as her reddened eyelids began to flutter open, allowing her a tiny sip.

Still, despite his care, she began to choke. At once, he sat her up, held her to him as he circled her back with the flat of his hand, almost as if she were a baby. Anxious moments passed. Then he felt her head move against his shoulder.

"God."

She shuddered so hard he thought she was actually going into spasm, but it subsided soon enough.

"God, God, God..."

"You're okay now." He detached himself, held her at arm's length so he could look into her eyes. "Rebeka, you're okay."

"Yes." A faint, watery smile. "Yes, I am."

"The Rohypnol must have caught up with you." He studied her face, as he had when she was unconscious. "What the bloody hell did you do to fight it off?"

"Did you ever see yogis—real yogis—walk on red-hot coals or lie on a bed of nails?"

"In fact I have," Southern said. "When I was a teenager."

"Same thing," Sara said. "More or less."

"I could've used some of that over the last four days."

Sara's eyes started to lose focus, and Southern slapped her cheek hard enough to startle her awake. "Here," he said, handing her the glass of tea.

"It's always tea with you Brits, isn't it?"

"Mother's milk." He grinned. "That's better, isn't it?"

When she nodded, he held out his hand palm up. "I found treasure."

Sara's eyes opened wide. "Chocolate!" She popped a square into her mouth, chewed as it began to melt. "Mmm. Manna from heaven." Then she gave a deep sigh as she began to come fully back to herself. She regarded him critically. "Hell, you look like shit, Lieutenant."

He laughed. "I must stink like it, too."

"No comment." She held out her hand, and he gave her more chocolate.

"The good news is I feel a ton better than I look."

She grinned as she devoured the chocolate. "A reprieve from a beheading will do that to you."

"Right. No bad news at the mo, except we're smack-dab in the middle of a hot war zone. A shower, shave, and a change of clothes will do me up right."

"No time for any of civilization's niceties," Sara said, feeling more herself with every tick of the clock. She rose. "We've got to find a way out of here before ISIS troops get here, otherwise we'll—"

"Don't even say it," Southern said with a shudder. "One threat of a beheading is more than anyone should face in a lifetime."

They went through the house, looking for weapons, but apart from several carving knives from the kitchen found nothing of use.

"Outside," Sara said. "Borz's men are all dead and they were heavily armed."

Together, they climbed through the rubble at the foot of the ruined wall, and were confronted by all manner of semiautomatic weapons, lying beside twisted corpses.

"Speaking of treasure," Sara said. "Here we go."

Which was when they were caught in a withering cross fire.

Poor Mr. Tesfey. The crestfallen look on his face when Bourne rose and excused himself without making that fantastic deposit was classic. However, Bourne had no time to worry about anyone else's disappointment. He had his own to contemplate.

Time was fast running out. If he couldn't find the hidden bank the Sovereign was using to fund his horrifying war, the resulting worldwide conflagration would be catastrophic. He put his head back against the seat as the taxi took him back to the airport. There were two other international banks in Asmara, neither of which had the word *commerce* in its name. Nevertheless, Bourne had dutifully visited them, repeating the stage show he had put on for Mr. Tesfey, both with the same result.

Dead end.

Bourne closed his eyes. "*So now I will show you the glyphs while I pronounce them in Russian*," Boris had said that year's-ago day in the Jerusalem café, "*and, naturally, you will memorize them as I draw them. Finally, we will each write a cipher for the other to decode. A game, if you will.* Our *kind of game. And like all our games, one with the possibility of deadly consequences.*"

Bourne wondered whether at that moment Boris could have had any intimation of just how deadly this one would become.

And then he sat bolt upright as another fragment of that same conversation rose into the forefront of his mind: "*And, of course,*" Boris had reminded him, "*there's always the false group hidden somewhere in the message in the event a hostile figures out the cipher key.*"

The moment Bourne had left, Mr. Gebre Tesfey stood looking at a door in his office he had hoped never to open. But now he knew he must. Using a key, he unlocked the door, stepped inside. As he pulled the door shut behind him the lights came on and the electronic antisurveillance system was activated. Three months ago, a cadre of workmen had outfitted this windowless room. It had taken them three days, working fourteen hours a day. Mr. Tesfey knew this for a fact; he had been required to be present in his office the entire time. When they were finished, they left as mysteriously as they had come. They never once talked to one another—at least when he was in earshot—he had no idea of their nationality. Just as well, he thought now as he crossed to a desk, unlocked the lower of the two drawers. He did not know the nationality or even the identity of the man who had contacted him by phone, the man who had arranged everything, including his ten-thousand-dollar-a-month stipend. That money guaranteed two things: the first, that Mr. Tesfey never, ever ask questions or seek to discover the man's identity. He was about to fulfill the second condition.

Inside the drawer was only one item: an encrypted mobile phone sent to him by international courier the day the workmen left for parts unknown. The mobile was always plugged in to an outlet in the rear of the drawer, ensuring the battery would never run down.

Mr. Tesfey was disturbed to discover his hands were moist as he gripped the phone, that his upper lip had grown a thin, itchy line of cold sweat. Unplugging the mobile, he punched in a three digit code. As if it were alive, the mobile sprang into consciousness, automatically dialing an overseas number.

"Yes," the man at the other end of the line said. It was both a greeting and a question.

"He was just here," Mr. Tesfey said.

"You're quite certain?"

"He claimed to be Fyodor Ilianovich Popov, second vice president of Gazprom. Is that his real name?" The moment he asked the question, Mr. Tesfey knew it was a mistake.

Silence.

"Hello? Are you there?"

Mr. Tesfey's blood ran cold. The line was dead. He fervently prayed the same wouldn't soon be said of him.

"So the third group—the one with the oblique reference to Eritrea—was a false clue," Abdul said when Bourne returned to the plane.

"That's right, and I fell for it."

"Don't blame yourself, Jason. You couldn't know that Boris was using a double-blind cipher."

"The point is I *should* have known the moment I saw the Sumerian glyphs."

"Forget regrets. Forward," Aziz ordered. He held out a small plate. "Have some halvah."

"Abdul."

"What? It's sesame—brain food. Every good Arab knows that."

Bourne popped a square into his mouth, sat chewing it slowly while he wrote the Sumerian cipher down on a ruled pad provided by his friend. He pointed. "See, here, the first grouping is the date—tomorrow—when the invasion is set to begin. I can only think that ISIS is preparing a major assault—possibly on western Turkey—to coincide with the Sovereign's troops pushing across the border in Ukraine."

"The Western powers will be paralyzed. They won't know which way to look first. There will be chaos in the United Nations and the EU, with politicians and diplomats debating endlessly on what response to make."

"Precisely the point," Bourne said. His pen point moved to the second group. "Here, Boris writes, *Follow the money*."

"And the third group is when you ran into trouble."

Bourne crossed it out. "It's the double-blind, in case the cipher fell into hostile hands and was cracked."

"So that leaves us with the fourth group," Aziz said. "Logically, it would be the account number and security code."

"Yes, and the third group would translate as the name of the bank. But, as we've seen, Boris wasn't being logical. The double-blind is much too clever for that." Bourne considered for a moment. "More often than not it's an inversion."

Aziz pursed his lips in concentration. "Meaning the three active groups don't follow in sequential order."

"Correct," Bourne nodded. "Added to that is the fact that the fourth group doesn't translate into a number string as it would if it were the account number."

"Then what does it translate as?"

"That's the central enigma Boris has left me." Bourne tapped the pen point on the paper underneath the fourth group of glyphs. "Maybe I've been looking at this the wrong way."

"How d'you mean?"

"I've been assuming that all the information I need is right here in the cipher."

Aziz nodded. "That would be logical." His brows lifted, his eyes brightened. "But, as we now know, this cipher doesn't follow a logical course."

"Right," Bourne said. "There are three necessities for this bank: it needs to be officially unconnected with Bank Rossiya, but, preferably, with some back-channel proximity in case of emergency; it needs to be hidden away somewhere out of major banking centers."

"Like Asmara."

Bourne grunted. "That was the brilliance of Boris's double-blind. Asmara appeared to fit the bill, even down to—" He broke off, his eyes going out of focus.

Aziz became alarmed. "Jason, what is it? You look like you've had a stroke."

"A stroke of luck, maybe." Bourne's attention snapped back to his friend. "Listen, Abdul, the third and maybe most important necessity was that the bank the Sovereign chose had to be in need of a big account like his."

"Money coming in, going out in odd amounts and at odd times." Aziz nodded. "I understand."

Bourne's eyes were alight with a strange passion. "Where in this part of the world would fulfill those requirements better than any other?" He didn't wait for his friend to answer. "Cyprus."

Aziz snapped his fingers. "That's right! Cyprus's banking system almost failed less than two years ago. The IMF bailed them out—at least to some extent—but the infrastructure has been in desperate need of a substantial capital infusion since then."

"Now the island is home to banks from Greece, Lebanon, Jordan, Eastern Europe, and—"

"Russia!"

"Just so. Let's go on the premise the bank we're looking for is domiciled in Cyprus and see where that leads us." Returning to the fourth cipher group, Bourne stared long and hard at his translation in this new light. The last section of the rebus was still withholding its secret.

"The first two glyphs translate as 'shore bird,'" Bourne said. "The third is 'fair.'"

"I'm no expert on the language," Aziz ventured, "but that fourth glyph doesn't look Sumerian at all."

"That's because it's written backward."

"Why would Boris do that?"

"In this rebus a backward word means it's to be ignored." Bourne scribbled the word "fair." "The backward glyph is 'air.'" He put a line through the last three letters, leaving only the "f."

Aziz shook his head. "I don't understand."

"Here, look. 'Shore bird.'" Bourne wrote the word "gull." Then he added the "f" left over from the third glyph.

"Gulf?" Aziz said uncertainly.

"Yes. The shore bird is a gull."

"Hold on a minute." Aziz turned to his laptop, checking foreign banks in Cyprus. "There are three banks with Gulf in their names: Gulf Friends Bank, Lebanon and Gulf Bank, and—"

"Omega and Gulf Bank."

Aziz's head snapped around, staring at him. "How did you know?"

"Because I was right. Boris was counting on my knowing the bank's name all along." He told Abdul about Omega + Gulf Agencies in Doha, where friends of his had been held captive last year. "I had assumed the company was owned by Borz, but now I suspect he was only a minor partner. Omega and Gulf is owned by the Sovereign."

52

"DOWN!" SARA SCREAMED, and when Southern didn't move fast enough, she grabbed him by the belt, dragged him down beside her, behind a Jeep that looked like it had seen better days. She had gathered two semiautomatic rifles and now, with bullets whizzing over their heads, striking the metal shell of the Jeep, she offered him one.

"I'm an officer of Her Majesty's Armed Forces liaising with our American cousins, not a fighter."

She jammed the weapon into his chest. "Well, pretend for a moment you're an American and shoot the shit out of anyone who comes toward you."

As she began to scuttle away, he said, clearly alarmed, "Where are you going?"

"To find out who's shooting at us."

"It has to be ISIS."

"Lieutenant, the gunfire is coming from two opposite directions. It's not just ISIS bullets that can air us out." She looked at his white, pinched face. "We're almost out of this. What d'you Brits say, 'Keep calm and carry on.'"

"Actually, we never said that during the war, but no worries. It's entirely appropriate." His face darkened. "But, listen, before you go."

"Please don't tell me to let your wife and kids know you love them. They already know that and, besides, you aren't going to die."

He barked a laugh. "I've never married, I'm afraid. And you're right, my partner knows I love him." He shook his head. "But, listen, I overheard Borz talking on a sat phone. He spoke in Russian, which I don't know, but one word stood out: 'Vankor.'"

Sara frowned. "'Vankor? Never heard of it."

"Me neither." He shrugged. "But I thought you should know." He grinned suddenly, and it was like the sun had emerged from behind clouds. "Now go. I'm counting on you to save both our arses."

Sara sprinted away, and was at once submerged in the fog of war: particulates of churned-up dirt, larded with sticky droplets of coagulating blood, bone chips, bits of viscera, fistfuls of hair, tossed like grass clippings. The stench of death was inescapable, as well as the smells of cordite, overheated metal, the ozone-like scent of air burned by constant, rapid gunfire.

She made it to the corner of the second building without being hit. Inside, she found a crude wooden ladder that rose vertically to a trapdoor in the ceiling. Pushing through it, she found herself in a makeshift rooftop observation post. From her eyrie she could see for miles. The black-clad ISIS troops were arrayed to the south, while to the north a triple line of Kurdish freedom fighters were slowly advancing toward her position.

But now she could see that the Kurds had been joined by what must be outside forces. She counted two tanks, accompanied by a squad of soldiers in what were either British or American camo uniforms. When she heard the telltale *whup-whup-whup* of a military gunship quickening from the border to Turkey, she realized how she and Lieutenant Southern were going to get out of this war-torn hellhole.

She turned, on her way back downstairs to tell him the good news, when she ran right into a pair of ISIS advance scouts: Two pairs of implacable eyes, one muzzle of a semiautomatic rifle stuck under her chin, and she thought: Fuck!

Abdul Aziz's jet was refueled and ready to go. Peering through one of the Perspex windows Bourne could see the pilot striding across the tarmac toward them from the terminal. He was three-quarters of the way to the plane when he was shot dead. He fell facedown on the tarmac, unmoving, having been struck three times simultaneously.

Aziz pulled his head up from his laptop screen where he had been surveying their choices of routes to Cyprus. "What just happened?"

"We need to get out of here now," Bourne said, rising from his seat.

Aziz glanced out the window, saw his downed pilot and the cadre of Army troops advancing across the tarmac toward them. They had weapons raised and looked ready to fire the instant anyone started the engines.

"Jason!" Aziz shouted, tearing himself away from the terrifying scene. "What has happened? Where the hell are you going?"

Following Bourne up the aisle, he hurried into the cockpit. Bourne was already strapped into the pilot's chair, going through the final checklist the pilot had on a clipboard. "We'll never get out of here," he said. "Besides weapons on the ground leveled at us, we haven't logged a flight plan. The control tower in Cyprus will never give us permission to land."

"I don't need their permission." Bourne was throwing switches. Lights came on, dials sprang to life, quivering. "There are only three or four flights a day in and out. I'll take my chances."

"But what about the soldiers?"

He was about to get his answer. Bourne started the engines, and almost immediately the firing commenced.

"The chocks!" Aziz cried.

"I kicked them out of the way before I boarded. Now sit down and strap yourself in, Abdul. It's going to be a bumpy ride."

"If one of those bullets hits a fuel tank..." Now Bourne was hearing his friend through the com system, along with excitedly angry chatter from the tower.

"Think positive," Bourne said as he pushed levers forward and the jet began to taxi down the runway. "And pray to Allah."

As they gathered speed along the runway, Bourne saw an armored vehicle, no doubt borrowed from the adjacent military base, lumbering into his path. He gritted his teeth, increased speed to max, gave the jet maximum lift and pulled back on the lever.

Wheels up! he thought. Had he left them down seconds longer they would have been impacted by the armored vehicle.

"We're airborne, Abdul."

He no sooner said that then he saw the plane descending toward him on an intercept course.

Sara raised her hands over her head. As the ISIS terrorist gestured with the muzzle of the rifle he'd held under her chin, she slammed the edge of her hand into his throat with such force she sent him tumbling back down the ladder headfirst.

The second shrouded figure was savvy enough not to swing his rifle around in such close quarters. Instead, he whipped out a WWII American Army Ka-Bar—a formidable weapon in hand-to-hand combat no matter what decade they were in.

He lunged at her—a quick and vicious strike meant to rip apart her belly. Instead of moving back, as he had anticipated, she moved into his attack, allowing the blade to pass by her left side as she brought the power of her combined fists to bear on the side of his head. He staggered against her, and she kicked his back leg out from under him. He was so far extended he could not recover his balance and, as he tipped over, flailing, she ripped the Ka-Bar out of his grasp, buried it to the hilt in the soft triangle of tissue where the neck met the shoulder. He went down and stayed down. What breath was left him was soon extinguished.

Peering down through the hatch in the ceiling, Sara could see the first man hadn't moved. No wonder. His head was at an unnatural angle.

She climbed down, made it back across to where Southern was dutifully waiting. By this time fire from the gunship was no doubt causing the advancing ISIS front line to fall back. She wondered how long before they regrouped and came again. Apparently, the weapons operator was thinking the same thing. The gunship let fly an air-to-ground missile. Moments later, there was a flash like a thousand lightning bolts striking in concert, the ground shook, and the percussion rang in their ears.

Sara put her lips to Southern's ear, said as loudly as she dared, "That's our ticket to ride. Move out, Lieutenant."

Together, they broke cover. Zigzagging, she led him due north directly into the flight path of the gunship. The pilot must have spotted them, because the gunship tilted left, homing in on them.

Sara began to wave, realized she and Southern still carried the semiautomatic rifles she had picked up, was about to drop hers, when she heard Southern yell, "Bugger all!" from just behind her.

Turning, she saw he was down on one knee, holding the back of one thigh. Blood oozed from between his fingers.

"I've been shot," he said superfluously, but then people tended to say foolish things when they had received a direct shock.

Out of the corner of her eye, Sara saw the gunship bearing down on them, weapons bristling. Ignoring the ball of ice forming in the pit of her stomach, she threw down her weapon, hauled Southern up, and bending down, hoisted him across her shoulders. Her knees threatened to buckle under the weight, but drawing strength from her *hara*, her lower belly, she staggered on toward the gunship.

And, ironically, it was Southern getting shot that saved them from being torn to pieces by small-arms fire from the gunship. Instead of being mistaken for active hostiles, they were mistaken for noncombatants, fleeing the conflagration. That lasted only until the gunship was close enough, and the crew saw that they were Caucasians.

A nylon rope ladder was unfurled, one of the crew clambered down, took the lieutenant off her shoulders. And then everything fell in on her. The last, lingering effects of the Rohypnol, which her body had been fighting for hours, the utter shock of being held captive, tortured by a man who looked like Jason's twin, the savagery of her response, the fact that she had not—could not—honor Amira's promise to keep her brother safe, and, deadliest of all, the nightmare of Jason's death. She collapsed against the bottom rung of the ladder, sobbing, all strength, all hope gone.

From somewhere far away from the helo's incessant racket, she heard someone calling her name. At first, it seemed like a dream, and she ignored it because she could not endure another instant of false hope. But gradually, as the voice grew nearer, she tilted her head up, squinting and shading her eyes from the whirlwind downdraft. The crew member had taken Southern back up into the gunship. She assumed he had returned for her, but as he reached the end of the ladder, she saw it was someone else altogether, someone she knew well.

He reached down a strong arm and with an unthinking, automatic gesture she took it, swinging off the ground as he hauled her up against him.

"Rebeka," Dov Liron, head of her Caesarea unit, said, "sometimes even you require a bit of help."

And, leaning heavily on him, she climbed rung by rung up the ladder.

Bourne banked the jet hard over left. The other plane banked right, but Bourne could tell that with him ascending and the other descending they were too close: their wingtips would come at each other like crossed swords, sending both aircraft pinwheeling, plunging into the ground.

"What's happening up there?" Aziz said in his ear. "We're clear of the runway at least."

Bourne had no time to answer. He stood Abdul's jet on its left wing, so the aircraft was perpendicular to the ground. A moment later, the other plane flashed by, a near miss—too near, by far.

"Allah preserve us!" Aziz said, and then in a stricken voice, "I think I'm going to be sick."

"Calm yourself, Abdul. The worst is over. Just sit tight for a few more minutes." Bourne kept the plane in a steep climb, leaving all that was of danger to them behind. Gradually, he brought the aircraft back to level.

For some time, he heard nothing but the plane around him, which was, in itself, reassuring. It's when you didn't hear sound, when you didn't hit air pockets, that you knew it was time to be concerned.

"Abdul, have you worked out our flight plan?" he called. "I have an initial heading, but it won't be long before I'll need a definite waypoint."

Not long after, Abdul appeared. His face was chalk-white and his legs appeared rubbery. "This is not the sort of flight to which I've grown accustomed."

"Couldn't be helped." Bourne indicated the fold-down jump seat. "Take a pew."

"Where's my prayer rug when I need it?" Aziz said mournfully as he settled his buttocks on the narrow seat. Then he shook his head. "What d'you think happened, Jason?"

"One of the three bank directors I saw today must have called the wrong people—for us, anyway."

"Any idea which one?"

Bourne took the flight chart his friend had painstakingly written out, adjusted the heading accordingly. "My money's on Mr. Gebre Tesfey, but it doesn't matter who made the call. What interests me is who he called."

"Any thoughts on that score?" Aziz inquired.

"That's the problem," Bourne replied. "I've got too many."

53

ANGELMAKER THEY CALLED her, and Angelmaker she was. It was Timur Savasin, the first minister himself, sitting beside her in the commercial airliner, who had dubbed her, much as a king dubs a knight for extraordinary services rendered, and in so doing gave rise to a legend.

When Timur Savasin advised the Angelmaker of a commission, he asked her to "take care" of the offending creature, much as a supervisor would dispatch a nanny to an upper-class family home. Her bones were made—in literal fashion—when she took care of an avaricious up-and-coming *silovik* who had become something of a thorn in Timur Savasin's side. She lured this know-it-all into a honey trap, in the parlance of the shadow world, to a dacha away from the center of Moscow Savasin used for such purposes, fed him poison in glasses of champagne he guzzled after liberally availing himself of her considerable charms. The poison, part of an apothecary of more than five hundred it was believed the Angelmaker concocted herself, literally melted the skin and flesh off the offending creature's bones.

"Pig," was all she said when Timur Savasin arrived to drink in the successful outcome of her commission. And then she took the first minister right there on the dacha carpet, riding him bare-chested, very much like the Sovereign riding his horse.

Now, in the midst of a different kind of commission, she was an entirely different person. She was, in fact, the very paradigm of a major modern executive, clad in an oyster-gray Armani silk suit, sensible, low-heeled shoes, and a chiffon scarf tied loosely around her neck. Her hair, which in other circumstances could turn into a wild mane, was pinned sleekly back into a prim and proper bun. She wore diamond studs in her pierced ears and a simple gold wedding band on the third finger of her left hand. She was subtly made up to look a decade older than her real age, and almost plain. She had, in short, dialed down her natural charms to a bare minimum.

For his part, the first minister was attired casually but ever so elegantly, freshly shaved, the skin of his cheeks pink, his hair recently cut and coiffed in the European manner. He wore a matching wedding band. Were they president and vice president of a prestigious conglomerate? Husband and wife? Who could say? No one, as it happened, because no one gave them so much as a second look.

Her current commission was one she carried out each time the first minister traveled abroad on business that was not strictly official. On these infrequent trips there was no alarmingly large posse dictated by the Federation trailing after him. She was his sole companion, bodyguard, assassin. He would trust no one else, not even his string of seconds-in-command, to both guard his life and his secrets. Sadly, in this increasingly complex world, one had to trust someone, sometime. Given that, Timur Savasin had chosen someone who was not only supremely adept in all matters relating to coaxing death out of even the most hairy situations, but whose allegiance was never in question. Years ago, before she had become the Angelmaker, but after he had assured himself that her potential would eventually be fulfilled to his satisfaction, the first minister had done the Angelmaker a service of such desperate consequence to her that he was assured beyond any shadow of a doubt that she was, body and soul, bound to him for life.

The little chime rang out in the interior of the aircraft and the pilot came on advising them to stow away their tray tables and return their seats to the upright position and telling them that they would be landing in Nicosia, Cyprus, in twenty minutes. Then he announced the local time, and both the Angelmaker and the first minister adjusted their wristwatches accordingly.

It seemed altogether appropriate that their first meal in Nicosia should be at a restaurant along the Murder Mile, otherwise known as Ledra Street, for centuries the city's main shopping and eating thoroughfare that ran north-south through the walled Old City. The street got its nickname in the latter half of the 1950s, when colonialists were often shot to death here by nationalist fighters seeking to end the British rule.

Today, in the blue-gold coolness of the Mediterranean early evening, the former Murder Mile was as calm and serene as a bustling concourse could be. Even though indigenous businesses were in the process of being overrun by Starbucks, McDonald's, surf shops, and all other manner of Americana exported to the world, which Muslim extremists of every stripe bitterly resented and fought against, Ledra Street still retained its distinctly Cypriot flavor. As in most all of Cyprus, particularly in the often disputed north, the mark of the Turk was in evidence almost everywhere.

Every country had its battles, Timur Savasin thought as he savored a retsina, its piney resin taste bitter-tart on his tongue. In Cyprus it was the Turks who engendered animus among the fiercely independent locals.

They had gone directly to their hotel from the airport, checked in as Mr. and Mrs. Blaine, of the Sussex Blaines, unpacked, showered, dressed in more casual clothes, as befitted the Cypriot lifestyle, and then sought out a restaurant that had been recommended to the Angelmaker. By whom, Timur Savasin did not know, but since all her recommendations turned out to be stellar, their origins were of no interest to him.

Opposite him, the Angelmaker had eyes only for the pedestrians on the street, the shadowed doorways, the windows that had the best sight lines to their outdoor table, which the first minister had insisted on taking, rather than one indoors, which she had wisely advised.

"There is a time for prudence," he had told her, "and a time for living life."

"I suggest the former," the Angelmaker said in her peculiarly clipped speech, "so you can enjoy the latter."

The first minister smiled, raised his glass of retsina, touching the rim to her glass of tonic water. "Well, just this once, let us enjoy life together as if we were part of the real world."

"I have a job to do," the Angelmaker said. "Please allow me to do it."

"Hmmm." Timur Savasin sipped his resiny wine without enjoying it in the least. How could people drink this swill? he asked himself. Calling a waiter over, he placed his glass on the tray, and ordered a pair of triple vodkas on the rocks. In the meantime, he lit a cigarette, drew the smoke deep into his lungs.

"One hour," he said to his companion. "Is that so much to ask?"

The Angelmaker hesitated for just a moment, then she smiled. Something magical happened to her face when she smiled—what had been deeply, inarguably erotic became irresistible. Though it could never be said of the Angelmaker that she was unaware of her sexual allure, she was never bound to it. Her radiance was entirely effortless, and therefore all the more potent.

"Like a vacation?" she asked.

He nodded. "Like a vacation."

The vodka came, as icy as he liked it, and they toasted again, this time to their sixty-minute vacation, whatever that might entail besides food and a proper Russian drink. Not that the Angelmaker was Russian. She was, in fact, Estonian, a member of a people whose strange and vaguely unsettling language was entirely opaque to him. Much like the

Angelmaker herself. Which he believed was part of her allure. He was aware of only one small sliver of her past, the one he was able to mend for her. Perhaps he could have discovered more had he put his people to work. But he found the thought of others pawing through her intensely private past intolerable. Besides, she was part of his own intensely private life. Anything discovered about her would inevitably lead to him. And so these two remained as sun and moon, a binary system whose components were destined to be neither reconciled nor happy, circling one another in the secretive fastness of the Federation firmament.

Timur Savasin allowed her to order for them; this restaurant was, after all, her recommendation. The quality of the food was her responsibility. With their meal ordered, he said, "How's Liis?"

"You know perfectly well how Liis is."

"Of course. I have someone watching her day and night." He smiled. "But there is some news I prefer to hear from someone who loves her above all others."

She regarded him for a moment—one of her patented enigmatic expressions that so thrilled him. Until the Angelmaker, he had never met a woman he found unfathomable.

"She's just been made soloist in the Company." She meant the New York City Ballet.

"I imagine congratulations are in order."

The Angelmaker laughed, and it was like sleigh bells in the snow of a Christmas morning. "If you mean the three dozen pairs of toe shoes and the bouquet of red roses you sent, I believe you've already taken care of that."

"I'm proud of her."

"You sent the gifts in my name."

"What of it?"

"You don't know?"

"It was an altruistic gesture."

"No," the Angelmaker said. "It was egotistical. 'From your loving sister.' She read me the card."

"Why did she do that?"

"Because it didn't sound like me."

"She could tell that just from that one short sentence."

"You were an only child, weren't you?" She sat back, eyed him again as their food, a deluge of little plates, cold and hot, all fragrant, was set down in front of them.

He smirked, nothing more than a defense. She had his number—why couldn't he get a handle on hers? "I know from experience that gifts don't always make you angry."

She took up a fork, speared a bit of octopus ceviche. "I'm not angry. Disappointed, perhaps."

He was genuinely at sea. "By what?"

"That you didn't tell Liis who the gifts were from. She would have appreciated—"

"I don't want her thanks," he said a bit too coldly.

"I already conveyed her thanks."

"You never should have told her about me."

"Not tell her about the man who rescued her from the Albanian mob? Who got her psychiatric help for the anguish those fucks put her through—"

"Those fucks, as you so colorfully put it, are no longer among the living."

"It was important for Liis to know that. It would have meant the world to her to meet you."

"We've been down this road too many times," the first minister said. "What I did... It was personal, part of my other life only you are privy to."

"Fine," she said. "She knows who sent her the toe shoes and the flowers. She's very grateful."

He said nothing for a time. There was a point, at the very beginning, when rescuing the Angelmaker's younger sister was nothing more than a means to an end, but latterly he had come to realize that Liis's continued well-being contained meaning for him—meaning he never suspected would exist. He wondered about this, just as he wondered what the Angelmaker was to him. Her official duties were simple enough, but then there was the hidden side, as if she were a human black op.

Thoughts like these caused him to pick at his food. He didn't like any of it, especially the octopus ceviche she seemed so fond of. His mouth watered for a steak, thick and bloody, or, failing that, a rack of veal.

"You don't like that kind of attention, do you?" the Angelmaker said.

"In my world it's too often unhealthy."

"My God, FM, she's half a world away—safe in the arms of New York City. You ensure that."

"Stealth and prudence—two words I live by."

The Angelmaker put down her fork, having apparently lost her taste for the octopus. "Which brings us to why you're here." She never inserted herself into conversations regarding these clandestine field trips. It was as if she was invisible or didn't exist.

"So the vacation's over."

"As far as I can see it was just the right amount of time."

He nodded. Sometimes—and he was at a loss to understand this—he felt good bending to her will. Better than good, actually. He felt a stirring in his loins, an ache, which was so inappropriate he encouraged it to its full extent, until he had to shift in his seat because of the pain of his phallus against the crotch of his trousers.

"Anything the matter, FM?" Her full lips were half open, shining as if with the thinnest coating of saliva. "Something I can help you with?"

He said nothing, even when her shoeless foot slipped between his thighs and her exceedingly talented toes, in concert with the ball of her foot, began to stretch his trousers to the limit.

"It's you who should have been a ballet dancer," he murmured with half-closed eyes. "Such talent shouldn't go unnoticed."

"Is it unnoticed now?"

All Timur Savasin could do was groan softly through bared teeth.

54

ARE YOU TELLING me he's alive?"

Dov nodded. "So far as we know. Some of these Kurds here on the ground took Bourne in a Jeep to the military air base just outside of Suruc, north of here."

"It was definitely him."

"The man who skydived out of the helo seconds before it was hit. Yes."

Sara's heart turned over. She could feel it pumping new life into her. She and Dov were on the ground at a Kurdish base some miles beyond the border. The makeshift hut they were in was hastily constructed of stones, wood planks, waxed muslin, and God alone knew what other odds and ends. They sat facing each other on upended empty ammo crates. Beside her was a mattress that smelled as if it were stuffed with straw. It was covered in old, raggedy blankets and on it sat a hull pillow. To Sara, it looked like a little bit of heaven.

Lieutenant Southern had been airlifted by his people to a hospital in Istanbul. Sara had found their parting bittersweet, which was almost always the way when you spent time with someone under fire. This had been one of those odd times when she regretted not telling him her real name, but in the field there was, of course, no choice. She was Rebeka, and would always be to him, the angel whom he had saved and who, in turn, had saved him. There could be no stronger bond between two people.

"Where did Bourne go from the airfield?" she asked now. She was not going to call him "Jason" in front of Dov; their relationship was none of her boss's business.

"None of the Kurds know. But as they were leaving they saw a private jet coming in to land. It's likely he boarded that."

"Any markings?"

Dov waggled his head. "Sara, please. Right now, we need to concentrate on you, not Bourne."

It's the same thing, she almost said, but, biting her lip, didn't. She was appalled at how close her emotions were to the surface. The belief that he had died had harrowed her beyond anything she had ever known, and this both elated and frightened her.

"From what little you've told me, you've been to hell and back."

That I have, she thought, unable to keep Jason out of her head. He resided there now like every other part of her.

"Ivan Borz is dead," she said. "The wildly successful ISIS recruitment campaign has ended." Overcome by another bout of vertigo, she fell silent, head down. She massaged her temples with her fingertips.

"Despite the disaster in Cairo, you've made the mission a success. That's all that matters."

"You're wrong about that," she murmured, unable for the moment to speak any louder.

"The Director is furious," he said. Either he hadn't heard her or else he thought she was semidelirious.

"I can imagine."

"He wants you home ASAP." Dov shoved a canteen full of cold water into her hands. "Drink," he said. "Water's the best way to get the residue of the drug out of your system."

She nodded, drank until the canteen was empty. Dov replaced it with another, and she continued to drink until she felt as if she were drowning. "Enough."

He took the canteen from her. "It's not enough, but it'll do for now."

Her head was still down; she was staring at the dirt between her boots, trying to think and not think at the same time. She knew he was trying to read her by her body language, since she'd pretty much hidden her face from him.

"Rebeka, more than anything now, you need to sleep."

"I can't."

"Regain your strength."

"No time."

"Otherwise, you won't be of any use to anyone . . ." He paused, sighed deeply. "Including Bourne."

She lifted her head, looked him directly in the eye. There was absolutely nothing in his expression to reveal his thought process.

"There's something else going on. Something bigger than Ivan Borz."

He went very still. He certainly was listening now. "What, precisely?"

"I don't know," she said. "But a lot of people have been killed because of it."

"Don't make me wait too long for the other shoe to drop."

"There's only one person I know who does know."

For the next several, agonizing minutes Dov appeared to be putting his mind through a vigorous debate. At length, he said, "I'll see if the owner of that private jet can be identified, and, if so, determine where it was off to."

She smiled. "Thank you, Dov."

"For what?" He stood up. "I did nothing. Nothing at all." He began to turn away. "In fact, right about now I'm sitting in a café in Tripoli enjoying a Campari and soda, wondering where the hell you are." He grinned at her over his shoulder. "Now get some sleep. Hear me?"

"Yes, boss." With a groan, Sara slid off the crate, onto the bed. She had never felt anything so soft and inviting. She stretched out.

She had not prayed since she was a little girl, but now silent words came to her: *Dear God of our fathers, thank you*.

An instant later, she plunged into a deep and dreamless slumber.

"A bank," Timur Savasin said.

The Angelmaker turned from her contemplation of the view outside their top-floor hotel suite. "Name?"

"You've never heard of it."

She had the sliding glass door partially open. Beyond the rim of the terrace the Mediterranean pulled and subsided against the pebbled shore.

"Is that so?"

"It is," the first minister said. He was in a powder-blue polo shirt and jeans, huaraches on his feet. He felt ridiculous. But then everything about this island was ridiculous. Apart from the Turks, no one took Cyprus seriously. That was the point; that was why the bank was situated here. "No one's ever heard of it."

"And why would that be?"

"Designed to exist under the radar."

Night had fallen, a velvety fisherman's night he would never get used to. The western horizon was stained orange, bloodred. A line of teal divided them. Closer to, lights blinked out on the water, mutes trying to talk to him.

"But you know it exists. Who else does?"

He slid his hands into his pockets. "Why is it you give pleasure but refuse to receive it?"

She smiled. "How do you know that?"

"A man can tell."

"No. You mean *you* can tell." She came away from the door, from the salty slick breeze stirring the chiffon curtains. "That's not the same thing."

He shrugged. "I'm just curious."

The Angelmaker was near enough that he could smell her scent: musk and cinnamon and something more exotic he couldn't place. Her scent stopped him from pulling out a cigarette, even though he longed for the smoke. She did things like that to him.

"If it was simple curiosity," she said softly, "you wouldn't have asked." Her eyes slid away for a moment, as if she were watching the past unreel before her eyes. "My life before you became aware of me was very bad."

"Worse than Liis's?"

"Much, much worse. You've seen me naked."

"Those scars are nothing a good plastic surgeon couldn't—"

"No!"

It was almost a shout, startling him. She never raised her voice, at least not when she was with him.

"The scars are a part of me," she said in an undertone so far removed from her yell the words might have been spoken by another person entirely. "They are what made me who I am."

"I refuse to believe that."

A quirk of a smile played around one corner of her mouth. "The person who made them was an artist."

"An artist of pain." She wouldn't even divulge the gender of her tormentor. How grudgingly she let go of bits of herself, he thought.

The Angelmaker nodded imperceptibly. "That, too."

He found he did not want to take this line of questioning further. "To answer your question, the name is the Omega and Gulf Bank." Because that was what he thought she was aiming at. He was right, but he was also wrong.

"You want to know me, but that's all there is," she said. "You want to see clear through me so you can pin me to the bedroom wall of your underground train. You want another trophy."

"I don't think of you that way," he said stiffly, suddenly defensive. "I never have."

"I know." She laid a hand along his cheek. "You know I'm no man's trophy."

He searched her eyes. "Why do you do what you do? Is it for money, for the privilege this life affords you, is it for the freedom I give you between assignments?" He found himself willing an expression onto her face, a reaction to him. "Or is it only for Liis's sake?"

Her large eyes were of such a deep blue they seemed black in low light, starless. "I do what I do for the pleasure of it. Pleasure is provided by measuring out death in specific doses."

"You can control death, is that what you believe?"

"Death walks beside me every day. Death lays its head down on the pillow next to me each night. Death is here in this suite with us."

"Don't be absurd."

"Extending his benevolent arms."

"Benevolent? Whatever do you mean?"

"Death is the doorway out of pain, suffering, and misery. Death is the beginning of peace, of beauty—and of love."

"You don't really believe that, do you?"

Abruptly, she turned back to the open slider, stepped out onto the terrace, leaned on the railing, staring out at the glimmering water and, beneath her, the beach. When Timur Savasin followed her out, she altered the mood with the tone of her voice. It was clipped again, all business. "What happens tomorrow morning?"

"We go to the bank." The first minister was relieved to return to solid footing. He found the occult, ghosts, personifying death in the form of vampires or zombies, and other such outlandish notions risible as well as vaguely unsettling. "We safeguard it."

"Against what?"

"Unauthorized withdrawals."

The Angelmaker was caught slightly off guard. She gave him a sideways look. "I thought you said no one knows about this bank."

"I know," he said. "The Sovereign knows." He was watching her carefully. He seemed oblivious to the world beyond the terrace, and with good reason. "It's altogether possible that someone else knows."

"Such as?"

"General Boris Karpov."

"Karpov's dead."

"There are people in the world who are powerful enough to speak from the grave. I'm afraid the good General was one of them."

"Perhaps it would be wiser now to speak plainly, FM."

"Somehow, General Karpov found out about the Omega and Gulf Bank. Worse, he discovered its purpose. Worst of all, it seems as if he foresaw the possibility of his own death. Therefore, he went to great lengths to keep his discovery alive."

"How did he do that?"

"By sending it in code to his best friend, Jason Bourne."

"So you foresee the possibility of Bourne coming here."

"Oh, no," Timur Savasin said as he turned back inside. "I *know* he's coming."

55

THE DISTANCE BETWEEN Asmara and Nicosia was 1,415 miles, as the crow flies. It took Bourne three and a half hours via Aziz's flight plan to navigate the distance. The jet touched down just after sunset. The sky was indigo, shot through with orange, bloodred, teal. Bourne heard the plaintive cry of the wheeling gulls as they stepped out onto the tarmac. Aziz was already on his mobile, talking rapidly and excitedly.

"Well, that was fun," Aziz said, finished with his call. He stretched his cramped legs. "Unfortunately, there's no rest for the airsick. As soon as we're refueled and I can hire a pilot I'm off back to Istanbul." He looked chagrined. "As you know, Allah blessed me with two sons, one of whom is an idiot when it comes to his life. He needs me to extricate him from yet another pile of excrement he walked into with his eyes open."

He stepped in, embraced Bourne, loudly kissing him on both cheeks. "May Allah keep you wise and safe, my friend."

"And you," Bourne said. "Thank you, Abdul."

He had the taxi drive him three blocks past the Omega + Gulf Bank. He gave the driver money to wait, got out, and walked back. Though it was dark, the street illuminated only by poles and the lights of passing cars, Bourne was able to make out the details of the building. It was set back from those around it, looking for all the world like a boutique hotel. It took some doing to find the sign, though.

He toured around the two-story building and grounds, noting every detail, including the palm-tree-laden park along one side. Twenty minutes later, he was back in the taxi, somewhat surprised it was still waiting for him. The driver was eating a gyro out of a waxed paper wrap. He offered Bourne half, and Bourne accepted gratefully. Piloting an aircraft did wonders for his appetite.

He asked the driver to suggest a hotel on the water, and, in due course, checked into a new boutique hotel next to the immense Golden Tulip resort. Bourne did not go immediately to his room, but stepped out of the rear of the lobby into the dimly lit bar. He sat at a curved granite-and-pearwood bar at some remove from those around him. Ordering a gimlet, he took in the room, which was perhaps half filled. A murmur of low conversation mingled with the pianist's repertoire of songs he'd never heard before.

"You here on business or pleasure?" the bartender asked as he set the drink in front of Bourne.

"Business," Bourne said. "The Omega and Gulf Bank."

"Huh," the bartender said. He was a Cypriot with leathery skin and a whole lot of crow's-feet around his eyes. "You'll be the only one."

Bourne sipped his gimlet. "How's that?"

The bartender leaned in. "That building's been up for close to a year. No business yet, so I hear. Don't even think the place is finished."

"No one comes and goes?"

"Small group of men from off island." The bartender swiped at the bar top with a cloth. "They come and go now and again, so I hear. Said to be a cleaning crew, but there seems to be some conflicting views on that score."

A customer hailed the bartender, who nodded at Bourne as he drifted away. Bourne finished his drink, slipped some money under the empty glass, and strolled out onto the dining terrace, where every table was full. Broad sandstone steps led to the beach. He needed to detox. Other men went to brothels, or perhaps S&M dungeons, got massages or lap dances, or simply took drugs and slept for eighteen hours straight. Proximity to the sea was what worked best for Bourne.

At this hour of the evening the only people on the strand were young couples, lovers with their sandals dangling from one hand, their shoulders and hips pressed together. Not too many of them, either. He removed his shoes and socks, picked his way down to the water's edge, and let what passed for surf in the Mediterranean rush and withdraw over the tops of his bare feet. He breathed deeply of the salt air and tried to rid himself of the events of the past eight hours.

Time was running out. Tomorrow evening the full-scale invasion of Ukraine would begin, the world leaders would be shaken out of bed, and nothing would be the same again as the Sovereign sought to mold a new world order in his image.

But until the bank opened tomorrow morning there was nothing Bourne could do. In fact, if he were to be honest with himself, he didn't know what would happen after the bank opened. He did not have the code for the Sovereign's account. Without it, he couldn't stop the flow of money to ISIS or turn off the spigot that would fund the Sovereign's expanding war in Eastern Europe. The Sovereign needed ISIS to keep advancing, to keep gaining territory, to keep winning. Without the distraction the terror group provided, the Western powers would turn their collective eye east, they would unite against the Russian Federation, and the Sovereign would have no choice but to withdraw his troops or risk devastation and, worse for him, personal humiliation beyond imagining.

For a time, he sat on the pebbly sand, arms clasped around drawn-up knees, listening to the water lap against the hulls of small boats close by, the rhythmic slap of rigging, the plaintive cries of night birds, the lulling susurrus of the wind. His eyes began to close as his body relaxed, his mind following its lead.

In times like these his thoughts turned to Sara. He wondered where she was, what she was doing. He projected his thoughts to help keep her out of harm's way. Not that she needed any help from him. His lips curled up at the thought, as he tried to conjure her up.

"Anyone sitting here?"

He looked up to see a very beautiful woman standing beside him.

"No one but me."

She sat down next to him, close, but not too close. She wore a loose-fitting ankle-length midnight-blue dress, which she tucked under her as she drew her knees up. She was barefoot, which meant she was staying at his hotel or the behemoth next to it.

"May I ask you a question?"

He turned his head toward her.

"Do you think what I'm wearing is appropriate?" She laughed self-deprecatingly. "For the beach, I mean. I decided to come here at the last minute." She shrugged her shapely shoulders. "Fight with my boyfriend. Only now I don't think I want him to be my boyfriend—or any kind of friend." She sighed. "Anyway, like I said, last minute." That self-deprecating laugh again. "I forgot to pack a bathing suit, and the lobby boutique was closed. Is this dress as bad as I think it is?"

He said nothing. He really didn't want company at the moment, especially someone as attractive and lonely as this woman. But far away, in the darkened recesses of his mind, a bell was tolling.

"Worse, huh?" She picked her head up, stared vacantly out to sea. "Serves me right."

He knew she wanted him to ask, *For what?* Any response would be part of a game he didn't want to play.

She gave him a rueful smile. "Serves me right for coming over here and disturbing your peaceful solitude. What an idiot I am. Sorry."

Rising, she brushed sand off her the back of her dress, momentarily revealing the contours of her buttocks and the backs of her thighs.

"Have a good night." She shook her head angrily. "Wow, that sounded lame."

She walked away from him down the beach, carefully putting one foot in front of the other, as if unsure of her footing. Without warning, she collapsed and didn't get up.

"I'm fine," she said, pushing him away as he crouched down beside her.

Her dress was rucked up, her legs were out from under her, the right one, with its ugly jagged scar running up the outside of her calf, exposed to the knee. She couldn't help seeing where he looked, but instead of pulling her dress down, she let it be.

"I was studying to be a ballet dancer," she said, "but then—" Her arm waved over the scar.

"What happened?" Bourne said.

"He speaks!" She smiled shyly, like a little girl. She couldn't have been more than twenty-four or twenty-five. "Would you like to see the whole thing?" Without waiting for a reply, she drew the dress up her long, glorious legs until the fabric was bunched around her hips. The scar went that far.

"This couldn't have been the result of an accident," Bourne said.

"What makes you say that?"

"It was made in stages, over a period of time."

She stared at him. One moment her large eyes were midnight-blue, the next they were pure black—a trick, he was sure, of the indirect lights from the hotel restaurant terraces. All at once, she jumped up, her magnificent legs vanishing beneath her dress. He rose with her. They stood side by side, not quite touching, gazing out over the sea.

"Have you ever wanted to sail in darkness, on a night like this?"

"I have done."

"Of course you have."

A corner of her mouth twitched up. A dusting of freckles arced across the bridge of her nose. He hadn't noticed them before, but then he hadn't really been looking.

"So tell me how you knew—about the scar, I mean."

"I've seen one very much like it."

"Really?"

"Really."

"Where?"

"On a woman."

"No, I mean where in the *world*."

"In Somalia."

There was still the ghost of a smile on her lips. "What? Pirates, I suppose."

"Pirates, slave traders, terrorists, call them what you will. She was a girl, actually. She looked twelve or thirteen, but with children who have been so abused it's difficult to tell their real age."

When she turned to him her smile had vanished. Her eyes were on him, and they were very still. "And you saw this girl? With the same scar as mine?"

"The wound at her hip was dark and swollen. It hadn't completely closed over yet. There were droplets of blood around the edges."

A certain vibration had sprung up between them, a quivering in the air, as of a swarm of soundless insects.

"And?"

"And then," Bourne said, "I disappeared her."

First Minister Timur Savasin, lounging in the shadows of his hotel room terrace, watched the couple stand with their backs to him as they gazed out to sea. They seemed close as lovers. He felt no jealousy seeing the Angelmaker with Jason Bourne, only a keen anticipation. It seemed to him now that tomorrow was the culmination of a fated life. He was overcome with the sensation, not of déjà vu but of the opposite: that he was meant to be here now, at this very moment, on the shore of Cyprus, watching the creature of his design and Bourne, close enough to have sex or to kill each other. She had taken only the briefest glance at the photo of Bourne, but that was all she needed. She had a knack for taking in entire subjects in the blink of an eye and never forgetting them. Keeping an image from a photo in her head was child's play. Now here they were together. However she had handled the first contact, she had succeeded. He would have been stunned if she had failed.

A frisson of presentiment passed through him then, like a chill ribbon invading a tropical ocean's warm current. With startling clarity, he recalled the Angelmaker telling him that death was in their room with them. Idiotic as that had sounded to him then, he thought he felt death's presence now, as, like him, it watched, godlike from above, its two principal objects of affection.

Time to make some calls. Digging out his mobile, he dialed the first of two local numbers.

"And this girl, this refugee from Somali pirates," the Angelmaker said, "where is she now?"

Bourne's gaze remained fixed on the lights at sea. "Wouldn't it be strange if she were standing here beside me?"

"I don't believe in coincidences," she said dismissively.

"Neither," Bourne said, "do I."

She looked at him again with that curious sideways glance. "What are you implying?" When he remained silent, she said, "Do you know how many complex factors would have to align in order for me to be that girl?"

"A thousand angels dancing on the head of a pin." Into the silence that now arose between them, he said, "You recognized me, Mala. I have no doubt about that. The question is, why are you here at the same time as me?"

“I’m not that girl anymore.”

“No one is the same.”

“You are.” Her dress swirled around her ankles like a sail. “And for the record, I was a good deal older than I looked.”

“That’s disturbing.” He shifted in the sand. “You’ve learned a great deal in the interim.”

“I am wiser as well as older.”

“Mala,” he said, “when are we going to stop playing this game?”

“Why stop something that’s so pleasurable?”

He saw the wisp of a smile play across her lips. Then it was gone. “There’s only one reason why you’re here now,” he said. “You’re working for the Russians.”

“I work for myself.”

“A very specific Russian.”

“Who could that be?”

“Tomorrow is zero hour,” he said.

“Zero hour? That means nothing to me.”

“You know.”

“But I don’t.”

Bourne knew there were many ways to lie; there was only one way to express true ignorance. “Tomorrow—in nineteen hours, to be exact—the Sovereign is going to order his troops into Ukraine for a full-on invasion.”

“You’re hallucinating.”

“He’s been arming ISIS, fueling their advance as a distraction for the Western powers.”

“How could he do that?” she said. “Even the Sovereign couldn’t come up with such a plan. Besides, the committee that runs Bank Rossiya wouldn’t—”

“But he did,” Bourne said. So she wasn’t working for the Sovereign. Who then? First Minister Timur Savasin. “He bypassed even his inner circle at Bank Rossiya. The money is in a secret account at the Omega and Gulf Bank, which he owns.” He turned his head, studying her profile. She was already a beautiful girl when he had come upon her in the Somali camp. But, as a young woman, how she had flowered open.

"You're making this up. The Western powers would never allow such a thing."

"The EU derives eighty percent of its natural gas from Russia. It's getting on toward winter. What do you think will happen when the Sovereign turns off the tap, leaving millions of people shivering in the dark?"

She crossed her arms over her chest.

"In Somalia, after I liberated you, after I shot dead the creature who had marked you over and over as his possession, his slave, his chattel, do you remember what you said to me? How you survived those long months?"

Nothing from her. Nothing at all.

"You told me that you became expert at deluding yourself. You convinced yourself that you were somewhere else, that you were someone else. 'I would have gone insane.' Those were your exact words. That iron will was ingenious, admirable, but now it has worked against you. I was wrong—some people don't change. What is different here than it was in Somalia? You have traded one master for another."

He moved so that he was facing her, his back to the rolling sea and its mysterious winking lights neither of them could decipher. "Mala," he said, "Russia is going to war. It's going to invade Ukraine. You know the Sovereign's stated claim on Eastern Europe. The populace of the West cares very little about what happens to Ukraine—think of the dithering and nonresponse when Russia took over the Crimea. Most people in the West don't even know Estonia exists, let alone want to risk lives to save it. Unless the plan is stopped now, before it begins, how long after Russia absorbs Ukraine do you think it will take before the new Union of Soviet Socialist Republics invades Estonia?"

56

SARA ROSE FROM delta sleep chased by dreams that had latterly insinuated themselves into her sleep, as if her unconscious was preparing her to leave the delicious nothingness in which she floated.

"Rebeka!"

Her eyes snapped open, she found herself looking up at Dov.

"Are you awake?"

"What d'you think?" she said crossly, because her head was still muzzy.

"The private jet belongs to Abdul Aziz, a businessman from—"

"Istanbul," she finished for him. That had snapped her to full consciousness.

"You know him?"

"He's a friend of Bourne's."

"Well, I hope he doesn't end up like Bourne's other friend, General Karpov."

She sat up. "You knew about that?"

"It didn't make us happy."

Her vertigo seemed to be gone. "D'you have more?"

"God, yes. A whole lot more. And very fast transport standing by for you."

"Is it stocked with food?"

He laughed. "Yes."

She stood. "Fill me in while we board. Suddenly, I'm ravenous."

"When do you want me to kill him?" the Angelmaker said when she returned to their room.

Timur Savasin had ordered room service: a pink saddle of lamb, grilled vegetables, halloumi cheese, and *loukaniko* sausage. Out of respect, he had ordered her a salad as well, something he detested.

She sat down opposite at the laden table in the sitting area of their suite and began to serve herself. "Tonight would be good."

"Very possibly."

"In his sleep. Moonlight stealing into the room. Very romantic. I'd like that. All romance ends in death."

"So that's what you started?" he said neutrally. "A romance?"

"Christ, no." She laughed, showing small white teeth. "I was using a figure of speech."

"Very poetic."

The hint of an electric current in his voice caused her to glance up, between transferring a spoonful of artichokes, carrots, and onions to her plate.

"FM, you aren't jealous, are you?"

"I've no idea what you're talking about."

Smiling slyly, she speared a chunk of lamb on the tines of her fork. "I'll say this for you, FM, you do love your meat." She popped the morsel in her mouth, chewed slowly and lasciviously, swallowed. "Human and otherwise."

Pushing back his chair, he crossed to the sideboard where the three bottles of premium-grade vodka he had ordered each stood in the center of its own sweating ice bucket. He poured himself a shot, downed it with a violent backward thrust of his head, sloshed in a triple. Turning around, he watched her eat with slow, methodical precision; he'd never seen her wolf her food.

She lifted a shapely arm. "Come. Sit. Eat your meats." She speared a sausage. "They're really rather wonderful."

He took a sip or two of his vodka, strolled back across the room, and, moving his chair, sat down beside her. Taking up a fork, he began to eat from her plate.

"Here's the table leg." She tapped it with a forefinger. "Why don't you piss on that, too?"

He grunted. "No worries there. I've already marked my territory." He chomped down on a sausage. "Many times." He chewed slowly, thoughtfully. "So you've bonded yourself to him."

"I've bonded him to me."

"By giving him your confidence."

"The foundation of all con games. That's right."

"And he bought it—your confidence."

"I believe so."

"This is not just any mark. This is Jason Bourne."

"I know who he is, FM," she said levelly. "What eludes me is your intense antipathy toward him."

"He and Boris Karpov were close friends. I don't need any more incentive."

"But you do have more."

He set down his fork, wiped his lips with a napkin. "I believe we shall continue this conversation in the bedroom."

"I haven't even started on my salad yet," she pointed out. "Shall I take it with?"

He was like an animal, ripping off her clothes, growling in the back of his throat. The Angelmaker had seen him like this once before, with one of his mistresses. He had insisted she watch, from a shadowed corner where she was to remain absolutely still. At the end of the session, Savasin's victim, as she became in the Angelmaker's mind, had emerged spattered with bite marks, roundels already turning from oxblood to black-and-blue. As she had stumbled out, half insensate, the First Minister had called the Angelmaker to his bed for the first time, which was when she saw the blood on the sheets.

Now, as his hands and mouth roamed over her body, the Angelmaker felt the well of time open up, felt herself falling into it, down and down, until she was back in the Somalian pirate encampment. Her body was crisscrossed, swirled, circled, triangled with wounds, turning with time into scars, remnants of unthinkable rituals, which her captor called art, and which, for decades after, she held on to as desperately as a drowning woman clutches a dead body in order to keep afloat.

It was in the Somali encampment, at the hands of her captor, a Yibir, one of a clan of Somali magi so ancient they predated the coming of Islam, that she had been desensitized to sex without pain. She had been trained, he had trained her—she knew all this—but somehow the circuits in her brain had been rewired, and now her body responded only to the stimuli the Somali had laid out for her. There was, therefore, a ghastly agony inside her, an itch that could never be scratched. Never be assuaged. Except by pain. Bourne was right. Even after time and distance, she was still the Somali's prisoner, with no hope for escape.

Breaking away, she rolled off the bed.

"Where are you going?" he asked as she walked away.

57

BOURNE LAY ATOP the bed in his darkened hotel room. Moonlight, sliced into cool bars by the wide, wooden jalousies, stretched across the tile floor like mercury. And like mercury, the moonlight had turned poisonous since his encounter with Mala on the beach outside his sliders. Winter was coming. Even here, a certain chill had invaded the Mediterranean night. He tried to turn his mind off, but the coming events of tomorrow kept returning to vex him. Only hours to go, and still he had no answer as to how to get into the Sovereign's account at the Omega + Gulf Bank. He knew Boris must have included it in his cipher, but after racking his brains for hours on end he remained at a loss to discover where it was. He had deciphered the entire rebus—all four groups of Sumerian glyphs.

All at once, he sat up, drenched in cold sweat. Had there been a fifth group, written in invisible ink? It was an old-school trick, but one Boris might very well have used. If so, Bourne was screwed, having destroyed the scrap of paper in order to keep it from falling into the wrong hands. If so, if the information he needed wasn't somewhere embedded in the four groupings of glyphs stored in his memory then, by tomorrow evening, the entire world would be at war.

Unless First Minister Savasin possessed the account code. In which case, there was still a chance, though a slim one. But slim was better than none.

Bourne was about to lie down again, to sink himself, if not into sleep, then into deep meditation, when he picked up a corruption of one of the bars of moonlight, as of a shadow crossing in front of it on his polished concrete balcony.

Bourne lay very still, slowing his breathing until the rise and fall of his chest was barely discernible. The shadow was there, moving so slowly as to be almost imperceptible. Arranging the pillows to resemble a body under the sheets, he slipped off the edge of the bed farthest away from the sliders, crept to the end, keeping his head and shoulders low enough that that bed blocked his progress from view.

Several thick bars of moonlight slanted in between the jalousies. A bullet from a noise-suppressed handgun would have to first pierce the plastic safety sheet sandwiched between the double-hung glass, making a poor-percentage shot. Whoever was on his terrace would have to expose themselves to the moonlight in order to get to the bed. On the other hand, if he pressed himself against the far wall, he had a route to the sliders that was completely in darkness.

He was at the slider when it opened ever so slowly from the outside. Still, the jalousies prevented him from seeing who was trying to gain access. He stood very still, watching as a hawk will the last movements of its prey before the strike. The slider was now open enough for a slender person to enter sideways. An arm entered his field of vision, briefly rippling a bar of moonlight. In a lightning-like move, Bourne reached out, grabbed the wrist, jerking the arm in toward him. An instant later, a hand closed around his throat, he drew the intruder through the gap, clamped the throat in a reciprocal strike, locking them together in what could only be a mutual death grip.

And stood face-to-face with Sara.

A peal of laughter so clear and pure it might have come from a bell emerged from Sara's throat, surrounded Bourne with a warmth he hadn't felt since they'd said their silent good-byes what seemed like both an age ago, and at the same time no more than hours.

They took their hands away from each other's throats, but Bourne kept hold of her wrist, pulled her tight against him. Feeling the contours of her body mold themselves to his delivered back to him a sense of reality, which had begun to slip away from the moment he had recognized Mala on the beach.

"How did you find me? How did you get here?"

Sara told him what had happened to her at Borz's camp. How she had captured Borz, tortured him, and was beginning to interrogate him only to have Amira's rogue brother, El-Amir, shoot him dead. How she was in turn captured by El-Amir, thrown into a cell with the British lieutenant Southern, and how she managed to kill El-Amir so they could escape and, ultimately, be rescued by helo.

"I thought you were dead," she said now. "I saw the helo you were flying hit by a missile. I didn't know until we were taken across the border into Turkey that you had escaped. My boss found out where you had gone and rounded up transport to take me here to Nicosia.

"Now tell me what you're doing here. What trail are you following?"

"The one laid out for me by Boris."

Talk of his mission here brought him out of the parallel track he had been revisiting, a rare occurrence, for so many reasons. The Somali who had worked his despicable magic on Mala, as he had so many other young woman, girls, and children, as a supposed means of keeping himself young and virile, haunted the dark recesses of his mind only infrequently. Bourne had lied to Mala; he hadn't killed the Somali. When he had destroyed the encampment, he had had to make a choice: save her or go after the Somali. He had made his choice without a moment's conscious thought. Preserving lives—including those far younger than

Mala—was far more preferable than taking one, even if it meant also lying to his Treadstone masters, who had ordered the Somali's termination. Thankfully, he had slunk off into the shadowy underbelly of his war-torn country, never to be heard of again. Still, encountering Mala again had stirred the darkness in which the Somali lay slumbering, and the question of what had happened to him, where he was, rankled Bourne's consciousness.

Sara must have picked up on his mood, for she laid a hand along his cheek. "Jason, what is it?" she whispered. "What's happened?"

Instantly, he knew he couldn't tell her about his history with Mala; it would set up too many alarm bells for her, both personally and professionally. He remembered only a fraction of his time as a Treadstone assassin, but of one thing he was certain: though he could not recall a name or time period, he could picture himself in Jerusalem, shooting dead a Treadstone target, who he was fairly certain was a Mossad field agent.

Instead, he went with another facet of the truth, refusing to lie to her. "The Russian first minister is here."

"Timur Savasin?"

He nodded. "Savasin was Boris's sworn enemy. He was jealous of Boris's power—a power all the more solid because it wasn't built on lies, deceit, and corruption, as Savasin's is."

"Speaking of the first minister, Boris's widow has disappeared."

"She called me from Amsterdam. She was certain she was being followed; she was afraid for her life."

"She made it to Cairo, according to Dov. Outside the airport, she vanished."

"They got her." Bourne's heart sank. "Savasin had her killed."

"Supposition?"

"More than that," Bourne said grimly. "She found material Boris had left in his dacha. Material that the first minister would not want discovered."

"So Savasin had both Boris and his wife murdered."

Bourne nodded. "Which means that Borz has been working both sides of the street: the Sovereign and Savasin."

"Borz is working for the Sovereign as well?"

Bourne nodded, told Sara about how the Russian president had hired Borz to recruit for ISIS, all the while stealing from him through Mik, the man who made money disappear from one place only to reappear in another as if out of thin air.

The fires of rage he had so painstakingly banked while trying to complete the mission Boris had set out for him now flared up. Like paper burning, his fingers curled up into fists.

Sara could not help but notice the change that had come over him. "Does the first minister know you're here?"

Bourne nodded again. "He's brought along his personal bodyguard."

"You know him, this bodyguard?"

"Her," Bourne said. "She's known as the Angelmaker."

Sara laughed uncertainly. "You're joking, yes?"

His answering smile was not a pleasant one, and Sara sobered at once. "I wish I were. The Angelmaker is exceptionally formidable."

"So he's here to stop you."

"That's who I thought you were, the Angelmaker."

She watched him thoughtfully. "Why has Boris led you here?"

"There's a bank that belongs to the Sovereign. It holds the vast sum he's using to fund his aggression both in Ukraine and in Syria, underwriting ISIS."

"Which bank?"

"You'll like this," Bourne said. "The Omega and Gulf Bank."

"Full circle," Sara said. "So really it's all one immense ball of wax." She told him about Vankor. "Do you know what it refers to?"

Bourne nodded. "A highly lucrative oil field owned by Vankorneft, a subsidiary of Rosneft, the Federation's largest oil company." He thought for a moment.

"What is it?"

"I'm not sure. Something Boris's widow said to me, about a secret deal the Sovereign had made with CNCP, the Chinese energy company. She said it was the start of a formerly unthinkable change in the Federation energy policy."

"You mean the Chinese government is basically funding the Sovereign's new wars."

"That's precisely what I mean," Bourne said. "The amount needed was astronomical, far exceeding what could be skimmed off of Borz's accounts. And all of that vast fortune is turned on and off at one spigot: the Omega and Gulf Bank."

This would be the point where he would reach for her. That he didn't disturbed him in a way he could not fathom.

58

THE DAY DAWNED cloudless and preternaturally warm, the last gasp of Mediterranean late summer before the invasion of winter. In stark contrast to its neighbors, the Omega + Gulf Bank stood out, as all new construction will. But there was something different, something anomalous that hadn't been apparent at night. Even in the raking morning light, the anomaly was difficult to pinpoint, until Bourne was close enough to see that the building was constructed of steel-reinforced concrete. Either the builder had neglected to add an outer facade or it hadn't been part of the architectural plan. Either way, the bank was unlike any other building in its immediate vicinity, possibly in all of Nicosia.

"Are you armed?" Bourne had said just before dawn.

Sara shook her head. "I came direct from the airport. There was no time to find a local dealer. You?"

"Same as you. No time."

Sara smiled. "There are those who say man cannot live by wits alone."

"They never met us," Bourne had said.

Now they stood deep in the shadow of a doorway across the street from the Omega + Gulf Bank.

"Not a creature is stirring," Sara said, "not even a mouse."

"Or a car."

"So I noticed."

Sometime in the dead of night, the street had been swept clean of parked vehicles. There was no traffic whatsoever, though neither of them had seen barriers anywhere along the street.

"Savasin's already here," Sara said.

Bourne nodded. "It would seem so."

"Are you sure he brought only the Angelmaker with him?"

"Right now, I'm not sure of anything." Bourne was staring hard at the bank's rough facade. "But it would be prudent to assume he's hired local talent."

"Well," Sara said, "it's clear we can't simply waltz in through the front door."

"I can't," Bourne said. "But Savasin doesn't know you're here. He might not even know who you are."

"I was made leaving Sheremetyevo. My face is now known to the Russians."

"That's why I cut your hair short, why you're wearing lipstick, a sundress, and sandals."

"Praise God for hotel gift shops that open early." She made a face. "But I hate this straw hat."

He gave her a crooked smile as he glanced at her. "You know what to do."

She tossed her head. "Jason, we've been over it a hundred times."

"Okay, then. Give me ten minutes, then walk directly across the street and—"

"Enough!" She was impatient to reach the mission's end-game, but she was also confused and a bit put out that they hadn't made love in the hours before dawn. What was up with that? she wondered, then immediately stifled the thought; they had so much on their plates. She cleared her mind of negative thoughts. "Get going."

He left her, then, went left to the end of the block, crossed over, and vanished down the street that ran perpendicular to the one they had been on. A quarter of a block in, he reached the stained and garbage-strewn alleyway he had discovered during last night's reconnoiter.

As he had seen, the bank's rear door was composed of reinforced steel. It was also alarmed—an expensive bleeding-edge system, which he saw no quick way to disable from the outside. No matter; he hadn't planned to enter that way.

Several mature date palms rose up from the garden he had noticed the night before. He climbed the one closest to the bank until he reached the roof, which was flat, made of corrugated steel. Apart from a dense copse of antennae, it was bare. Bourne swung across, landing silently on the steel. The moment he did so, two men appeared from behind the antennae cluster.

They ran at him very fast, crouched over, scimitar-blade dirks held in front of them. Their hard plastic eyes reflected his image; there was nothing in their universe but him. Clearly, they were fanatics. Halfway to him, they split up, to come from him from two sides simultaneously. Instead of retreating, Bourne held his ground until they were committed to their respective paths, then he launched himself, not at them, but as if they were coming at him head-on. He sprinted so fast and surprised them so thoroughly, they were obliged to change direction so abruptly that when he reached first the one on his right, then the one on his left, they were both off balance.

His forearm knocked their knife hands away from him while, at the same time, he drove a fist into first one, then the other. As the breath rushed out of both of them, he kneed one in the forehead, slashed a kite with the edge of his hand into the side of other's neck. Two well-placed kicks drove them both deep into unconsciousness. Grabbing their dirks, he moved past them.

Circling around the antennae display, he came upon a service hatch, which the mercenaries Timur Savasin had hired had used to gain access to the roof. He grasped the recessed handle, turned it, then pulled back the hatch. A quick glimpse revealed a metal ladder straight down to what might be the monitoring room. His glimpse afforded him no sign of life, but he didn't feel comfortable climbing down. If anyone was in the room waiting for him, that was what they'd expect him to do.

Instead, he positioned himself over the open hatch, grasped the side railings and slid down, using the insides of his shoes against the edges as a kind of brake. Someone inside the room fired at him.

The street was the epitome of calm, but the lack of movement, of the small, quotidian activities endemic to any city or town struck Sara as downright eerie. She didn't trust what she saw at all. Nevertheless, she had no choice but to stride purposefully across the street, her stupid straw hat shading her eyes—indeed, the entire upper half of her face—from view. The Omega + Gulf Bank's massive front door seemed to be composed of vertical slabs of rosewood, until she got close enough to see that the slabs were bolted onto a brushed metal door, studded between the slabs like the door of a medieval castle keep.

To her surprise the door opened easily when she pulled on the handle, as if it were set on a complex set of gimbals. Inside, the bank was like nothing she had ever seen before. There were no stands on which to write out deposit or withdrawal slips, no ATMs against the wall. There were no tellers, no place for inquiries, no sitting area in which to wait for an officer's attention. That was because there were no officers. In fact, there was no one, and the sound of her sandals against the marble floor was the only sound, echoing off columns with an aching loneliness.

Off to the left, a door stood open. Upon close inspection, this led into a short corridor off which were a series of offices—all deserted. They contained identical desks, rotary phones, bulky intercoms, IBM Selectric typewriters, stacked in- and out-boxes, paper cutters, blotters, pencil sharpeners, a round container of freshly sharpened pencils. Black metal file cabinets stood against one wall, the others were blank. The offices looked time-warped, beamed in from the sixties and seventies. The carpeting, lush and expensive, smelled new.

Stepping into the first one, she went immediately to the file cabinet. The three drawers were locked. Working her hand along the top of the cabinet, she encountered the key. She unlocked the top drawer: empty, did the same with the middle and bottom ones: empty, empty.

The same held true for the drawers in the desk, none of which were locked. Not even a speck of dust lay within. Her hands roamed over the desktop, upended the holder, spilling the pencils out onto the desk. She peered into the holder: nothing there, either.

Unfathomable, Sara thought.

That was when she heard the quickening sound from behind her.

Because of the swiftness of Bourne's descent, the bullet from the noise-silenced pistol passed just over his head.

An instant later, he was on the floor, turning into a crouch, as the second shot was fired. The ricochet almost caught his left cheek, chips of plaster flicked past his eye. Then he had loosed one of the dirks, which, owing to its curved blade, wasn't ideal for throwing. Nevertheless, because he had calculated for its shape, the tip struck home, the dirk burying itself above the man's sternum.

Now he was alone in the comm room, with a dead man bleeding out, two more men on the roof over his head. Only it wasn't a comm room; it was nothing at all. Whatever data was being fed into the bank from the antennae array wasn't here. "Here" wasn't even finished; it looked like a mock-up of a room. Iron beams and joists made a jigsaw puzzle of the space. Below: blackness of the place between floors, where nothing but mice and roaches would want to live.

He went out of the room, into a hallway of sorts: a circular space, bare plywood that, like in the room he had just left, seemed to serve no purpose save to fill up the interior so that from the outside, the structure looked like a two-story building. A casual observer might very well think that he was in a partially built floor, but there was no sawdust, no power tools, no generator or stacked cans of paint waiting to be opened. The lack of even a grain of dust or soot was almost pathological.

If it wasn't a two-story building housing a working staff, then what was it? But then, if the Omega + Gulf Bank was for the sole benefit of the Sovereign of the Russian Federation, what need had it of a second story? Where were the funds kept? How were they disbursed when needed, often at a moment's notice? The antennae array on the roof had to lead somewhere in the bank.

He went down a circular staircase with a sinuous, polished cherrywood handrail, gilt balusters, as grand as any in an eight-figure mansion. It was carpeted, but the carpet had no imprints on it. Bourne might have been the first person to walk on it after it had been set in place. Black-and-white photographs of what appeared to be oil fields and refineries hung at regular intervals on the curving wall. Gouts of gas-fed flame, blackened, cindered ground lent them an atmosphere of the apocalyptic.

He was halfway down when he heard the first cry of pain. It wasn't the last.

59

NO TIME FOR thought. Instinct was what saved Sara. Instinct and training. Whipping off her straw hat, she threw it, whirling, at the figure rushing toward her. His forward momentum was momentarily arrested as he swatted the hat away from his face. That was all the time she needed. Scooping up one of the pencils she stepped into his attack, inside his Taser-holding hand, jammed the pencil point first into his left eye. As he reared back, roaring in stunned agony, she slammed the eraser end with the heel of her hand, driving the point through the viscous back of his eye, the optic nerve, into his brain. He screamed. She stepped back to avoid his flailing arms, his fingers clawing at the foreign object. But before he could remove it, he was dead, collapsing onto the carpet as if he were a marionette with its strings cut.

She was struck then, a titanic blow that knocked her sideways against the edge of the desk. A bolt of pain ran up from the tips of her ribs, filling her chest with fire, making her gasp. Her attacker was upon her, bending her backward, his foul breath in her face. His knuckles were clad with something that gleamed in the light, and when he hit her in the side, she almost blacked out. Her knees filled with water, her legs were like rubber, and the agony was so intense she could scarcely put two thoughts together. She felt stupid and weak, and this filled her with a black rage; her meticulously honed survival instinct turned her wicked, ruthless, implacable. Remembering her first sight of the desktop as if it were still before her, she reached back. Even that motion was difficult. One of my ribs must be cracked, she thought, even as her fingers scrabbled to find the heavy paper cutter.

At that instant, her assailant flipped her over onto her stomach. Bent over the desk, she felt him pull her dress up, drape the hem over her waist, exposing her. He pressed himself against her, rubbed up and down like an animal in heat. In her mind, he was barely more than that.

He held her hips, he was working the zipper of his trousers but was so engorged he was having difficulty freeing himself. Sara grabbed the paper cutter. Her angle worked against her, reducing the leverage she could apply. But she was possessed by the strength of righteous rage, which overrode both the poor leverage and the blinding flashes of pain in her side. Wrenching the long blade from the heavy base of the paper cutter, she pressed one hip into the edge of the desk and, though it was also painful, torqued herself from her hips up through her torso, swung first the flat of the blade into the small of her attacker's back, then, as he reacted, slashed his throat from side to side, nearly decapitating him in that single prodigious blow.

Blood fountained, pulse by pulse, inundating both the carpet and his fallen comrade. As he fell, a blurred figure coming through the doorway at speed brought a last savage response from her. She raised the bloody blade, ready to strike, but was halted at the top of her attack arc by a powerful grip on her wrist. She began to struggle, knowing her life hung in the balance, that if she let herself be stopped now she'd be dead within seconds.

"Sara."

The blood ran down the blade, over her fist, thick, still warm. If she didn't have that, she had other weapons at her disposal.

"Sara!"

Her entire body was a weapon. This was how she had been trained; this was how she would use it now in the last defense of her life.

"Sara, it's me, Jason."

She blinked sweat out of her eyes, saw him before her frenzied brain recognized him. Then, flooded with excruciating pain, she dropped the paper cutter blade, and, with a gasp of both agony and relief, fell against the blessed solidity of his chest, clung to him like an orphan in the adrenaline storm still thundering through her body. She shivered, began to shake uncontrollably, as if with a high fever.

"Jason," she whispered. "Jason."

"It's all right now," Bourne said, stroking her sweat-slick hair.

"If only that were true," an urbane voice said from behind him.

They both turned to see First Minister Timur Savasin aiming a massive .357 Magnum at them.

He doesn't leave anything to chance, Bourne thought. That thing will stop a rampaging lion in its tracks. He saw no sign of Mala, and this worried him more than the threat of the Magnum.

"What is this place?" Bourne said.

"What? No greeting? No prelude to formal talks among nations?" Timur Savasin was smirking. "Well, what can you expect from an American and an Israeli?" He spat out the last three words as he shook a cigarette out from a pack at his hip pocket, lit it, all with one hand. Apparently, he had practice with this maneuver. He inhaled deeply, expelled a cloud of smoke toward the ceiling. He appeared exceptionally fit beneath his open-collared shirt and lightweight linen trousers; a healthy glow suffused his face. "First, drop the gun."

Bourne did so.

"Kick it away." Savasin nodded. "That's a good lad. Now get rid of that dirk you have stuffed at your back."

Bourne grasped the hilt, began to slide it out.

"Slowly," Savasin said. "Very slowly." He nodded again. "Now drop it and kick it away, too."

When Bourne had done as he was ordered, the first minister took another puff on his cigarette, said, "To answer your question, this place is precisely what it purports to be: the Omega and Gulf Bank."

"Bullshit!" Sara snapped. She appeared to have recovered a bit of her core energy. "There are no tellers, no safes, no money. It's no bank at all."

Timur Savasin looked only at Bourne. Smoke drifted past one eye. "It is a bank because I say it's a bank."

"That, unfortunately, isn't enough, First Minister," Bourne said, even as he squeezed Sara, warning her to keep her mouth shut. "Rebeka is correct. There's nothing here to indicate it's anything but a hollow shell, a half-finished stage set."

"That's because you haven't seen the vault." Savasin's eyes gleamed like unholy lamps in the dark. "You haven't taken the journey down to level one. The journey we're going to make right now." He gestured with the barrel of the Magnum as he backed carefully out of the doorway. Dropping the butt, he ground it out beneath his heel. Then he gestured in a mock bow. "After you."

They took an elevator, so large it could have served as a freight lift, down one level. The door slid back, and they found themselves in a small, almost claustrophobic space excavated out of the island's bedrock. Savasin turned on the electric lights, revealing the immense circular steel door of the bank's vault, gleaming like the pot of gold at the end of the rainbow. He had not lied. Here before them lay the repository of the Sovereign's new wealth, courtesy of the mainland Chinese.

As the three of them stood before the vault door, Timur Savasin said, "Here is the nub of my dilemma, Bourne. I need to open the vault, yet I do not have the code to open the door." He stepped closer to the vault, but at the same time kept his distance from Bourne. "You, I believe, do."

"In that," Bourne said, "you're mistaken."

"Well, you see, I don't believe you, Bourne." Savasin leveled the Magnum. "And to prove it I will give you precisely one minute to input the code into the keypad at the center of the door."

"I can't do it," Bourne said truthfully. "I don't have the code."

"You have fifty seconds left, Bourne. At the end of that time I will shoot your inamorata, though how you can bear to touch Israeli animal flesh is beyond my ken."

Sara made to move, but Bourne restrained her. "Don't," he whispered in her ear. "Don't do or say anything. He *will* shoot you at the least provocation, of that I'm sure."

She subsided, but he could feel her seething just as if he shared her body. "How will you stop him?" she whispered in return.

"By opening the vault."

Her eyes opened wide. "How?"

"Well, that's the enigma I need to solve." He released his grip on her. "Can you stand on your own?"

Her eyes flashed fire. "Don't be absurd."

He gave her a hard grin before stepping to the input plate on the vault door. It was a touch screen with numbers from one to zero. No letters. This confused him.

"Thirty seconds," Timur Savasin called from behind him. "Twenty-nine, twenty-eight..."

No letters, only numbers. But there were no numbers in Boris's message. It had said, *Follow the money*, it had contained the place and the bank name, but no clue as to the code. The only numbers were today's date—the commencement of the Russian Federation's full-scale invasion of Ukraine.

"Fifteen seconds, fourteen, thirteen..."

Bourne stared at the touch pad. No letters, only numbers. And then he had it. The date! The date was the code!

"Ten, nine, eight..."

He inputted the date, turned the bar. It wouldn't budge.

"Six, five..."

Sweat broke out on his forehead and upper lip. The nape of his neck was wet.

"Four, three..."

Then he saw his mistake. He had inputted the date in the American manner with the month first, then the day. Now he reversed it, tapping the day first, then the month, in the European fashion. He finished with the year.

"Two, one..."

He gripped the handle. It released down, he heard the tumblers clicking away, a whirring as the thick solid steel bolts retracted, and the vault door swung open.

The three of them stepped in to find that the interior was completely barren. No skids of dollars, euros, or yen. No bars of gold. No thick stacks of bearer bonds or stock certificates. They were confronted with nothing at all.

"Jesus Christ," Timur Savasin said. Clearly he was as surprised as Bourne and Sara. "What the hell—"

Then the door slammed shut behind them, the bolts slid to.

60

THEY WERE LOCKED inside. This was Mala's work, Bourne knew. The devil's work.

"The Angelmaker has fucked you, First Minister," he said.

"The bitch has fucked us all," Savasin howled.

He turned the Magnum on Sara, as if she, not the Angelmaker, had betrayed him, and in a more fundamental way, she had. She was a Jew. Worse, she was Israeli, his implacable enemy, the ready tip of the bayonet that had been thrust through so many of his comrades.

He fired at her at the same moment Bourne's shoulder slammed into him. Sara went down, but whether she had been hit or had simply ducked out of harm's way Bourne had no way of telling. He had his hands full with the first minister.

Timur Savasin, the martial arts expert, possessed a fierce will not merely to survive but to triumph. Anything other than victory was not only unacceptable, it was unthinkable. Beyond that, he completely surprised Bourne with his understanding and practice of *haragei*—the art of balance and power emanating from the lower belly. *Haragei* was the basis of all Japanese martial arts, from sumo to karate to the almost extinct *harakei*.

The first minister's chosen expertise was, like Bourne's, in aikido. While firing his Magnum—a distraction, nothing more—he slid into Bourne attack, bending his torso, while sweeping his feet in a shallow arc that struck Bourne's leading ankle, taking him off his feet.

With the Magnum out of bullets, Savasin reversed his grip, swinging the butt into Bourne's chin. Bourne's head slammed back against the rock floor. On the verge of blacking out, Bourne raised his arms in defense, but Savasin was already inside his semicircle of defense, and he smashed his fist three, four times into Bourne's side, aiming for the muscle over Bourne's kidneys.

But even while being battered, Bourne gathered himself. The true beauty of aikido was that it taught not only the inner centralization and coordination of power, but also emphasized the building up of the mental core, eliminating normal inhibitions in order to attain a single focus, so that even injured a proponent could not only persevere but gain victory.

But, again, Savasin was turning out to be an aikido savant. He immediately knew that Bourne had retreated into *haragei*, knew what he was doing, and sought to counter it by attacking Bourne's source of power, his lower belly. Again and again, he struck Bourne as he raised up over him, his thighs locked against Bourne's hips to keep him from rolling or wriggling away.

Bourne could feel the darkness of unconsciousness lapping at the edges of his vision, while blinding sparks exploded like fireworks in the center, making him effectively blind. But none of that mattered, because, in fact, Savasin did not know Bourne; he had only files and hearsay to go by, and those were not nearly enough. Not by a long shot. Now he found out.

Bourne grabbed the cigarette pack out of Savasin's hip pocket, ground the cigarettes, tossed a blizzard of tobacco in his face. Savasin could not see the calloused edges of Bourne's hands rising up like serpents, but he certainly felt them strike him, causing him to loosen his grip on his prey's hips. He stared sightless, helpless, while Bourne tossed him aside, and was just about to regain a semblance of his faculties when the hammer came down.

Blood filled his cracked lungs, rose up into his throat and mouth. He was drowning in his own fluids.

Bourne stared into First Minister Timur Savasin's bloodshot eyes, watched more and more blood overflow the corners of his mouth.

"It wasn't enough that you murdered my friend," he said, "you had to kill Svetlana as well."

Savasin's mouth worked spasmodically. Animal noises emanated from him that might once have been intelligible words. Then he turned his head to one side, spat out a gobbet of blackish blood with a shard of his own lung embedded in it. When he turned back to Bourne, he spoke. The hateful words, though slightly garbled, were unmistakable as he spat them at Sara: "Jew bitch should never have been born."

Those were also the last words he ever spoke. Bourne took up the empty Magnum, shoved the long barrel through the top of Timur Savasin's palette, through his sinuses, into his brain. There, he stirred the pot until all light faded from the first minister's eyes. Life abandoned him, as if it could not flee fast enough.

61

"THERE'S NO STOPPING YOU," Bourne said, as he raised Sara to a sitting position.

Her smile was leavened with the pain from her ribs. "There's no stopping either of us, it seems." She indicated with her head. "What the hell did you do to him, anyway?"

"Nothing less than he deserved." He pulled her to her feet with one arm at the small of her back. "How badly are your ribs hurt?"

"Let's find a way out of here first."

He shook his head. "No chance. As long as the filtration system is working we'll be—"

At that instant complete silence engulfed them. Someone—most likely Mala—had turned off the internal air in the vault.

"All right?" Sara asked archly. "Is that what you were going to say? Now what do you say about finding a way—"

But Bourne had already stripped off the first minister's shirt and was tearing it into lengths he knotted together. He bound her midsection, tying the material off tightly.

"I can hardly breathe. I feel like I'm wearing a corset."

"Good. Now let's see where we stand." He crossed to the closed door. "There's always a safety mechanism to open a door like this from the inside." He found it. "Ah, here we go." He pressed the emergency release, but nothing happened.

"The Angelmaker has disabled it," Sara said. "It looks like she's living up to her name. I guess it *is* possible to hate someone you've never met." She glanced at Bourne. "And, by the way, why did your good friend Boris Karpov lead you here? There's no staff, no money. To me, it looks like a dead end. It's time to face the fact that he was conned, and so were we. There's nothing here for us. The Russian invasion will begin this evening dead on schedule."

Bourne shook his head. "I'm convinced this place is ground zero for the Sovereign's Chinese money. I'm missing something." He spun slowly, looking around the bare vault. "Something vital."

"Like what?"

His eyes lit up. "Like *this*." He recrossed the vault to the wall where Savasin's shots had chipped away at the rock face. And rock face it was, in every sense of the word. His fingertips roamed over the surface beneath. "Look here."

Sara winced as she bent stiffly to look at where he was pointing. "It's smooth!" she exclaimed. "And it's metal!"

Retrieving the Magnum, Bourne wiped off the barrel on the First Minister's trousers, then returned to the chipped wall, hacking at the thin facade—which, as it turned out, wasn't stone at all, but plaster molded and painted to resemble stone—until he revealed an array of electronic equipment. Checking the monitor, he saw that the array was connected to the Dark Web, a place in cyberspace where illicit matériel of every sort imaginable was bought, bartered, and sold.

"There's a powerful antennae array up on the roof," Bourne said. "It's invisible from the street. I wondered what it connected to. There was nothing on the second floor."

"And all the offices on the ground floor are empty—looking like dummies—a stage set," Sara said. "And yet spotless, which means someone must come in periodically to clean."

"I'm willing to bet it isn't anyone local," Bourne said.

"So now we know the bank is used for something. But what? If there are no banknotes, no bonds, no certificates of deposit, no gold, then what is the bank for?"

"I think I know," Bourne said. "But first we need to get out of here."

"As I was saying." Sara was watching him carefully. "Any ideas?"

"Just one," Bourne said. "The Angelmaker."

Sara blinked hard. "I beg your pardon?"

"She's not going to let us die in here."

"That's why she turned off the air, right?"

The air! Bourne thought. Of course.

"The Angelmaker knows this place better than we do," he said. "I would wager she's been here before—more than once."

"Doing what?" Sara said. "Mopping and dusting?"

At last, he found what he was searching for. The air vent was almost as cleverly hidden as the banks of electronic equipment it serviced. Any form of stacked electronics threw off tremendous heat, requiring powerful fans and heat sinks. The heat problem was bad enough out in the open, but when the components were secreted as these were, they required an immense amount of cooling.

Cooling meant air—a lot of it. And the cooling system had to be vented somewhere close so that the heat would not build up and destroy the components.

And there it was. He pulled off the grate, camouflaged to look like the surrounding rock wall.

"Big enough for a human body," Sara said. "Where does it lead?"

"Let's find out."

Bourne crawled inside, Sara following. The shaft, which was very cold indeed, led them horizontally for only twenty yards or so, before tilting upward so steeply they were obliged to press their knees and the outsides of their shoes against the freezing metal sides. This was particularly difficult for Sara, since she was wearing a sundress and sandals, which afforded her minimal protection in this arctic environment. In fact, she found the sandals a hindrance, and shook them off. They fell down behind her, two small plops like birds hitting a window.

It quickly got worse: the shaft turned vertical. Now they used elbows as well as knees and feet. Sara shivered. Even that involuntary motion sent shards of pain through her side, but the ties that bound her also saved her, and she thought it a fitting legacy of First Minister Savasin's despicable life, one he'd hate. And, in fact, it was his inimical hatred that helped her keep going when the agony swept over her, threatening to make her lose her grip. How easy, she thought, to just let go, to let the darkness come rushing up to greet her, to fall into its open arms and rest there for a while before dropping into sleep.

As if psychically bonded to her, Bourne's voice broke apart her black thoughts at just the right moment: "Sara, I can see light up above. We're almost there."

Each word was another rung in the lifeline extended to her, pulling her inch by inch out of darkness's seductive embrace. She had never felt so tired or in pain in her life, not even when she was bleeding out in the back of a taxi in Mexico City. There, she was basically self-anesthetized; here, she was all raw nerve endings and rage.

Up ahead, she heard Bourne working on another grate, knew that he had stopped, that they were at the end. She clutched her Star of David and said a short prayer. Moments later, Bourne was lifting her out of the air shaft. She wanted to cry out, but her training took hold, and she just gritted her teeth and let the pain wash over her once more. But now she was in the arms of the man she loved, felt his heartbeat and, beyond that, the solace of human warmth.

Bourne set her down gently. “I’ve got to get you to a hospital.”

“Later,” she said, and smiled at him as she got to her feet. “Or maybe not at all.”

She looked around. They were on the unfinished second floor. It was just as Bourne had described it. “Tell me what you’ve discovered.”

“I’ll do more than that,” Bourne said. “I’ll show you.”

He led her down the wide, curving stairs. “The photos, Sara. What are they of?”

She frowned. “An oil field,” she said. “Refineries.”

“Not just any oil field. Vankor.”

“The oil field the Sovereign sold part of to the Chinese.”

“The same,” he said, nodding.

As they moved slowly down, tread by tread, he lifted off each photo. “Of course this bank doesn’t hold banknotes, bearer bonds, stock certificates, or gold. They’re all too cumbersome to transport efficiently at a moment’s notice, which is how this bank’s assets are deployed.”

Behind the third photo down was a metal plate with a large keypad on it.

“Oh my God,” Sara said. “Diamonds!”

Bourne nodded. “Now look at the keypad. It’s not like any other I’ve ever seen.”

“Me neither,” Sara said. “It’s got thirty-three keys, all of them blank.” She looked from the keypad to Bourne. “How on earth will you open it?”

“The answer is staring right at us from these photos.”

“Vankor.”

“The Russian alphabet is composed of thirty-three letters.” Bourne touched the keypad six times, inputting the Cyrillic equivalent of VANKOR. The door popped open. He put his hand inside, drew out a single red silk bag. It was embroidered with a gold Chinese dragon, and was tied with a drawstring. Opening it up, he spilled a pile of diamonds into Sara’s open palm, shimmering and winking like stars in the night sky.

“But…” She looked at him. “Surely, that’s not all there is.”

"There are hundreds of others," Bourne said.

"But there won't be for long."

They turned to see the Angelmaker. She held a machine pistol on them, threw a doctor's satchel made of worn pigskin at Bourne. "Fill it up."

Sara stiffened. "You're not going to let her—hey!"

Bourne was sweeping the red silk bags of diamonds into the satchel.

"Thank you for finding the safe and opening it," the Angelmaker said. "I knew whether I asked you politely or not you'd refuse." She nodded. "Now set it down and step back."

Bourne did as she asked, dragging a reluctant Sara with him.

The Angelmaker stepped down, put her boot through the satchel's handles, lifted it up with her leg. When she had hold of it, she peered into its depths, then, pushing the satchel up her arm to hold it in place, put her hand inside the safe, presumably to make sure Bourne had emptied it completely.

"Now," she said, "I must be going." As she backed up the stairs, Sara broke away from Bourne, took a step toward her. "Don't even," the Angelmaker said in a tone of unmistakable menace. "I will shoot you dead." She continued up the stairs. "One shot."

Then she vanished into the unfinished upper floor.

Sara turned to Bourne. "You're not going after her?"

"She's a trained assassin. She meant what she said. I plan to live at least another day."

"The better part of valor. All right." Sara ascended to his level, hefted the diamonds still in her palm. "Why didn't she threaten to kill me in the vault in order to coerce you into telling her where the diamonds were? That worked for Savasin."

"I didn't know then. I think she suspected that."

She shot him a skeptical look, as if she knew something more was at work. But she was too canny to press him. If he wanted to tell her, he would have. "Okay, leaving that aside, can you at least tell me why she left these behind?"

Breadcrumbs, Bourne thought.

"No again. You can't mean after all this the Sovereign will get his money, after all."

Bourne shook his head. "He won't. I need to go back to Moscow." Where it all began.

"And the invasion?"

"Will not now happen. Without these diamonds, the Federation will have trouble feeding its own people, let alone anyone else, including its standing army in Eastern Ukraine."

She gave him a puzzled look. "You know this for a fact?"

"As much as anyone can know anything in this life. And in a few months a twenty-one-billion-dollar loan to Rosneft will come due. Where will the Kremlin get the money? If Rosneft, the largest state-run energy company, fails, Russia will be in ruins."

At last, she acquiesced. "I'll accept that. I mean do I have a choice? We'll go to Moscow together."

He shook his head. "You need treatment and then a bit of rest." He spilled the remainder of the bag into her hand. "Then I'd like you to take on a special mission. As a personal favor."

"Of course." She watched him carefully, searching for a clue to his odd behavior, but none presented itself. Okay, then. She needed to exact some form of concession from him, a test, perhaps—minor perhaps, but significant to her. "But only if you promise to see me afterward."

"That," Bourne said, with a quick kiss to her lips, "was never in doubt."

62

IGOR MALACHEV WAS reading the morning's *New York Times* when he saw the Angelmaker enter the subterranean station. Savasin had a personal copy flown in daily. He was properly suspicious of electronic editions of any newspaper or magazine, believing they could be hacked at any time by anyone, their stories turned into propaganda or, worse, disinformation.

WESTERN POWERS READY TO ACT ON RUSSIA'S NEXT MOVE, ran the headline of the above-the-fold front page story he had just read. Another beside it: IRAQI ARMY RETAKES MAJOR OILFIELD FROM ISIS. And another: ALLEGED ISIS COINAGE NOW A MIRAGE. And still another: UKRAINE IN MAJOR TILT TOWARD NATO. The news was all bad and getting worse. The first minister had better have answers for this, he thought sourly. Otherwise, I'll be out of a job. Guilt by association was a favorite death sport inside the Kremlin.

As the Angelmaker approached, he folded the paper under his arm, automatically looking for his boss. It was two days past the deadline Timur Savasin had told him about. Russian troops and tanks were still inside Eastern Ukraine—though this was vehemently denied by their foreign minister and, last night, in a televised speech, by the Sovereign himself—but they had stalled. Now there was even some talk of a gradual withdrawal, a slow slinking back into the shadows of Crimea. Malachev did not know what had transpired over the last forty-eight hours to turn the tides, but he was both eager and anxious to find out from the first minister himself. Savasin had been out of contact since leaving the country with the Angelmaker. He had not asked their destination and the first minister had not volunteered it. He understood the need for compartmentalization and deniability, plausible or otherwise, as well as any *siloviki* inside the Kremlin.

Now here came the Angelmaker, an old-fashioned doctor's satchel swinging easily from her left hand. She smiled as she approached him beneath the domed tile ceiling of the first minister's private subway station. But it was an odd, inward smile, as if she had just told herself an amusing joke. On this morning, Malachev's vestigial sense of humor had vanished.

Already on edge, having ingested the Kremlin's panic-mode stress level over the last two days, Malachev took a step forward, anticipating his sighting of the first minister; he needed explanations that were not forthcoming in the offices or even the gossipy halls of the Kremlin. Soon enough, however, it became clear that the Angelmaker had arrived by herself.

"Where is he?" he asked the Angelmaker when she stopped in front of him. "Where is the first minister?"

"Timur has been unavoidably delayed," she said.

Her smile was so completely gone, he wondered whether he had imagined it.

"Delayed by the cluster-fuck at the Kremlin, I imagine." When she made no response, he added: "When can I expect him?"

"He told me to board his train, and wait."

Malachev immediately blocked her path. Just behind him Timur Savasin's opulent train stood waiting, its doors open. But he had strict orders not to allow anyone on the train without direct orders—oral or written—from the first minister.

"You didn't answer my question. How long is the first minister expected to be delayed?"

There was that off-kilter smile again. Malachev hated it and her.

"His delay," she said, "is permanent."

Then she swung the satchel, catching him flush on the face. As he staggered back, she shot him three times in the chest, making a neat isosceles triangle. Malachev had just enough time for his brain to register shock and outrage before he fell backward onto the platform. Around him, the pages of the paper settled like nesting cranes.

"Time," the Angelmaker called. "I've cleared the way."

A small figure, his greatcoat swirling around his ankles, removed himself from the deepest shadows behind her, moving swiftly into the light.

"Pity about Malachev," she said, her critical eye appraising the corpse.

"He was an idiot." Ivan Volkin fastidiously lifted the hem of his greatcoat as he stepped over the bloody corpse, into the parlor car.

The Angelmaker followed him, the door closed behind her, and, as Volkin, the eminence gris of all the Russian *grupperovka*, took his seat in the chair normally reserved for Timur Savasin, the train lurched into motion, sliding out of the station, into the tunnel burrowed under all the others, snaking beneath Moscow.

Volkin looked around the interior of the car. "I've dreamed about this moment for years." A wolfish smile overtook his face. "And now I know just how comfortable this chair is."

The Angelmaker, feet spread wide, balanced easily to the rocking motion. She swung the doctor's satchel up onto his lap.

He looked up at her. "And difficulties?"

"None I couldn't handle."

"Good." He nodded. "Good." He flipped open the brass catch, opened the satchel's jaws, peered into the interior. He removed one of the red silk bags, the gold dragon glinting in the car's warm lamplight. Spilling the diamonds into his cupped palm, he said, "How many bags?"

"One hundred seventy."

"Have you calculated the amount?"

"North of seventy-seven billion dollars, depending on the final examination of the diamonds."

"You looked at them?"

"I took a random sampling."

"And?"

"High grade," she said. "Very."

"Then I have it all. All the Sovereign's wealth."

"Not all," Bourne said, opening the door and stepping out of the bedroom car. He held up the red silk bag Mala had left for him—her breadcrumb through the last section of the dazzling mirrored labyrinth Ivan Volkin had built. The bag was empty of diamonds. It was weighted by pebbles from the Nicosia beach, but no point in telling the old man that.

A slow smile creased Volkin's face. "By God, Jason, you are persistent. I won't even ask how you got in here unobserved. That's your stock in trade, after all." He waved a hand. "Do sit down. You look like hell."

When Bourne made no move, Volkin shrugged. "Suit yourself."

Bourne, standing with legs apart, faced Mala, with Volkin between them. Volkin turned, picked a green bottle out of a bucket of ice, bracketed to the floor. "Champagne? No?" He grinned. "Considering the company, me neither." He dropped the bottle back into the bucket, the sound of a body falling through thin ice.

Crossing his hands in his lap, he said, "So, Jason, what can I do for you? I have the diamonds now. I've saved the world from the psychopath who runs this country—at least for the moment. Honestly, I think I deserve a medal."

"You deserve more than that," Bourne said. "It took me a while—longer than it should have, maybe. But you were counting on that. You knew how very few friends I have. You knew the only way to shake me up was to kill one of them. You picked Boris for many reasons, though only now are they fully clear to me."

"I have no idea what you're talking about."

The train slowed, going around a bend in the tunnel. Both Bourne and Mala leaned more heavily on their flexed left leg. Volkin closed the satchel, placed it beside his chair.

Bourne, watching everything, said, "I started to wonder how Boris had obtained the information he sent me. One of his lieutenants at FSB? I didn't think so. The intel on what the Sovereign was up to was too hot for anyone but Boris to have seen. So the enigma remained, and got more knotty when I realized that his ciphered message to me contained the means to stop Russia in its tracks. Now *there's* intel you don't pick up from contacts or from the usual rumor mills."

Volkin stared at Bourne, unblinking, hands still folded placidly on his lap. "So how do you think Boris got the intel? I'm curious to hear your theory."

"He got it from you, Ivan. And that's no theory."

One of Volkin's eyebrows arched up. "No?"

"It's a fact."

"Now you sound like a madman."

Bourne smiled. "I'll admit that for the longest time you had me fooled. I was sure Savasin had ordered Boris's death."

"You mean he didn't?"

"He had Svetlana killed in Cairo. That much I can pin on him. But Boris . . . ?" He shook his head slowly. "You see, I had assumed that Borz was working on Savasin's orders. It made perfect sense. The first minister hated Boris, would have done just about anything to destroy his reputation. But order his execution? No, that was not his way."

"I've known Savasin longer than you do, and far, far better. It would be a mistake to underestimate how badly he wanted Boris out of the way."

"But you see, Ivan, I underestimated how badly *you* wanted Boris out of the way."

Volkin's upper lip curled in a sneer. "You couldn't be more wrong. I liked Boris. He saved my twins from certain death."

"True enough. And your fondness for each other might have survived, except that for you the world wasn't enough. You decided to step out of the shadows, to straddle all three upper layers of Russian rule. You became a friend and advisor to everyone, but underneath you played the mobs against the oligarchs, the oligarchs against the Kremlin's *siloviki*. All to increase your power exponentially.

"But Boris was smarter than you in many ways. He saw through you, saw what you were up to, and he found it intolerable. Worse for you, he proved incorruptible. You tried every way you knew how to keep his nose out of your business, but he wouldn't listen. That's Boris, through and through."

"Do you hear this?" Volkin said, addressing the Angelmaker. "Can you beat this? He's raving like a madman."

"What I forgot about in the morass you were throwing at me, Ivan, was right in front of me all along. Your hall of mirrors began with your grandson pretending to be Boris's courier, handing me the false coin in Hamburg. He intercepted Boris's real courier. How did he know Boris had dispatched a courier, let alone where he was going and who he was going to meet?"

"Savasin could have—"

"No, Ivan. Boris knew every one of Savasin's people—even the ones embedded inside the FSB. No, it had to be someone else. And once I knew the impersonator's real identity, I should have put it together. But I didn't. I had more pressing things on my mind, including the loss of my best friend. You were dead on about that, anyway.

"You saw to it I received Boris's cipher, but only under your control. You knew about the Sovereign's plans, about the Omega and Gulf Bank. What you didn't know—and neither did Savasin—was how to get the money out. That's why you needed me."

Volkin was all but goggling at him. "I misjudged you, Jason. You need to be locked up."

"And then," Bourne went on, ignoring Volkin's outburst, "we come to Irina Vasilýevna's seemingly inexplicable behavior at Mik's. Why did she lead me to the money launderer in the first place? I thought it was because it would bring me one step closer to Borz. Only much later did I realize that she had taken me there to unmask you. She wanted to let me know that Mik was *your* money launderer."

When the old man made no comment, Bourne went on. "Irina Vasilýevna had had her fill of you controlling her life. She said as much to me. But, again, I was too preoccupied to see it as a key piece of the puzzle. No, she had broken away, but was too scared to tell you. She was going to *show* you when I exposed you through Mik's ledgers."

Volkin's eyes were half closed, as if he were on the verge of sleep. "That never happened."

"Of course it never happened," Bourne said. "You saw to it that it never happened. Why would Mik blow himself up? I asked myself this question over and over without coming up with an answer."

"But of course there is an answer," Volkin said. "There always is."

"For a man who's lost two generations of his family," Bourne said pointedly, "you're awfully pleased with yourself."

Volkin screwed up his face, pricked by Bourne's words. "And so I fucking should be. Mik didn't commit suicide, he wasn't the type. But I had to have a fail-safe in case Mik made a mistake. I arranged to have an explosive device planted in his office." Volkin spread his hands. "You understand, Jason, I couldn't risk the evidence of money transfers falling into the wrong hands. Like yours, for instance."

"Or Irina's."

Volkin frowned. "That was . . . unfortunate. It was only a week ago that I discovered that she and Aleksandr had gone into business on their own." He shook his head. "Without proper upbringing children can be so foolish."

"How was the bomb rigged?"

"I had remote surveillance installed. I knew everything before it happened." His smile was as thin as a razor blade. "One of the few benefits of old age is hard-learned knowledge. When it comes to business, never leave anything to chance."

Bourne took a step to his left. "So. How does it feel, Ivan, to know that you've murdered your grandchildren?"

Volkin leapt at Bourne, a stiletto in one hand, drawn from inside the cuff of his greatcoat. Bourne took the thrust, allowed it to pass between his side and his arm. He grabbed Volkin by the throat, and squeezed.

"Don't just stand there gaping. Do something!" Volkin said in a strangled voice. "Why don't you do something?"

The Angelmaker remained perfectly still, save for the motion caused by the train's progress across the diameter of Moscow.

Bourne turned his head. "Why didn't you kill him yourself? Why did you need me?"

"Your reason for killing him is emotional," the Angelmaker said. "Mine is purely financial."

Bourne shook his head. "The time for deluding yourself is over, Mala. Volkin was using you just like the Somali. Their methods might be different, but what they wanted from you was the same."

"You won't kill him? Have you become a coward?"

"You know me better than that," Bourne said. "But I'm tired of other people leading me around by the nose, including you."

With that, he hurled Volkin across the car. He fetched up against a table, which immediately canted over, crashed to the floor. Volkin rolled onto his stomach, and at last the Angelmaker moved, crossing the car to scoop up the satchel with the diamonds. Then she reached up to pull the emergency stop cord.

"I can't let you go," Bourne said. "You're culpable in all this."

"You won't harm me. We both know that."

And in that moment, while their eyes were fixed on each other, Volkin reached inside his greatcoat, pulled out a small .22 pistol. He aimed squarely at the Angelmaker's head, which, this close, he couldn't fail to hit. And he would have, had not Bourne, catching the movement out of the corner of his eye, pushed Mala away. The bullet caught him instead, twisting him to one side. But he rose, advancing on Volkin, who squeezed the trigger a second time an instant after the Angelmaker pulled the emergency cord.

The train lurched, losing speed with such rapidity that the shot, which otherwise would have penetrated Bourne's heart, struck his shoulder instead. Bourne kicked out, the toe of his shoe catching Volkin on the point of his chin. His head rocketed back at such an angle that when it slammed into the upended table edge, his neck cracked, fracturing multiple vertebrae. He was dead in an instant.

The train shuddered, lurching again with such violence that Bourne, bleeding from both wounds, lost his balance, slid to the floor. The train, jerking and juddering, came at last to rest in the middle of the tunnel, where it crouched panting, as if after a too-long run. In a moment, the engineer, no doubt armed, would be racing back to deal with the emergency.

The Angelmaker slammed the heel of her hand onto the manual override, and the car doors slid open. Staggering, Bourne regained his feet, launched himself after her, but as he reached her he lost consciousness.

As he slipped down, she caught him in her free arm. For a moment, she stood with him in her arms, uncertain as to what to do. The anxious sound of hurried footfalls galvanized her. The engineer was coming. Setting the satchel down for a moment, she bent her knees, hoisted Bourne up over her shoulder in the classic fireman's lift and, at the edge of the car, leaped the two feet onto the tracks.

She headed away from the engineer, hurrying down the tunnel the way they had come. She could feel Bourne's blood running down her neck, into the channel of her spine. It dripped down her arm, scrolling across the pigskin of the satchel she gripped with a kind of desperation.

She heard an alarmed shout from behind her. "Hey! Hey, wait! Come back!" A warning shot had her scurrying to the side of the tunnel. In the shadows between two caged bulbs, she found a narrow metal maintenance door. It was locked. Setting down her precious satchel, she fiddled with the lock, using one of the dozen picks she carried with her. The lock was no match for her expertise. She gathered up the satchel, opened the door, stepped through, pulled it shut behind her.

Using the light app on her mobile, she took a look around. Flicking a switch on the wall beside her gave her all the illumination she needed. Stuffing the mobile into her pocket, she went on, unmindful of the weight on one shoulder. She had carried heavier weights than Bourne for longer distances. She possessed the endurance of the long-distance runner.

She found herself on the edge of a maintenance air shaft that ran vertically, upward to the public transport tunnel, downward into God alone knew what. It was black as pitch down there, impossible to make out a thing. An iron ladder bolted to one wall led up the vertical shaft. She heard the sound of the engineer's voice calling, and knew it was only a matter of time until he pulled the maintenance door open and found her.

Only one way out. She started to climb, one rung at a time. The ascent was awkward. Owing to Bourne's body, she was obliged to lean out farther than she would have liked, and her only grab hold was with the hand clutching the satchel. No matter. She'd had more difficult obstacles to overcome; she would overcome this one, as well.

She was perhaps a hundred yards up the ladder when Bourne suddenly came to. He started to flail, knocking her sideways so violently she was forced to stab out for the next rung. In so doing, she lost her hold on the satchel, which plummeted straight down. Down and down it sailed, until it was lost to sight in the blackness of the shaft. She listened for it to hit bottom, to get a reading on how far down she'd have to climb to retrieve it. She counted off the seconds, and when she heard it hit bottom, she did her calculation. At almost the same time, a fresh gout of blood from Bourne's wounds inundated her. She had her choice starkly laid out before her. If she went back down for the satchel Bourne would surely bleed out. If she took him up into the light and safety, the diamonds would be lost forever. The engineer would have raised the alarm, and when Volkin and Malachev were found the lower tunnel would be crawling with FSB agents. Then it would be sealed up for all time.

She couldn't save both. It was either the diamonds or Bourne. It took her less than a minute to make her decision.

Forty Days Later

CHRISTMAS EVE. A fresh snowfall lay on Manhattan's sidewalks, obliterating the crunchy overlay of salt crystals. The gutters ran with filthy water, and already the heavy holiday traffic had churned the street beds to slush. Cars hissed by Lincoln Center, where, in the David H. Koch Theater, the evening's performance of Balanchine's *The Nutcracker* was just getting under way. The New York City Ballet production was, as usual, both lavish and impeccable, the audience—adults and children alike—was alight with the dance, the music, and the spectacle that for many epitomized Christmas.

Their excitement reached a fever pitch during the Arabian dance. There was a new soloist, recently promoted from the corps, and reviewers in plum orchestra seats and dancers in the company not onstage at the moment strained to see how the newcomer, Liis Ilves, would perform the sinuous dance. Liis was Estonian, the program informed the audience. Her surname meant "lynx," and she was proving to be every inch the lithe animal her family was named for as she whirled and pirouetted. The applause, when it came, was a tidal roar of acclamation, and much later, at her stall backstage, bouquets of flowers were brought in, lined up as on a florist's bench, in green glass vases.

Sara watched the young girl, with whom she had bonded over the past five days, with a growing sense of pride and affection that surprised her. The girl was an unusual mixture of naïveté and mental toughness. She still seemed lost in New York, grateful for the hermetically sealed world of ballet. She fed off the toughness of the exercises and rehearsals, reveled in the constant pressures imposed on body and mind. It was only latterly that Sara came to understand that this was a form of seeking shelter from a larger world which was frightening and, in every way, senseless. A drowning princess, she clung to her emaciated company with all the considerable will she possessed.

Bourne arrived, as he always did, unexpectedly, while Liis was in the tiny room she used to change in and out of street clothes.

"Did you get here on time?" Sara asked, after their first, fierce embrace. "Did you see her?"

"I did."

"She was magnificent!" Sara's eyes were shining. "Thank you for introducing me to her."

"You're wearing a brace," he said.

"Leave it to you to kill a good mood."

"Seriously. How are your ribs? And don't tell me 'fine.'"

She gave him a wry smile. "It only hurts when I breathe, doc." Then she laughed. "It only hurts when I twist too quickly. Israeli doctors—they're all grin-and-bear-it types."

"And your father?"

"Pissed as hell."

"But he's forgiven you."

"Not exactly," she said. "I'm on what you might call probation."

Bourne nodded. "That sounds about right."

It was then, as she drew back, that she got a good look at his face. "Jason, what happened to you?"

He told her what had transpired in the tunnel deep within the bedrock of Moscow.

"So it was Volkin all along," she said. "Volkin, who helped you. Volkin, your friend."

"He helped me," Bourne said, "because it also benefited him. And as for being my friend . . ." He shrugged. "He was Boris's friend once, when it suited him."

"And the diamonds?"

"Gone," Bourne said, moving out of the way of two corps members. "All except for the ones I gave to you."

"Which I had appraised and sold in Amsterdam, after which I flew back to Cairo, and, as you instructed, gave one-third of the proceeds to Amira. She can buy a new houseboat now. Hell, she can buy a fleet of them."

"More likely, she'll leave Egypt forever."

Sara nodded. "That's my guess, as well." She paused, waiting until one of the tall male dancers passed by on what seemed silent cat's feet. "Then it was on to Paris, where I met up with Soraya and her daughter." Soraya was a longtime friend who had worked alongside Bourne, before marrying and having a child. Her husband had been brutally murdered last year. "A third went to them."

"Then you flew here."

"The final third was turned into the trust you had me set up for Liis. She'll have use of the interest until she turns twenty-five, when the principal is hers, just as you wanted."

"I would have been here sooner, but I took a couple of days to visit old sites."

"Boris's grave."

He nodded. A cloud crossed his face. "His dacha was razed. It's as if it had never existed."

"The famous Russian revisionism at work. I'm sorry."

Seeing so much of Boris's life's work erased had been difficult to stomach, and he had been shadowed all the time. No one had dared approach him, though. Lucky for them; he'd been in a homicidal frame of mind. In shadows, he had mourned his friend and compatriot on so many adventures. He felt Boris's absence as a child feels a hole in his pocket through which he had lost something personal, something valuable. There were tears inside him, but they refused to budge. They stayed hidden as he traced the nighttime streets of Moscow, looking for trouble, finding only a life apart. A solitary man shadowed, always shadowed. His expression was grimly determined. "They can't erase my memories."

She studied him closely, moved her hand experimentally under his coat. "Volkin shot you twice before you got to him."

"Once in the shoulder, once in the meat of my biceps." He had not told her that he'd taken the first shot protecting the Angelmaker, though he could not quite figure out why. "The arm wound was nothing, the bullet went clear through, but the first shot nicked an artery. I lost a lot of blood. I don't remember much after that, I was out cold. The next thing I knew I was in a Moscow hospital. No one could tell me who had brought me in."

"But you knew. It was the Angelmaker who saved you." Her eyes were wide and staring. "Why did she do that? And why . . . Helping Amira and Soraya now that she's a widow I understand. But why have you done this for Liis?"

At that moment, Liis stepped out of her changing closet, saw Bourne and, with a shriek, flew into his arms. She swung against his chest like a perfect porcelain doll. "And now here you are in the flesh! My very own Christmas present! Thank you! Thank you for everything!"

She hugged him again, and then, almost immediately pushed back. "Mala. Where is she? I know she'd want to be here. I was so counting on seeing her."

"She'll come," Bourne said with a wide smile. "She'll come," he repeated without knowing whether it was the truth or a lie, "one of these days."

The Angelmaker sat in the last row of the theater balcony, off to the side, in a darkened corner. She had shrunk her presence down, clung to the shadows, so that when, one by one, the banks of spots winked off, until only one light remained on at center stage, no one noticed her.

It was from this high eyrie that she had watched her little sister perform, her eyes moist, her heart fluttering like a bird's in her chest. There were no words to describe what she was feeling. High emotions clogged her like a stopped-up drain, made whatever words she wished to say to Liis impossible for her to voice. Besides, considering her profession, it was far wiser to keep her distance from her sister, painful though it was.

But, then again, pain was her life. She had lived with it from the moment she had been abducted. It had never occurred to her that the pain would lessen, let alone go away, when she was saved by Jason Bourne. He had removed her from the basis of her physical pain, but the rest of it, nesting at the emotional, the psychic levels of her being, could not be exorcised, even by the phalanx of psychologists, psychiatrists, neuroscientists, and cognitive therapists she had been subjected to, like a butterfly pinned to a sheet of paper. There was nothing anyone could do. The pain had been embedded so deeply inside her there were days when her bones ached from it. But it was a familiar ache, which, in time, had morphed from a parasite to a passenger to a form of symbiosis, until she had convinced herself that it had always been a part of her, waiting for the right circumstances to step out into the light. Bourne meant well, and she was eternally grateful to him, but he didn't understand. How could he? How could anyone?

At length, she rose, slipped from the silenced building to wait with the crowd of balletomanes, oblivious to the snow and the bitter cold that was not so different from Moscow this time of year. She watched her sister, in the intoxicated arms of excitement and cheer, emerge from the stage door. The expectant clutch of people rushed forward, Playbills and autograph books extended toward the New York City Ballet's newest rising star. She resisted the tide, pushing back against it until she was at the outer fringe, almost in the gutter.

Liis, her cheeks flushed with her triumph as much as the cold, handed off a bouquet of roses—the very ones the Angelmaker had sent—to Rebeka, the beautiful woman who had been with Bourne at the Omega + Gulf Bank in Nicosia. Had she saved him for this? For Rebeka? He stood on the other side of Liis, almost unrecognizable in a suit and tie, a beautiful tweed overcoat. He'd had his hair trimmed, his stubble scraped off. He could pass for anyone in the real world of bright lights and nine-to-five jobs. Almost. She smiled to herself. But not quite. She saw how his eyes darted from person to person, his brain assessing risk, always and forever. She saw how he stood, very still but at the same time ready to spring into action at an instant's notice. In that, they were the same: the instincts of a feral creature, faculties undulled, unsullied by human civilization.

She followed the trio as they broke at last from the bubbling crowd, went down the block, and into a restaurant. For a moment, she stood gazing through one of the enormous windows, as the three removed their coats, handed them to a young woman, and were led by the maître d' to a choice table. Their small movements were like that of a family—intimate, secure with each other. Her pride in Liis swelled once again, making her eyes enlarge with tears, and glow brighter than the blighted streetlights overhead. Her fingertips traced an unknown pattern on the icy glass.

Abruptly, she turned, stepped decisively away, placing herself within the safety of the holiday throng. The rhythmic sound of a Salvation Army bell ringer floated to her from farther down Broadway, packed so tightly with pedestrians she couldn't see across to the east sidewalk. Boys shouted to one another, and a brief snowball fight erupted before an errant missile struck an old man in the back, and they ran away, laughing.

It's life and life only, she thought. But it had nothing to do with her. She took out her mobile, blew on her fingertip to warm it, then pressed a speed-dial key. With the phone against her ear, she listened so intently her sense of the frenetic activity around her vanished. She might have been in a vacuum. Her body trembled.

A moment later, she was talking with the Somali Yibir. His name was Keyre. Every scar on her body resonated to the sound of his voice, set up a yearning like a tide irresistibly bearing her back into the past.

Moments later, she was a speck in the crowd. After that, she was gone.

Acknowledgments

Once again, thank you to all the people who helped with the research for this novel. Most of you have asked to remain anonymous, but you know who you are. Without your invaluable assistance *The Bourne Engima* would not see light in its current form. Having said that, any and all alterations (for dramatic effect) and (inadvertent) errors are mine alone.

Biggest thank-you of all to my wife, Victoria Schochet Lustbader, my first and best editor. You make my writing so much easier.